A
COMMON
HEARTH

Book I
Second Edition

C.D. NELSON

WOODBRIDGE
PUBLISHERS

276 5th Avenue Suite 704 #944

New York, NY 10001

ISBN: 978-1-918130-45-4 (Paperback)

ISBN: 978-1-91830-46-1 (Hardback)

ISBN:978-1-918130-47-8 (eBook)

Cover Design by Woodbridge Publishers.

Find out more about our upcoming releases and authors at www.woodbridgepublishers.com and sign up for our newsletter to stay updated!

DEDICATION

To my bride, Tiffany, without you, I have no idea where I would be today in life. We have been through so much: war, loss of family and friends. Life has not been easy, and sometimes it has been downright horrible, but one thing that has always been consistent and solid is you. Even when I was at my worst, you were there to show me what Agape love is. The one thing in this world that has always been lacking is this type of love. God has truly blessed me with someone I can share this life with, and I am deeply grateful. You are stronger than anyone I have ever met or known; you truly exemplify what it means to love others more than yourself.

TABLE OF CONTENTS

Contents

Asa and Astrid:
Roots in the Iron Soil

In the late 800s, by the Anglo-Saxon reckoning, a time when life in the Northlands was engraved in struggle and tempered by iron. In a cluster of longhouses clinging to the edge of a fjord inside the expanse of Norway, the village of Njardarheimr clawed existence from the harsh, unforgiving land. Here, underneath a sky, often greyer than the fabled midnight sun, a child entered the world. She was named Asa (Gunnarsdóttir), a weightier name than its simple meaning of "goddess." Her parents, like all who lived before, bound to the cycles of scarcity and sudden violence, hoped she would embody the strength and stern favor of the Æsir they propitiated, not simply their divine grace.

Her father was Jarl Gunnar Gydasson, not a king ruling vast tracts but a Jarl whose authority was earned through strength, cunning, and the ability to hold his folk together against the twin wolves of starvation and rivals. His stature was not so much about physical height as about the heavy set of his shoulders, the calloused competence of his hands, and the grave, calculating look in his eyes. He ruled with a pragmatism born of necessity, his fairness measured by what ensured survival for his *hirð* (household warriors) and the *karlar* (free farmers) who looked to him.

Her mother, Yrsi (Ketillsdóttir), was no frail beauty but a woman whose hands were as adept at mending torn hides and salving burns as they were at spinning wool. Her gentleness was an understated strength, essential in a community where a fever could decimate a family or a poorly healed wound could cripple a needed worker. Her knowledge of herbs and poultices was practical magic, valued far above idle charm.

Asa's birth, like any successful passage from the womb, was met with grim relief and a round of celebratory ale, a brief respite before the grind of life restarted. There were no grand feasts that risked depleting precious stores; survival was the ongoing feast. From the start, Asa had a sharpness, a quickness of eye that missed little, indicating her father's vigilance. The flash in her unnervingly brown eyes, where a glint of the cold fjords seemed to catch the light, was almost wary, intelligence, a necessary trait for seeing the world as it was.

Her shadow and closest companion was Astrid (Knutsdóttir), two years her elder, a girl whose name, 'divinely beautiful,' seemed almost a jest given the smudges of dirt and the perpetual knot in her flaming red hair. Astrid wasn't just a "shield maiden in the making" in the legendary sagas yet to be written. Still, a girl grows into the demanding roles expected of women, with tireless energy and a powerful will that chafe against purely domestic tasks. Her emerald eyes wore not just mischief but a fierce, almost challenging glint.

Their families' closeness was forged through shared labor and mutual defense, huddling together during blizzards, helping during harvests, and standing side by side when rumors of rival raiders circulated. The girls learned the rhythm of the seasons, the brutal lessons of animal husbandry, the elaborate web of kinship and obligation, and the stark, often violent, history of their ancestors told in the dancing firelight.

Training wasn't a sport; it was preparation for inevitability. While boys learned the heft of an axe and the thrust of a spear, girls were taught to handle knives, tend to wounds under duress, and the vital skill of the sling or bow for hunting and defense. Asa, smaller than most, found her advantage in her wiry strength and unnatural swiftness. She moved just as a fox through the snow-covered pines, her black hair often a tangle from clambering over rocks. Her focus was absolute, her small, strong hands learning the pull and release of the bowstring; each arrow loosed a potential meal or a deterrent to danger. Astrid, taller and broader-boned, was a physical presence. Her flaming hair was a light against the subdued landscape. Her strength was evident, but her acute intellect and ability to assess and respond set her apart. She learned the weight and balance of a round shield, how to brace against a blow, and understood that survival in the press of bodies regularly came down to brutal, simple physics.

Together, they were a pragmatic unit, Asa, the eyes and quick strike from a distance; Astrid, the grounded force capable of holding a line. Their relationship was less a thing of legend and more a vital necessity, two young women negotiating a world which demanded constant watchfulness and repaid weakness with swift oblivion. Their story wasn't just beginning; it was unfolding as it had for generations, a fiber in the course, resilient cloth of Njardarheimr.

Their friendship, a constant fire against the cold, was formed not in idyllic adventures but in shared hardships. They learned the biting sting of the fjord winds together, the exhausting labor of the brief summers, and the piercing emptiness of lean winters. As they shed childhood, their relationship became a practical alliance. Training sharpened their instincts and their trust in each other. Asa's precision with the bow became Astrid's early warning, her ability to pick off a far-off threat, saving Astrid from needing to meet it head-on. Astrid's strength and shield mastery offered Asa cover should her arrows fail or the enemy close. They were two parts of a necessary whole.

Their learning wasn't confined to combat. They absorbed the *Eddas* and sagas, not as imaginative tales but as blueprints for behavior, cautionary warnings, and explanations for an often-capricious world. They learned the lore of the land, which plants were healing and which were poisonous, how to track game, and how to read the subtle cruelties of the weather. Their arguments were less intellectual sparring and more sharp exchanges born of differing perspectives on practical problems, the best way to salt meat for winter, and the most defensible position for the herds.

By the time they were considered young adults, they stood ready to defend their homes and families. Side by side, not always in the shieldwall with the men, though sometimes women occasionally fought alongside men out of necessity, wielding what weapons they could, but on the flanks, applying their skills to protect their community. They saw the brutal reality of conflict, severed limbs, gurgling last breaths, the pungent smell of fear and spilled blood. Victories remained grim affairs, celebrated with exhausted relief and the grim task of burying the dead. Losses were a gaping wound in their small community, felt by everyone. They carried the implicit burden of knowing their efforts meant the difference between their families eating and starving, living and dying.

Their friendship wasn't a gentle bloom; it had thorns. Disagreements flared, sharp and cutting, born of stress and clashing approaches. Instances of tension were inevitable in a life lived in close quarters with high stakes. But these clashes were weathered. They learned the reluctant respect that comes from seeing someone stand their ground, even when you disagree. They discovered that a trusted hand in a crisis was worth more than easy companionship. Their relationship was resilient, tested, akin to a blade against a whetstone.

A turning point, sharp and cold as a snapped bone, came during a winter that aimed to consume them all. Another clan, driven by hunger, cast a covetous eye on Njardarheimr's meager stores. As the snow fell thick and fast, word came that they were on their way. In the smoky, crowded main hall, the air laden with the aroma of damp wool and nervous sweat, Gunnar gathered his folk. The discussion was grim: how to face the coming threat.

Asa, her mind always calculating angles and

distances, argued for defense from the high ground surrounding the village, using their knowledge of the treacherous winter landscape as a weapon, channeling the enemy into kill zones where her archers could rain death from above. It was a strategy of attrition, one that let the environment do half the killing. Astrid, gripping a practice shield, her face set, argued about meeting them on the frozen fjord or the open, snow-swept fields bordering the village. A confrontation, a brutal, decisive clash of shieldwalls and blades, to break their will swiftly before they could dig in or probe weaknesses.

Their disagreement was sharp, with voices elevated; the hard edge of conviction had replaced the usual easy cadence between them. The inhabitants watched, silent and tense. It was unusual for women to speak so forcefully in such a council, but Asa was the Jarl's daughter, and Astrid's ability was undeniable. Yet, they did not descend into petty squabbling. They laid out their reasoning, stark and practical, each accepting the grim merits of the other's plan even as they supported their own.

The final decision rested with Jarl Gunnar. He listened, his gaze moving between his daughter and the girl who served as her shadow. He saw the clear logic in Asa's defensive plan, the wisdom of letting the land fight with them. He saw the fierce courage in Astrid's call for a direct clash, the understanding that sometimes you had to break the enemy's spirit with a brutal show of force. His decision was a Jarl's compromise, borne of necessity: they would secure their perimeters, creating traps and advantageous firing positions as Asa suggested, but they would also prepare for the shieldwall, ready to meet the enemy in a bloody embrace if the defenses were breached or the opportunity arose, as Astrid advocated.

The winter clash was a brutal, desperate affair; the snow was stained red. It tested the inhabitants, pushing them to their limits. It tested Asa and Astrid. Forced to trust in the combined plan, they saw the wisdom in both their perspectives play out in bloody reality. They learned that disagreement was not a betrayal within their bond but an indication of their strengths and the harsh calculus of survival. Their friendship, tested amidst the crucible of conflict and differing ideologies, emerged harder, more resilient, and stripped of any lingering childish idealism.

The rival clan, harried by arrows from unseen positions and then met with unexpected, savage resistance in close combat, broke and fled, leaving their dead scattered across the snow. Njardarheimr had held. Safety wasn't a warm blanket; it was the cold, hard fact of survival earned through blood and ice. Asa and Astrid stood next to each other afterward, not in a triumphant embrace, but side by side, gazing across the horizon, their expressions stern and scored by the recent violence. The moment wasn't one of glorious legend but a muted acknowledgment of shared ordeal and an unbreakable bond shaped in the iron soil of their home and the cruel realities of their age. It was a defining moment, yes, but less about being shining beacons and more about being survivors together.

Aedelric and Eadric:
The Roots of Warriors

In Wessex, Winchester rose within the chalk hills, a city of timber frames, smoky thatch, the smithy clang, and the Old Minster's rising stone skeleton. Here, among the mud and bustle, Aedelric (Æthelric, son of Wulfric) first drew breath, son of a thegn favored by the king.

Aedelric's father, thegn Wulfric(Æthelwulf), held lands from Aethelred I, and his loyalty was sworn in the great hall and tested on the campaign trail. He was a man whose word was his bond, tough yet fair. Leofwynn, his wife, managed the household with a firm hand and pious heart, known as much for her skill at the loom as for her discreet acts of charity.

Not far off, in a sturdier cottage near the barracks, Eadric was born, son of a warrior whose renown was earned in sweat and blood. Eadric's father, Cynric, carried the scars of a dozen campaigns, a veteran whose loyalty to his Lord and king was unquestioned. His strength had carved out respect where birthright had not. Eadric's mother, Mildrith, possessed the healer's touch; her knowledge of herbs and poultices was a vital, sometimes feared, skill in a world where sickness could strike faster and more swiftly than any dagger.

Proximity and their fathers' shared service brought the families together. The boys grew up in each other's shadow, tumbling among the chickens and dogs in the yards, daring each other into the cold rush of the River Itchen, and learning the secrets of the nearby woods. Their voices resounded, sometimes joyful, sometimes charged with the bitterness of childhood rivalry.

Childhood's freedom soon yielded to the harsh discipline of weapon training. Under his father's stern eye and the tutelage of veteran warriors, Aedelric learned the shieldwall, the bite of the spear, and the elaborate, deadly movement of the sword, a costly weapon and a symbol of his station. Eadric, lacking the coin for such fine steel initially, first mastered the shield and the fearsome reach of the war-axe, his raw strength making the heavy blade sing. Inheriting his father's well-worn axe, he learned its ways, his power turning chopping blows into devastating finishers. He favored a heavier blade, a pattern-welded beast, some called 'Maelstrom' for the ruin it left.

Their learning went beyond the practice yard. Aedelric, guided by a stern priest, wrestled with Latin prayers and the Psalms, learning the histories of the kings and saints from scrolls painstakingly copied onto precious parchment. Eadric absorbed history differently, through the boastful songs sung in the mead hall, the sagas of heroes and monsters recited by firelight, and his father's practical wisdom. Both learned the harsh lessons of loyalty, the burden of an oath, and the merciless demands of the world they inhabited.

Their lives took a decisive turn when they were still in their teens. Recognizing their fathers' service and their rising skills, King Æthelred called them into his hearthweru, his hearth-troop, his sworn household warriors. Taking the oath, they became closer than brothers, an honor demanding absolute loyalty, often sealed in blood.

Their oaths were soon tested. Welsh raiders, probing the borders with sudden ferocity, struck near the coast. They came in swift, disciplined bands, hardened by the mountains and valleys of their homeland. Æthelred dispatched a force, and Aedelric and Eadric marched with his hearthweru, young but already tempered by training and expectation.

Deflecting raids became the forge of their brotherhood. They faced warriors who fought with a fierce, almost ancestral hatred, men who moved with the speed of hill wolves and struck with the precision of hunters. Their numbers pressed hard against the Wessex shieldwall, a living tide that slammed into them with bone-shaking force. The air grew dense with the iron smell of blood and the stench of sweat, mud, and fear. The roar of the shieldwalls meeting was deafening, wood splintering, iron ringing on iron, the guttural shouts of men fighting for their lives.

Spears thrust over and under the rims of shields, punching into flesh with wet, sickening sounds. Welsh axes hacked into flesh and bone. Short swords flashed in brutal arcs, carving through limbs and leather. The ground churned into a slick, muddy slurry of trampled earth and blood, sucking at boots and bodies alike.

Aedelric's voice, hoarse from shouting commands, kept his place in the line steady. His shield was battered, his arm numb from the constant impact, but he held. He felt the shake of each blow through his bones. Beside him, Eadric fought like a storm given human form, his heavy axe rising and falling with ruthless precision. Each swing crunched through shield, leather, and bone, sending men sprawling.

In the chaos, Eadric overextended. His shield collapsed under a vicious strike, splintering in his grip. Three Welsh warriors advanced toward him, snarling, blades stabbing for the gaps in his mail. Eadric staggered, exposed, his teeth bared in a snarl of resistance.

Aedelric saw it. A cry ripped from his throat, raw and instinctive. He smashed his way through the press, shoulder-charging one foe aside, his sword catching another's blade before it could pierce Eadric's ribs. He reached his friend just as Eadric felled one attacker with a desperate swing.

Back-to-back, they became an island in the storm. Their breath came in labored gasps, their bodies slick with sweat and blood. They covered each other's blind spots, turning and striking with the desperate ferocity of cornered wolves. Aedelric's sword opened a man from collarbone to sternum. Eadric's axe shattered another's knee, dropping him screaming into the mud. Together, they overwhelmed the last of the attackers, driving them back into the chaos.

Wessex held the field that day, though the cost was carved into every survivor's face and heard in the groans of the wounded as they were carried from the carnage. For Aedelric and Eadric, soaked in sweat and grime, spattered with blood not entirely their own, it was more than victory. In the shared terror, the desperate fight for survival, and the fierce loyalty that had driven Aedelric to his side, their bond was reforged in the fire of battle, harder and sharper than any sword steel.

From that day forward, Aedelric and Eadric were no longer simply friends. They were brothers in arms, bound by blood, by fear, by triumph, and by the grim understanding of what it signified to stand together when death pressed close enough to taste.

PROLOGUE

In the heartland of the West Saxons, in the years when the Dragon Banner of Wessex strained against the winds of change, Aedelric moved with the hushed confidence of a man whose place was hard-won and secured by blood-oath. His service in the *hearthweru*, proven in battle, had marked him. Gallantry was less about glory and more about standing fast when the line wavered; honesty was a blunt necessity in a society where shattered trust could mean a blade in the gut. These qualities gained him the respect of his peers and the cold, appraising nod of his Lord. Yet, beneath the mail shirt and the load of expectation, a unease stirred. Not a fanciful longing, but the ambition common to capable young men: a hunger for greater responsibility, for lands of his own, for a name that might echo beyond the mead hall, a destiny formed not by idle fate but by strength and favorable fortune.

Miles across the treacherous sea, where the fjords bit deep into the land of the Northmen, life in Njardarheimr represented a stark equation of effort and survival. Here, Asa, was designated not just by her lineage. She owned a keen mind that missed little and a reserved intensity that held attention. While tales might later speak of beauty rivaling the goddesses, in the here and now, her value lay in sharper things: a clear head in a crisis, a functional understanding of their world, and a growing mastery of skills vital to the community's survival. She, too, experienced a pull, a sense that the expected path of marriage to a suitable Jarl managing a household was too small for the energy coiled inside herself. She craved the ability to protect her own, to influence their fortune in a world that demanded strength from every soul, regardless of gender.

Their universes were separated by more than leagues of grey, storm-tossed water. They were separated by different gods, different laws, and distinct ways of viewing the sun and the stars. One lived under the growing light of Christ, and the other still paid homage to the old, demanding powers of Asgard. Yet, the *wyrd*, the elaborate, frequently severe, web of fate that linked all beings, was indifferent to distance and custom. The fibers of their lives, spun by the Norns or guided by God's inscrutable will, were drawn taut. Events were stirring across the sea, hints of distant sails and burning steadings that would soon weave their separate paths into a single, perilous design.

Aedelric continued to hone the deadly craft demanded of the *hearthweru*. His training with Wulfric and the seasoned veterans wasn't a graceful dance but a grueling, repetitive trial of endurance, strength, and reaction. Hour after hour, in the harsh wind or under the weak sun, he practiced the brutal economy of the shieldwall, the sudden violence of the spear thrust, the hacking, cleaving power of the sword, an extension of his own will and strength. Mastery was not a destination, but the grim necessity of being slightly faster, slightly stronger, and somewhat more skilled than the foe who sought to kill you.

Asa, from a young age, had shown an uncanny skill for the bow, a tool vital for hunting on the lean slopes and for raining death from a distance should raiders appear. It wasn't a sudden discovery of latent talent, and yet the tireless pursuit of proficiency. The old bow and arrows, her father's from his younger days, became her constant companions. She didn't just loose arrows; she *practiced*. Drew the sinew-backed wood until her arms ached, loosed arrow after arrow till her fingers were raw, and learned to judge distance and wind with an instinct born of repetition. Each shaft sent whispering into the air remained a devotion to skill, to survival, to become a needed asset within a world that had little patience for weakness. The villagers observed her dedication, the unnatural precision with which her arrows struck their marks, and they talked about her with a combination of pride and awe, the Jarl's daughter, sharp-eyed as an eagle, deadly with a bow.

Their lives, so far apart, were converging. They weren't simply carving out personal destinies. Still, they were being molded by the forces of their time: the continual threat of violence, the demands of loyalty, and the brutal realities of survival. Unseen by them, the currents of history and the detailed tapestry of fate were pulling them towards a collision, a convergence that would not just change their lives but, perhaps, in some small way, the shape of the world around them.

And so, the grim saga of a pair of souls caught in the currents of a world burning in conflict.

CHAPTER 1

Part 1: Heathen Come Ashore

The delicate veneer of peace in the West Saxon kingdom was easily shattered by the shriek of war horns resounding from the coast, and as in winters past and increasingly through the leaner summers, this year brought the dread sound of longships scraping shingle. They were Vikings, sea wolves from across the great water. Northmen and Danes alike, their sails carrying plunder and misery to the shores of Britannia. They fell upon coastal settlements not with ritual but with brutal, expert efficiency, taking coin, goods, and captives, leaving behind smoke and corpses. This summer, a fleet from Njardarheimr, known among the Northmen for their lean ships and hard-fighting men and women, had set their sights on Wareham, a place of known wealth where the frame met the ocean, a knot in Wessex's modest trade network.

The coast was not purely disrupted; it was plunged into terror. Yet, Wareham had a sliver of luck. Word of the approaching raids, dark marks on the horizon, settled the day before. It was not a speedy journey by modern standards, but a desperate and challenging ride for the man who spurred his horse inland, carrying the stark news. From village to village, the warning spread, a ragged cry ahead of the storm, until the lathered rider finally burst into the Great Hall of Winchester, the fear stark on his face, demanding an audience with the King.

King Æthelred, his countenance marked with the intimate worry that these ceaseless pagan raids brought, sat bent over a campaign map, its parchment edges tattered from constant handling. The wavering lamplight cast deep shadows under his eyes, betraying the sleepless nights he had endured. He raised his head, his look sweeping over the trusted thegns and hearthweru assembled before him within the quiet chamber. The air remained thick with tension, the silence marked only by the occasional crackles of the hearth and the distant, hushed sounds of the sleeping royal burh.

"Aedelric, Eadric." The King's voice was tense with haste, lacking any grand flourish. This was not a formal court, but a war council in the shadow of an imminent threat. "The heathen have returned. Word reached us but an hour past. They strike at Wareham. My gut clenches for the folk there, for the monastery, for the same stones of our kingdom."

Aedelric moved forward, his bow economical, the movement ingrained by years of devoted service. His countenance was grim, but his voice remained a steady, calm anchor in the room. "My Lord, we will ride. Wessex must stand, and by God's grace, we shall make it so." The calm certainty in his tone was the calm expected of an experienced hearthweru, a man whose existence was dedicated to protecting his king and country.

Eadric, an impressive presence beside him, his hand unconsciously resting on the hilt of his heavy axe, gave a sharp, grim nod. "My Lord," he stated, his speech a soft growl, "They will find steel awaits them. Every blow they strike against our people, they shall feel tenfold." His words were few, but the set of his jaw and the hard gleam in his eyes revealed much about his firm determination.

Æthelred ran a weary hand over his short beard, his look fixed on the two men who represented the immediate strength of his house. "Your courage is a stone for us all in these times," he said, his voice suffused with the load of his burden. "But Wareham is vital. A strategic holding, a bulwark on the coast. It must not fall entirely. Drive them off if you can. Preserve what can be saved of the folk, the sacred relics, the innermost fabric of our Christian land." He paused, his look hardening with cold resolve. "Break them. Make them regret setting foot on these shores."

"We know the ground, my King," Aedelric affirmed. However, 'stratagem' for this desperate ride meant using the terrain for ambush, for forcing a disadvantageous approach on the pagans, not elaborate maneuvers on a battlefield. "We will make them pay for every foot of ground they defile."

Eadric added, his manner blunt and direct, "And kill any who stand against us, my King." The unvoiced understanding was grimly clear: shielding the innocent, protecting the kingdom, meant killing the attackers before they could continue their brutal work. It was a brutal equation of survival, one they all understood.

The King rose, stepping forward to lay a heavy hand on each of their shoulders, a rare, profound gesture from the monarch. "Go. Ride with the speed of the wind and the fury of God's righteous anger. May the Lord shield your arms and guide your blows against these pagan dogs who defile our lands and our Christ. I will muster the ford, gather my remaining nobles, and follow you to Wareham as fast as my horse can carry me."

There was no time for elaborate farewells or lengthy preparations. Aedelric and Eadric moved with the urgent efficiency of men used to sudden calls to arms. They roused their hearthweru companions, who responded to the alarm with the disciplined readiness of loyal warriors. They packed only what was necessary for a forced march: weapons sharpened and mail gleaming, sturdy shields, a few days' worth of hard bread and jerky, and filled water skins. Speed was paramount. Every hour lost meant more lives ended, more wealth carried off, more sacrilege committed against their faith. They moved out of Winchester, a dark, silent column of mounted warriors, riding with the forced pace of men racing the dawn and the longships, their destination engraved in the burning hope of rescue and vengeance.

Meanwhile, back at Wareham, the Northmen's fleet, consisting of about eight longships, drove towards the coast. Among the warriors packed shoulder-to-shoulder on the vanguard ship were Asa and Astrid. Asa, the Jarl's daughter, her bow strung and ready, felt the familiar knot in her gut, the grim necessity of the raid, struggling with the knowledge of the violence to come. This was how her people survived, by taking what others had. But it came at a cost.

Astrid, her axe head glinting dully in the grey morning rays, stood at the side of her. Her flaming hair was pulled back tightly. She was a warrior, formidable and unflinching, more comfortable in the press of bodies than managing a household. She was not a "legendary shield maiden" yet; perhaps such tales were years away, but within Njardarheimr's fighting folk, her competence with axe and shield was already well-known and respected, even among the men.

As the ships scraped on the shallows, the air thrummed with a savage, primal energy. "Landfall." Asa's voice sounded like a soft growl over the sloshing waves, less an order than a grim statement of fact. Her stare swept the distant shore, already anticipating the resistance.

Astrid's grin, a feral flash of white in her grime-streaked face, split the gloom. "Wealth for the taking! My axe hungers!" No doubt, no pause for thought, just the pure, unburdened anticipation of the kill.

With jarring thuds, the longships beached. Before the hulls had fully settled, the Northmen flowed into the icy water, a howling tide of steel and wrath. Asa, already nocking an arrow, proceeded with a hunter's precision, her eyes seeking for leaders. She spoke quietly to no one in particular, "Remember who fights," a quiet, pragmatic reminder that inside the turmoil of a raid, only the armed mattered.

Astrid's laugh came as a sharp bark, like a fox's yelp as she splashed ashore, shield already up, a red-haired whirlwind. "Look at them scramble! Like fish on the drying racks!"

The beach erupted into controlled chaos. Warriors of Njardarheimr coalesced, a dark wave of axes and spears. Asa positioned herself slightly back, near a small contingent of bowmen, her war bow already singing. Her arrows flew fast and accurately, each ring of the bowstring a death toll, targeting the scattering figures attempting to form a defense line near Wareham's flimsy palisade hastily. The Northmen's shieldwall was already forming as they advanced with calculated efficiency and deadly skill in the art of warfare.

The defenders, a desperate amalgamation of town guards, farmers, and panicked townsfolk, responded with a clumsy, frantic, yet ragged efficiency. Slowly, agonizingly, a shieldwall began to form, a desperate, defiant barrier. Though fewer than the fresh Norwegians pouring ashore, their faces, pale with fear, were set in grim, firm determination. The Northmen, a disciplined tide, did not rush. They advanced with a measured, deliberate walk, their shields locked, their footsteps made a heavy, measured thud against the wet sand. In sharp contrast, the defenders took an even slower, more defensive, almost nervous stance, their line faltering faintly as each man braced for the inevitable.

Then, the world exploded. The two shieldwalls collided with the bone-jarring impact of colliding mountains. The initial clash was a jarring crack of wood, the rasp of steel, and a simultaneous roar of primal rage.

The air became a storm of noise and gore. Axes bit deep into wood and bone with wet, tearing sounds. Spears splintered, their tips seeking throats and bellies. The ring of iron on iron was ear-splitting, an unrelenting percussive rhythm toward the symphony of death. Men cried, their cries cut short as the Northmen, a tide of unrelenting brutality, pushed. Blood, warm and thick, sprayed across shields, mixed with the churned mud and icy spray from the shore. The reek of sweat, fear, and fresh blood clogged the air.

Asa, from her vantage behind the main push, was an unrelenting bringer of death. Her bowstring vibrated ceaselessly, her arrows finding gaps in the desperate Wareham line, felling those who tried to rally, breaking their faltering cohesion. She observed the fear in their eyes, as well as the courage, and had a cold, professional respect for their valiant stand. It was a mutual, harsh dance of skill, but only one side would walk away.

On the flanks, Astrid was a demon unleashed. Her axe, a streak of polished steel, rose and fell with brutal, efficient grace, carving a bloody path. She didn't just strike; she hacked, she cleaved, she tore. One defender's shield broke under her blow; the next had his head split from shoulder to jaw. She was a wedge of pure destruction, slowly, relentlessly prying open the Wareham shieldwall.

The Saxon line, already bent by the Northmen's unrelenting pressure, now began to shatter under the concentrated assault. Step by bloody step, the defenders gave ground. The shieldwall, once a defiant barrier, broke into desperate pockets of resistance, then turned into a panicked rout. Wareham was falling, succumbing to the Norsemen's stern determination. It was another victory, another tally of spoils, but for Asa, the essence of ash in her mouth was already familiar, the bitter byproduct of necessary violence.

As the fighting receded, replaced by the sounds of triumph, the true sacking began. The splintering of wooden doors, the lowing of stolen cattle, the terrified cries of captives, and the raucous shouts of the victorious Northmen filled the surroundings. Asa moved through the plundered settlement, her look somber. This was the price. The silver and goods were tangible wealth for Njardarheimr, food and security for her people through the coming winter, but the wreckage and suffering were hard to ignore.

Astrid, however, was in her element. Her commanding voice, hoarse from battle cries, now fractured like a whip, directing warriors who hauled chests overflowing with coin from shattered shops, overseeing the collection of livestock driven bawling from their pens, and pointing out the finer goods being stripped from homes. "War is the gift of Odin!" she roared, her face alight with triumph. "The wealth flows! Take what is ours! Empty their coffers and their larders! Strip this town bare!" To her, the dead were merely the cost of the bounty. "They have found their halls," she said, dismissively waving a hand towards a fallen Saxon, just glancing at Asa's quiet contemplation. "We have bellies and people to serve. Our people are fed for the winter now." Asa nodded quietly, the words reflecting her own pragmatic, if unwelcome, truth. This suffering, she knew, was a grim necessity, a brutal equation for the survival of Njardarheimr.

The Northmen, their bellies full of plundered food and their hands loaded with loot, established a temporary camp near their beached ships. Fires flickered, casting moving shadows on the sand as darkness fell. The air, heavy laden with the scent of burning wood smoke and the sweet, metallic flavor of drying blood, now filled with the smell of roasting meat and the drunken revelry of men sating their immediate desires. Laughter, coarse and loud, merged with the occasional wail from a captive, quickly silenced. Asa sat apart, her back against an overturned boat, watching the unfamiliar stars of the southern sky. Hamingja (luck) had favored them this day, granting them an easy victory and rich spoils, but the burden of it pressed down on her. She wondered about the souls departed, violently torn from their lives today, bound now for Helheim's cold halls or, if they were Christian souls, some other realm she did not understand, a domain perhaps less forgiving than Odin's. She saw the faces of the fallen, young and old, their eyes wide with fear or defiance, and felt the familiar hollowness in her gut.

Astrid joined her, her arms already loaded with looted silver and a fine wool cloak. Her eyes gleamed, showing the firelight and the avarice that drove this life. "Look at that star," she said, pointing not in contemplation of souls but of navigation. "Clear skies. Good sailing. Where to next, Asa? More wealth awaits. Perhaps the village upriver, or across the strait?"

Asa shook her head, the dim smile on Astrid's face fading. "No, Astrid. We sail at first light." Astrid frowned, her brow wrinkling. "But why? The pickings are good here. We could easily."

"We have enough," Asa interrupted, her voice assertive, leaving no room for argument. "This raid, this town… it has given us sufficient stores for the winter. Our people will not starve. There is no need for further bloodshed, not at this time. The cost, even to us, grows with each prolonged venture. Better to secure what we have, return home, and prepare for the seasons ahead." She watched out at the dark, restless sea. "We go home. For now, there will be no more raids." The words rested between them, a quiet, unyielding declaration. The dead were gone; the living had needs and desires that, for now, had been satisfied.

The following dawn appeared grey and cold over Wareham. The haze off the water softened the edges of the destruction. Outside the broken palisade, a new sound sliced through the sorrowful cries of gulls, the measured movement of trained men.

Aedelric and Eadric's force, travel-worn though resolute, had arrived. They had ridden hard through the night, pushing their horses, their mail clanking softly. Now, dismounted, they formed their ranks, shields locked, spears held ready. Aedelric, his face grimed with dust and sweat, scanned the port, his eyes alert beneath a plain iron helm. The signs of the raid were everywhere: smoke, quiet where there should be noise, the raw smell of plunder. Beside him, Eadric, a tower of tired muscle, hefted his heavy axe, Maelstrom, feeling its familiar, soothing weight. His gaze was locked on the still-silent settlement, ready for the work ahead.

Suddenly, a shout cut through the calm. From within Wareham, a Norse guard spotted the new threat on the horizon. Asa heard it, her head snapping up. There they were, a line of armed men silhouetted against the early sun at the edge of the settlement. Her brown eyes narrowed, scanning the approaching Anglo-Saxons. She recognized the disciplined formation, a force to be reckoned with.

"Astrid," Asa called, turning to the red-haired warrior who was already rising, axe and shield in hand. "You and Skarde," she added, nodding to a burly male fixing his helmet. "Go. Meet them. See what they want. Let's not shed blood needlessly, yet." A wave of adrenaline, not of fear but of shrewd calculation, flooded her introspection. Astrid nodded, her countenance grim but ready. Skarde grunted his assent, grasping his axe.

Meanwhile, Eadric strode across the torn ground towards the edge of the Norse position. Aedelric had given the nod. "Go, Eadric. See if... if words mean anything to them." It was a slim hope, born of a warrior's instinct to understand his foe, perhaps foolhardy. Astrid, her face set, axe still in hand, detached herself from her companions and walked out to meet him. Next to her, Skarde took up a position, axe held loosely.

Eadric stopped a spear-length away, the quiet between them crackling. He stared at Astrid, the red hair, the firm eyes, the battle-stained axe. He had heard the gossip and dismissed the accounts of women fighting alongside these heathens as unlikely sagas. But there she stood, real and dangerous. The fact was a gut punch. His gaze flitted past her to Skarde, then, for a brief moment, it met the intense brown eyes of Asa, standing further back, observing them. A shock went through him. Another woman, clearly a leader, was judging him.

He tried to speak, his voice harsh. He used the tongue of Wessex, words wholly foreign to her. "We... cessation?" He pointed between them and made a gesture of laying down arms. "Talk?"

Astrid watched him, her features unreadable. A light smirk curved her lips, a trace of something that wasn't quite amusement, more like assessing a strange creature. She made no sound, no gesture in return. Skarde remained impassive next to her.

Frustration tightened Eadric's chest. He tried again, louder, more emphatic, pointing to the dead bodies, then shaking his head. "No more killing! Speak! Why attack?" It was useless. The words bounced off the wall of incomprehension between them. The gulf was enormous, filled with centuries of different tongues and different ways of life.

Astrid felt no urge to bridge it. His attempts at communication were inept, his words meaningless noise. Her initial shock at his approach faded, replaced by a warrior's curiosity. She studied his size, the way he held himself, and the heavy axe. *I could put the blade through his neck right now*; the thought was cold and practical. But the moment passed. She had seen enough for now. She had assessed this large, strange man who didn't immediately try to kill her.

Eadric saw the understanding fail. He saw the blankness in her eyes, the slight, unsettling smirk. The quietness stretched, heavy and insurmountable. He had failed. With a final, frustrated glance at the implacable woman, the watchful Skarde, and the Norses behind them, he turned and walked back towards his lines, every step burning with frustrated energy and a revived, cold determination. He had seen the enemy up close, seen their ruthless capability, seen the woman who looked like no other woman he'd ever seen. They had to be stopped.

Astrid watched him go, the tall Saxon with the heavy axe. His retreat wasn't one of fear but of frustrated purpose. His grim expression revealed her anticipation. Good. The battle was on. She looked forward to meeting that heavy axe again.

Eadric reached Aedelric, his boots heavy on the churned earth. The exhausted faces of their warriors turned towards them, hope and exhaustion warring in their eyes.

Eadric's voice was low and rough, with a grim certainty. "They won't parley. She, the woman with the axe, seeks only blood." He paused, his breath frozen. "And they have archers. I saw them, a woman, stringing her bow, cool as winter ice."

Aedelric's jaw stiffened. His eyes were already locked on the distant Norse line, a dark, growing mass. He knew then that the hope for a delay, for reinforcements from King Æthelred, was a vanishing dream. They would have to hold or die. "Shields!" he cried out, his voice harsh, still resolute, resonating over the tense ground. "Brace! We hold them as long as we can!"

The Northmen, a howling wave of blade and fury, charged ahead, their roars tearing through the air. From behind their foremost ranks, Asa, an unceasing bringer of doom, moved with experienced calm. Her bow sang, and the first barrage of Norse arrows descended, a deadly rain. Arrows hissed through the air, thudding with splintering force against shields, embedding in the earth, and finding flesh.

"Shields up! Hold the line!" Aedelric roared, shoving a man into place, his shield already braced. The Wessex warriors instinctively hunkered down, a wall of wood and iron rising to meet the onslaught. The thrumming impact of arrows striking their defenses was booming, a prelude to the storm that was to come. There was no more choice, no more hope for parley or retreat. Aedelric gripped his sword, his look hardening as he prepared to meet the surging wave of charging warriors. He had to meet them face-to-face.

Aedelric's command cut through the air, keen as a whetted blade. "Shields!" The Wessex line braced, a stoic wall of oak and iron rising to meet the onslaught, their feet digging into the earth. Eadric, Maelstrom swinging in a deadly arc, met the first wave of attackers, his sheer, brute power a bulwark against the furious Norse charge. The opposing lines slammed together with a concussive crash of wood and bone that snatched the air from a man's lungs. The shieldwall was not a static barrier, but a grinding, heaving mass of bodies, muscle straining against muscle, a terrifying, claustrophobic press, inches were fought for with brutal ferocity. The air immediately grew thick with the metal tang of hot blood, the pungent stench of sweat and fear, and the iron-like taste of adrenaline.

From slightly elevated ground behind the main Norse press, Asa worked her bow with tireless efficiency. Her arrows weren't just finding marks; they were aimed at faces, necks, anywhere mail didn't cover, anywhere a hit would cripple or kill swiftly. Each release was a focused breath, her mind cold and calculating. Yet, it wasn't infallible; some shafts splintered harmlessly on reinforced shield bosses, and others went wide in the eddying bedlam below, but enough flew true to make the Wessex line shudder.

In the belly of the grinding mass, Astrid served as a force of nature. She fought on the edge of the shieldwall, where the fighting was most desperate, a maelstrom of red hair and shining steel. Her circular shield absorbed or deflected blows with jarring impacts as her axe swept in arches, every blow delivered with bone-shattering power. There was no finesse, only brutal, effective killing, a snap of bone through the mail, a wet, tearing sound as the blade bit flesh. She roared challenges and grim jests, her red hair an intimidating, blood-spattered banner in the melee, her cackle a cold counterpoint to the screams.

Within the Wessex wall, Aedelric and Eadric held their ground, the unflinching heart of the desperate bulwark. The ground under their feet quickly became a slick, treacherous mire of mud and gore, footing constantly shifting as men fell or were pushed forward. Aedelric battled with a shield braced against the constant shove, thrusting his spear into the gaps that briefly appeared in the Norse line, pulling back and switching to his sword for the tighter, hacking work when they pressed close. His arms screamed with the effort, his vision narrowing to the immediate threat. Eadric, a bull of a man, used his immense strength to anchor their section of the wall. His axe, Maelstrom, was a deadly extension of his will, capable of splitting shields or rending through arms that reached too far. He cried out in defiance, his face a mask of exertion and fury.

The noise was a roaring ensemble of hell: the constant CRUMP of shields impacting with nauseating force, the shriek of steel sliding off steel or grating on mail, the guttural roars of the attackers, the grunts and cries of pain from the wounded and dying. Men stumbled, fell, and were immediately trampled into the bloody earth, their lives quashed underfoot.

In the churning, bloody heart of the struggle, a brief, impossible gap opened. For just a heartbeat, through the spray of blood and the press of bodies, Aedelric's eyes met Asa's across the carnage. He saw the archer, her bow drawn, her face grimly focused, and the sudden, jarring realization occurred to him again, the woman fighting in their ranks, not screaming in terror, but dealing death with icy precision. The sight was sharply out of place in the brutal, masculine scene of the shieldwall, a trace of the unexpected amid overwhelming violence. The moment was momentary, erased by the next shove of the line, the next enemy thrust.

The fight was a brutal, agonizing push-and-shove. Hours merged into one another, indicated exclusively by the shifting sun and the mounting piles of dead. Neither side broke easily. Muscles burned, lungs screamed for air, and exhaustion began to claw at their limbs. Men moved with leaden slowness, their swings losing power, their shouts turning to hoarse gasps. Aedelric felt the strain in his shoulders, the pain in his sword arm a persistent throb. Eadric's breath came in labored gasps, sweat combining with the blood on his face, but Maelstrom continued its deadly work, though every blow took a visible toll.

The battle settled into a grinding, bloody stalemate. Every inch gained was paid for in lives, every loss was met with grim, desperate resistance. The initial fury had given way to a deep-seated weariness on both sides. The Northmen pressed, but with less raw vigor. The Saxons held, but their shieldwall, though unbroken, was thinning, its members bruised and battered. Neither side could deliver the decisive blow, nor could they dislodge the other entirely.

Aedelric, seeing his men falter from sheer exhaustion and knowing that every fallen warrior was a loss he could ill afford, made a difficult decision. His eyes scanned the horizon, longing for the sight of King Æthelred's banners, but the forest stayed motionless. He could not throw more lives into this meat grinder without a definite path to victory. He needed to preserve his strength for when reinforcements might arrive. He yelled, his voice harsh, "Fall back! To the forest! Withdraw, slowly, shield by shield!" The command passed through the Wessex line, met with a combination of relief and frustrated grimness. Slowly, with trained discipline, they began to disengage, facing the enemy even as they retreated, pulling back towards the sheltering trees.

From her position, Asa observed the slight change in the Saxon line, the way they began to draw back, not in rout, but in a controlled, defensive maneuver. She saw the heavy toll the battle had taken on her warriors, their grimaces of pain, the flagging energy in their thrusts. The ground around them was a validation of the cost. She had achieved her objective: the town was sacked, the spoils secured. To continue fighting now, simply for the sake of it, would be to invite unnecessary losses. Her gut churned at the thought of more of her people dying for no strategic gain. Her look swept over her fatigued Northmen, then across the field to the slowly retreating Saxons. Enough. She raised her hand, signaling her horn-blower, then gave a sharp, distinct calla call to disengage. Slowly and grudgingly, the Northmen began to pull back, peeling away from the shieldwall and retreating toward the sacked port, their faces furrowed with exhaustion.

The abrupt silence that fell was heavy, marked solely by the horrific sounds of the battlefield's aftermath: the gasping breaths of the wounded, the ragged coughs of men choking on blood, and the low moans of those beyond help. Across the torn, corpse-strewn ground, Aedelric's eyes found Asa again, still standing near the rear of the retreating Norse. Their looks held across the bloodied earth, a muted acknowledgment of the deadly duel they had just shared as well as the grim certainty that this was merely a pause.

As the weary Wessex force pulled back towards the relative safety of the dense forest bordering the battleground, Aedelric and Eadric slumped to the ground, mail heavy, muscles trembling from the clash. The odor of blood and waste wafted densely in the air of their temporary camp, a grim sign of the day's brutal work. Asa, too, watched her warriors regroup within the plundered walls of Wareham, directing the last of the wounded until they all made it back into the sacked town.

"By God's teeth," Eadric gasped, pushing his helmet back and wiping grime from his face with a quivering hand. "They're hard bastards, these heathens. Man or woman, they mean to kill us all." His tone was flat, pragmatic. There was no room for wonder, only the bleak reality of the threat. He thought of the woman who had met him across the short distance during the parley attempt, the cold steadfastness in her eyes, and the other, the leader.

Aedelric watched the retreating Norse figures, his look lingering on where Asa had been seen near the rear ranks entering the town. "She fights with a bow," he spoke quietly, almost to himself, remembering her armed stance even in the pause. The archer. The warrior. The unforeseen sight of her skill burned in his mind. "She cut down men before we even met the line." He shook his head, the sheer, brutal capability of their foe sinking in.

"Don't go soft," Eadric warned, his voice harsh. "They're the enemy. Remember that." Eadric had a slight smile on his face, and he looked at Aedelric. "Maybe if we capture her, you can hump her."

Aedelric's grim expression didn't waver. "I don't think they would ever surrender," he said flatly, his gaze still on the distant Norse line."

Aedelric's mind still contended with the image of the archer's fierce gaze and the unexpected realization of fighting women. The simple truth of enemy and friend felt less simple now.

Back in the Norse encampment, within the perimeter of the sacked town, the air was laden with a different kind of weariness and fatigue, the dark satisfaction of survival, blended with sorrow for their fallen and the practical tasks of caring for the wounded and securing the spoils. Asa sat near a crackling fire, not reveling but meticulously inspecting her bow. The yew limb, sought deep in the forest for its perfect strength and toughness, was sound, but the nock was chipped. Her hardened hands, working with experienced care, made minor repairs.

She pulled her dark hair from its battle braid, letting it fall heavy around her shoulders; the warrior's face softened a little by the hearth light, though the fierceness in her brown eyes remained. Her thoughts, too, drifted back to the clash. "That one," she spoke quietly, her voice subdued, thinking of the Saxon leader. "The one with the swift sword. He moved well in the line." And the larger one... he stood his ground." There was a warrior's respect, a cold, assessing recognition of formidable challengers.

Astrid limped from the makeshift healers' area, a grimace on her face, nursing a strained muscle and a minor cut. She was cleaning the blood and grime from her axe and shield with salt water drawn from the nearby sea, the sting a well-known sensation against scrapes and cuts. Her flaming hair, damp and clinging to her face, contrasted with her pale skin. She overheard Asa's quiet words.

"Asa," Astrid said, her voice keen, practical, her eyes glinting in the hearth light. "Their skill means they are dangerous. Not fodder for quiet thought. They didn't break entirely. They pulled back, yes, but their gazes still held defiance." She motioned towards the dark forest where Aedelric's men had retreated. "We took the town, but the head of the snake still lives. We need to cut it off." She looked at the piles of loot being sorted, the grim necessity of their raid illustrated by the wounded groaning nearby.

Asa knew Astrid was thinking only of killing, of conquest. The admiration for skill, the strange trace of connection inside the chaos, was a distraction they couldn't afford. Their purpose here was to plunder, not annihilation.

Astrid walked over, her movements stiff, and she sat beside Asa, beginning to sharpen her axe with a whetstone, the harsh sound a counterpoint to the fire's crackle. "They are Christians," Astrid stated, the word charged with difference, with inherent opposition. "Their god is not ours, their wealth ours to claim. That is the way of things. And they are still out there, bleeding, regrouping. We should finish them tonight."

Asa looked at Astrid, then back at the unfamiliar stars, her look hardening. "You are right," she said, her voice firm now, the brief instant of reflection hardening toward resolve. "They are the enemy. And we have taken enough from the enemy." She turned her look to the darkened harbor, calculating the tides. "We have what we came for. The ships are loaded, the winter stores secured. We sail at first light."

Astrid's axe scraping stopped abruptly. "At first light?" Her speech was flat, incredulous. "But the tide..." She trailed off, then her eyes flared with a different kind of anger. "No. The tide will be against us for hours after dawn. Sailing in the dark is perilous, a fool's gamble, but so is waiting here for them to return emboldened. We should press the advantage now, while they lick their wounds! Strike them in their sleep!"

Asa fixed her gaze, unyielding. "We have what we need, Astrid. To endanger our ships in the dark, or to lose more warriors in a needless skirmish, is foolish. Our mission is complete. We leave with the dawn tide." Asa's tone allowed no room for argument, a direct order from the leader to kin.

Astrid's jaw tensed, her grip firming on her axe. She wanted to argue, to rage, but the finality in Asa's voice was absolute. Her eyes, however, continued to burn with a frustrated, dangerous fire. She said nothing, but a cold, defiant resolve fixed deep inside herself. First light, you say? The tide may change before then. She rose, turning her back to Asa, and walked towards her warriors, her mind already forming a plan that did not involve waiting for the sun.

Part 2: Ambush

The deepest part of the night hung heavy over Wareham, wrapping the plundered port and the surrounding forest in a cloak of cold darkness. A biting wind whispered through the trees, carrying the distant, rhythmic slap of waves against the beached longships. Inside Wareham's shattered perimeter, the Northmen slept soundly, their bellies full, their bodies heavy with exhaustion after the day's brutal work. Fires had long since died to embers, casting only faint, dying glows. Asa, too, was deep in a fitful sleep, the grim weight of victory and its cost pressing down on her.

Outside the port, in the relative safety of the dense forest, Aedelric and Eadric's remaining Wessex warriors were equally lost to sleep. Huddled together against the chill, their wounds aching, they sought what little rest they could find. A few weary sentries, similarly exhausted, shivered by a dying fire, their gazes unfocused with fatigue, dreaming of the dawn they hoped would bring reinforcements.

Astrid moved like a ghost through the slumbering Northmen. Her mind, a forge of relentless ambition, had already made its own decision. She roused a select, eager few, the most bloodthirsty, the ones who chafed under Asa's cautious leadership. No signals, no horns, no shouted commands. Just the quiet scrape of steel, the muffled clink of mail, and low, guttural whispers as they gathered, their shadows stretching long and thin in the pre-dawn gloom.

A chill wind, carrying the scent of pine and something sharp and metallic, stirred Asa awake within Wareham's walls, but it was not the wind alone.

Astrid led her chosen few through the silent, pre-dawn forest, each step placed with unnatural quiet. Aedelric's camp was barely a camp, more a collection of exhausted men huddled against the cold, some wrapped in cloaks, others simply slumped against trees. A lone sentry shivered by a dying fire, his breath misting in the cold air, his gaze unfocused with fatigue. Astrid approached him from behind, her movements fluid and silent as a hunting cat. Before the man could even turn his head, her hand clamped over his mouth, pulling him back into the shadows. The quiet, wet gurgle of a slit throat was the only sound, quickly swallowed by the forest's stillness. The body was lowered gently and noiselessly to the ground.

Then, with a shared, unspoken signal, Astrid and her Northmen exploded into the sleeping camp.

The world erupted for Aedelric's men. Sleep-dazed Wessex warriors scrambled, fumbling for weapons, their cries of alarm quickly turning to screams of terror and pain. Axes bit deep with sickening wet thuds, cleaving bone and shattering desperate defenses in the dim light. The metallic tang of fresh blood immediately choked the pre-dawn air, joining the screams in the dim light, wet thuds punctuating the silence of the forest that had only moments before been absolute. This was no battle; this was a slaughter.

Eadric, stirring from a deep, uneasy sleep, instinctively reached for Maelstrom. He rolled, bringing his shield up, as a hulking Norseman bore down on him. But it wasn't the hulking figure that struck the blow. Astrid, a phantom of brutal efficiency in the pre-dawn gloom, was already through the meager defenses. She moved with a predator's grace, her axe a blur. Eadric, turning to meet one threat, had barely registered her presence when her heavy axe struck. It landed with a horrifying crunch, cleaving into his exposed side where his arm had momentarily lifted, tearing through flesh and ribs. Maelstrom, his trusted axe, fell from his numb grasp, clattering onto the bloody ground near his feet.

Eadric roared, a sound of agony and disbelief, stumbling as his world tilted. Before he could even try to draw a knife, Astrid was upon him, a red-haired fury. With a final, brutal swing, her axe came down on his head and on his raised arm, grinding across it with a sickening tear of muscle and bone. He fell heavily, his body hitting the ground with a sickening thud, already dead before he landed, his eyes staring blankly at the greying sky. The oak had fallen. The beacon of hope for his men was extinguished.

Aedelric, roused from sleep by the first shouts and screams, had stumbled from his makeshift bedroll, sword half-drawn. He saw it all unfold in the flickering torchlight: Eadric, his rock, his brother in arms, falling, his life brutally extinguished by Astrid's axe. A primal roar of grief and fury tore from Aedelric's throat. Blind rage consumed him. He charged towards Astrid, sword raised, cutting down any Northman unfortunate enough to be in his path, his grief lending him a terrible, desperate strength.

The cacophony of the ambush, brief but absolute, reached Asa's ears, pulling her entirely from sleep. The screams were too sharp, too sudden, to be anything but a surprise attack. Her heart hammered with a cold, furious dread. Astrid. The thought was a burning ember of rage. She hadn't ordered this. This recklessness, this blatant defiance! She cursed under her breath, scrambling for her bow.

"To me!" Asa bellowed, her voice cutting through the fading sounds of slaughter. The few warriors who hadn't followed Astrid, caught by surprise by the pre-dawn chaos themselves, rallied around her. They hurried towards the sounds, towards the forest edge where Astrid's brutal work was already done.

Asa reached the carnage just as Aedelric, a wild figure of grief and fury, was making his desperate charge towards Astrid. Asa saw the raw, suicidal intent in his eyes, and her gaze turned cold and calculating. There was no hesitation. She would deal with Astrid later. He was a threat, a leader, and a valuable prize.

With a swift, fluid motion, she nocked an arrow and loosed it. The shaft flew true, finding its mark in Aedelric's side, just below the arm where the mail was weakest, where his furious, desperate swing had exposed him.

Aedelric gasped, the force of the impact staggering him. His hand instinctively clutched his side, feeling the fletching buried deep. His sword, the silver blur, slipped from his weakening grasp, clattering onto the bloody ground, a stark, terrible sound announcing his fall. He crumpled to his knees, then pitched forward onto the churned earth.

The fighting around them faltered, men turning to stare as Aedelric and Eadric both lay broken. Asa walked towards the fallen Saxon, her boots crunching on the debris of battle. Her bow was still in her hand, a silent symbol of her deadly skill. She stood over Aedelric, his mail-clad body prone in the mud, his face a mask of pain and disbelief. The Wessex leader, moments ago a whirlwind of rage, was now at her mercy.

Aedelric lay there, pain searing through his side with every ragged breath. His face, grimy and blood-streaked, was proof of his defiance. His eyes, though clouded with agony, still held a spark, a refusal to break, even now. His jaw was clenched tightly, his muscles twitching, as he held back cries. Frustration warred with the pain, frustration at being brought down, at failing Eadric, at the fate of his men. But beneath it all was a hard kernel of resolve. He was a warrior. He would not yield. He was wounded, captured, but unbroken in spirit.

Asa looked down at him, her face unreadable, the intensity in her brown eyes unwavering. His pain was evident, his defiance clear. It stirred that same flicker within her, a strange, unsettling recognition in the face of an enemy. She wouldn't name it, not even in her thoughts.

Suddenly, Astrid was there, her axe still in hand, ready to finish the job. "The other one is down," she grated, her eyes fixed on Aedelric. Her axe began to rise.

"Asa, what are you doing?" she demanded, seeing Asa step forward, her arm outstretched, blocking the killing blow. The few remaining Norse warriors near them paused, watching.

Asa didn't answer Astrid immediately, her gaze still on Aedelric. Then, her voice, cold and commanding, cut through the tense air. "You disobey me." She gave Astrid a sharp, unyielding look, pushing her aside with a forceful hand. "No more killing," she stated, her tone leaving no room for argument, turning bloodlust into practicality.

Astrid stared at Asa, then back at the wounded Saxon. Her jaw worked, but she slowly lowered her axe, frustrated but respecting Asa's decision.

Asa roughly grabbed the arrow that pierced his side and ripped it out, with no emotion or empathy. This caused Aedelric to scream in pain and become even more wounded than he was. Then Aedelric's arm, hauling him to his feet, ignoring his painful gasp. Seeing their leader captured, hearing his cries, the spirits of the few remaining Wessex warriors finally broke. They had undeniably lost. Their survival instinct taking over, they turned and fled, scattering across the land in their desperate search for escape.

The ambush was over. A new chapter had begun. Aedelric, their enemy turned captive, was being dragged across the bloodied ground towards Wareham. The pain in his side was a constant reminder of his defeat, but the image of Eadric falling, of his men scattering, was a deeper wound. Failure. Worry for Wessex gnawed at him. His gaze fell on Asa, her grip firm, her face impassive. He saw no mercy, only the stern face of the victor. He was at her mercy, a chilling dread mixed with that strange, unwanted respect for her brutal effectiveness.

He was brought into the Norse camp, the smells of death and victory heavy in the air. With a forceful shove, the kind that could send a man reeling like a longship in a storm, Asa pushed Aedelric down onto the hard, unforgiving ground. His body hit with a jarring impact, a cloud of dust rising around him. His vision swam, the edges of his sight blurring, his consciousness fraying.

Asa stood over him, her gaze as intense as a hawk's. There was something in her eyes as she looked down at the wounded Saxon, a flicker of... something... that she immediately suppressed. Her face was a mask, her lips a tight, grim line. Whatever the feeling, it would remain unspoken.

Suddenly, Astrid's figure blocked his view. She stood over Aedelric, her chest still heaving from the pre-dawn exertion, her eyes alight with the triumph of the ambush. "The camp is cleared. The big one is dead." Her voice was low, almost gloating. "A true victory. We shattered them!"

Asa's gaze snapped from Aedelric to Astrid, cold fury simmering in her brown eyes. "You defy me," she stated, her voice dangerously quiet, devoid of the usual warmth. "You launched an attack without my command. You risked everything for a pointless slaughter!"

Astrid's triumphant grin faltered. "Pointless? They were broken! They would have fought us again at dawn! I simply"

"You simply decided you knew better." Asa cut her off, taking a step closer, her presence radiating a raw power that made even Astrid hesitate. "We had what we needed. Our people are fed for the winter. This... this was for your bloodlust, not for Njardarheimr."

Astrid's jaw tightened. "They were enemies! A threat! I removed it!"

"And what of the cost?" Asa gestured vaguely to the carnage in the forest, then to the few remaining warriors standing around them, their faces weary. "We lose men needlessly! This is not how we survive, Astrid. Not by throwing lives away for vengeance or pride."

A tense silence stretched between them, thick with Asa's anger and Astrid's simmering defiance. But then, Astrid's shoulders slumped almost imperceptibly. Her gaze dropped, avoiding Asa's searing stare. "I... I respect your command, Asa," she muttered, the words strained but firm. "Always."

"Then you will obey it," Asa said, her voice still sharp, but with a hint of resolution. She turned to the warriors now gathering around them. "Load the ships! All of it! The loot, the captives, the wounded, and him!" She gestured to Aedelric. "Everything we have. We sail with the tide. Now!"

Astrid, her earlier excitement thoroughly doused, moved to supervise, though with less of her usual fervent energy. The Northmen, accustomed to Asa's decisive commands, moved with practiced efficiency, loading the plunder, securing the few captives, and preparing the longships.

Aedelric, barely conscious, felt himself roughly handled, his body a dull throb of pain. He was hoisted and suspended between two burly Northmen, towards the longships.

The first pale light of dawn crept over the horizon, painting the sky in cold greys and soft blues as the last of the Northmen boarded. The longships, heavy with their grim cargo, slipped silently from the shore, their prows cutting through the calm, dark waters. As Wareham, stripped bare, receded into the burgeoning dawn, Asa stood at the helm of her ship, her face grimly set, watching the receding coastline. Astrid stood nearby, quiet, her gaze fixed on the sea, the conflict between them momentarily silenced by the vastness of the ocean.

Part 3: Storm's Gift

Aedelric's return to consciousness was a slow, painful ascent through murky water. His eyes fluttered open to a world that refused to settle, a blurry expanse of grey wood and rope against a blinding sky. The coppery tang of blood was strong in his mouth, the ache in his head a dull throb beneath the searing pain in his side. He wasn't on solid ground. The rhythmic lift and fall beneath him, the groaning of timber, the slap of water against wood, he was on a ship. Bound.

Rough rope bit into his wrists, securing him to the mast. Every shift in his weight sent a fresh wave of agony through his wounded side, a brutal counterpoint to the hypnotic sway of the longship. Salt spray kissed his face, the sharp, clean smell of the sea a stark confirmation of his predicament. How long had he been out? A day? More? The sun was high, a pitiless eye in the vast sky, offering no answers about the passage of time.

He strained against the bindings, the rope biting deeper into his flesh. The ship creaked and groaned around him; the great square sail overhead snapped and billowed with a sound like thunder. Where were they going? His mind, still sluggish, reeled with fragmented memories, the ambush, Eadric falling, the arrow... Astrid's face loomed before darkness claimed him.

Squinting against the glare, he could make out the shapes of Northmen moving on the deck, their voices a foreign, guttural murmur. He saw the helmsman, a grim figure at the steering oar, guiding them towards a horizon that stretched endlessly, blue melding into pale blue. The uncertainty was a cold heavyweight in his gut. All he could do was endure. Survive.

And then he saw her. The Northwoman from the fight, the archer who had brought him down. Asa. She stood near

the stern, her silhouette sharp against the sky, her gaze
fixed on him, cold and unwavering as the sea itself.

She moved closer, her voice carrying over the wind
and waves, a stream of harsh, unfamiliar sounds. "The
Gods have spared you." The words meant nothing to him,
but her tone was stark, matter-of-fact. "You are lucky to be
alive."

Aedelric's consciousness flickered. The pain, the
exhaustion, the relentless motion of the ship, Asa's
unintelligible, stern voice, it all blurred into a suffocating
haze. He was a captive, wounded, adrift. But alive. The will
to survive is buried deep, stirred. But his eyelids felt heavy,
impossibly heavy. The rhythmic creak of the ship and the
murmur of foreign voices became a strange, distant lullaby,
pulling him under.

Before he finally succumbed, he saw her again, a brief,
sharp image. Asa, her hand raised, not towards him, but
towards the sky, her gaze fixed on something unseen in the
distance. Astrid, the one who had slain Eadric and ended
his fight, stood beside her, following her gaze. Then,
darkness.

The sea voyage became a nightmare: no gradual
worsening, but a sudden, savage descent into chaos. The
sky turned a bruised, angry purple. The wind rose to a
shriek, tearing at the sails, whipping the sea into monstrous,
unforgiving waves. The longship, built for speed and raid,
was a fragile shell against nature's fury. Water crashed over
the deck, icy and relentless. Thunder boomed, not like war
drums, but like giants smashing the heavens with mallets.
Lightning split the sky in jagged, terrifying cracks,
momentarily illuminating the terrifying peaks and troughs
of the waves.

Aedelric was ripped from unconsciousness by the
violence of it. Cold water slammed into him, the ship
rearing and plunging beneath him with sickening force.
Rain lashed down like icy needles. He saw his captors now,

not grim warriors, but desperate men and women fighting for their lives, scrambling across the pitching deck, yelling orders lost to the wind, hauling on ropes, securing cargo, fighting the sea with every ounce of their strength and skill.

He saw Asa and Astrid near the helm, their faces stark white masks in the gloom, gripping the steering oar as they battled the storm's pull, their bodies braced against the ship's violent movements. "This is no natural storm!" Asa yelled, her voice raw, barely audible over the wind's howl. "The gods are against us!" Astrid nodded grimly, scanning the impossible waves. "Hold fast!" she screamed to the crew, her authority clear even in the maelstrom.

A colossal wave, a liquid mountain, rose above them, blotting out the sky. With a thunderous roar, it slammed into the ship's side. For a blinding instant, Aedelric saw Asa's face, her eyes meeting his across the chaos and terror, just before the world went dark again, not from unconsciousness, but from the crushing force of the water.

The wave capsized the longship. Timber groaned and splintered. The cold, black sea swallowed them whole. Men, women, warriors, prisoners, they were all plunged into the churning abyss. The storm devoured their cries, their struggles futile against the ocean's overwhelming power. Few survived. The sea, vast and indifferent, claimed most.

Somehow, amidst the chaos, Astrid was torn free, swallowed by the currents, swept away from the wreck, and the struggling few clinging to splintered wood. Her fiery hair, her fierce spirit, lost to the storm's wrath.

And by some grim twist of fate, two enemies were spared. Asa and Aedelric. Battered, half-drown, they found themselves clinging to a broken piece of the longship's hull, tossed about like driftwood by the still furious waves. The sky still bled lightning, revealing the monstrous waves that towered above them, threatening to drag them under. But in one blinding flash, through the spray and the driving rain,

Asa glimpsed a dark shape on the horizon, a distant, uncertain promise through the storm.

It was a shred of slim hope. The storm that had tried to kill them was, in its unrelenting fury, driving them towards salvation.

They were vomited onto a desolate beach, collapsing onto the cold, gritty sand, gasping for air that burned their raw throats. Their bodies hurt with a thousand bruises, lungs aching from saltwater. They lay there, two broken figures against the vast, indifferent expanse of sand, chests expanding, hearts pounding on their ribs, the raw, grim truth of survival settling in.

Slowly, painfully, Aedelric pushed himself onto hands and knees, then one knee, his wounded side howling in protest. His eyes, wild with exhaustion and shock, fixed on Asa. His clothes, sodden and torn, stuck to him, stained with blood and the filth of the sea. His mail and weapons were gone, stripped away long before the storm. Asa, too, was in a tunic and trousers, no armor, shivering, her dark hair a matted mess stuck to her face and shoulders, streaked with sand. They were two battered, stripped-down creatures on a wild shore.

Asa, mirroring his movement, pushed herself into a seated posture. Her dark hair, usually braided tight, was a disorderly tangle against the grey-white sand. Her eyes, wide and still haunted by the storm, flitted across the empty beach, the towering cliffs behind them, the dense, dark edge of the forest beyond. Confusion and perplexity whirled inside her; the violence of the past few hours was still too raw to comprehend their present reality fully. Where were they?

The tension between them, thick and primal, was a third entity on the beach. They were enemy survivors, stripped bare of rank and allegiance. Their stares locked, a silent challenge, an assessment. Then, propelled by exhaustion, adrenaline, and the ingrained instinct to fight, they charged, without weapons but with raw, desperate fury. Fists clenched, they ambled towards each other, a blind, clumsy brawl sustained by everything that had happened, by sheer survival instinct overriding reason. Grunts and the impact of skin-on-skin resounded over the quiet beach. It was a brutal, pathetic dance, but it was the only language they had left.

Asa, drawing on her warrior's strength, landed solid blows, but Aedelric, powered by a desperate defiance and the ghost of Eadric's fall, met her with equal ferocity. They fought, battered bodies colliding, each clumsy strike a demonstration of their refusal to yield.

Yet exhaustion, a far crueler enemy than either of them, dragged them down. Their movements slowed, and blows lacked force. Finally, with a shared look of complcte depletion, they both collapsed onto the sand, breaths tearing in harsh gasps, bodies bruised and spent.

They lay there, side-by-side, the marks of their desperate struggle already blooming on their skin. The immediate storm had passed. They were alone on a desolate beach in a wild, untamed land that Asa, despite her confusion, gradually recognized as likely a remote corner of her homeland. Far from any familiar longhouse or settlement, their only company was each other and the vast, indifferent wilderness.

The future was a terrifying blank. Difficulties loomed, unseen and unknown. But for this moment, lying there, they allowed themselves the simple grace of survival. They lay and breathed, bodies aching, minds numb, anchored only by the even rhythm of the waves and the slow beat of their hearts against the earth. Two souls, enemies, shipwrecked, alive.

As Asa lay there, the cold, gritty sand against her cheek, her mind, although tired, began to race. The battle, the storm, the wreck, a cascade of disaster. Her people, her warriors, her friends, all lost to the sea. Astrid... where was Astrid? Was she even alive?

And this man is near her. The Saxon leader. Her enemy. The strange, disconcerting mix of feelings resurfaced: respect for his raw grit in the fight, curiosity about his strength in the storm, and that trace of something else, a tug she refused to name.

Their situation was dire: they were stranded, alone, with no weapons, no supplies, and no obvious path forward. How would she survive? How would she find food in this wild place? How would she pass through these lands, even if they were her own?

Still beneath the fear and uncertainty, the hard core of her being remained. She was a survivor. She had confronted death and disaster before. She would face this. She would rise. She would fight. She would survive. The thought remained a quiet pledge in the vast wilderness.

In that vulnerable moment, Aedelric stirred, turning his head towards her. His voice was an unrefined croak, faintly audible over the sound of the waves. "What do we do now?" The words were foreign, meaningless sounds to Asa, but the utter exhaustion, the raw need for direction, the simple gesture of reaching out for a common purpose, spoke a tongue she understood. It was not the voice of an enemy thegn, but a fellow survivor.

Their mutual predicament stripped off the layers of nation and war. Here, on this bleak shore, they were merely two people, stranded, facing the same stark reality. Aedelric broke the silence again, his voice still rough but stronger now, locking eyes with her across the small distance between them. "We need each other."

Asa understood the sentiment; the stark truth of his foreign words was conveyed by his eyes, his posture, and the sheer logic of their situation. Alone, they might not last. Together, they stood a chance.

With a slow nod, she extended her hand, a gesture he understood perfectly, an alliance. Brought forth by desperation, shaped in saltwater and blood. "An alliance, then," she uttered in Norse, the words foreign to him, but the offered hand and the shared look spoke the agreement.

Below the vast, impassive sky, on that remote, wild beach, an uneasy truce was struck. Their destinies, violently twisted by the storm, were now bound together in ways neither could have imagined.

As the sky began to darken, the bleak reality of the coming night spurred them into action. They needed shelter and warmth. They moved slowly, stiffly, searching the immediate area. They found a small rock overhang nestled against the towering cliffs that rose sharply from the beach, offering some protection from the wind and potential rain.

The cliffs towered above them, ancient, worn features carved over millennia by wind and sea, giving their refuge a sense of wild grandeur. The beach extended out, a swathe of white sand dotted with rocks and smooth pebbles, the mild lapping of the waves a constant, relaxing rhythm in the sudden quiet of their world. Behind the shelter, the dense, dark forest started abruptly, a knotted, impenetrable wall of green, alive with the unseen sounds of the wilderness.

Finding shelter was one thing; fire was another. They had no flint, no steel, nothing except the raw materials of the land, and the knowledge of ancient ways. Building a fire by friction was a grueling task, demanding strength and patience, neither of which they had in abundance after their ordeal. Asa, despite her aching muscles, took on the task. She found a dry piece of driftwood, weathered smooth by the sea, and a strong stick. Settling on the sand, she notched the wood and began to spin the stick rapidly between her hands, the effort burning her own palms as sweat beaded on her brow. Her breaths arrived in gasps, but she worked with tireless focus. They needed fire. Desperately.

Aedelric watched her, helpless, his body too injured and exhausted for such strenuous work. His eyes, fatigued yet hopeful, were fixed on her hands, on the point where wood met wood, waiting for the first wisp of smoke, the first glimmer of warmth. Asa gathered dry leaves and fine twigs, ready to nurture the fragile spark.

Finally, after what appeared like an eternity, a thin thread of smoke twisted upwards. Then, a tiny, hesitant spark caught on the dry leaves. Asa shielded it with her body, her breath held, adding small twigs and coaxing it to life. Slowly, tentatively, it grew, a delicate flame licking at the wood until it grew into a steady, crackling flame.

They sat opposite each other, the fire's glow dancing on their faces, throwing long, moving shadows. Asa looked across at the Saxon, who had contributed nothing physical to the fire's birth but had watched with an intensity that indicated his need. They were still utterly exposed, completely alone, utterly far from home. But for now, they had warmth, shelter, and the dancing comfort of the flames. And, though neither fully grasped the enormity of it yet, they had each other. Their story of survival, bound together, had truly begun.

Asa watched the fire; its glow was soothing against the cold and the soreness in her bones. The day played back in her mind, the storm's fury, the ship breaking apart, the desperate struggle in the water, the brutal, necessary fight on the beach. Her warriors... lost. Astrid... gone. A chilling knot of grief tightened her chest.

But the man across the fire was real. Alive. Her enemy, now her... ally? He knew nothing of living in the wild; that was clear. He watched her with the fire-making as if she were performing some strange magic. Yet, his determination, his sheer refusal to die, was something she couldn't help but respect. The fight on the beach... the unexpected strength he had found... and that other feeling, still unsettling, still present.

Her glance fell on his side. The dark, spreading stain on his torn shirt. Her arrow. It looked bad. He was useless to her, dying of infection. He needed help. Tonight, if possible.

She looked at his wound, then back at him. He fixed his eyes on hers, pain carved on his face, but awareness dawning in his eyes. He knew what needed to be done. There were no supplies, nothing. Only what they had.

Without a word, Asa began to tear at the bottom of her rough tunic, the fabric ripping with a harsh sound. She pulled a long strip, then another, circling the hem with experienced, rough efficiency. She motioned to his bloody shirt, then made a pulling gesture.

Aedelric, wincing, fumbled with the tie of his shirt. As he pulled the blood-soaked garment away from the wound, exposing his side, his gaze was drawn to Asa. Her dark hair, now loose and tangled, framed a face wrinkled with lassitude but still held that core of firm strength. Her brown eyes, in the firelight, were intense, focused on the task, not him. She was beautiful, yes, but in a fierce, practical way, utterly unlike the shielded women of Wessex. There was a wildness about her, a self-possession that pulled him in, an undeniable attraction born not of courtly manners but of shared, brutal experience.

His eyes dropped lower as she began to clean the wound as best she could with a piece of moist cloth torn from his shirt, preparing to bind it. He saw the elaborate patterns of tattoos adorning her skin, swirling across her shoulder, down her arm, vanishing beneath the torn material of her tunic. Dark lines and symbols upon her skin, a language he couldn't read but knew, was significant. They told of journeys, of conflicts endured, of gods, perhaps, of who she was. They were distinctly Norse, alien, and fascinating, each denoting a piece of an account etched permanently onto her body.

In the dancing light of the fire, the roar of the sea a distant lullaby, Aedelric watched Asa tend to the wound she had inflicted. He saw her more than the deadly warrior, the terrifying enemy, but as a woman. A complex, capable woman whose wordless language of scars and ink was as captivating as her unforeseen act of binding his wound.

As Aedelric's look lingered, attracted to the stories written on her skin, particularly the patterns visible on her arm and shoulder in the flame light, she noticed. Her hands halted for a fraction of a second. A sudden rush of feeling, indignation, or a fierce guarding of her privacy shone in her eyes. With a quick, sharp movement, she pushed his hand away from the wound and leaned back slightly, putting a small distance between them.

She spoke then, a sharp retort in swift, icy Norse. The words were meaningless to him, but the sound was unmistakable, an apparent, cold demand for respect, a drawing of a line. It was an unmistakable reminder that, despite the shared ordeal, despite the alliance, she was not his to gaze upon without leave. Her fierce independence was as sharp as any blade.

Yet, as she pulled away, Asa found her look flicking back to him, drawn against her will. His face bruised and spent but set with that stubborn resilience, his unfamiliar features... it aroused something inside of her, a raw, unexpected attraction that conflicted with the ingrained knowledge of who he was, who he had been. Enemy. She turned her head away quickly, her mind in turmoil of conflicting feelings.

Within the quiet of the night, with only the glowing fire and the sound of the waves for company, they sat, weighed down by the heavy, unspoken load of their mutual past, their uncertain future, and the tempestuous, unexpected emotions stirring between them. Survival had thrown them together, and now their journey was taking a turn neither had expected. Their story wasn't just about withstanding the wilderness; it was about traversing the treacherous, unmapped territory of their unforeseen connection. The tattoos on Asa's skin, quiet witnesses to her past, watched over this new, unfolding chapter. Though Aedelric could not read their specific tales, he knew they were part of the complex, formidable woman who had brought him down, saved him from Astrid, and now tended his wound within the desolate night. They were a story he was now, unexpectedly, a part of.

CHAPTER 2

Part 1: Price of Survival

Aedelric's eyes shot open to the raw soreness in his body. The steady throb of the arrow wound in his side, the battered soreness from the desperate, clumsy brawl on the sand. He lay on the hard ground beneath the rock overhang, his meager bandage feeling insufficient. The initial light of dawn passed through the gap in the rocks. He was alone.

A jolt of deep dread shot through him. That woman. She was gone. Had she simply left him to the mercy of this brutal, alien land? Or worse, was she nearby, watching, waiting for him to lower his guard, to finish what she'd started? His insides clenched. He was a warrior, a King's hearthweru, but he knew nothing of surviving like this, stripped of his armor, his companions, his familiar world. Alone here meant a swift, miserable end.

With a grimace of pain, he pushed himself up, his muscles objecting after the cold night. He ambled out from the shelter into the pale morning sunshine. The beach spread before him exactly as they had left it, strewn with seaweed, driftwood, and the scattered wreckage. And there, in the shallow water near the shoreline, stood Asa, waist-deep in the icy waves.

His wariness spiked, but then he saw what she was doing. She moved with swift, silent grace, her eyes focused on the water. With sudden, darting movements of her hands, faster than a striking adder, she snatched small fish from between the rocks and pooling water. She was fishing with her bare hands. He watched with a grudging, bewildered admiration rising in him. Despite their past, despite his fear, he recognized the stark, beautiful efficiency of a survivor. For now, at least, their uneasy alliance held.

Asa secured a wriggling fish and turned back towards the shore. She stopped when she saw Aedelric watching her from the edge of the sand, his face wrinkled with weariness, evident, and something that looked like awe. His persistent gaze, even across the distance, was a presence. She had a familiar trace of annoyance at being scrutinized, yet a small, unwelcome part of her registered the attention. Holding up the fish, she made a simple gesture, pointing from the catch to her mouth, then towards the remains of last night's fire pit. Food. A shared necessity.

Their communication was a clumsy, vital movement of stores, expressions, and raw action. Words were useless, sounds that meant nothing across the gulf of Norse and West Saxon. Asa pointed to the fish, mimed putting it over a fire, and then rubbed her belly. Aedelric nodded, understanding the basic need. He watched her face, her eyes, and the set of her jaw, trying to read intent, emotion, anything beyond the literal movement. She watched him just as closely: his wincing movements, the steady, focused gaze that seemed to miss nothing, the fundamental strength in his posture even when wounded.

It was a slow, often frustrating process. Points were missed, and gestures were misinterpreted. Even with each mutual moment of understanding, the nod that confirmed a meaning, the exchanged glance that acknowledged a task, a different kind of connection began to form. It was built not on common stories or uncomplicated conversation but on observation, necessity, and a developing, reluctant empathy. They were learning from each other, not through language, but through the stark, shared struggle to stay alive.

Back at the overhang, they shared the roughly cooked fish, devouring it, and discarded the bones onto the sand. The quiet between them was not empty; it was still filled with the tacit pressure of their situation, the contrast between the fish in their hands and the lives they had known. They were not Saxon and Northwoman here. They were merely two people chewing tough meat, trying to survive another sunrise.

Asa would point to things, firewood, the water's edge, the forest, and mime actions: gathering wood, drinking, walking inland. Aedelric watched her intently, his brow knitted in concentration, then attempted to replicate the gesture, a wordless question in his eyes. A sharp nod from Asa confirmed his understanding; a slight shake of her head sent him back to puzzling it out. His movements held the solid, grounded quality of a shield-wall fighter. Hers were quicker, lighter, the focused economy of an archer and hunter. Trust remained a seed, fragile and new, planted in the infertile soil of necessity. Every common, understood gesture, every successful task completed together, nurtured it.

Sharing the meal, the rough, smoked fish filling his empty belly, Aedelric contended with the sheer strangeness of it all. Eating with the Northwoman who had shot him down, who had stood over him before taking him prisoner, and whose companion had killed Eadric. It was beyond surreal. He was astonished by her, her fortitude, her utter competence in this wild place. She caught fish with her hands, read the land, and knew what to do. He had been taught to fight, to command, to govern within a system; she had been taught to live, raw and direct, from the earth itself. He admired her deeply.

And the unwelcome tangle of feelings remained. Admiration mixed with the unquestionable pull he felt towards her, a pagan warrior whose culture was the sworn enemy of his own, whose gods were alien demons. He watched her, her face intent as she ate. Did she feel anything similar? Or was this purely a cold, practical alliance of survival?

The language barrier was an ongoing, frustrating wall; yet, their mutual struggle seemed to bypass it, forging a connection that words might have complicated. He wanted to know about her, about her life across the sea, about the symbols on her skin. But the chasm was huge, different worlds, different loyalties, different Gods. What would happen if they survived this? If they found their way back to other people? Would they simply become enemies again, their mutual ordeal forgotten in the face of old hatreds? The thoughts were a heavy counterpoint to the simple act of eating.

Asa ate, her eyes scanning the beach and the forest edge, constantly assessing. Sharing food with this Saxon was deeply ironic. Enemies by birth, bound by shipwreck. He was strong; that was clear from their fight and the brief clash the day before. His determination was formidable. But his helplessness here was equally apparent. He knew nothing of this land, how to feed himself, how to read the signs. It was a strange contrast to his warrior's strength.

The disturbing feelings persisted for him. She was drawn to his strength, his unforeseen resilience, and the stark honesty in his eyes, even as her arrow had brought him down. But he was Christian. An enemy. What did these feelings mean? What purpose could they serve?

She watched him, curious about the world he came from, the life of a then in Wessex. She had heard myths of their single, all-powerful God, a concept so strange compared to her teeming pantheon. *One God? How could one God encompass everything?*

As they finished the fish, the immediate gnawing of hunger dulled. Aedelric lowered his head. Asa watched, puzzled, as he closed his eyes, his mouth moving silently. It was the strange ritual he had performed before. He was speaking to his God.

He looked up, seeing her questioning gaze. He tried to explain, gesturing upwards and then placing his hand on his chest, but a complex concept was reduced to clumsy hand movements. He was giving thanks to his God. Asa watched, understanding the gesture of devotion, perhaps, but the depth, the nature of his single, unseen deity, remained a mystery, a silent, unbridgeable gap between them.

Hunger sated, their attention turned to the vital need for survival. Supplies. Fresh water. They needed to search the debris of the wreck again and venture inland.

With a common understanding of the current task, they moved down to the beach, scanning the high-water line, where a knotted mess of fragmented wood and cargo had washed ashore. It was a grim indication of the storm's power. Among the lots, they found a length of thick rope, applicable for countless tasks, and then, a glint of steel, a dagger, well-made, its blade remains sharp despite the saltwater. Asa spotted it first, her eyes quick, her hand closing around the hilt. Aedelric watched her, a trace of unease playing across his face. A weapon. In her hand. The power balance shifted subtly.

But Asa showed no intention of using it against him. Anger was a tool for survival, not a means to renew conflict. Their lives depended on cooperation now. Besides, the feeling towards him... it had moved. He wasn't just an enemy. He was... the Saxon who had survived with her.

Having salvaged what little they could, Asa gestured towards the forest, the dark, imposing wall that marked the edge of the unknown. Inland. They needed water, food, and perhaps better shelter.

They entered the dense wood. The air immediately changed, becoming cooler and thicker, bearing the scent of moist soil, moss, and rotting leaves. Sunlight fought to penetrate the canopy overhead, filtering down in shifting patterns of brightness and shade. Every murmur of leaves, every crack of a twig under their feet, appeared intensified within the quiet of the forest. Aedelric, his wound paining with every step, gritted his teeth, pushing down the pain, resolve carved on his face. He kept pace with Asa, trusting her lead.

His trust was soon tested. They came upon a patch of fungi, bright red caps standing out against the brown leaf litter. Aedelric, seeing potential food, instinctively reached out. Asa's hand shot out, grabbing his arm with surprising strength, stopping him cold. Her eyes, sharp and severe, fixed on the mushrooms. Then she drew her finger across her throat, a clear, unmistakable sign of poison.

A wave of cold realization rolled over Aedelric. His ignorance here was a deadly vulnerability. He nodded his understanding, relief struggling with a fresh awareness of his helplessness.

As they moved on, Asa paused, crouching next to a low-growing plant with broad green leaves. She recognized it instantly: a healing plant, good for poultices, for cleaning and binding wounds. She picked up a handful of the leaves, her eyes flickering briefly towards Aedelric's bandaged side.

Aedelric followed Asa through the forest, his mind a jumble of pain and new understanding. His wound throbbed, a constant, dull ache, yet the sheer fact of his continued movement, his fortitude despite it, amazed him. He was surviving.

And knowledge of this wild place was staggering. The poisonous fungi, the healing plant, she passed through the forest with an innate understanding that he, for all his training in warfare, utterly lacked. He was dependent on her. Gratitude seemed a new, humbling feeling.

His growing fondness for her strengthened with every revelation of her competence. Her strength, her termination, and this surprising, quiet care pulled him in, tugging at the strands of his ingrained beliefs about enemies and pagans. *Did she feel anything similar? Or am I just a tool, a temporary convenience?*

The uncertainty of their situation was a heavy veil. Stranded, alone, facing unknown dangers. Fear served as a constant companion, but alongside it grew an unusual sense of peace, fragile but persistent. They had survived the shipwreck, the fight on the beach, and his wound. Perhaps, simply perhaps, they could face whatever unfolded next together.

Asa led the way, her senses keen, reading the faint signs of the forest and listening to its sounds. Finding food and water, these were the immediate driving needs. She felt Aedelric's presence behind her and heard his occasional wince of pain. He pushed himself; that was clear. His determination was formidable, even when wounded. It aroused a sense of responsibility in her.

And the feelings for him. Still unexpected, still confusing. This Saxon warrior was her enemy on the battlefield. His strength, his fortitude, the glimpses of something beneath the warrior's hard shell... it engaged her. She was seeing him not as a faceless foe but as a man.

Their mutual ordeal had undeniably changed something. Could they ever truly reconcile and become enemies again? The thought was equally unsettling and strangely liberating.

As they moved deeper into the forest, the air grew heavier, dense with the scent of wet ground and old trees. The wind murmured through the high branches, a constant, low murmur. Still beneath it, another sound emerged, a rhythmic gushing, the unmistakable sound of falling water.

Asa's head lifted, her senses at full alert. She moved with quiet purpose, tracking the sound, her eyes inspecting the undergrowth, alert for any movement that wasn't the forest's own. Aedelric followed silently, trusting her feelings implicitly.

Emerging from the dense screen of leaves, they found it. A small waterfall tumbling down a moss-laden rock face into a clear, dark pool below. The sight brought a wave of raw relief, fresh water. Asa's face eased, the tension draining from her shoulders. Aedelric saw the subtle change and understood its significance instantly. Water meant life.

They approached the pool, sunlight shimmering through the boughs onto the still surface. Aedelric, his throat sore with thirst, started to move towards the water but paused, his look fixed on Asa. The implicit rule of the wild had been established; her knowledge was paramount. If she deemed it safe, he would drink.

Asa knelt near the pool, her experienced eyes taking in everything: the clarity of the water, the life teeming within it (small insects, larvae), the lack of unnatural foam or smell. She tested the edge with her fingers and tasted a drop. Safe. With a silent nod, she cupped her hands and drank, the cool water a shock against her tongue. Only then did Aedelric kneel next to her and drink, burying his face in the water, gulping it down, rinsing the taste of salt and fear from his mouth.

The water was life. It quenched their physical thirst, yes, but it also seemed to wash away some of the tension in a brief moment of joint, simple necessity. Trust solidified in the act of drinking water deemed safe by one and accepted by the other.

Thirst sated, another need became apparent. Cleansing. Without hesitation, Asa moved back from the pool's edge and, with uninhibited practicality, began to strip off her torn, stained clothes. The tunic and trousers were not the norm; her clothing was simpler, with fewer layers. She shed them quickly, revealing a lean, muscular body honed by a life of hard work and warfare. Her long, dark hair, still partly braided, fell around her shoulders.

She plunged into the cool water with a sigh, the shock of the cold a bracing, cleansing sensation touching her skin. It washed away the grime, the sweat, the blood, the salt of the air, a visceral feeling of renewal, of shedding the ordeal.

Aedelric froze, his eyes growing wider. His upbringing in Wessex, his Christian faith, all shouted modesty. He averted his gaze sharply, shoulders tense, and lifted a trembling hand to trace the sign of the cross over his heart, as if by reflex seeking an invisible shield. Lips moving in a silent, hurried prayer, he turned his back to her, a wave of heat rising in his face, a collision of embarrassment and the sudden, aching pull of desire. The urge to look, to witness her easy freedom, gnawed at him. Despite his best efforts, he found his gaze drawn over his shoulder in quick, guilty glances, stealing moments of her in the water: her effortless comfort, her strength, the dark, flowing motifs of tattoos coiling over her back and shoulders. Faith, duty, and instinct warred silently within him, the tension alive and raw beneath his skin.

Asa, washing vigorously, noticed his reaction, the stiff posture, the averted face, and the quick, stolen looks. She splashed water playfully and intentionally in his direction, a sharp, unexpected gesture that relieved the tension. She motioned to herself, then to him, then to the water, miming washing. A clear invitation. A need to cleanse themselves, wounds and all.

Aedelric hesitated. Modesty, ingrained since childhood, warred with the desperate need to wash the salt, the grime, and the dried blood from his own wounded body. Asa's gestures were clear and insistent. The attraction of the clean water, of feeling truly clean after the horrors, was powerful. Slowly, reluctantly, he began to unfasten his remaining clothes. He carefully peeled away the improvised bandage, exposing the raw, inflamed wound on his side. The breeze was cool upon the injured flesh. He stepped into the water. It was a shock, biting cold, but then, a strange relief, a soothing sensation against his weary, aching body.

Asa moved towards him through the water. He was still unsure, self-conscious, and acutely aware of their nakedness, of her proximity. She stopped before him, her look falling to his wound. With a gentle and firm hand, she reached out, pointing to it, then mimed washing that spot on her own body, a question, a gesture of assistance.

He paused for only a moment. The vulnerability of his injury, the trust already built through the shared ordeal, and her care with the plant, he nodded.

With gentle, practiced movements, Asa began washing the wound. The cool water stung, but it also cleaned, removing the filth that clung to it, lessening the immediate risk of infection. Her caress was impersonal, focused on the task, yet the act itself, in this wild place, in their nakedness, was profoundly intimate. A silent bond intensified in the clear water under the forest canopy.

The forest around them was a living, breathing world. Sunlight shone amid the leaves, painting the forest floor in shifting patterns of gold and shade. The air remained thick with the fragrance of growing things.

There were myriad bird songs, of invisible creatures, and the constant murmur of the waterfall. Life teemed everywhere, indifferent to the two human figures who had a moment of stark, simple peace.

After the cleansing, a new awareness emerged between them. The easy bond of the shared task gave way to a heightened sense of vulnerability and a deeper awareness of their physical presence. The implicit tension returned, a perceptible pull. They dried themselves on the warm rocks, stealing glances, acutely aware of each other's nakedness, the attraction seething beneath the surface, held in check by exhaustion, past enmity, and cultural barriers.

A faint rumble, startling in the relative quiet, broke the moment. Asa's stomach. Hunger. A visceral, undeniable reality. The brief pause of cleansing and contemplation evaporated. Practical need reasserted itself with brutal urgency. They dressed quickly, the awkwardness of their mutual vulnerability replaced by the sharp focus on survival.

Asa, dagger now back at her belt, began searching for the right kind of wood, straight, sturdy, something that could be trimmed into a spear shaft. Aedelric watched her, admiring her immediate, functional focus and her knowledge. She found a bright branch, testing its weight and strength.

With the makeshift spear fashioned, Asa turned towards the deeper forest. Food. She needed to hunt. Her eyes scanned the ground for tracks; her ears tuned to the slightest sound. The pursuit had begun.

Asa moved into the thick foliage, disappearing into the green depths, every sense focused on the task at hand. Aedelric watched her go. His side ached, a steady throb beneath the roughly tied bandage. He had expected her to re-tie it after the bath, but the immediacy of hunger had overridden it. With a grimace, he fumbled with the wet cloth, tightening it himself, securing it as best he could.

He couldn't be left behind. Not here. Not alone. Despite the radiating pain, he pushed himself forward, following the path Asa had taken, moving as quickly as his wound allowed, determined to catch up, to stay with her.

He found her frozen, utterly still, just inside the tree line. She was crouched low; her eyes focused on the ground before her. Tracks. Delicate, cloven prints in the moist earth. Roe deer. Aedelric, though a warrior and hunter of men, knew little of tracking animals in the wilderness. He watched in muted awe as Asa read the story left in the mud and leaves.

For hours, they followed the weak trail. Asa moved with silent intent, a predator shadowing its prey, her movements economical and quiet. Occasionally, she would stop, raising a hand to signal Aedelric to halt, listen, scan, and confirm the path. He followed her lead, his trust in her advice absolute.

Finally, she stopped, motioning for him to crouch next to her. They had arrived at a small clearing. They waited in silence, the forest brimming with the sounds of birds and the swish of hidden life. Forty minutes lingered into a timeless stretch of tense expectancy.

Then, a shape appeared from the trees at the far side of the clearing, a Roe deer, walking cautiously into the open. Its soft brown coat appeared to absorb the mottled sunlight. Its eyes were wide, alert. Asa watched it, utterly still, her body coiled. Slowly, with deliberate, silent steps, she began to move, closing the distance between them.

When she was close enough, she paused, breathing a deep breath, tightening her hold on the makeshift spear. Then, with a sudden, explosive burst of speed that startled Aedelric even from his state of improved awareness, she threw. The spear flew straight and true, a streak against the green. It struck the deer with a solid impact, knocking it to the ground.

Aedelric stared, amazed. The speed, the accuracy... he had seen her with a bow, but with a spear, at close range, she was just as deadly. Asa looked back at him with a trace of quiet pride in her eyes. Success.

She motioned towards the fallen deer, then towards the beach shelter. While she approached the fallen deer, clearly still alive, she slit its throat, finishing it off. The deer was not large, but its weight was a challenge to their weary, injured bodies. But they worked together, lifting and dragging, a common burden, a mutual triumph.

By the time they ambled back to the overhang, the sun was starting to sink towards the horizon, coloring the sky with muted colors. They had returned to their temporary home, successful in their hunt, their survival ensured for another day. The day's trials, from the initial shock of finding each other alive to the struggle of the hunt, had forged their delicate alliance into something more substantial, a bond born of joint effort and mutual reliance.

Standing over the kill, a blend of emotions flooded them. Aedelric felt awe at Asa's skill, a strong respect for her competence in this brutal world, relief that they had food, and gratitude for her presence. It proved a humbling experience for a warrior accustomed to leading men in battle to be so utterly dependent on this woman, his former enemy, for the very basics of survival.

Asa had a surge of pride in her skill and in her ability to provide for them both. Exhaustion was a heavy burden on her limbs, but the success of the hunt was a powerful affirmation of her capabilities. There was subtle satisfaction in proving herself, especially to the Saxon.

Underlying these feelings was a growing sense of fellowship and a hard-earned respect for each other's strengths.

They had encountered the wilderness together and prevailed.

The grim, necessary task of processing the kill began. They worked in silence, their movements coordinated, understanding conveyed through looks and simple gestures. First, hanging the deer from a sturdy branch near the shelter, a joint effort, arms flexing.

Then, the skinning. Asa took the lead, her movements exact, and the newly salvaged dagger unexpectedly sharp. She made the initial incision along the belly, her hands firm, separating skin from the flesh. Aedelric watched as a necessary observer, learning.

Then arrived the gutting, a raw, visceral task. Asa moved forward, her face set, her hands shifting with skilled efficiency. The smell of blood and viscera saturated the air. She worked quickly and cleanly, removing the internal organs. It was a gruesome sight, the warm, slick insides exposed.

Aedelric's insides contracted. He gulped sharply, suppressing the rush of nausea that rose in his throat. This was the brutal, undeniable reality of survival, a world away from the relatively clean violence of the battlefield or the prepared meals of Winchester. He had killed men and seen blood spilled, but this... this was different. It was the raw process of taking a life to sustain your own, exposed. His face looked pale, but he forced himself to watch, to learn. He had to accept this.

Asa, immersed in the task, noticed his reaction, the sudden paleness, the tight set of his jaw. A trace of something that might have been mirth brushed her lips. He was strong, yes, and could swing a heavy sword and lead men, but this simple, fundamental reality of preparing a kill unsettled him. It served as a stark reminder of the differences among their worlds, and she found a sullen satisfaction in witnessing it. The pampered Christian is confronted with the actual cost of his next meal. It was a small, private moment of levity during a necessary, bloody task.

She continued her work, her hands firm, but the occasional glance towards him contained a hint of something that verged on teasing, a quiet recognition of his discomfort. Survival wasn't just enduring; it was finding these small moments, these unexpected degrees of understanding, even in the grimness. And right now, the Saxon's pale face was one such moment.

Nothing was wasted. Asa carefully separated the organs, heart, liver, and kidneys, setting them aside. Even the intestines would be cleaned and used. Every part of the animal had a purpose, a sharp lesson in the economy of survival.

Finally, they began cutting the meat. Asa showed Aedelric the different cuts, guiding his hand with the dagger and teaching him which parts were best for immediate cooking and which for preserving. They worked in near silence, the only sounds being the slicing of the blade, the quiet whispering of leaves, and the remote murmur of the waves.

They had a substantial amount of meat. Some they cooked over the fire, the smell of roasting venison a welcome aroma in the dusk air. The rest, using Asa's knowledge, prepared for smoking, making sure they would have food for several days.

Sitting by the fire, eating the hot, cooked meat, there was a strong feeling of accomplishment between them. They had encountered the day, faced the wilderness, and they had won. The hard-earned meal tasted like victory. They dined quietly, the setting sun throwing long shadows, tired yet alive. It had been a long, brutal day, but they had survived together.

Part 2: Somber Shore

They sat by the fire, the smell of roasted venison, a potent aroma of success. Exhaustion was a heavy weight in their limbs, but beneath it was the grim satisfaction of the hunt, the fundamental accomplishment of having secured food in a place that offered nothing freely. She looked at the meat, a life taken so theirs could continue. A silent, practical gratitude for the deer filled her. And she looked at Aedelric, eating the meat she had provided. His reliance on her was absolute. Their silent bond, forged in shared ordeal, tightened.

Aedelric ate slowly, savoring the taste of hot meat, a contrast to the cold fear and pain of the past days. He watched Asa across the fire, silhouetted against the flames. Awe was a constant companion now. Her skill with the spear, her knowledge of the tracks, her effortless command of this hostile world, it was humbling. He was a man, yes, but here, she was the true master of survival. Relief washed over him with each bite, gratitude for this moment of simple peace, for the food in his belly, for her presence. He wondered about tomorrow and the days to come, but for now, there was only the meat, the fire, and the quiet presence of the North woman.

They ate in silence that was no longer merely the absence of everyday language, but a shared space of exhaustion and simple need. They watched each other, learning in ways words could not convey.

Asa watched Aedelric. He ate with the focused intensity of a warrior, but his movements, even when lifting meat to his mouth, held the controlled economy of his training.

Despite his wound and his unfamiliarity with actual wilderness survival, he carried himself with quiet strength and an unbroken quality that she admired. She saw his eyes catching the firelight and noticing the rare, open look of gratitude he sent her way, a warmth that unsettled her even as it stirred something unexpected.

Aedelric watched Asa eat. The firelight softened the warrior's hardness in her face, revealing a weariness he hadn't seen on the ship or the battlefield. He saw the slight, almost imperceptible smile as she chewed the hard-won meat, a flash of satisfaction that spoke volumes. Her movements were fluid and efficient, even in the simple act of eating, a constant reminder of the deadly grace she possessed. Resilience radiated from her.

In these quiet moments, they saw beyond enemy and captive, beyond Saxon and Northwoman. They saw survivors. They saw the raw, capable human beings beneath the layers of culture and conflicts. Small, silent understandings formed, building a bridge of shared experience across the language barrier. There was a fragile comfort in this companionship, born of shared desperation and the simple fact that they were not alone.

Meal finished, the practical needs reasserted themselves. Asa reached for the leaves she had gathered earlier, the unassuming plant with the potent healing properties. She looked at Aedelric, then at his bandaged side.

She placed a few leaves in her mouth and chewed them into a pulp. The taste was bitter, green, a harsh contrast to the savory meat. She chewed steadily, her face set. This was knowledge hard-won, a necessity of life here.

Aedelric watched her, curious, then apprehensive as she gestured to him, then to his wound, then to the paste in her mouth. She wanted to tend to his wound. *With that chewed pulp?* Hesitation flickered in his eyes, doubt, wariness. But he had seen her knowledge at work today, had seen her save him from poison, and had seen her provide food. He trusted her. More than he trusted himself in this place. Slowly, wincing, he pulled away his torn shirt and the rough, blood-stained bandage, exposing the raw, inflamed gash on his side.

Asa's expression softened slightly, a fleeting moment of shared vulnerability. The wound looked angry and inflamed. The greenish paste was ready. Taking a deep breath, she leaned forward, her touch gentle but firm, applying the cool, wet pulp directly to the raw flesh.

Aedelric flinched, the initial contact a shock, cool against the throbbing heat of the wound. But almost immediately, a soothing sensation spread outwards. The sharp, burning pain began to recede, replaced by a duller ache and a gentle numbness. He watched Asa work, her brow furrowed in concentration, her movements precise as she spread the paste, covering the wound. Her knowledge of this land, of its hidden remedies, was incredible. Gratitude, profound and humbling, filled him. He was in her hands, and those hands, though capable of lethal force, were now tending to his life.

As the light faded, Asa finished applying the paste, covering it with a fresh strip of torn cloth that was secured tightly. She was focused, intent on the task, knowing that proper care now could mean the difference between healing and the creeping rot of infection. Every movement was weighted with the awareness of Aedelric's trust, the vulnerability he had shown her. She had provided food; now she was giving medicine. Her capabilities were being tested, and she was meeting the challenge. There was quiet satisfaction in that, a confirmation of her strength and resourcefulness.

But worry still gnawed at her. The wilderness remained vast and unpredictable. One successful day did not guarantee another. What dangers lie unseen in the forest? What challenges would tomorrow bring? Yet, as she finished tying off the makeshift bandage, a hard knot of determination settled in her gut. Whatever came, she would face it. She would survive.

As the paste dried on his skin, drawing out the heat, Aedelric felt a profound sense of relief. He looked at Asa, her task complete, her face illuminated by the fire. His eyes met hers, conveying his thanks in a silent, heartfelt glance. A new respect for her, even deeper than before, filled him. She had saved his life, not with a weapon, but with knowledge and care. With her by his side, they might survive this.

In the quiet of the evening, the sounds of the wild filtering into their small haven, Aedelric turned to Asa. He had to try. He had to express it. "Thank you," he said, his voice low, raspy with exhaustion and emotion.

Asa looked at him, firelight dancing in her brown eyes. The words were foreign, meaningless sounds. But the tone... the raw sincerity, the soft cadence... she understood the feeling. Gratitude. Acknowledgment. She tried to echo the sounds, her tongue clumsy around the unfamiliar syllables. "Than-koo?" Aedelric smiled, a weary, genuine smile. He repeated the words slowly and patiently. "Thank you."

Asa tried again, this time closer. "Tha... thank you."
And then, breaking the final barrier of language, Aedelric
reached out, his calloused and strong hand gently taking
hers. Asa started, her eyes widening in surprise. His grip
was warm, firm, and reassuring. He held her hand, looked
into her eyes, and repeated, simply, "Thank you." In that
touch, in his steady gaze, in the repeated foreign words,
Asa understood. Not just the meaning of the sounds, but the
depth of the feeling behind them. He was honestly thanking
her. For the care, for the knowledge, for the hope she
represented in his grim situation. She squeezed his hand in
return, a silent acceptance, a shared acknowledgment.
A moment of profound connection, born of necessity and
forged in the wilderness, passing between them.

But the moment, in its unexpected intimacy, shattered
something within Asa. A surge of cold unease, sharp and
sudden, washed over her, immediately followed by a wave
of fierce anger. The warmth of his hand, the sincerity in his
eyes, it triggered memories, stark and brutal. This man. A
Christian. One of them. One of the people who had fought
her warriors, who had stood against her kin. The faces of
the fallen, the blood spilled, it all rushed back, a cold tide
of the past threatening to drown the fragile present. How
could she feel about this connection? How could she let her
guard down, even for a moment, with one of them?

Anger, hot and sharp, directed primarily at
herself, stiffened her spine. She snatched her hand back, her
eyes hardening, the brief warmth extinguished, replaced by
the familiar, icy coldness he had seen on the ship. Without
a word, she turned sharply away from him, moving her
makeshift bedroll further away from his, putting physical
distance between them.

Aedelric, left reeling by the sudden withdrawal and the
abrupt return of the ice, felt a wave of confusion and
hurt. He watched her move away, the space between them
widening, a palpable void opening where, a moment

before, there had been a connection. His face, softened by gratitude, hardened, mirroring the coldness in her eyes with his own bewildered anger. He, too, moved his bedroll, turning his back to her, settling down in the sand. Sleep felt impossible; his mind was in turmoil about what had just happened.

Asa lay in her solitude, the sand cold beneath her, the firelight a distant, flickering presence. The tension in the air was a physical weight. Despite their proximity under the same rock overhang, they had never felt more distant, separated by the sudden, stark return of their past, by the unresolved anger and confusion that hung between them.

Sleep, when it finally came, was restless, filled with fractured images. Aedelric dreamt of home, the familiar walls of Winchester, the faces of his comrades, Eadric's booming laugh... but the images were blurred, overlaid with flashes of green forest, the taste of raw fish, the sharp pain in his side, and always, her face, the fierce eyes, the unexpected gentle touch, the quick, cold withdrawal. His dreams were a battlefield of longing for the familiar and the jarring reality of his new, entangled existence.

Asa dreamt of the wild, the endless trees, the sound of the waterfall, the thrilling tension of the hunt. She saw her warriors, their faces lost to the waves, and Astrid's fiery hair vanishing beneath the storm. But in her dreams, too, his face appeared, the gratitude in his eyes, the warmth of his hand, the bewildered hurt when she pulled away. Her dreams were a raw blend of survival, loss, and the confusing, unsettling presence of the Saxon warrior who had become her unexpected shadow.

Their dreams, though different, shared a common thread: survival, yes, but also the indelible mark they were leaving on each other, the bond, however fraught, that had formed between them. As the night deepened, carrying them toward another uncertain dawn, their dreams mirrored the complex and dangerous path they now walked together.

Part 3: Across the Divide

The first pale early light of dawn shone through the overhang, stirring Asa and Aedelric from their uneasy sleep. They rose to the constant, subtle murmur of the waves, the unfamiliar calls of seabirds, and the soft sigh of leaves at the forest's edge. The air remained cool and fresh, carrying the piercing tang of the sea and the more profound, natural scent of the woods. The fire from the night before was reduced to a heap of glowing embers, throwing a faint, warm light around their small haven.

Nearby, the smoked deer meat, wrapped in large leaves, lay safely where Asa had placed it. The sight brought a quiet, somber satisfaction, sustenance for the coming days, a confirmation of yesterday's effort. Despite the lingering stiffness in their muscles and the tension from the night's abrupt separation, they rose with the immediate, fundamental purpose of survival.

They stretched, bodies stiff from the cold ground, movements gradual and deliberate. The rising sun colored the beach in pale gold and long, dark shadows. They ate a simple breakfast of smoked meat, chewing in silence, the sole sounds the occasional crackle of the embers and the faraway cry of a bird. The grim reality of their situation, momentarily softened by sleep, returned with the daylight.

Asa finished eating first, standing with the smooth grace of a hunter rising from a crouch. Her eyes scanned the forest perimeter, her gut feeling already assessing the day's needs. Aedelric watched her, the pain in his side a steady throb, but his trust in her knowledge was absolute. He winced as he pushed himself up, movement slower than usual, and hesitant, pressing a hand to the bruised flesh beneath his tunic. The prospect of a long trek made him uneasy; every step had grown heavier since the injury. Sensing his struggle, Asa paused, eyes narrowing. Without a word, she adjusted her original plan, gesturing for a detour along the firmer sand near the waterline, an easier walk, but riskier if the tide turned or if wreckage was hidden beneath the surface. Aedelric nodded, grateful for her wordless concession. Today, their course would be shaped by what his body could bear.

They passed the morning scouring the beach, walking along the high tide line, the wide expanse of sand extending out before them. Their eyes and ears were tuned to the environment, the debris from the wreck, the sounds of the sea, and the bordering forest. They needed valuable salvage, they needed to understand this stretch of coastline, and find a potential closer water sources.

As they walked, skirting the edge where the sand met the trees, Asa paused, her gaze sweeping across the immense curve of the shoreline. An involuntary noise escaped her lips, a soft exclamation of... awe? She motioned with her arm, encompassing the immensity of the sea and the land that met it, her eyes open, showing the raw, untamed beauty of the place. Aedelric, following her stare, nodded, a trace of mutual wonder in his own eyes. Then, to bridge the silence itself, to articulate the unutterable vastness before them, he proceeded to mimic the noise of the waves crashing, his hands curving, rising, and descending like the swell of the tide along the shore.

Asa turned to him, a trace of surprise on her face. His clumsy, earnest mimicry of the waves was... strange. Unexpectedly. A small, unexpected giggle escaped her, a light, airy sound that seemed completely alien in this harsh place. Aedelric, hearing it, sensed a wave of relief sweep through him, a brief victory in lightening the grim mood.

But the moment remained fleeting. Almost as quickly as it had appeared, Asa's laughter vanished. Her expression stiffened, the cold, stern look from last night returning sharper in the morning light. Without a word, without a backward glance, she turned away from him, facing the infinite stretch of beach, and began walking, her stride purposeful, leaving Aedelric alone and confused by the abrupt shift. The unremitting crash of the waves accentuates the sudden, inexplicable rift between them.

Aedelric stood statue-still, confusion battling with the hurt of her sudden coldness. But they were in the wilderness. Dwelling on it was a luxury they couldn't afford. Shaking off his bewilderment, he quickly moved to follow her, jogging lightly despite the pain in his side, closing the distance she had put between them. When he caught up, she cast him a brief, icy, sidelong glance that conveyed her annoyance, but she didn't slow her pace. Her focus was elsewhere, back on the grim task of survival.

The beach was a long, scattered graveyard of longships. Splintered timber, broken oars, shattered shields, fragments of cargo, the detritus of their lost world. Combing through it was a brutal indication of how much had been lost. A dagger and rope were meager salvage from such destruction. And there was the ever-present, morbid possibility of finding the bodies of their fallen comrades, washed ashore by the tide. The thought of seeing Astrid among them sent a cold tremor down Asa's spine. She forced her sight to remain focused on the wreckage, suppressing the fear of focusing on finding anything useful. Miles of coastline extended ahead, a daunting prospect, but every valuable item found meant a slightly better chance of survival. She fortified herself for the grim search.

After what appeared like an age, walking mile after mile through the scattered relics, Asa stopped dead. Her stare was fixed on something further up the beach. A body. Lifeless, prone on the sand. A chill came upon her spirit. Aedelric, noticing her sudden halt and the direction of her gaze, saw it too. His heart sank. He recognized the shape, the likely attire. He remained silent, respectful, knowing this was one of her people.

They advanced slowly. The effects of the sea were obvious; the body was bloated, pale, and grey against the sand, facedown, a bleak, brutal tribute to the ocean's indifference. Asa knelt near the fallen figure, her heart burdened with a rising, dreadful suspicion. She had to know. Placing her hands carefully beneath the cold, decaying form, she rolled it over, the odor of death rising thick and overpowering, a foul difference to the briny air.

The face was recognizable. An older man, Brynhild. An old farmer from the outskirts of Njardarheimr. A widower who had lost his wife the previous winter. He had pleaded with her father, Gunnar, to join the raid, seeking an honorable death in battle, a seat in Valhalla, with nothing left to live for at home. He had not been on her ship, confirming that the storm's reach had been broad, claiming others from their fleet.

Asa had barely known him, yet sorrow constricted her chest. As the Jarl's daughter, she was tied to her people, even those on the fringes of village life. Their fate was her concern. This was who she was. But she dared not show this depth of feeling to Aedelric. It seemed like a weakness he might take advantage of. Still, as she reached for the dead man's belt, her voice caught a faint, unintended rasp as she tried to steady her breath. Aedelric's gaze flicked to her, catching the slip, a momentary fracture in her control. In response, Asa's eyes steeled; she gave nothing more away, determined to mask this glimpse of vulnerability. She quickly wiped away a single tear that escaped, her hand moving almost instinctively to Brynhild's waist. A leather belt. Sturdy and likely useful. She unbuckled it, examining it. Yes, a worthy spoil of the dead.

Looking down at Brynhild's sightless eyes, devoid of the trace of life, a shock of sadness struck her again. His wish for Valhalla, for a warrior's death, had been denied.

Closing her eyes for a moment, she offered a silent prayer to her gods, to Odin, asking for mercy on Brynhild's journey and for his acceptance into the great hall despite the manner of his death.

Finding nothing else of use on the body, Asa rose. All the while, Aedelric had watched her in silence. He had seen the slight change in her posture, the brief trace of emotion before she masked it. He couldn't understand fully, but he sensed the burden of her sorrow, her connection to the dead man. He understood loss.

Asa turned away from the body, looking further down the beach. Aedelric's gaze went from the dead man to the forest edge. The body couldn't be left here for the tide or the scavengers to find. It needed burial. It was the only way he knew to show respect for the dead, for Asa's grief. He knew he had no proper tools, but he resolved to try, even with his bare hands if necessary. As he turned towards the forest to find something, anything, to dig with, he saw Asa watching him.

He had taken only a few steps when Asa's hand grasped his shoulder, stopping him. She spun him around to face her. Their eyes met in a silent, intense exchange. He experienced an urgent need to communicate his intention despite the language barrier and his ignorance of Norse burial rites. He pointed to a stick on the sand, picked it up, and made a digging motion in the earth. Asa watched him, still confused. He repeated the gesture, then pointed to Brynhild's body and back to the digging motion with the stick.

Comprehension dawned on Asa. He wanted to bury the body. The Saxon. She hadn't expected this. Did he... understand her? The thought flashed, quickly extinguished by the ingrained prejudice. He was a Christian. Ignorant of her people's ways. They were meant to die, to be enslaved, not to be honored. Anger, sharp and hot, blazed inside her, battling with the unexpected sign of respect. Her rage was cut short as she saw Aedelric, stick in hand, walking towards Brynhild's body.

He approached the fallen warrior with a solemn respect that Asa couldn't ignore. He knelt, taking hold of Brynhild's arms. With evident effort, he began to drag the heavy body away from the high tide line towards the shelter of the trees. It was a difficult task, made harder by the sand and the body's weight.

Just as he began to strain, Asa was there, stepping in beside him without a word. She gripped Brynhild's legs, lending her strength to the grim task. Together, the two moved the body, a common burden, a quiet agreement to offer this basic dignity to the dead man. They dragged him far enough from the sea's reach, then lowered him gently to the ground.

Finding whatever sticks and driftwood they could, they began to dig. The sand here was soft, but the effort was taxing, their improvised tools inadequate. They dug in silence; the only sounds were their breaths and the scraping of wood against sand. It was slow, back-breaking work.

When the hole was perhaps three or four feet deep, enough to offer some protection, they carefully lifted Harald's body and placed him in the shallow grave, covering him with the sand they had displaced. They sat for a moment, then, side by side, in weary reverence.

Aedelric's gaze wandered to the sea, and then he rose. Asa watched him with quiet curiosity. He found two pieces of driftwood, one longer than the other, and a length of vine near the edge of the forest. With simple, practiced movements, he began to bind the wood together, fashioning a rough cross. He knew this man was not of his faith, but it was the only marker he knew, the only symbol of remembrance that appeared right to him. He planted the makeshift cross firmly in the sand at the head of the grave. Asa, though the Christian symbol meant nothing to her, she understood the sentiment behind his action, a marker, a sign of respect rooted in his own beliefs.

Brynhild would not have the burial of a true Norse warrior, but Asa could offer what she had. Scanning the beach and the forest edge, she searched for smooth stones and other natural objects of beauty. Finding a few which seemed right in her hand, she kneeled at the foot of the grave. As Aedelric stood silently, head bowed in his prayer, Asa placed the stones one by one onto the sand covering Brynhild. She uttered her prayers to her gods, Odin and Freyja, asking for Brynhild's safe passage and his acceptance into the halls of the honored dead, despite the manner of his passing.

They prayed in their ways to different gods, their rites distinct but united in the shared act of honoring the fallen warrior. A Saxon thegn and a Norse Jarl's daughter, burying a Viking farmer on a desolate shore, their faiths side by side in an instant of shared, grim respect.

As the afternoon sun began its descent, sending long shadows across the beach, they trudged back towards their overhang shelter. Their bodies ached, muscles groaning from the day's unexpected labor. Their spirits felt subdued, weighted by the bleak reminder of death, of the lives lost. Yet, they had dealt with this bleak task together. In the face of adversity, their relationship, shaped in the crucible of common hardship and grim necessity, grew stronger with each mutual effort.

Once darkness settled, they sat crouched around the fire, the flames casting a mellow, fluttering glow that pushed back the advancing blackness. Despite the day's somber events, there was comfort in each other's silent company. They ate smoked deer meat, the hard-earned bounty a counterpoint to the life they had put in the ground. Actions were minimal, words scarce. This silence was not awkward but a common understanding, a silent acceptance of the day's reality. They had each other, and in this bleak place, that was everything.

While they settled into their makeshift beds, the sand chill beneath them, they knew they would face tomorrow together, whatever it might bring.

The day was long and hard, defined by death but also by a mutual act of humanity that overcame their enmity. What would dawn reveal?

Part 4: Embrace

The weeks that followed merged into a rhythm dictated by the severe demands of survival. The easy optimism of that first morning faded, replaced by the weary, relentless effort required to stay alive. They woke stiff and aching, gathered precious firewood against the ever-present chill, and scoured the tide line for anything helpful, a constant, often fruitless task. Asa taught Aedelric which berries wouldn't poison him, which roots were edible but bitter, and how to identify the tracks of small game. Their meals turned into a monotonous rotation of smoked deer meat, occasional foraged plants, and the rare, hard-won fish or rabbit. They fashioned crude waterskins from the dried bladders of hunted animals, a necessary but unpleasant task. Water from the nearby found stream acted as a lifeline, a brief moment of simple abundance in a world of scarcity.

As their immediate surroundings yielded fewer resources, they were compelled to venture further along the coastline, driven by the critical requirement to find more sustenance and usable wreckage. The monotony of their days was now cut with a sharper edge of anxiety. The weather, too, was shifting; the wind grew colder, and the threat of days of rain loomed ever nearer. Each failed hunt, each empty-handed morning, was a reminder that if the coastline gave them nothing new within the week, starvation or exposure would soon press in. Miles of shore extended out, an endless, tiring trek. The remains of Asa's ships became scarcer, picked clean by tide and time, useful only now as dwindling sources of firewood.

On one such day, walking along a stretch of sand further than they had gone before, Aedelric's foot struck something hard under the surface. A stab of pain shot up his leg. Curious, he knelt, brushing away the sand. The curved edge of wood appeared, painted a washed-out blue.

His pulse quickened. He dug with fresh urgency, pulling at the buried object. It was a shield, round and heavy, weighted by its waterlogging and the sand clinging to it. The wood was solid, and the leather rim remained intact, despite the ravages of the sea. The paint, a bright blue, was surprisingly well-preserved, and below it, etched or painted in black, was a familiar, intricate symbol, the branching shape of Yggdrasil.

As he struggled to free it, his fingers brushed against something wrapped tightly around the leather grip on the back. He unwound the binding, a length of sturdy cordage, disclosing a piece of shaped wood. With more effort, he managed to pull the entire object free from the sand. He saw it clearly now, the upper limb of a bow snapped cleanly below the grip, still bound to the shield handle. He detached it, the shield falling with a thud onto the sand. He held the broken bow part, its familiar curve unmistakable.

He knew he had to show Asa. Spotting her further down the beach, examining a pile of driftwood, he raised the shield and the bow piece high, letting out a loud call, not a hoot, but a sharp, attention-grabbing shout that carried over the waves.

Asa turned at the sound. She saw Aedelric, standing alone on the vast beach, holding a shield aloft. A blue shield. Her breath faltered. As she narrowed her eyes, recognizing the familiar color and shape, then the distinctive symbol, a flood of emotion hit her with the force of a breaking wave. Astrid.

With a sudden, desperate burst of energy, she sprinted towards him, her feet flying over the sand. She reached him, breathing hard and almost stumbling in her haste. She scarcely noticed Aedelric as she took the shield, pulling it from where he had set it down, grasping it to her chest. It was real. Astrid's shield. A physical link to her lost friend.

Holding the shield, a storm of longing and fear tore through her. Astrid's shield. Could she be alive? Somewhere along this brutal coast? Injured? In need of help? The thought felt a desperate, fragile thing, immediately battered by the cold, complex reality of the storm's ferocity and the sea's mercilessness. Chances were... vanishingly small.

Tears, hot and sudden, welled in her eyes, dimming the stark image of the Yggdrasil. "Astrid," she choked out, the name torn from her in her native tongue, raw with grief and bitter hope.

Aedelric, startled by her intensity, the sudden tears, the foreign word, repeated it tentatively. "As-trid?"

She looked at him and heard the name upon his lips, acknowledgment in his voice. The red-haired warrior. He knew. He understood. The heaviness of her grief, the desperate, fragile hope, the sheer, overwhelming reality of holding this piece of her lost world, it all converged. In a sudden, impulsive movement, powered by raw emotion and a desperate need for comfort, she dropped the shield and threw her arms around Aedelric, burying her face in his chest and clinging to him.

Aedelric stood stunned for a moment, taken aback by the surprising force of the hug and the unfamiliar experience of holding a weeping woman, especially this woman, pressed against him. Then, instinctively, his arms went around her, holding her tight, offering what little comfort he could in the face of her sudden, raw grief. It wasn't about Saxon or Norse at that moment, not about enemy or ally. It was one human holding another against a wave of pain. Neither could have articulated why it felt so necessary, so right.

It was then, as she gripped him, that Asa noticed the broken piece of wood still held in Aedelric's hand. Her bow. Her bow, the one she had handcrafted, was cracked but recognizable. Another piece of her lost self returned.

A complex wave of emotions flooded her: the aching sorrow for Astrid, the slight, desperate trace of hope, the return of her prized weapon, and the unexpected comfort of Aedelric's arms around her, his silent empathy in the face of her loss. This day, meant for scavenging, had delivered far more than expected, tearing open old wounds even as it offered unexpected peace and strengthened a relationship she still didn't fully understand. As she turned the cracked bow piece in her hands, a new determination settled over her. If she could mend the bow, she and Aedelric could expand their hunts inland, increasing their chance of finding more food as winter pressed closer. Repairing it would become their priority when they returned, a task that would give shape to tomorrow. The discovery of the broken weapon did not simply reopen the past; it offered a tangible way to fight for their future, a goal to drive them on.

Pulling back, wiping her eyes, she looked at the shield, then at the bow piece. They needed to get back to the shelter. Urgently. She handed the still-heavy shield back to Aedelric. "Home," she said, the word in Norse, but pointing towards the overhang, a word he had surely picked up by now through her constant use. The word was clear.

Aedelric took the shield, strapping the aged leather handles to his arm, marveling again at the craftsmanship's resilience. As he tested the weight, a pang of worry edged beneath his admiration. The shield was made for war, for skillful hands. He glanced at Asa, grasping her cracked bow, striding up the beach ahead of him. In battle, she would fight with a ferocity and knowledge that felt foreign to him, perhaps even greater than his own. The thought unsettled him. *What if her strength outmatched his, her experience deeper? Was he only a companion here, or falling behind?* Still, her pace was quicker now, her spirit somehow lighter despite the tears. She seemed... different. Less guarded, perhaps. Was it the hope for Astrid? The return of her bow? The unexpected embrace? He didn't know.

His thoughts floated back to the red-haired warrior, to Astrid. And with that thought came the sharp, recognizable pang of sorrow for Eadric, the sudden, visceral memory of his friend falling, brought down by that woman. The pain he had hidden deep amidst the chaos of shipwreck and survival resurfaced, a dark shadow on this moment of delicate hope.

He watched Asa walk ahead, her dark hair swaying. He inhaled the smell of the sea, the slight, lingering fragrance of her, always present, like her. Another feeling, something confusing and powerful, arose inside him, pushing back the sorrow and anger. Could this... this confusing, strong pull he felt towards her... be love? He didn't know what "love" felt like, not the kind sung about in the halls, not this raw, visceral connection born of shared blood, storm, and silence.

At that moment, watching her, a decision formed inside him. He couldn't change the past. Eadric was gone. Astrid was gone. Dwelling on the anger, the sorrow served nothing. Asa was here. And the feeling she stirred in him... it was unquestionable. It made the old loyalties and hatreds feel distant and less important. Speaking the words into the wind, a private apology to his fallen comrade, he said,

"I am sorry, dear Eadric. Forgive me."

With the burden of the past acknowledged and set aside, he turned and followed Asa back towards their temporary home, leaving the painful memories on the sand.

He followed her into the prospect of a future that, while uncertain, seemed slightly less daunting because he wasn't facing it alone. He followed her towards the overhang and towards whatever complicated path was ahead.

Yet as the sky darkened and the surf hissed in the distance, a question lingered in his mind, unresolved and persistent. What if Astrid was still out there, or worse, what if she wasn't and Asa's hope would be crushed anew? And would he ever find a way to confess to Asa the weight he still carried, or the feelings that now unsettled him with every step? The uncertainty shadowed his heart, never quite dispelled by the comfort of her presence. With each footfall, the unspoken question pressed closer: what would tomorrow bring, and would either of them be strong enough to face it?

Part 5: A Bond Sealed

With the burden of the past acknowledged but set aside, he focused on the present. On the walk back. On Asa. He followed her, leaving the ghosts on the sand, walking towards the shelter, in the direction of a future that was still terrifyingly uncertain, but which he would face with her.

The sun was starting its descent when they reached the overhang, arms heavy with Astrid's shield and Asa's broken bow. Exhaustion claimed Aedelric swiftly after their meager meal. He fell into a deep sleep, the sound of the waves a dull roar in his ears.

He awoke in the early morning to the quiet scraping and tapping sounds nearby. Wiping sleep from his eyes, he looked towards the soft gleam of the embers. Asa was awake, sitting near the fire, her figure glowing from the mild light. In her lap was her bow. The snap below the grip was gone. It was whole again, strung with new cordage. She drew the tensioned string across her thumb, and for a moment, Aedelric could see the frayed ends of the old fibers caught beneath her nail. Arrows lie beside her, fletched and nocked, neatly arranged on the sand. The scents of charred wood and sinew drifted in the air, a tacit evidence of her midnight labor.

She noticed him stirring, her face turning towards him. A rare, genuine smile brushed her lips, not the fierce grin of battle or the tight smile of grim amusement, but a soft, subdued smile of satisfaction. It changed her face, chasing away some of the hardness. Aedelric experienced a warmth rise in his face, a blush he couldn't control. He rose stiffly and walked over to sit beside her.

She reached for a piece of smoked meat and offered it to him. He accepted it gratefully, his fingers touching hers. As he ate, she watched him, then lowered her bow, meeting his gaze directly. In slow, deliberate words, using sounds she had learned from listening to him, she spoke. "No... mmm... more." There was the faintest hesitation and a stumble on the first syllable, her brow tightening as she concentrated, determined to get it right. The bridge between them, fragile and unfinished, hung in the breath between her words.

Aedelric paused, a piece of meat halfway to his mouth. "No? More?" He repeated the unfamiliar phrase, recognizing his own words, puzzled. Her pronunciation was clear, astonishingly so for someone beginning.

Asa nodded, her look steady, then stood. The quiver, fashioned from salvaged hides and Harald's belt, was slung over her shoulder, filled with newly made, makeshift arrows. She held the repaired bow, a picture of calm strength and readiness. Aedelric watched her, awe returning. The quiver, the arrows, twenty, perhaps? They spoke of hours of meticulous work while he slept. Her ingenuity with the salvaged materials was remarkable.

She stood before him, no longer an enemy, but a capable, vital companion. The sight of her, armed and ready, stirred that known warmth in his chest, the bewildering, powerful feeling that had claimed him on the beach. A breeze slipped through the trees, swaying Asa's hair across her cheek and sending a brief flutter through the leaves above them. A patch of sun appeared, shifting the shadowed ground at their feet. Just for a moment, all the world seemed to hold its breath along with him. Was this... was this what it meant to be falling in love?

"Let's go," she said, her voice muted but clear, using the few West Saxon words she knew. "We... hunt."

Aedelric blinked, marveling again at her ability to pick up his language, to piece together meaning from his unconscious mumbles. Her intelligence was indisputable. And her leadership, even with this limited vocabulary, was absolute.

They set off, retracing their steps into the forest. The familiar path now felt less daunting, softened by repetition and Asa's guidance. Aedelric walked beside her, his mind drifting back to their previous journeys here: the near-fatal mistake with the mushrooms, saved by her knowledge; the discovery of the waterfall; the unexpected moment of absolute vulnerability; and the shared cleansing. He remembered the sensation of the cool water on his skin, her hands on his wound, the rugged yet beautiful sight of her, and the yearning he had felt. He glanced towards where the waterfall rested concealed, a flash of longing for another such moment, even as he knew the immediate need was for meat.

Asa moved through the undergrowth with focused intent, her eyes observing, her ears listening. She now knew this area, its secrets concealed. But she also knew its limitations. The game was scarcer here now, hunted, wary. The need for meat, for fat, was constant, gnawing. The return of her bow, whole and strung, gave her fresh purpose and confidence. Hunting with the spear was effective, yes, but the bow was her accurate weapon; her reach extended.

They reached the clearing where they had brought down the Roe deer weeks ago. How much time had passed? It looked much the same, quiet and still. They settled into their waiting spot, finding comfortable positions with a view of the clearing's edge, preparing for the long, patient vigil.

Hours passed in silence. The forest sounds were muted, distant. No deer appeared. No smaller game stirred the underbrush. The clearing remained empty. At first, Aedelric tried to keep still, but tension wormed into his hands. Without realizing, he began to tap a nervous pattern against his knee, three quick beats, then a pause, the same pattern he used to count down before battle. He mouthed a silent prayer halfway through, lips moving with no breath, an old appeal from his childhood buried deep in memory. The quiet pressed in, and beneath it, the restless tapping betrayed his anxiety, the worry that food would not come, that they would fail. Eventually, the quiet, coupled with exhaustion, claimed Aedelric. He drifted into a light sleep; the world contracted to the feeling of the soil beneath him and the still presence of Asa beside him.

A gentle shake roused him. Asa. She was still utterly still, her look fixed on the clearing, but her face was scratched with disappointment. "Nothing," she whispered, her words soft, the few West Saxon sounds clear.

Aedelric looked out. The clearing was empty. The sun was high, throwing long shadows. The hunt here had failed. "We head back," Asa said, her voice subdued, pragmatic. "Too much time here."

They turned to retracing their steps. But instead of following the exact path back to the beach, Asa led them on a slight detour. Aedelric's heart lurched in recognition as the faint, familiar sound of falling water reached his ears.

Anticipation wound in his gut. Were they going back to the pool? Would she shed her clothes again, plunge into the cool water? Would he see her again as he had that day, raw and free? Did she want to recreate that moment? His heart pounded on his ribs, sweat prickling his palms. Why did her opinion of him feel so crucial? Why did he care so deeply about pleasing her? These foreign, powerful feelings whirled inside him, confusing and exhilarating. He glanced at Asa, walking ahead, her profile set with purpose. Did she sense his turmoil?

She stopped at the edge of the pool, knelt, and cupped her hands, drinking deeply. The scene was achingly familiar, a direct resemblance to their first visit. He knelt next to her, drinking, his mind in turmoil.

He wished to know whether the powerful attraction he felt was shared. He couldn't ask in words. He decided to try the language of action. He would mirror her previous action. He would undress. It would seem natural, a simple act of washing, but it would be a question, a hopeful gesture towards intimacy.

He began to unfasten his shirt, trying for an air of ease he didn't feel. He kept his movements deliberate, his eyes on hers. Asa watched him, her expression impassive at first. A trace of something, surprise? Curiosity in her eyes? She was attracted to him; he knew, had sensed it before. But her focus was so often on the grim necessities.

As he continued, their gazes met. The moment stretched, charged with unvoiced words, unacted desires. He was close enough to see the fine lines of exhaustion around her eyes, the way her hair stuck to her neck, close enough to imagine reaching out, touching her face, tasting her lips. The desire was a physical ache.

But then, her expression changed. Not towards him, but past him, towards the trees. Her eyes widened, sharpening with immediate, predatory focus. With breathtaking speed, she snatched her bow, nocked an arrow, and drew the string taut, aiming past him.

Fear, sharp and cold, lanced through Aedelric. Had he misread everything? Pushed too far? Was she going to kill him now, in this moment of vulnerability? But the arrow whizzed past his head with a vicious sound, thudding into something in the undergrowth behind him.

He spun around, heart beating, pulse pounding. A small, black, furry shape lay twitching in the leaves: a pig. A wild pig was brought down instantly by Asa's arrow.

Asa lowered her bow, a triumphant grin forming across her face, chasing away the hunter's intensity. Relief, so sudden it left Aedelric weak-kneed, flooded him. For an instant, he felt the jarring crack of the moment, the thin thread of intimacy between them snapped abruptly, just like the bowstring had in her hands before. Survival had intruded with the swiftness of a loosed arrow, shattering tenderness and replacing it with necessity. "We have food," she said, her voice even, stating the simple, vital truth.

She walked over to her kill and examined the shot. The arrow had gone clean. She cleaned the fletching and pointed at the edge of the pool, then returned to Aedelric, who was still standing rooted, half-undressed, shock warring with relief. She reached out, touching his bare chest, her fingers chilly against his skin. "Scared?" she asked, a hint of teasing in her voice, a light entering her eyes that hadn't been there moments before. "Don't worry. I like"

Aedelric could only stare, speechless. She liked him. The depth of his feeling, the shock of the near-fatal arrow, the abrupt return to the grim reality of hunting, it was too much to process.

Asa smiled, a knowing, almost flirtatious smile now. "We can later," she spoke quietly, the promise hanging in the air. "We eat, go home."

The shift was complete. The moment of potential intimacy, the fraught emotional tension, had been shattered by the sharp reality of survival, replaced by the simple, vital triumph of the hunt. Aedelric's bewildered emotions took a backseat to the undeniable truth: they had food. They had, at least for a few more days.

Asa began walking back towards the overhang, her steps light and purposeful. Aedelric, still processing, fell into step behind her. He opened his mouth to speak, perhaps about the arrow, about what she had said, but she cut him off with a casual reminder. "Get pig."

Aedelric turned back for the kill. It wasn't large, perhaps weighing forty pounds, which made it manageable. As he hoisted the pig over his shoulder, the weight a known comfort, he found his voice. "How... how do you speak my language?" he asked, the words flowing out, wonder overriding his recent shock. "Have you... been practicing?"

Asa glanced back at him, a look of mirth in her eyes. "You talk," she said. "In your sleep." Aedelric stopped dead. He talked in his sleep? And she had been listening? Learning? "You... you've been picking it up from me talking in my sleep?"

She nodded, a slight smile flickering on her lips. "Yes. You talk yourself. You loud." The mutual moment of amusement felt like a new step in their connection, a lifting of some of the old weight.

Back at the processing area near the shelter, Aedelric dropped the pig. They moved with skilled efficiency now, a grim, wordless choreography born through necessity. Aedelric took the dagger, his hands firm. He cut the tendons on the pig's hind legs, inserted a stick, tied a rope, and, with Asa helping steady the branch, hoisted the carcass clear of the ground. He then bled it out, a quick, brutal cut to the neck artery, the dark blood pooling on the sand. It was a task he had learned from Asa, and he performed it with grim competence.

Asa tended the fire, adding fuel and coaxing the embers back to life for cooking and processing. They worked in silent harmony, each knowing their role. Aedelric, resting for a moment while the pig bled, sat on their makeshift log seat. The waterfall, the missed moment of intimacy, the arrow, the kill, her words ("I like you"). His mind reeled. He was about to speak, perhaps to revisit that moment, when Asa interrupted his thoughts.

"I'm thinking," she said, her voice serious, pulling him back to the present reality. She approached him, her look steady. "We don't stay here."

Aedelric blinked. He had thought this was home, this small haven they had built, this rhythm of survival they had found together. "What do you mean?" he asked, confused.

Asa struggled to find the words in his language, resorting to simple phrases and gestures. "This place... here... animals... flee." She motioned to the increasingly barren forest. "Crops... food we eat... little."

Comprehension dawned slowly, then with full force. She was talking about resources. About the dwindling game, the limited foraging. They had depleted the area. "Yes," he said, the grim reality coming over him. "I know. We can't live here forever. The food won't last."

Asa nodded, sinking to the sand, her look fixed on him. "This... this...not home." Her voice was quiet now, the simple words carrying a heavy weight. Tears welled in her eyes, reflecting the firelight. She looked down, tracing patterns in the dirt, then back up at him, her voice scarcely a whisper, full of unfallen tears. "You... you not my kin."

Aedelric felt the impact of her words, the depth of feeling behind them, even as his mind pieced together their meaning. Not her kin. Not her tribe. "Yes," he said, his voice subdued. "I see. We... we are not the same." He paused, the truth stark and unavoidable. "Our people... are enemies."

Asa nodded, a single tear flowing and tracing a trail down her cheek. "Yes." Her voice was hardly audible now. "My people... kill. They hurt... You people. They hurt... you." The brutal history, the lives lost, the arrow in his side, it all rested between them, a dark veil.

The gravity of those words, of the history they embodied, came upon Aedelric. Enemies. Yes, that was the truth of their births, the truth which had brought them to this point. By all rights, they should have remained on opposite sides of a shieldwall, one of them dead by the other's hand. But the war had shipwrecked them, stripped them bare, and forced them together.

He slid off the log, kneeling in the sand beside her. He looked into her eyes, red-rimmed with unfallen tears, and held her gaze. All the confusion, longing, fear, hope, and overwhelming feelings for this woman converged into a single, undeniable truth. "My heart is yours," he confessed, his voice husky, the words raw with emotion.

Asa looked at him, surprise widening her eyes, the tears briefly forgotten. He reached out, his strong, scarred hands cupping her face, his thumbs gently wiping away a tear. "My heart is yours," he repeated, his gaze locked with hers, pouring every ounce of his feeling into the words, into the touch.

Understanding, profound and overwhelming, dawned in Asa's eyes. Before she could speak, Aedelric leaned in, kissing her. It was a kiss born in desperation, of survival, of profound relief, and irrefutable connection. Long and tender, a joining of two lost souls. Yet, even as the warmth grew between them, a shard of memory pressed in: the clash of shields, a dying man's last cry on the muddy battlefield, the memory of Asa looming from behind an enemy standard. It flickered behind his closed eyes, a ghost intermingling with the living press of her lips. For a second, the burden of the past threatened to pull him under, the knowledge that this was forbidden, a betrayal of fallen friends. Still, he cupped her face, his hand tracing the line of her jaw, then tangling in her hair, all resolve bowed before the depth of feeling. Asa responded, melting into the kiss, her arms going around him, pulling him close. It was a kiss of mutual vulnerability, of acceptance, of a love which, somehow, even with old wounds aching in the dark, defied the boundaries of nation and religion.

As their lips parted, she buried her face in his shoulder, and the dam of unfallen tears finally broke. She sobbed, not from pain or fear this time, but from the overwhelming release of emotion, grief for her people, sorrow for the brutal history, but also the deep, overwhelming happiness and comfort of this connection, this love, this mutual moment that existed outside the grim realities of their worlds. Aedelric held her tight, no words needed now. He understood. They shared something precious, something that exceeded the battlefield, something the outside world would likely never comprehend. They were enemies by birth, survivors by chance, and bound by something neither could explain, here, on this desolate shore.

They stayed wrapped together as the night thickened, the calm of the tide just within hearing. Cool air slipped in from the sea, brushing Asa's tear-damp cheeks and raising goosebumps on Aedelric's arms. The sensation echoed the first chill he had felt that morning on the sand, the start of a day, and of everything that had brought about this. Now, as the last of Asa's sobs faded, the same rising coolness pressed close. It was the world returning, unchanged and yet slightly altered, a silent benediction on their fragile union, binding the end of this night to its uncertain beginning.

CHAPTER 3

Part 1: A Family Begins

The comforting familiarity of the beach, their haven, was slowly fading. It was no longer a place of relative abundance, but a larder scraped thin. The signs were obvious: scarce game trails near the camp, depleted foraging patches, and the constant, demanding need to range further for firewood. Survival here was becoming a more brutal, faster grind. The decision had been unspoken at first, a grim knowledge shared in quiet glances, before Asa, using her growing vocabulary and gestures, had voiced it. "We go," she had said, tapping her chest, then pointing inland. "No food here. No more."

Aedelric had nodded, jaw tight. "Go… yes. Inland." They had to leave. Venture inland. Find her way home. Preparations for such a journey were basic but vital. Using hides from their hunts, cured and softened as best they could, they fashioned simple, practical backpacks, essentially pouches cinched with thongs, designed to carry essentials without impeding movement too much. Into these went carefully selected provisions: the remaining smoked meat, dried berries and roots, bundles of medicinal herbs, Asa identified, the precious flint and steel, lengths of salvaged rope, and their weapons, Asa's bow and arrows, the salvaged dagger, and Astrid's shield. Every item was a weight, a trade-off between necessity and the need to travel light through dense, uncharted terrain.

Amongst these tasks, the relentless work of building a shared language continued. Asa, with strong determination, spent hours teaching Aedelric basic Norse words, pointing to water, fire, food, tree, path, danger, sleep, and rest. She would tap the water skin. "Vatn," she'd say slowly. "Vat… n," he repeated, frowning. She smiled faintly. "Better."

Her grasp of West Saxon, gleaned from listening to Aedelric's mutterings and sleep-talking, was advancing more rapidly. She could now form simple sentences, stringing together words to convey needs and even some thoughts. Aedelric struggled more, his Saxon tongue wrestling with the sounds of Norse, his accent thick and clumsy, sometimes drawing a rare, common moment of amusement from Asa. Once, when he butchered the word for "danger," she laughed softly and corrected him. "Hætta. Not… het-ta." He groaned. "Your words… sharp stones." "Your words… mud," she countered, tapping his chest lightly. They both laughed.

By this time, the absolute barrier that had separated them had significantly diminished. Their communication was still elementary, limited to the practicalities of survival and simple expressions of feeling, but it was enough. Enough to plan, to share burdens, to offer comfort beyond touch. This fragile shared language was evident in their deepening bond, strengthening their resolve for the terrifying journey ahead.

It occurred during one of these halting conversations. At the same time, Aedelric sat on a log, sharpening the dagger; the familiar scrape of stone on steel was a counterpoint to their words. Asa proposed the destination, her village, Njardarheimr. Using the words she knew, she drew the shape of a fjord or a settlement in the sand, revealing her lineage, that of Jarl Gunnar's daughter. She tapped the drawing. "My home. Njardarheimr." Aedelric blinked. "You… jarl's… daughter?" She nodded. "Gunnar. My father." She hesitated, then added, "He… takes you. He does not kill."

The prospect unsettled Aedelric deeply. Walking into the heart of the people his own had fought, a land where his face, his very being, represented loss and vengeance to countless families. He paused in his sharpening, the stone silent. He looked at Asa, busy wrapping smoked meat in broad leaves for their journey. She looked up, her look a question. "You… sure?" he asked quietly, tapping his chest, then miming a blade across his throat. "Me… Saxon." Asa shook her head firmly. "You with me. They see." She pressed her palm to his. "Safe."

Caught at a crossroads of fear and commitment, Aedelric hesitated. Return to Wessex? An impossible sea journey, risking capture or death on hostile shores. What awaited him there anyway? His parents? The King? What did he want, stripped of his rank and world?

Asa watched him wrestle with the choice. "Aedelric," she said softly, searching for the right words. "Come. Home… with me." He exhaled, slow and unsteady. "With you," he said at last. "I go."

He looked at Asa, at their meager preparations, at the vast, unknown forest behind their shelter. He returned to sharpening his dagger, the sound a rhythmic acceptance. "No… other… choice," he conceded slowly, using his limited Norse, gesturing inland. "Cannot… stay. Cannot… sail back." His voice was quiet, weighed down by the burden of the decision. He met her gaze. "Your… village. Best." A grim acceptance. He motioned vaguely. "Go… to your village. Where?"

Relief, sharp and visible, eased the tension in Asa's face. She knew the risks, knew the uncertainty of their location. But it was her land. "Yes," she confirmed, her voice clearer. "My land, my home." She spoke with more certainty than she felt, trying to reassure him. She knew they were far from Njardarheimr, perhaps days or weeks of hard travel, but it was a destination, a hope.

They had survived. Learned. Built a bond stronger than the barriers of language or heritage, forged in the brutal heat of shared survival. They could face this together.

Engrossed in the final preparations, Asa suddenly stopped, turning to Aedelric. She moved towards him with a quiet seriousness, kneeling before him, taking his hands in hers. Her gaze met his, steady and empathetic. "Understand," she said, her West Saxon clearer now, a soothing balm to his unspoken fears. "Not... easy." Aedelric held her gaze, nodding, a myriad of emotions reflected in his eyes, fear, doubt, trust, commitment.

With a tender gesture, she leaned forward, pressing a kiss to his forehead, a wordless promise of support. Rising, she continued to hold his hands, her fingers intertwined with his, her grip firm. A rare, radiant smile lit up her face, chasing away the weariness. "Have... grown... to love you," she confessed, her words simple, profound. Her voice held a fierce hope. "My parents... love you? Maybe. Time."

Aedelric's doubts did not vanish, but Asa's words, her firm belief in them, were a powerful anchor. Their bond, tested by fire and sea, strengthened by mutual respect, felt like the only solid ground in his world. With her beside him, he thought he could face anything.

Returning to her task, Asa resumed wrapping the dried meat, her movements efficient, as she placed the bundles into the finished hide packs. Aedelric finished sharpening his dagger, sheathing it in the crude scabbard Asa had made him. He looked around their small camp, the firepit, the rock overhang, the scattered remains of their time here. A sense of profound calm settled over him. They had done all they could to prepare. The journey into the unknown awaited.

As the last night before their departure drew near, they checked and rechecked their packs, ensuring nothing essential was left behind. In the quiet hours by the fire, Asa continued teaching Aedelric essential Norse words and phrases, greetings, warnings, and questions. If they made it. The uncertainty was a tangible presence, a long shadow cast over their preparations. But they faced it together, their resolve unwavering.

They sat huddled by the fire, the last fire they would share in this small, known haven. The packs were ready.

The destination is terrifyingly uncertain. The past, battle, shipwreck, loss, appeared both distant and ever-present. The future, a vast, dangerous unknown. All that was certain was the fragile, powerful bond that had grown between them.

Asa looked at Aedelric, the firelight dancing in his eyes. He looked at her, his gaze steady. The air sizzled with wordless words, with emotions held in check by weeks of shared hardship and the raw, physical reality of their lives. They were two souls, stripped bare of their old worlds, finding everything in each other.

Aedelric reached out, his hand finding hers, calloused fingers intertwining. Asa turned fully towards him, her heart beating against her ribs, reflecting the firelight in her eyes. The unspoken desire and the strong connection pulled them closer.

He leaned in, his look steady, as he asked the question not with words but with his eyes, his hand holding hers shaking gently. As he mirrored his movement, her breath caught in her throat. And then, their lips met.

It was a kiss long in coming, a culmination of shared fear, shared hope, shared vulnerability. A soft, hesitant touch that deepened with sudden intensity. A silent confession of love, given and received. Their bodies moved together, seeking comfort and closeness in the vast, isolating landscape.

Under the vast, indifferent sky, by the flickering light of the fire that had sustained them, they committed themselves to each other. No priest, no family, no formal vows, only the two of them, the wilderness, and the undeniable truth of their hearts. They explored each other with a tenderness born of profound respect and deep-seated affection.

That night, they consummated their relationship. It was an act of raw, honest intimacy, a physical expression of the emotional and spiritual bond they had established. Passion and tenderness intertwined in the quiet of their shelter, sealing their union most fundamentally.

Unbeknownst to them, at that moment, their joining had sparked a new life. A tiny, fragile promise conceived in the heart of the wild, it would change everything. As they finally drifted to sleep in each other's arms, utterly exhausted but bound, they were on the cusp of a new journey, not just into the unknown forest but into the future of a family they had created against all odds. They had prepared for the wilderness, for the dangers ahead, but the most profound preparation, the commitment to each other, had just been completed. They slept, lovers, poised to face whatever came next together.

As they embarked, leaving the coastal haven behind, they entered the forest proper. It was a world both beautiful and daunting. Towering ancient trees formed a dense canopy overhead, filtering the light into shifting patterns on the leaf-strewn ground. The undergrowth was thick, a tangled, formidable barrier. It was a labyrinth of green, silent save for the sounds of nature.

They moved steadily, conserving energy; their packs were light, but their limbs were weary. Asa took the lead, her senses heightened, eyes scanning, bow at the ready. Aedelric followed, his gaze shifting between the path ahead, searching for obstacles, and Asa's purposeful figure, his anchor in this alien world. The forest was alive, the constant sigh of leaves, the calls of unseen birds, the murmur of the wind high in the branches. They moved in silence, their footsteps muffled by the soft earth beneath them.

Days blurred into a rhythm of travel dictated by the sun and their endurance. They rose at first light, ate cold, dried meat, and walked until their legs ached, finding a place to make camp before dusk. Hunting and foraging were constant necessities, successes, and failures that determined the nature of their meager meals. They drank from streams, the cool, clear water a profound relief.

Each sunset brought the challenge of finding a place to shelter. Sometimes it was a small cave, a makeshift lean-to constructed from branches and moss, offering scant protection from the night's chill or unexpected summer downpours. They huddled together for warmth, for comfort, the simple act of sharing a rough fur blanket on the cold ground deepening the unspoken trust between them.

It was during these shared, quiet moments, and throughout the long days of travel, that their language truly began to intertwine. Now, driven by necessity and a growing desire for genuine understanding, they became tireless teachers and eager students for one another.

Asa taught Aedelric the names of the trees, the calls of birds, and the subtle signs of the forest floor. He learned "skog" for forest, "fugl" for bird, and "dyr" for animal. Aedelric, in turn, taught her the West Saxon names for the stars they watched from their camp, the words for comfort, for hunger, for hope. He'd tell her simple tales from his youth, in broken, halting Norse, his hands painting the pictures his words could not yet fully convey. Asa would listen intently, her brow knitted in concentration, piecing together meanings, occasionally interjecting with a Norse word or a clarifying gesture.

Their understanding grew not only through words, but also through shared experiences. A glance, a touch, a shared breath as they stalked prey or navigated a brutal stretch of terrain, these became their most actual language. They learned each other's habits: Aedelric's quiet, meticulous preparation of a fire, Asa's quick, decisive movements when setting a trap. They saw each other's strengths and vulnerabilities, the stoicism that masked fear, the fierce determination that drove them forward.

They were no longer just two strangers thrust together by fate; they were companions, partners, a nascent family carving out an existence against impossible odds, their very survival dependent on the deepening understanding and unfaltering loyalty they found in each other. They spoke not just with their tongues, but with their eyes, their hands, their very presence, building a bridge between two worlds, one word, one shared moment at a time.

Amidst the hardship, moments of stark beauty pierced through, the forest floor illuminated by the first beams of dawn, dew sparkling like dispersed jewels; the sky ablaze with color as the sun set, a breathtaking contrast to their grim reality. At night, they huddled together for warmth against the chill, their bodies exhausted but spirits resilient, sharing quiet words and fragments of their pasts pieced together through limited language and the shared intimacy of their journey. They learned each other's fears, Asa's quiet dread of being truly alone, Aedelric's pangs of homesickness, sharper in the isolation. They knew each other's quiet strengths, Asa's unwavering hope, and Aedelric's steady patience.

As the months went past, the passage of time became evident in subtle ways: the changing foliage, the cooler bite in the air, and the increasing difficulty of finding certain plants. Their shared language grew, allowing for more complex conversations, understanding extending past immediate needs to nuances of feeling, shared memories, and tentative dreams.

A new, profound change started to manifest. Asa's body began to shift subtly. The exhaustion was deeper, more persistent. The simple nausea she had initially dismissed became a regular morning sickness. The gnawing hunger was different now, demanding specific foods. Pregnancy.

The realization was a quiet, mutual moment of shock and awe. A new life, conceived in the raw aftermath of shipwreck and loss, growing here in the indifferent wilderness. It added a new layer of urgency, of fear, and purpose to their journey.

Their travel pace slowed significantly. Shorter distances and more frequent stops replaced long days of strenuous trekking. Finding safe, sheltered campsites became even more critical. Aedelric's protectiveness intensified; his hand was always ready to help her over rugged terrain, his eyes constantly scanning for any potential threat. Asa, despite the physical toll, remained resolute, her maternal instincts adding a fierce determination to find a way out, to find safety for their child. Finding nutritious food and clean water was no longer only about their survival, but the survival of the fragile life within her.

They were lost, undeniably. The forest was a vast, confusing maze. The heavy canopy and the sheer scale of the wilderness hindered their attempts to navigate by sun, stars, and landmarks. Paths wound, often leading nowhere. But they continued, their love for each other and the child, Asa, carrying them, becoming their compass and motivation. They were no longer simply navigating towards a village; they were navigating in the direction of a future, a future for their small, improbable family, forged in the heart of the wild. Their bond, tested by hardship and now carrying the weight and wonder of a new life, was their unshakable guide.

Part 2: Survival's Sharp Edge

Months had passed since they left the beach haven. The sea was a distant memory, replaced by the unending, disorienting expanse of the forest. The initial hope fueled by their union and the promise of Asa's village had been worn thin by relentless travel, dwindling resources, and the gnawing certainty of being lost. Asa's belly was now rounded and prominent, a constant, visible sign of the new life she carried, a life that added immeasurable purpose and terrifying vulnerability to their every step. Their pace was slow, dictated by Asa's increasing discomfort and limited mobility. Every incline was a struggle, every fallen log an obstacle. Finding safe places to rest was paramount.

They rose, bodies stiffened by the forest floor, the morning chill biting deep even through their layers of hides. The fresh air, sharp with the aroma of pine, held the first subtle hint of approaching winter. They needed food. More than ever, with winter coming and the needs of the growing child pressing. Asa could no longer move with the fluid speed the hunt demanded. Her bow remained her weapon, but stalking game through thick undergrowth with a swollen belly was a dangerous, slow effort. Aedelric did most of the active hunting now, relying on snares and his dagger, but the larger game remained elusive.

They moved through the dense woods, Asa's breath coming in ragged gasps on inclines, Aedelric's hand often at her back, helping her over roots and rocks. He was constantly scanning and listening, his protectiveness a fierce, firm presence.

Suddenly, a crashing sound, far too heavy for a deer, tore through the quiet of the woods. A primal smell, rank and terrifying, filled the air.

A bear, gaunt, desperate, and starving, burst from the thicket. Its fur was matted, eyes frantic with a terrifying, singular hunger. Its gaze set on them, on Asa, its need overriding any natural caution.

Instinct spurred Aedelric into immediate, desperate action. "Asa! Back!" he yelled in, shoving her firmly behind him, shield ripped from his back, dagger in hand. Asa recoiled, her belly making quick movement impossible, her hand going to her bow, but knowing she could not maneuver effectively.

The bear charged, a terrifying, ground-shaking rush directed at Aedelric. He met it with a harsh roar, shield braced, as he attempted to deflect the immense force. Asa, rooted to the spot by her condition, could only draw her bow, her movements slower, more deliberate, her breath faltering in her throat. She aimed, a desperate prayer on her lips.

The bear's charge slammed into Aedelric. Astrid's shield splintered and cracked under the brute force, offering little defense. The bear swiped, tearing through Aedelric's clothes, claws ripping gashes into his arm as he twisted desperately to avoid its full weight. He fell back under the impact, shield lost, dagger slipping from his bloody hand.

Asa loosed her arrow. A desperate shot from a static position, hampered by her breathing, her condition. The arrow struck the bear's shoulder, a solid hit, but only served to enrage the desperate animal further. It turned, snarling, moving towards Asa, its hunger a terrifying, visible force.

Aedelric, pain exploding through his body, scrambled to regain his footing, grabbing for his fallen dagger. Asa, rooted by her pregnancy, searched for another arrow, her usual fluid speed gone, her hands quivering. The bear advanced.

Then, a miracle of desperation and skill. Asa found her mark. Her second arrow flew, a single, precise shot born of instinct and grim necessity. It found the bear's eye. The animal roared, a sound of agony and rage, its charge faltering as its head shook violently.

Aedelric seized the moment the bear faltered and surged forward, adrenaline sharpening his hands into iron. He drove the dagger into its flank once, then again, twisting and thrusting with a grim, mechanical insistence over and over, each stab seeking the dark hollow beneath the ribs where the hope resided that it might die; blood slicked his palm, and the blade sang as it found its mark. The great body convulsed, legs buckling; with a last terrible shudder, it collapsed.

They stood, chests heaving, Asa leaning against a tree for support, Aedelric bleeding heavily, watching the massive form of the bear. That silence that fell was heavy, broken only by their rough breaths and the pounding of their hearts. Danger now passed, leaving behind the raw, brutal reality of their injuries and the sheer terror of the encounter. Aedelric's arm burned with pain, blood soaking his clothes. Asa, pale and shaken, clung to the tree, her hand reflexively going to her belly.

In the quiet aftermath, kneeling by the dead bear, the sheer terror of the encounter lingered. Aedelric's arm bled freely, the gashes deep and raw from the bear's claws. Asa moved with slow, careful steps, her pregnancy obvious in every movement, her face furrowed with concern as she knelt next to him. Using water from their pack, she carefully cleaned his wounds, her hands composed despite her condition, her brow knitted in concentration. "Hold still," she murmured in West Saxon, her voice rigid with worry. "Might sting."

Aedelric clenched his jaw against the pain of the cleaning, managing a weak smile. "I trust you," he whispered hoarsely, his voice harsh, echoing the words he had used months ago. His gaze went to her belly, then back to her face. "More than just us now."

Asa nodded, her eyes meeting his, reflecting the same grim understanding. She took the bundle of dried Usnea, crumbling the lichen, and applying the cool paste to his wounds. "This helps healing," she said, her voice mild but firm. "Cannot get infection." She carefully bound the wounds with strips of salvaged cloth, her movements precise despite the awkwardness of her belly pressing against him. "We will make it," she vowed, her voice quiet but fierce, looking not just at him but at the life she carried. "For... us."

Sitting by the fallen bear, its sheer size was a terrifying token of the threat; the reality of their situation pressed down on them. They had faced nature's desperate hunger and won, but at a cost. The bear's gauntness, its "hunger rage"; it was the harbinger of the coming winter, its dangers magnified tenfold by Asa's advanced pregnancy. The wilderness was unforgiving, and their vulnerability was increasing with every passing week.

But the bear also offered a vital, if grim, bounty. Its meat would provide sustenance for many weeks; its thick hide, once processed, would offer crucial warmth against the deep cold that was coming. They began the arduous, bloody work of butchering the massive carcass, a task made infinitely more complicated by Asa's limited mobility. Aedelric, despite his fresh wounds, bore the brunt of the heavy labor.

Using branches and salvaged rope, they built a makeshift stretcher, lashing heavy portions of meat and the rolled hide onto it. It was a crushing weight, requiring immense effort for Aedelric to lift and carry, even with Asa's limited help. As they prepared to move on, their gazes met, a wordless promise passing between them, a vow to protect each other, their precious, vulnerable burden, and the unseen life that tied them, no matter the cost.

As the sun started its descent, throwing long, mysterious shadows through the trees, they continued their journey. The weight of the bear's gifts, meat and hide, was a physical burden on the stretcher. Still, the weight of their new reality, Asa's advanced pregnancy, Aedelric's fresh wounds, the grim promise of winter, was heavier still, a constant, pressing presence shaping their slow, arduous path through the ancient, indifferent forest.

The hope of finding Asa's village felt more distant than ever, but the resolve to survive together, for their child, burned brighter than the fear.

Part 3: Winter's Edge

Daylight came, a grey, frigid light piercing the thick blanket of snow that had silently descended overnight. Winter had come, not with a gradual descent, but a sudden, brutal fist. The cold was a physical presence, seeping into their deep bones, each inhalation a sharp ache in their chests. Months of relentless travel through the forest had honed them, stripped them bare, and left them bone-weary. Asa's belly was large and heavy, a constant, undeniable weight that slowed her steps and made every fallen log a monumental effort. With each passing night, the cold deepened, resembling the dwindling hope that they would find a way out before the harshest season claimed them. Yet, they moved forward, a silent, fierce vow to endure for the life burgeoning within her, fueling their exhausted limbs.

On this fierce morning, through the swirling snow and the skeletal shapes of the trees, a darker mass resolved itself in the distance. The shape was not forest or rock. A sign of man. A sign of desperate hope against the overwhelming white and grey. It was a village. Wooden palisades, rough-hewn but sturdy, jutted defiantly against the snow-laden landscape. Asa squinted, straining her weary eyes, searching for familiar signs, the style of the longhouses, the symbols on the banners that snapped in the biting wind. Nothing registered. It was neither the familiar architecture of the Norse villages she knew nor the Saxon settlements Aedelric had described.

"Look," Asa said, her voice as a raw murmur against the wind's howl, pointing with a mittened hand. "A village."

Aedelric strained his eyes, able to discern the tops of the palisades, the faint wisp of smoke. He turned to Asa, his face drawn with a combination of disbelief and desperate hope. "Is this... your village?"

Asa shook her head, disappointment a bitter taste. "No. I recognize nothing." Her mind raced, grasping for any fragment of knowledge, any mention of a settlement in this deep wilderness, but found only emptiness. Lost. Utterly lost.

Aedelric's voice was grim. "Do we approach?" The question hung densely in the biting air.

Asa paused, exhaustion at her bones, yet every sense razor-sharp; she listened to the wind and scanned the silent woods around the distant settlement for any sign of watchers or danger. "I am not sure," she admitted, eyes locked on the palisade gates. This could be salvation or a curse.

Just then, a movement within Asa's belly made her gasp, a strong kick upon her ribs. A rare smile brushed her lips, one that always broke through the weariness. Aedelric saw it and placed a hand gently on her belly. "He's kicking again," he said, a smile easing the tension in his face. "Strong. Like his mother."

Asa placed her hands over his, her gaze meeting his. "How do you know it's a boy?" she asked.

"So much... movement," Aedelric reasoned, grinning slightly. "Must be a boy."

Asa squeezed his hands, her smile confident despite the cold. "If it's a boy," she said, her voice tender but fierce. "May he be strong like his father." Aedelric knew, deep down, it didn't matter, boy or girl. A boy would have her strong spirit and his strength. A girl would have her intelligence and skill and his steady heart. Either would be a miracle.

The biting cold forced a decision. They couldn't stand still, couldn't wait. "Okay," Asa said, rubbing her hands together, breath misting in the air. "What do we do?" She gestured towards the endless, snow-covered forest, then towards the distant palisades. "Winter is coming. Do we find somewhere outside? Shelter for winter?" The prospect was bleak. "Or do we seek refuge here?" The risks were immense. Hostile people? A fight they weren't sure they could win, not with her condition.

Aedelric looked at the unforgiving wilderness, then at Asa's heavy belly. The notion of facing winter's full fury, of Asa going into labor unprotected, was a cold terror. The village, however unknown, offered walls, warmth, and people. A risk, yes, but perhaps their only one.

"Approach the gate," Aedelric finally decided, his voice resolute.

Asa nodded, accepting the choice, the gamble. She saw no guards; this seemed odd to her. What price would refugees demand? Did these people know her father, her village? Would that be a blessing or a curse? Time, a luxury they had almost run out of, would tell. With caution guiding their every step, weapons ready but not openly displayed, they began to approach the village gates. As they drew closer, the scent of firewood smoke reached them, a powerful lure of warmth and life. They could see smoke drifting from the rough rooftops beyond the palisade.

Stopping a short distance from the gate, they called out, their voices resounding through the stillness. "Hello! Travelers seek refuge!" Calling out was a sign of peaceful intent, announcing their presence rather than sneaking up on them.

The heavy gate creaked open slowly, and a face peered out, wary but curious. A young man, his features obscured by the low light and palisade shadows, spoke in a language neither fully understood, but the intent was clear. "Who... you?"

Asa replied in Norse, speaking slowly, using simple words. "We are... wanderers. Seek... shelter." She kept her identity and her pregnancy concealed as best she could for now.

Suddenly, the young man was yanked back, a stern voice speaking sharply from within. A ripple of unease passed between Asa and Aedelric. An older man, bald with a long grey beard, replaced the boy at the gate. He repeated the question in the same fragmented language, then, to their surprise, tried a few halting words in Norse. "Who... are... you?"

"Travelers," Asa repeated in Norse, keeping her tone calm. "Seek... shelter." She subtly motioned for Aedelric to lower his hand from his dagger hilt, which he did with a quiet nod, though his muscles remained coiled. Asa kept her bow hand behind her back, fingers wrapped around the grip, ready to nock an arrow in an instant while maintaining an outwardly non-threatening posture.

The elder's eyes, sharp and assessing, swept over them, their worn clothes, the packs, the weapons. He spoke again in halting Norse. "Where... from?"

"Lost," Asa replied. "Journeyed... from south." She watched him, sensing his caution, his attempt to glean information. Time for a calculated risk. "We... from Njardarheimr. Under... Jarl Gunnar." She tightened her grip on the bow, braced for a reaction, recognition, hostility, anything.

The elder looked up at the grey sky for a long moment, pondering the name. Aedelric felt Asa's tension spike, and his muscles coiled tighter. The elder finally shook his head. "Unfamiliar... with this place... or man." This brought a small, shared flicker of relief. No immediate, known enemy here, perhaps. "No, Jarl... here. A... Magnate... governs us."

Asa didn't know the word "Magnate" but understood it meant leader. They waited, letting the elder speak, reveal more about this unknown place. Impatience flickered in his gaze. "Have... goods... trade?" he finally asked.

"Yes," Asa confirmed, the word immediately brought their bounty from the forest. "Bear meat. Hide."

The elder's eyes lit up. Trade. Valuable resources. "Hunters?" he asked, excitement entering his voice.

"We are."

His assessment seemed complete. Satisfied, the elder stepped back, and the heavy wooden gate began to creak open. The boy appeared again, helping the elder strain to push the massive doors wide enough. The elder gestured them forward.

Asa and Aedelric stepped through the gates into the village. Their hearts hammered, not just from fear but from the possibility of refuge, warmth, and a reprieve from the relentless wilderness. The air was warmer here, laden with the smell of firewood smoke and the sounds of human life, distant voices, the ring of hammers.

The elder was surprisingly small, even shorter than Asa. The boy was a mere youth. Aedelric felt like a giant towering over them, but neither seemed intimidated.

The gate groaned shut behind them, cutting off the view of the endless snow. The elder turned, his ancient eyes meeting Aedelric's. "Come," he said, a single, clear word.

Asa understood. "He wants us... to follow him," she translated into West Saxon for Aedelric, then turned to the elder and boy, who were watching her with renewed curiosity. "He... not speak... Norse," she explained in her native tongue, gesturing to Aedelric. "I... tell him... follow." She saw their surprise, the dawning understanding that the Saxon wasn't just a silent brute but needed her to understand their words. It was a slight advantage.

The elder nodded, seemingly accepting her explanation. He turned and began walking towards the heart of the village, a jumble of rough-built longhouses and smaller structures. "Come," he repeated over his shoulder.

Asa and Aedelric followed, their senses absorbing everything around them. The village was unlike any they had seen, a mix of architectural styles, suggesting a community built by people from various lands. Villagers stopped their tasks, watching the newcomers with wary curiosity, but the rhythm of daily life continued, people mending nets, working hides, carrying water, and children playing.

At the center of the village stood a massive rune stone, unlike any they had encountered. Its surface was covered in intricate, swirling carvings from base to top, towering three men high, equally broad. Its meaning was a mystery to both of them.

As they stood before it, engrossed, a deep voice resounded from behind them, speaking in fluent, clear Norse. "Welcome."

They turned, startled. A rotund man stood there, jovial-faced, despite a receding hairline, pulled into a neat ponytail bound with a golden band. His clothes were an obvious contrast to the villagers' simple garb, rich robes of deep purple and red, a cloak adorned with miniature carvings or symbols of various colors. He was a man of apparent wealth and authority.

"You speak my language," Asa stated, surprise in her voice.

"Indeed, I do," the man replied, his tone smooth, welcoming. "And we welcome you... all."

Asa stepped forward, taking his hand. "I am Asa. This is my husband," she said, gesturing to him, a faint, almost imperceptible shift in her stance indicating he didn't speak their tongue. "He does not speak Norse."

Pall nodded, his gaze returning to Asa, a trace of understanding in his eyes. "A pity. However, I am confident that we can still find common ground. Again, welcome."

Asa's brow furrowed. "You all?"

The man's eyes twinkled. He looked at Aedelric, then down at Asa's prominent belly, then back to her face. "Yes. You, the big man here, and the new life you carry."

A tremor ran down Asa's spine. He knew. How could he know? She had tried to conceal it. However, his tone wasn't accusatory; it was simply a statement of fact.

Accepting that concealment was impossible, she decided honesty was their best path. "Yes," she said, her voice unshaken despite the shock. "We seek shelter. My child is due soon."

His face lit up, a genuine, broad smile beaming across it. "A wonderful occasion! You are indeed fortunate that fate guided you to our humble village in this season." He gestured warmly. "But forgive my lack of manners. I am Pall Thorfinnsson, the Magnate of this settlement."

Magnate. Asa hadn't heard the title, but the man's bearing, his clothes, and his presence spoke of clear leadership. Who was this man, this community that seemed to appear out of nowhere, led by a man who spoke her tongue perfectly and knew her secret?

Aedelric had not been idle. His gaze swept over Pall, the villagers, and the surroundings. He had followed the conversation, understanding the exchange about their origin, the bear meat, the trade, and the offer of entry. He understood Pall's fluent Norse. But the moment Pall had spoken of the child, Aedelric's command of Norse wasn't complete enough to catch every word, but the tone, Pall's gaze on Asa's belly, Asa's reaction, he understood the essence. Pall knew.

A burst of relief, mixed with deep caution, went through Aedelric. This Magnate welcomed them and offered shelter. But how did he know about the child? He watched Pall, with his jovial face and rich clothes, so out of place here. He noticed the elder and the boy discreetly melting away into the background. Why hadn't Pall addressed him directly, the larger of the two newcomers? Aedelric remained silent, vigilant, letting Asa lead the conversation, his perceived ignorance a potential advantage.

With a grand gesture, Pall invited them, in a tone of genuine joy, towards a large, central building, *'The Great House'*, he called it, promising warmth, food, and introductions. Pall told them they would take care of the trade items, meaning the bear meat and hide. To which people, just as small as the older man and the younger, took their haul and headed back into the village. They had little choice but to accept. Intrigued, warned with caution. This place was a mystery. Its leader, even more so. But winter was here. And they had a child coming. They had to take the risk. Asa instinctively assumed it would be like her father's Longhouse.

Part 4: From Wild to Warmth

They approached the Great House, its sheer scale unfolding as they drew near the edge of the village center. It was vast, a formidable structure stretching perhaps a hundred and fifty feet in length, maybe fifty in width, far larger than any Norse longhouse Asa knew, though still a single-story timber hall, unlike the stone structures Aedelric had seen in Winchester. Its size alone spoke of Pall's power and status in this wilderness setting.

The exterior was a blend of familiar materials and skilled artistry. Walls of massive, interlocking oak logs were carved, the surfaces bearing patterns and symbols that corresponded to those on the central rune stone. The roof, thickly thatched, sloped gently, culminating at either end in carvings of dragon heads, fierce and ancient. Yet, despite its grandeur, the house seemed to settle into the landscape, its design hinting at a respect for the natural world around it.

The entrance was framed by towering wooden pillars carved into the likeness of ravens, Odin's ravens, Huginn and Muninn, Asa recognized instantly. The sight served as a stark reminder of their pagan hosts, a detail that settled cold in Aedelric's gut, even as he was still in the midst of his awe. Stepping inside, they entered a vast central hall, dimly lit despite the large central hearth sending a plume of smoke towards a vent in the roof. Pall led them to the main floor of this massive communal space. Servants, creeping, awaited their arrival near a long, heavy table laden with a generous array of food and provisions, a bounty that seemed impossible in this remote, winter-struck land.

Pall guided them towards the table, the scent of roasted meat and spiced bread a powerful lure after weeks of gnawing hunger. He strode with easy confidence, settling into a sturdy chair at the head and gesturing for them to sit. Asa and Aedelric hesitated, their eyes wide, taking in the sheer abundance, the well-crafted table and chairs, the quality of the craftsmanship implying a strong, prosperous hall.

Before they could sit, Pall's sharp gaze rested on Aedelric, noting the subtle stiffness in his posture and the way he instinctively favored his side. "That wound," Pall observed, his voice deep and perceptive, a glint in his eye that suggested he knew more than he let on. He then addressed one of the servants nearby. "See that our guests' wounds are seen before the meal. Wounds deserve swift attention." Aedelric nodded a silent acknowledgement of the Pall's perception, and the servant, a brisk woman with knowing hands, stepped forward to offer a quick assessment and the promise of proper care after the greeting.

She began to observe Aedelric's wounds. In Norse, she stated that it is "Not too bad, and it will need to be cleaned". Aedelric looked to Asa, still pretending not to know what was being said. Asa then thanked the servant. She nodded with a quick nod and left the room to fetch clean water and a bandage. When she returned, she had a basic array of remedies: warm water, rough cloths, and a pungent-smelling poultice made from ground herbs. She worked efficiently, cleaning the wound of dried blood and grit, then applying the fresh poultice, explaining its properties as she did. "This will draw out the ill humors and speed the healing. Best to keep it covered and warm." She rewrapped it with fresh, somewhat finer linen. She worked quickly and then promptly returned to her place in line. Pall thanked her and returned his attention to Asa and Aedelric.

"Please," Pall said, his voice kind and inviting, gesturing to the feast. "Sit and partake."

They moved stiffly, packs still on their backs, weapons clutched or slung, survival instincts shouting caution. They had lived off the land, off desperate hunts and meager foraging. The sight was almost overwhelming.

Pall watched their hesitation, his gaze perceptive. "I understand this is... much," he said, his voice soft. "You wonder how this is possible."

Asa found her voice, her innate noble bearing reasserting itself despite her worn clothes and the early curve of her belly. "Indeed. This land... I know some of it. But this place... I have never heard."

Pall nodded, his hands resting on the sturdy wood of the table. "Your perception serves you well, Asa. This place... everything you see... it is built on trust." His gaze seemed to go beyond them, looking into the distance. "Trust from the people who live here, work here, and raise their families here." He paused, his face changing. "I was once... like you. A wanderer. A warrior, partaking in raids." He used the term "Viking" with a certain detachment, as if speaking of a past life. "But that life... too much chaos. Once I had... enough silver, enough gold... I left it. Searched for something different."

He continued his tale, his voice acquiring a subtle intensity. "In my travels, I learned. From every culture, every person." His gaze settled on them again. "Then, in a distant market... a place untouched by the chaos of raids... I met a man. A trader. Not of silver or gold. But of knowledge. He asked nothing in return. Only to teach me... a way of life. I thought it was impossible."

He paused, his gaze holding Asa's, then Aedelric's. "So... I learned. Lived with this man. Learned his ways. I became... a better man."

Asa and Aedelric remained silent, riveted by his words, by the mystery of this man, this place. Pall clapped his hands, drawing their attention to the servants standing quietly nearby. "These people," he said, a warmth entering his voice. "They are my family. This is their home, as much as it is mine. I have no wife, no child... in the way others do. But I have a family."

"So... you were like me?" Asa asked, her voice hesitant. "From what village?"

Pall sighed slightly, a trace of sadness in his expression. "Many questions, all in good time. For now... please. My hospitality." He gestured to the food. "You will see... I have not even asked for your weapons. You are safe here. I mean you no harm."

With a reassuring gesture, Pall took a leg from a whole roasted chicken on a large wooden platter, tore off a piece with his teeth, chewed it thoughtfully, and then handed the rest to a nearby servant. "Eat," he commanded gently. The servant took a large bite, grease dripping down his chin, his eagerness evident. Seeing this, the palpable reality of food offered without immediate demand, Asa and Aedelric finally began to eat. The taste of rich, cooked meat, fresh bread, and simple fruits, after months of deprivation, was almost overwhelming. It felt like a dream, a hallucination brought on by hunger and exhaustion. But it was real. This place was real.

After the feast, having eaten until they could hold no more, Pall rose. "The hour grows late," he said, addressing Asa. "Personal affairs require my attention." He promised to speak with them further in the morning. Servants appeared, discreetly guiding them towards a part of the Great House clearly reserved for private chambers, a rare luxury in most dwellings.

They were led into a chamber that left them breathless. It was vast, warm, and filled with a level of comfort and luxury they had only dimly imagined. Dominating the room was a grand, high bed crafted from dark, carved oak, draped with fine linen, and piled with feather-stuffed bedding. At its foot sat a large oak chest, echoing the carvings of the bed. A sturdy writing desk with quills, ink, and parchment stood against one wall.

Their eyes, accustomed to the rough simplicity of their wilderness camp, took in the details, the elaborate carvings on the furniture, the glint of what looked like gold artifacts placed on shelves (cups, vessels, small statues, their purpose unknown, hinting at diverse origins or beliefs), the sheer cleanliness of the room. Just hours ago, they had been dirty, ragged, constantly cold, foraging for roots. Now... this.

A knock at the door interrupted their stunned silence. A young female servant entered, head bowed, holding a bucket of steaming hot water. Behind her, a line of others stretched, each carrying a similar bucket. "To fill the bath, master," the servant said, her voice mild, addressing Aedelric.

A large wooden tub sat in one corner, lined with a linen sheet. They were familiar with bathing, yes, but not like this. Not hot water, brought to a private chamber, bucket by painstaking bucket.

Soon, the tub was filled, steaming invitingly. The last servant bowed, leaving them alone, closing the heavy wooden door softly behind her. "Your bath is ready. Leave garments outside," she instructed softly before the door clicked shut.

Aedelric, survival instincts still paramount despite the luxury, immediately checked the door, ensuring it was secured. He pressed his ear against the wood, listening intently. Silence. Satisfied, he turned back to Asa, his face furrowed with disbelief. "Can you... Believe this?" he murmured in West Saxon, his voice full of wonder.

Asa was already moving through the room, her eyes sharp, scanning, checking corners, and running a hand along the walls, a lifetime of vigilance impossible to switch off. "I know," she said, her words soft, her awe warring with ingrained caution. "Overwhelming." Aedelric joined her, their hands and eyes exploring, checking the chest, looking under the bed, examining the walls. Nothing seemed out of place, no hidden dangers apparent. The room felt as secure as it looked.

After weeks of raw survival, the sheer comfort felt surreal. They sat on the edge of the grand bed, the softness of the feather mattress contrasting with the hard ground they were accustomed to. "Well," Asa finally said, breaking the silence, a weary resolve in her voice. "Let's not waste a good bath." It had been months since their last proper cleansing. Her hand reflexively went to her belly, sensing the familiar stir of the life within.

Aedelric readily agreed; the thought of hot water washing away the grime and cold was irresistible. He went to the tub, testing the water, still wonderfully hot. Asa began to undress, folding her worn, dirt-stained clothes neatly on the floor. Her bow and quiver were placed carefully on the writing desk. Seeing the size of the tub, built for one person's comfort, Aedelric knew Asa would take her turn first. She deserved this.

Asa, now bare, climbed into the tub, using a small wooden stool provided. A sigh of pure, unadulterated relief escaped her lips as the heat of the water shrouded her body. Aedelric, sitting on a chair he pulled up to the tub's edge, watched her, a soft smile on his face. "How does it feel?" he asked.

"Oh," Asa murmured, her voice almost a whisper, utterly relaxed. "This is... what I needed."

Aedelric reached for a bar of soap from a small dish, it looked and felt identical to the ones used in Winchester. "Lean forward," he instructed gently, his eyes automatically scanning the door. "We are safe. Relax. Let me wash your back." His dagger remained at his belt, a quiet contradiction to the intimacy of the act.

His hands, strong and calloused, took the soap, lathering it as he washed her back with slow, deliberate strokes, a tender massage that washed away not just dirt but weeks of tension. "This is unreal," Asa murmured, leaning back her head, looking at him with a soft smile.

"It is," Aedelric agreed, his voice suffused with quiet wonder. "I have seen comfort before... but not like this."

When he finished, he handed her the soap, and she took over, washing herself with thoroughness. She unbraided her hair, now long and heavy, letting it fall down her back, washing away the grime of months. She leaned back in the water, eyes closed in contentment. "The water is dirty now," she murmured, referring to the grime washed from her body.

"It's alright," Aedelric dismissed her concern. "Still hot?"

"Yes," she confirmed, opening her eyes, a soft smile on her lips. "Very much."

"I'll bathe," Aedelric decided. "After you."

"I am done now," Asa said, her voice echoing slightly in the large room. "I will find something in the chest to wear."

Aedelric rose, his interest sparked. He lifted the heavy lid of the ornate oak chest. Inside, an array of garments, soft to the touch, lay folded in rich colors. He picked up a shift of fine linen, incredibly smooth, holding it up.

As he turned back, Asa stepped from the tub, water streaming from her body, highlighting the curve of her belly and the lines of her muscles, honed by survival. Aedelric paused, a sense of quiet awe filling him. Even now, heavy with child, after weeks of hardship, clean in the firelight, she was breathtaking. Her beauty was not diminished but seemed amplified by the strength in her form, the visible promise of life. His thoughts drifted back to their time in the wilderness, the brief moments of intimacy, and the stark reality of their shared lives. Seeing her clean now, her body a portrait of strength and impending motherhood, was a moment of profound appreciation.

It was Aedelric's turn for the bath. Asa, drying her hair with a soft towel, slipped into the delicate linen shift Aedelric had found, its fabric softer than anything she had felt in months. She settled cross-legged on the grand bed, watching him.

Aedelric eased himself into the still-warm water, a sigh of profound relief escaping him as the heat soaked into his aching muscles and stung his fresh wounds, but still it was washing away the last remnants of the cold journey. He leaned his head back against the tub's edge, his eyes closing for an instant of pure, unadulterated comfort. When he opened them, he met Asa's gaze. She was watching him, a soft, warm expression on her face. A smile brushed his lips. "What?" he asked quietly.

Asa smiled back, her eyes sparkling in the dim light. "Nothing," she replied softly. "Just... watching you." Her heart felt full. Love for this man, who was experiencing simple comfort for the first time in months, who had just faced a bear to protect them, who was the father of her child.

Aedelric closed his eyes again, sinking deeper into the warmth.

Asa could see he hadn't washed yet; he was soaking. "Don't forget to wash," she reminded him gently.

He laughed quietly. He knew. But the simple luxury of hot water was too good to rush. Eventually, though, the need for cleanliness won. He washed himself thoroughly, the soap a lavish pleasure. Clean, he stepped from the tub into the cooler air of the room, drying himself off. He found clothes in the chest, soft linen undergarments, and a tunic.

By the time he had dressed, Asa had fallen fast asleep on the vast, soft bed, utterly exhausted by the journey and the day's events. He pulled a heavy flax blanket from the chest and covered her gently, tucking it around her. He knew what came next. Rest was vital for Asa and the child. But vigilance was his duty. Even here, in this place of unimaginable comfort, the instincts honed by survival and warfare could not be turned off.

He pulled a chair from the writing desk and placed it near the door, facing it. His dagger remained at his belt. He settled into the chair, his eyes fixed on the heavy wooden door, listening to the quiet sounds of the sleeping house, ready for whatever the night might bring.

CHAPTER 4

Part 1: Hidden Truth

As the morning light, softened by heavy curtains, filtered into the chamber, Aedelric stirred from his uncomfortable vigil. His body ached from the night in the chair, but his mind remained sharp, senses alert. Asa still slept deeply in the large bed, her breathing soft and even, the blanket rising and falling gently over her swollen belly. He watched her for a moment, the harsh lines of the past few months softened by sleep and comfort. Then, with a quiet sigh, he rose, stretching cramped muscles, and returned to his post by the door, listening for sounds of the house waking.

Soon, there were footsteps in the hallway outside, the rustle of voices. A soft knock came at their door. Aedelric hesitated for a fraction of a second, hand going to his dagger hilt, then opened it. A young servant stood there, bearing a tray laden with bread, cheese, and steaming mugs. "Good morning, master," the servant said softly, bowing his head. "Magnate Pall awaits you below when you are ready."

Aedelric nodded his thanks, accepting the tray. He closed the door quietly, placing the food on the writing desk. He looked back at Asa, still sleeping. The reality of their situation rushed back to guests, perhaps prisoners, in a place of impossible luxury, in a village that concealed secrets, led by a man who knew too much.

He ate a piece of bread, chewed the hard cheese, his mind already working. He needed to wake Asa. They needed to speak before meeting Pall. There was much to discuss: the village's strangeness, the wealth, Pall's unsettling knowledge, and the disturbing feeling that this sanctuary, however comfortable, might hide a dangerous truth.

Asa stirred as he approached the bed. Her eyes fluttered open, a soft smile touching her lips as she saw him. "Morning," she murmured, her voice husky with sleep.

Aedelric returned her smile, reaching out to touch her hand. "Morning, my love." He used the endearment instinctively, a word that felt right, that encompassed everything he felt for her. "Food." He gestured to the tray. "Servants came. Pall waits." His voice grew serious. "Asa... this place." He hesitated, looking at her, at her belly. "It is so much."

Asa nodded, her expression sobering as she looked around the opulent room, the events of the previous night and the day before returning with full force. The luxury, the strange customs glimpsed yesterday, Pall's unsettling knowledge, Aedelric standing guard... "Yes," she said, her voice muted. "Much." She sat up slowly, leaning back against the feather pillows. "We need to speak before Pall."

Aedelric agreed. They shared the bread and cheese, a simple act of eating that grounded them after the surreal hours that had passed. Their conversation was conducted in a low murmur. They spoke of Pall's knowledge, his apparent ease, his wealth that seemed to appear from nowhere. They spoke of the villagers, the mix of peoples, the wary curiosity, the quiet rhythm of life that appeared both genuine and somehow... incomplete. They spoke of the anxiety that lingered beneath the comfort. This served as a sanctuary, yes, but they were warriors, survivors; their instincts warned them that such a place did not simply exist without a cost, without secrets.

Later that morning, they descended to the hall to meet Pall. He greeted them with his usual calm demeanor, offering more food and hot ale. The conversation began tentatively, with Pall asking about their rest. Asa, seizing an opening, pressed gently. "Magnate Pall," she began, her voice respectful but firm. "This village is unlike any we

have seen. Its bounty in such a remote land, its people...
how is it sustained? How does it operate?"

Pall leaned back in his sturdy chair, his gaze distant.
"It is, as I said, built on trust," he reiterated, then
elaborated. "But also, on careful planning and mutual
endeavor. We do not raid. We trade. We cultivate. We
nurture the land and each other. The abundance you see is
the fruit of many hands, guided by knowledge from many
lands. Our people come from diverse origins, everyone
bringing skills and wisdom. We share resources and work
for the common good. There is no Lord here, no thrall.
Only those who choose to contribute." He spoke of
specialized crafts, skilled ironworkers, gifted weavers,
resourceful hunters, and farmers, all of whom contributed
to the community's self-sufficiency. He spoke of
disciplined resource management, of reserves built over
years of careful stewardship, allowing them to weather the
harsh winters.

Asa listened intently, her eyebrows knitted. "Yet, such
harmony... it is rare, even amongst kin. There must be
governance, a way to keep order?"

Pall met her gaze. "There is, not by force, but by
consensus. Disputes are heard, judgments rendered by
those chosen for their wisdom. And by example. My
example. When a community thrives, when each person has
enough, when they feel secure... the need for harsh rule
diminishes." He paused, his eyes softening slightly. "You
have endured much, both of you. And your child will soon
need a stable heart. This chamber, while comfortable for a
night's rest, is not a home. There is a longhouse in the
village, unoccupied since its family journeyed south for the
winter trade. It is warm, well-built, and has served many
travelers and new families before they found their place. It
will be yours while you are here."

The offer, though practical, held a weight of
expectation. Aedelric and Asa exchanged a glance. The

luxury of the chamber had appeared both unsettling and temporary. A longhouse, located within the village itself, implied a deeper integration and a commitment to staying. It was a far more familiar and grounding prospect than the opulent room.

That afternoon, they were moved from Pall's Hall. Pall himself walked them a short distance through the village to a modest but sturdy longhouse. It was clean, its central hearth well-swept, and the sleeping platforms lined with fresh rushes and thick animal hides. It was a *ból*, a true home, though simple in comparison to the great hall or the lavish chamber they had just left. It was practical, cozy, and filled with the subtle scent of seasoned timber and lingering wood smoke. It felt solid, safe, and undeniably real. They unpacked their few belongings, including their weapons and furs, which found their place in their new temporary dwelling.

As the weeks churned on, and the deep winter was truly setting upon the land, blanketing the village in a hushed, relentless snow, Asa and Aedelric began to live within the rhythm of Pall's community truly. They adapted to the daily routines within their longhouse, sharing responsibility for warmth and food preparation. The longhouse served as a sanctuary, its walls deflecting the fierce winds and its hearth radiating a constant, comforting warmth.

As the days passed into routine within the village walls, Asa and Aedelric began to see the layers of the community Pall had built. It was a crossroads, indeed, a place where people of varied origins Norse and Saxon, but others too, from lands they didn't recognize had come together. Stories were indeed shared here, fragments of lives left behind, tales of journeys taken. Their own story, they knew, would soon be another thread in this fabric woven at the edge of the known world.

The village itself, though modest compared to Pall's Great House, exuded a palpable sense of warmth and shelter against the approaching winter. The longhouses, built in varied styles reflecting their inhabitants' origins, sent curls of smoke into the fresh air, promising hearth and home. Laughter and the sounds of work echoed within the palisade walls. The local dialect was a hurdle, akin to Asa's Norse tongue but with enough differences to make complete understanding difficult, particularly for Aedelric. Yet, the villagers' faces held a familiar weariness, a shared knowledge born of being lost or displaced, that overcame language.

With Asa's pregnancy steadily advancing, the simple fact of having walls, a roof, warmth, and consistent food felt like salvation. The village, with its aura of hospitality, offered a crucial respite they desperately needed. The villagers, noting Asa's condition, showed a surprising readiness to help. Women, weathered and kind-eyed, knowledgeable in the ways of childbirth, approached Asa with offers of comfort and assistance. The men, seeing Aedelric's protective stance and calm strength, showed him respect, offering him work tasks around the village, such as repairs and helping with the communal stores, allowing him to contribute and earn their keep, a welcome return to purpose.

Asa and Aedelric slowly began to pick up phrases of the local dialect, adding another layer to their growing linguistic bridge. They learned, through gestures and fragmented conversations, that this village was a refuge for many who had been lost to the wilderness, displaced by war or misfortune. Here, all were seemingly welcome to share their stories, to find a temporary haven, to start anew under Pall's governance.

The coming winter months emphasized the need for stability, for a safe place for their child's arrival and the first vulnerable weeks of its life. Though still far from the lands they called home, they were learning that 'home' here wasn't just a place, but the people they were with, the bonds they were forging with each other, and, tentatively, with some of the villagers. In this sanctuary, which felt neither entirely Norse nor entirely foreign, Asa and Aedelric found a temporary home. The birth of their child here would be more than just the extension of their lineage; it would be a physical embodiment of the blending of cultures; of the improbable future they were building. Yet, beneath the surface of welcome and routine, lay an assortment of customs and rituals that were both intriguing and unsettling. Each morning, the villagers gathered in the central square, facing the rising sun. They chanted a melodic hymn, the sounds foreign to both Asa and Aedelric, a tune that seemed to resonate with the land's energy. The hymn was followed by a communal dance, their movements precise, flowing in patterns that suggested the weaving of a complex story.

Meals were shared, and before eating, a small, ornate bowl filled with water was passed around. Each person dipped their fingers in the water and flicked droplets over their shoulders, a gesture Asa and Aedelric learned was meant to ward off spirits who might envy the living's sustenance. This ritual felt both familiar in its pagan echoes and foreign in its specific form.

At dusk, a period of silence fell upon the village until the first star appeared in the dusk sky. During this silence, candles were lit in windows, paying homage to the transition from day to night. Asa and Aedelric noticed that the villagers would occasionally glance skyward during this time, their faces showing a mix of reverence and apprehension, as if they were watching for something.

Once a week, the village held a festival, vibrant affairs of music, feasting, and storytelling that lasted from midday until dawn. But the stories were always cryptic, tales of otherworldly beings and mysterious forces, leaving Asa and

Aedelric with more questions than answers about the beliefs and history of this place.

The most peculiar ritual was observed whenever someone chose to leave the village, a passage ritual. The departing individuals would walk down a corridor lined by two rows of trees leading out of town. Villagers would line up on either side, muttering phrases that sounded like a blend of farewells and warnings. The ritual ended as the traveler exited the tree line into the forest, with the villagers turning their backs, never to speak of that person again, as if they had ceased to exist.

These customs, while strange and sometimes unsettling, did not seem inherently evil. The villagers performed them with a sense of ingrained normalcy, suggesting they were fundamental to their way of life. Asa and Aedelric, though bewildered, began to see these rituals as an integral, if enigmatic, part of the village's identity.

As evening came, painting the village in shades of indigo and soft gold, Aedelric experienced the familiar itch of restlessness, the need for a solitary walk. He needed to think, to process. The longhouse he shared with Asa felt warm, the hearth comforting, but questions worried him. He stepped outside into the cold air, the cold biting on his cheeks, his breath misting before him.

He walked through the village, the well-trodden paths leading between the timber and wattle-and-daub buildings, around the communal spaces. Small gardens lie fallow, waiting for spring. He passed the smithy, the last embers in the forge glowing red like a dying eye. The villagers he encountered nodded, their countenances a mix of Norse, Danes, and other origins, a jumble of diverse backgrounds. Children played in the dwindling light, their chuckle a sharp, poignant sound that cut through his warrior's thoughts.

His gaze lingered on the elders, seated outside their homes, their eyes following him with an amalgam of curiosity and something he couldn't quite decipher, wariness, perhaps, or the guarded assessment of those who have seen too many winters. The large, longhouse at the village's heart, distinct from Pall's Great House, was adorned with carvings depicting hunts, battles, and intertwining human and animal forms, a belief system that was both alien and familiar in its pagan echoes.

As he walked, his hand reflexively went to the hilt of his dagger, a habit ingrained by years of conflict. Here, in this place that was not home, surrounded by strange customs and wary eyes, the dagger felt like a relic of a life slowly receding into memory. The village was a mosaic, a blend of cultures, a place that offered comfort even as it remained profoundly confounding. He knew, with conviction that chilled him, that he and Asa could not stay forever. The call of their lands and their people would one day demand that they leave this sanctuary. But for now, it was their refuge.

He continued to wander, a knot of questions tightening in his gut. The answers felt hidden, woven into the shadows between the flickering torches, held behind the villagers' eyes, buried deep in the history of this place.

As Aedelric's walk carried him beyond the village's familiar boundaries, he stumbled upon a path concealed by the low-hanging branches of ancient trees. It wound through the dense thicket, leading to a hidden entrance to a cave mouth almost swallowed by vines and moss, merging naturally with the natural landscape. Curiosity, a powerful instinct second only to survival, drew him towards this hidden portal. He crouched behind a cluster of ferns, their fronds offering perfect cover, his warrior's eyes scanning the approach. The entrance exuded an air of secrecy, a threshold guarded by nature itself.

He settled in to watch. Villagers approached the path with quiet purpose; their movements deliberate and measured. Some carried bundles of herbs; others bore tools or objects wrapped in cloth. Each person paused before entering the cave's maw, glancing over their shoulders, ensuring they were not followed, with a silent, furtive check. They exchanged subtle nods, a wordless language of consent or acknowledgment. One by one, they disappeared into the darkness, only to emerge later with a countenance of serenity, their earlier burdens seemingly lifted, their faces lighter.

The cave was clearly a place of significance, a sanctum for rites, counsel, or something else entirely. Aedelric's warrior instincts prickled. Mystery often hid danger. Yet, the villagers' expressions held solemn reverence, not fear, as they left.

As nightfall approached, the visitors dwindled, the path left deserted, bathed in the moon's silver glow. Aedelric remained hidden, a still watcher, processing the puzzle. The cave was central to this village's life; a secret kept from outsiders. He knew he needed to share this discovery with Asa. Together, they would decide if they dared delve deeper into the village's secrets or if prudence demanded they respect the hidden boundary.

Back in the warmth of their temporary dwelling, the memory of the cave burned in Aedelric's mind. He burst through the door of the longhouse, his eyes bright with the urgency of his discovery. "Asa," he began, his voice echoing slightly in the room, "My walk today... found a path. Hidden. Untouched by our routine. Covered by trees... it seems they wanted it to remain unseen."

Asa stopped what she was doing, turning to him, her face reflecting his urgency. "What did you find?" she asked, her voice sharp with curiosity.

In a hushed tone, Aedelric recounted his observation. "A cave. Hidden. Where villagers go... carrying things, they return lighter. I watched from the shadows. I watched them disappear into the rock."

"A cave?" Asa exclaimed, a hint of worry in her voice. Her hand went to her belly. "We've been here for moons... never a whisper. A sanctuary? Or... something worse?"

"Cannot say for certain," Aedelric admitted, stroking his beard thoughtfully. "The air was laden with enigma. But it's not malevolence that I see. But their faces... not fear, maybe reverence."

Asa's gaze settled on him, her concern palpable. "This is unsettling. We've been welcomed. But to stay here, safe for winter, we must understand them, their secrets. If they hide something dark, it is dangerous for us. For our child."

Aedelric nodded, his resolve hardening. "I share your concerns. That is why I must venture into this cave. Find its purpose. Know if we are truly safe here."

"But what if you are discovered?" Asa questioned, uncertainty clouding her features. "We cannot anger our hosts. Not when they are so kind to us."

"I will make sure I am treading lightly," Aedelric reassured her, the seasoned warrior resurfacing. "I have navigated shadows in enemy camps. This will be no different."

Asa searched his face and saw the determination there. It was a risk. But staying ignorant felt riskier with a child on the way. "Then, let it be so," she conceded. She stepped forward, wrapping her arms around him in a tender embrace, her voice low and fierce with emotion. "Promise me, Aedelric. You will not put yourself in unnecessary danger. Our family... needs you."

"You have my word," Aedelric vowed, holding her close. "I will return with answers. We will chart our course together."

With that shared vow, the decision was made. Aedelric would investigate the mysterious cave, a risky endeavor necessary to understand their hosts and secure their family's safety. His experience as a warrior and a scout would be put to a different, perhaps more dangerous, test.

Part 2: Shadow Walker

Within the cloak of deepest night, Aedelric made his way to the hidden path, moving with the practiced silence of a shadow. His heart was a steady drumbeat in his chest, a warrior's rhythm. The entrance loomed before him, a dark maw that appeared to swallow the light and sound of the world outside. He slipped through the vines, into the cave's cold embrace, his eyes adjusting to the gloom. The air remained heavily laden with the scent of moist earth, moss, and something else-something still and unsettling. He advanced further, guided by the faint, dim flickering light of torches hinting at human presence underground.

The path descended, winding, the darkness absolute save for the distant, moving lights. The silence of the cave was profound, broken only by his breathing and the slight echo of water dripping somewhere in the stone.

The passage opened into a chamber. Not a natural cavern, but a space clearly shaped by hands, cold and damp. It was a dungeon. Cages lined the walls, their iron bars dark and forbidding. And within the cages, silent figures. People. Still, their forms huddled or slumped, their eyes, catching the torchlight, reflecting a haunting resignation. The air here was saturated with despair, and beneath the moist soil smell, something else... the faint, unmistakable smell of sickness and... death.

Aedelric's breath paused. His warrior's mind snapped into focus: assessment, threat, escape routes. He moved with deliberate slowness, hugging the deepest shadows, his look scanning from cage to cage. He saw men and women, young and old, some seemingly healthy, others clearly wasted by illness, their skin sallow and their eyes glazed. They wore varied clothing, hinting at different origins, some in furs, some in coarse tunics, and some in remnants of finer cloth. None stirred at his presence, their gazes fixed on nothing, their despair so profound they seemed to exist in a world beyond his intrusion.

Then, his gaze fell upon one figure in a cage nearer the edge of the torchlight that stole the air from his lungs. The woman was huddled in a corner, her back partially turned, her head bowed. Her form was gaunt, her clothes ragged, and what hair he could see was dull and matted. He frowned, a vague familiarity stirring, but her face was obscured, streaked with grime, her body so broken down by captivity that recognition eluded him.

As she shifted slightly, a strand of her hair, caught in the dim torchlight just so, revealed its actual, fiery color beneath the grime, a vivid, unmistakable red.

Aedelric's mind reeled, a sudden, jarring image flashing before his eyes: Astrid, a whirlwind of fury and red hair, her axe falling, and the brutal, swift finality as Eadric crumpled.

He knew. Without a shadow of a doubt, it was her. Astrid. Her once vibrant hair was dull and matted, falling limply around her shoulders. Her face was gaunt, streaked with grime, her eyes sunken, but it was undeniably her.

She was alive.

A wave of profound shock, relief, and cold dread flooded over Aedelric. Astrid. The woman Asa had mourned, whose shield he carried before he lost it to the bear. Here. Imprisoned. Just yards away, yet behind bars. The impulse to call out, to let her know she was seen, was overwhelming. But his training, his newfound responsibility, slammed it down. Reveal himself now, and he would endanger not only his escape but also Asa and their child. He could not. Her eyes, weakened by captivity and hardship, held no trace of recognition for the shadowed figure watching her.

He retreated slowly, melting back into the shadows of the passage, his mind a whirlwind of thoughts. How? How had she survived the wreck? How had she ended up here, in this hidden dungeon? Who were these people? What did they want with prisoners? The genial Magnate, the seemingly harmless villagers, the strange customs, it all took on a sinister new light.

He had to get back. To Asa. To tell her. This changed everything. His earlier investigation, meant to ensure their safety, had uncovered a horrifying secret. He moved softly through the dark passage, a wraith in the stone, unseen and unheard, but his heart throbbed with a fierce, terrifying purpose. He had to free Astrid. But how, without destroying the fragile sanctuary they had found, without jeopardizing the lives that now mattered most?

Back in the quiet of their longhouse, Aedelric recounted his discovery to Asa, his voice low and urgent, the grim reality of the dungeon contrasting with the warmth of the hearth. Asa's initial reaction was raw disbelief. She dropped the garment she was mending, her hands flying to her mouth, her eyes opened wide in shock. "Astrid? Alive? It cannot be..."

Aedelric nodded grimly. "It is her, Asa. I saw her. Imprisoned. Below the cave. In cages."

Asa's face scrunched, a tumult of emotions: relief that her friend lived, joy that her hope had not been entirely in vain, and a cold, sharp fear for Astrid's fate, for the darkness hidden beneath this seemingly welcoming village. Astrid. Her sister in spirit. "We must free her, Aedelric. We cannot leave her there." Her voice was fierce, unwavering.

Aedelric's brow furrowed, the memories of their past battles, of Eadric's fall under Astrid's axe, of his capture, a sudden, sharp presence in the room. He looked at Asa, at the visible curve of her belly, at the life they carried. He swallowed hard. "I know what she means to you, Asa." He chose his words carefully, weighing the past against their future. "But we must tread carefully. Our first duty is to protect our child. I cannot risk everything for vengeance or debts of the past."

Asa nodded, understanding the importance of his words, the difficult truth of his position. Her life had been intertwined with Astrid's since childhood, but now they had new, more profound responsibilities. "It is not... vengeance," Asa replied, her voice muted. "But we cannot abandon her. In this darkness." She looked into Aedelric's eyes. "What she did to your man, your friend, it feels like a different life now. Not... this life. Here." She gestured between them, to her belly.

They sat in silence, the crackling of the fire punctuating their thoughts. The discovery of Astrid's survival and the hidden dungeon shattered the fragile peace they had found. The village that had been their sanctuary held a sinister secret. Their trust in Pall, as well as that of the residents, was irrevocably shaken.

"We will plan carefully," Aedelric said, his warrior's mind taking over, assessing the challenge. "I will free Astrid. Without alerting any guards or villagers. Then I need to escape with silence." He spoke with quiet confidence, mentally mapping out the initial steps.

Asa knew the stakes. Getting caught here meant disaster. "And if you're discovered?"

Aedelric met her gaze, resolute. "Then... we fight. As always. But this time we fight for a future. Not just survival." His words were quiet, but bore the weight of their grim reality. Their sanctuary was a lie, and their security would have to be won by their own hands, yet again.

They agreed. Aedelric, the seasoned warrior, would gather more intelligence. Map the dungeon's layout, the guards' routine, and potential weaknesses. Asa, despite her condition, would prepare supplies for a swift, sudden departure, reading their packs, drying what meat they could, and ensuring their vital gear was immediately accessible. Together, they would find a way. To save

Astrid. And protect the family they had built in this treacherous place.

Part 3: Out of the Cage

Once more, in the middle of the night. Aedelric returned to the hidden path. His heart was a steady drumbeat. He moved with practiced stealth, a shadow among shadows. The entrance loomed, a dark maw swallowing light and sound.

He slipped through the vines, into the cave's cold embrace. The air was laden with the same persistent scent of despair that had been present below. He descended the familiar passage, relying on memory and faint torchlight, all his senses alert.

He reached the dungeon chamber. The damp cold entered his bones. He moved across the shadows, assessing the situation. He had memorized the guards' patrol routes, the placement of cages, and the potential weak points. He found a vantage point, a place to observe while unseen.

He watched the guards; their movements were boring and predictable. He saw the prisoners, their still forms in the cages. And his gaze fell on Astrid.

She sat huddled, her face turned away. He watched for a long time, the minutes stretching into forever. He saw her shift, saw her interact with another prisoner through a silent gesture. He saw the trace of something in her as she looked towards the distant passage, resilience, or a desperate, buried hope.

He retreated from his observation point, satisfied he had enough information. He knew the guards' timing; the locks seemed like simple pin-tumbler mechanisms that improvised picks might be able to handle. The most significant risk was the surprise of noise or the appearance of additional guards from elsewhere in the cave system.

Returning to the longhouse with urgency, he spoke with Asa in quiet tones. They refined the plan. They would need to act during the shift change. Aedelric would use stealth and his dagger to kill the guards as silently as possible, then use the lockpicks to open the door. Asa, despite her pregnancy, would be needed at the cave entrance, ready with her bow, ready to signal, prepared to cover his retreat, or ready to fight if the alarm was raised before they were out. Her condition limited her role, but it was vital, nonetheless. They prepared their packs, tightening the thongs, adding extra dried meat, and layering on clothing.

As the planned night approached, Aedelric made final preparations. He checked the edge of his dagger, making sure it was razor sharp. He tested improvised lockpicks made from scavenged wire. He wore dark, soft clothing. His plan was to conduct a silent infiltration, swiftly neutralize the guards, quickly unlock, and make a desperate flight back to the village.

He found Asa by the hearth, tending to the banked embers, her silhouette quiet in the dim light. He approached her, the scent of wood smoke clinging to her hair. He drew her into a tight embrace, holding her close, feeling the subtle warmth of her belly against his own.

"The hour is near," he murmured into her hair, his voice subdued, a mix of grim resolve and tenderness. "The path is laid. I will go alone. Fewer shadows to cast."

Asa pulled back slightly, her eyes fixing on his, unwavering. "I know," she whispered, her hand rising to cup his jaw. "Be swift, Aedelric. And be unseen." Her gaze dropped to his dagger. "The guards... are you sure of their numbers? Their routine?"

"As sure as I can be without standing beside them," Aedelric replied, a grim line to his mouth. "One at the passage leading down, perhaps two in the chamber itself. They seem lax, complacent in their hidden strength. That is their weakness." He explained his movements: the precise angle of entry, the quiet steps, how he would use the natural shadows and the dungeon's despair to his advantage. "Once inside, it will be quick. A blade, a lockpick, and then... then we run."

Asa nodded, her gaze serious. "And if... if they are not so complacent? If they find you?"

Aedelric met her eyes, the implicit dangers hanging dense in the air. "Then I will fight. But know this," he said, his voice deepening, taking on a solemn weight. "I must bring Astrid back. We cannot leave her in that darkness." He then laid out the grave contingency, his instructions clear and final. "You will wait here, within the longhouse, for no more than two hours. The cold will bite, so you must stay warm. After that time, if I have not returned, please proceed to the cave entrance. Do not linger in the open." He gripped her shoulders, his thumbs tracing patterns on her arms. "But if I do not return at all, if word reaches you of my failure... then you must remain here. You must deny everything. They will not know of your hand in this. You will protect your life and the life of our child. It is your first duty. Promise me, Asa."

Tears welled in Asa's eyes, but she held them back, her willpower matching his. She understood the impossible burden he was placing on her, the agonizing choice he was asking her to be prepared for. "I promise, Aedelric," she said, her voice heavy with feeling but steady. "But you will return. You must."

He embraced her again, an unspoken pledge shared between them, the cold reality of their plan a sharp counterpoint to the passion of their common resolve. He released her, a last lingering touch, and then turned to face the unforgiving night.

With the return of the deep darkness of night, leaving Asa ready and waiting in the longhouse, Aedelric moved with practiced silence back towards the hidden cave entrance. The village was asleep, the longhouses dark shapes under the moon and snow. The cave entrance loomed, dark and menacing. Aedelric noticed the wind starting to pick up.

He slipped through the vines. The inside air was colder than it had been before. He descended, guided by the faint, remote glow of torches. He reached the dungeon chamber. The two guards were present, moving through their routine. He waited, hidden, timing his approach.

With practiced stealth, he moved. He surprised the first guard from behind, a swift, brutal application of the dagger silencing him instantly, catching his body before it fell heavily. He moved onto the second guard, using the element of surprise and the dagger's efficiency. It was brutal and messy, but quick. He relieved them of their weapons, which clinked softly on the stone. It wasn't entirely silent, but the sounds were muffled by the stone, hopefully not carrying far.

He moved quickly to Astrid's cage. The other prisoners stirred, watching with wide, fearful eyes. He knelt by the lock, fumbling slightly with the wire pick in the dusky light, the metal chilly against his fingers. It clicked. The lock sprang open. He pulled the heavy iron door inward.

He looked at Astrid, a gaunt shadow in the cage. "Astrid," he spoke urgently in Norse, reaching out his hand. "Come. Now. We must go. Quickly."

Astrid looked at him, a figure in the shadows speaking her tongue, her eyes wide with shock and disbelief. His voice... it sounded familiar, like a spirit from the long past. But in the fog of captivity, she couldn't place it. Freedom was offered, and that was all that mattered. She moved stiffly towards him.

Just as her hand reached for his, a shout ripped through the dungeon air from the passage leading up. "WHO IS THERE?! WHAT ARE YOU DOING?!"

Stealth failed.

The dungeon erupted into chaos. Guards from elsewhere in the cave system, drawn by the shout, came running down the passage, torches held high. Aedelric reacted instantly, pulling Astrid from the cage, shoving a sword from a fallen guard into her hand. "Go!" he yelled, spinning to face the incoming threat, clutching the stolen sword from the other fallen guard.

Astrid, though weakened, gripped the sword, adrenaline pumping through her system. Freedom. The taste of it, so close.

Aedelric met the first guards, his sword a deadly blur in the dim light, a silver streak of brutal potency. He fought with the desperate ferocity of a cornered animal, protecting their escape.

Astrid, despite her gauntness, moved with a surprising resurgence of warrior instinct, using the sword clumsily at first, then with growing effectiveness; her movements regaining a trace of their old fire.

"This way!" Aedelric yelled, cutting down a guard, gesturing towards the passage leading up. They fought back-to-back for a moment, a brutal, desperate duet of steel and flesh, bodies moving in a rough, effective coordination born of instinct and necessity. Guards fell before them, screams resonating off the stone walls, the smell of blood dense in the air.

They fought their way up the passage, Aedelric covering their rear, Astrid moving ahead despite her stiffness. They reached the cave entrance, bursting through the vines into the cold night air. The village lay dark and silent under the moon and snow. Pursuers' shouts and the clang of steel echoed from the cave mouth behind them.

"Village!" Aedelric gasped, gesturing towards the alleys between the longhouses. They plunged into the dark, narrow spaces, seeking concealment, escape.

The adrenaline of the fight, of the narrow escape, was still pumping through their veins. Still, beneath it, the pain and fatigue of Astrid's imprisonment and sudden exertion began to assert itself.

They were out for now. But they were exposed, and had traded one cage for another, the treacherous, freezing village that was now a place of open hostility. Their fight for freedom had just begun.

Part 4: Friend or Foe

Aedelric and Astrid plunged into the narrow space between two longhouses, pressing themselves against the cold timber walls, hidden for the moment from the guards flooding out of the cave entrance. The shouts from the dungeon echoed, followed by the clang of steel and the heavy tread of armed men. Aedelric's mind surged. His sword was effective in one-on-one combat but felt useless against the numbers he expected to face. Astrid, beside him, was a shadow of her former self, weakened by imprisonment, her breathing ragged from the short, brutal fight. They were concealed, yes, but for how long? Did the guards know it was him? Were their eyes already fixed on the longhouse they occupied, where Asa waited?

He glanced at Astrid. Her face appeared pale, marked with grime; her eyes were still glazed with the shock of freedom, but a weariness lay beneath the surface. She was frail compared to the warrior who had felled Eadric. He had to get her and Asa out now. Stealth was their only chance, however slim. Taking her arm gently, he began to move, a silent, urgent shadow pulling another through the narrow space, clinging to the deepest darkness between the buildings. It was a hopeless gamble, but time was not on their side. The plan to meet Asa at the cave entrance had been shattered; they had to return to her, gather their gear, and find an alternative way out.

As they crept through the village, slipping from one patch of shadow to the next, the sounds of alarm grew. Not just guards, but villagers' too doors opening, voices calling out in the local dialect, the dull gleam of weapons being carried into the streets. The entire village was stirring, arming itself. Panic tightened Aedelric's chest. He increased their pace, pulling Astrid along, urging her on silently.

They reached their longhouse, a dark shape against the snow. Aedelric eased the heavy wooden door open, a slow, agonizing creak. He slipped inside first, then pulled Astrid in behind him, closing the door with painstaking quietness. The interior was dim, lit only by the dying embers of the hearth. "Asa," he whispered anxiously into the darkness. Nothing. "Asa!" he called again, louder but still low.

A shape moved in the deeper shadows. Asa emerged, bow drawn, an arrow nocked, her face an expression of fierce readiness, her pregnant belly a prominent shape beneath her clothing. Aedelric moved towards her, relief pouring over him so powerfully that it made his knees weak. They embraced a tight, wordless clasp of shared fear and survival, clinging to each other for a brief moment of solace.

Then Astrid stepped fully across the threshold, her figure resolving in the subdued light. Asa pulled back from Aedelric, her gaze falling on the figure behind him. Recognition flashed, then shock, then disbelief. "Astrid?" Her voice was a choked whisper.

Astrid looked at Asa, seeing her friend, so real after months of believing her lost. Tears welled immediately in both their eyes. Disbelief gave way to overwhelming relief and sorrow. They walked towards each other, embracing tightly, tears streaming freely, clinging to each other as the reality of their reunion and everything that had happened crashed over them.

Aedelric, meanwhile, didn't hesitate. While the two friends wept in each other's arms, he moved through the dim longhouse, grabbing their prepared packs, securing his weapons, readying them for immediate flight.

Asa and Astrid finally eased their embrace, still holding on to each other, tears wet on their faces. Reality caught up swiftly. Asa looked at Astrid, taking in her gauntness, the dirt, the dullness in her hair and eyes. "What happened to you?" she whispered, her voice harsh with sorrow and shock. "Look at the state you are in."

Astrid looked at Asa in return, her gaze falling to Asa's greatly expanded belly, her eyes widening in astonishment. "Look at you, woman!" she exclaimed, her voice husky but filled with amazement. "You are as big as a house!" She motioned to the belly. "How did this happen?"

Then, as if a floodgate had opened, the memory of Aedelric, the battle at Wareham, his face, the moment he was taken prisoner on the ship, all rushed back. Her gaze snapped to Aedelric, who stood nearby, packs ready. Recognition, sharp and complete, slammed into her. Her eyes narrowed, her voice turning hard, accusatory. "You!" she spat out in Norse, pointing at Aedelric. "You did this... to her." Enraged, she started to move towards him. "What did you do... to her? What spell... You put on her?"

Asa reacted instantly, catching Astrid's arm, stopping her. "There is... much," Asa said, her voice firm but gentle, looking into Astrid's eyes, cutting through her friend's anger. "Need to catch up. Later."

Astrid's fury checked; her gaze returned to Asa's face, seeing the seriousness there. Aedelric, watching the exchange, knew there was no time for explanations, for settling old scores or addressing new misunderstandings. That conversation, complex and fraught, would have to wait if they made it out alive.

Outside, the sounds of the village grew louder, voices calling out, the jingle of mail, the heavier tramp of feet.

Though the words were in the local dialect, the mood was clear: alarm, search, urgency. Aedelric moved closer to the two women, his voice muted but firm. He reached out, taking a hand from each of them. "We need to leave. Now."

Astrid, though still visibly annoyed at Aedelric, with his hand on hers, understood the gravity in his voice and the urgency in his eyes. She nodded grimly. Asa agreed silently, her warrior instincts taking over, moving to grab her pack. Astrid had nothing but the sword Aedelric had given her from the dungeon guard.

Their preparation was swift, honed by months of necessity. Packs slung, weapons secured, they moved as one. Aedelric led them towards the back of the longhouse, towards the wall of logs and thatch, where a quiet exit through a window was possible. "Now," he whispered, urgency in his voice, his plan forming rapidly. "Move slow... quickly. Head... to the stables..."

But before he could finish, a voice, calm, clear, chillingly familiar, cut through the sounds of the village outside, seeming to come from directly in front of their longhouse door. "Aedelric."

The voice wasn't angry, not yet. It was Pall. And his tone was... almost pleasant.

All three froze. A shudder ran down their spines. Pall. He knew they were here. Aedelric's mind hurried. Did he know Aedelric had been in the cave? That he had released Astrid? Did he know what Aedelric had seen?

Pall's voice, still calm, answered the unspoken question. "Aedelric. I know... You were in my... house of worship."

There was no denying it. Not now. Aedelric's gaze met Asa's. Fear, sharp and cold, tightened his gut. They were trapped. *Should they fight? Die here? Or surrender?* They looked at Astrid, her face mirroring their grim realization. Surrender. The thought was abhorrent. To fall back into captivity. To be at the mercy of a man who kept dungeons.

All three knew the answer without needing to speak it. They would fight to the death. Even Asa, her hand going to her belly, the warrior's code was ingrained so profoundly that even the life she carried would not be taken captive. She would end it herself first. Aedelric felt the same cold resolve never to be held captive again.

But he wouldn't let them fight here, trapped inside. He made his decision instantly. He looked at Asa, love and grim resolve in his eyes. "Listen," he said, his voice firm, a commanding tone softened by love. "I know what to do."

"No!" Asa cried, cutting him off.

Aedelric didn't stop speaking; his mind made up, his only hope was to create chaos, to buy them time. He took Asa by the arms, his gaze holding hers, pouring his will into her. "Look. You go and hide. Let Astrid take you. Far from here." He was speaking quickly now, urgently, entirely in Norse, the words rushing out. "Go... to the back of the house... now, go!"

Outside, Pall's voice grew slightly sharper, a thin edge of irritation entering his tone. "I know you're in there. Do not be so rude. After all... we have done for you. I will fire the house... if I need to. Even if it means... killing you all. Even... the child."

The mention of the child, cold and casual, hit Aedelric like a sudden blow. There was no choice. He had to give them a chance. He kissed Asa fiercely, quickly, a kiss of farewell, tasting her tears as his own eyes burned. He looked at Astrid. "You. Take her when you hear fighting go. Take Asa. Take care... of her. Of my child." Astrid, though visibly bristling at his command, seeing the desperate resolve in his face, understanding the absolute necessity, grabbed Asa's arm and pulled her towards the back of the longhouse.

Aedelric turned towards the door, his mind a rapid mix of frantic planning how to maximize chaos, how to kill, how to buy time. He prayed silently, fiercely, for strength, for a chance. He pushed the door open and stepped outside, forcing himself not to look back, trusting Asa and Astrid to obey, trusting in Asa's understanding, and perhaps, begrudgingly, in Astrid's loyalty to Asa, overriding her animosity towards him.

He stood outside the longhouse, his gaze roaming across the scene. The full force of Pall's guard was assembled in a line of men in mail, some in full armor he hadn't seen before, armed villagers behind them, all standing silent, weapons ready, eyes fixed on him. Pall stood slightly in front, calm, almost relaxed.

"Ah," Pall said, his voice regaining its earlier, unsettling joviality. "Now... there you are."

Aedelric stood his ground, sword in hand, taking in the overwhelming odds. It was a David-and-Goliath situation, but he was no David. He was a cornered bear; his only thought now was to unleash fury, to kill, to buy seconds, minutes, for the two lives who were his world: his focus narrowed to targets, weak points, the armored guards, the armed villagers, Pall. Kill as many as possible, then somehow, reach Pall.

Pall showed no fear, only that unnerving calm. He stepped slowly towards Aedelric, hands behind his back, still in his rich robes, looking entirely out of place amidst the armed men and the snow. "Aedelric, my dear boy," he said, his voice mild, conversational. "What a predicament... You have put us in." He stopped a few feet away, his look meeting with Aedelric's. For the first time, Aedelric saw something beneath the jovial mask, something cold, utterly ruthless, pure evil. "You just had to go... snooping. Where you did not belong." Pall sighed slightly, as if genuinely disappointed. "You had to... interfere with my plans."

Aedelric had no idea what plans Pall spoke of, only that they involved a dungeon full of prisoners. Pall's look met his, and the chilling truth was revealed. "We just wanted... the child."

The words struck Aedelric with the force of a bodily blow. The child. His child. Rage, pure and consuming, flooded his being, overriding fear, overriding pain. "My child... my unborn child," he snarled.

Pall looked at him with unsettling confidence, a slight, sinister smile touching his lips. "Yes."

"Never!" Aedelric roared, the word torn from his lungs, his voice harsh with fury.

Pall's expression returned to its calm, matter-of-fact state. "You would have never known. You would have fallen in line. Just as all the rest. If you had just given it time." He shrugged. "But... everything has changed. So, you will die, and I will get... what I wanted." His gaze was chillingly direct. "We will hunt down... your lover... and her child, and there will be nothing you can do about it." He paused, a trace of cruel amusement in his eyes. "Or..." He turned slightly, looking over his shoulder at the house, then back at Aedelric. "Maybe... I will keep you alive. Let you watch... as your love... and child... become mine." His voice dropped slightly, a chilling whisper. "Oh. And for the red-head... she will suffer... as well."

That was the breaking point. The cold rage ignited into a roaring inferno. Every muscle in Aedelric's body coiled, adrenaline surged forward, his grip clenched on the sword hilt until it felt like an extension of his bone. His mind focused with terrifying clarity. Buy time. He was about to launch himself forward, a single, desperate charge into the assembled enemy, when a voice, loud, clear, and utterly unexpected, cut through the tense air. It was noisy and exhibited a strange, resonant quality, almost angelic in its power.

"Pall!" the voice boomed from behind Pall's assembled forces. "Your reign of terror... ends tonight!"

Part 5: From Fire to Frost

As the voice echoed, Aedelric saw torches flare into life all around the village on rooftops, in alleys, surrounding Pall's position. Figures arose from the shadows, holding weapons, challenging Pall's authority. Who were these people?

The voice spoke again, its tone now closer. "Tonight... you will meet your end!"

Pall stood before Aedelric, the assembled guards and villagers a silent, armed multitude behind him. Aedelric, sword in hand, braced himself for the inevitable charge. Then, the voice came again, sharp and resonant, cutting through the tense silence from behind Pall's ranks.

"Pall!"

It was a man's voice, clear and strong. Pall, his arrogant demeanor unwavering, turned slightly, his gaze roaming over the torch-lit crowd behind him. He spoke to the unseen person, his speech dripping with disdain. "I know not who you are... but you will fail and die... the same as all the others."

Aedelric watched, muscles tense, as the crowd parted, revealing the source of the challenge. He was a tall man, broad-shouldered, his skin dark a depth of color Aedelric had never seen on a man before. His features were strong, indecipherable in the torchlight. His head was shaved, save for a single braid. He wore simple, sturdy clothes, not mail, but carried a heavy, war axe. He was clearly a warrior. And he radiated an authority that commanded respect.

Pall's eyes narrowed, the easy smile gone, replaced by a look of grim recognition. Not shock, but a deep, cutting disappointment. "You," he said, his voice subdued. "Of all of them... it is you." He spoke a name that Aedelric did not understand, a man unseen and unspoken of in the village before that night. This man was clearly important. Never revealed, never highlighted until this moment of open defiance.

"Yes, Pall," he replied, his voice calm, resolute. "It is I." His gaze swept over the assembled villagers, then back to Pall. "I have watched. For too long. Planned... under your nose."

Aedelric's gaze followed the challengers. He saw then that the crowd was not just villagers in the streets. The group opposing Pall consisted of other armed villagers standing alongside the dark-skinned man. The village was split into two factions, facing each other on the brink of bloody conflict. Aedelric had a surge of desperate relief. It didn't matter who they were. He wasn't alone against Pall's might.

Pall gestured dismissively. "They are fools." He looked at the dark-skinned man. "Years... we built this. Security. Comfort. For all who bent the knee." His voice lowered, taking on a venomous tone. "Kidnapping. Taking... the children. It was necessary. To ensure our future. To bind them. To give us power." He looked at the opposing villagers, his voice hardening. "You have had such a life. Comfort. Ease. If you had just... stayed in line." He spat the words, contempt dripping from them. "Now... this defiance... will cost you. Cost you your lives. Cost you... your families." His gaze rested on the women among the opposition. "A worse fate... awaits your children."

The dark-skinned man was filled with sorrow and grim resolve. "No more, Pall. The taking of people ends tonight." His grip tightened on his axe. "This village... will be cleansed. Only your death... and the death of all who were complicit... will ensure it." He looked at his followers. "The sins... are heavy. But absolution... can be won. In blood. We do this... to be right with God!"

Pall's face contorted, rage finally bursting through his mask of calm. "Enough!" he roared, his voice resounding off the longhouses. He pointed at the opposing villagers. "Kill them all! Now!"

All hell broke loose. Pall's guards, heavily armed and mailed, surged forward, meeting the charge of the opposing villagers. The narrow space erupted into a chaotic, brutal battle. Steel clashed, men and women screamed, arrows flew from rooftops, finding targets in the milling mass. Torches, thrown, ignited dry thatch, sending flames licking into the night sky.

In the confusion, Aedelric saw his chance. As the first mailed guard charged, Aedelric moved with sudden, brutal speed. His sword flashed, finding the narrow gap in the mail at the guard's throat: a quick, silent slit, a fountain of blood, and the man crumpled. Aedelric roared, a Saxon war cry lost in the din, and plunged into the roiling melee, targeting the center where he had last seen Pall.

Behind him, the door of the longhouse burst open. Asa and Astrid emerged, silhouetted against the dim light within. "Asa! Stay close! Use that bow!" Astrid yelled, her voice cleaving through the noise. She held her sword, a grim smile of brutal efficiency on her face, and plunged into the close-quarters fighting near the house, a blast of desperate fury. Asa, her pregnancy making close combat impossible, positioned herself near the longhouse entrance, her bow humming, arrows flying with deadly accuracy into the ranks of Pall's men. The two women clearly did not heed Aedelric's instructions and decided to join the fray.

Aedelric fought with a desperate, killing rage, carving a path through the turmoil towards Pall. He brought down guards and swept aside villagers, his only focus the Magnate. But as he neared the edge of the primary melee, he was intercepted. Pall was calmly walking away from the fight, his men covering his retreat. Three figures stepped into Aedelric's path: the dark-skinned man and two of his followers. They were not attacking Aedelric; they were blocking him.

The dark-skinned man raised a hand, stopping Aedelric's charge. "Thegn!" he called, his voice clear even during the battle. "This is not your fight! Not truly!" He looked at Aedelric, his dark face furrowed with sorrow and conviction. "I prayed for this moment. For years." His gaze held Aedelric's. "Prayed... for a sign. That the time was right... to end this evil. You... your presence... your discovery... You are the answer to my prayer."

He gestured back towards Pall, towards the burning longhouses, the screaming, fighting villagers. "This cleansing... is ours. My sin... and the sin of those who stand with me." He spoke with a terrible calm. "The only way... to be right with God... is to end this. To kill all who were complicit." His eyes bore a profound sadness. "That includes... ourselves. For allowing it... for so long."

He looked directly at Aedelric, a man from another world, brought here by fate. "Take your women and get out of here." He pointed towards the edge of the village, towards the stables. "I have prepared a horse. Black stallion. With a pack." He spoke with a soft assurance. "It knows where... it needs to go.... ... follow it."

Before Aedelric could respond, they pushed him hard, shoving him back towards the longhouse where Asa was. "Go! Now!" Two of the dark-skinned man's followers grabbed Aedelric's arms, pulling him, dragging him towards Asa.

Aedelric looked back. "Your woman needs you now!" the dark-skinned man yelled over the din of battle. "Your child is almost here! Take care of them!" He turned then, axe raised, and plunged back into the heart of the fighting, heading towards the retreating Pall.

Aedelric was dragged towards the longhouse. He saw Asa, bow lowered, she was doubled over in pain, her hands pressed to her belly. She was standing in a pool of liquid. *Labor. Here. Now. It was early, too early,* Aedelric thought.

"Asa!" he roared, his voice suffused with sudden, desperate terror. "Astrid!"

Astrid, fighting nearby, heard his shout and Asa's state. Her eyes widened. She abandoned her fight immediately, running towards them. She reached Asa just as Aedelric did, helping to support her as her body was wracked by pain. The two-armed helpers from the dark-skinned man arrived, their countenances grim.

"Stables," one of them barked in their local dialect, gesturing. "Follow us. Now."

They half-carried Asa, Aedelric, and Astrid, supporting her, towards the edge of the village, through the turmoil of the peripheral battle, towards the stables. Outside a small building, a magnificent black stallion stood, saddled and packed.

"Get her mounted," the helper commanded, indicating Asa. "You with her," the helper pointed to Astrid.

Working quickly and desperately, they helped the groaning Asa onto the horse, Astrid mounting behind her and holding her friend. The helpers handed the reins to Aedelric. "The horse knows," one said. "Follow it. All... in God's hands now."

The two helpers turned and ran back towards the roaring battle, back towards their bloody cleansing. Aedelric looked at the black stallion, then back at the burning village, the sounds of battle fading slightly behind him. "Thank you," he said to the men he didn't know, to the helpers.

He took the reins, and the stallion began to move, a dark shape against the snow, heading to the main gate and away from the village, towards the wild. Aedelric jogged behind the horse, pulling his pack higher on his shoulders, urging the horse onward, away from the screaming, the fire, the death. Snow began to fall harder, whipped by the wind, the beginning of a blizzard. The storm rumbled around them, resembling the battle they left behind.

They traveled for miles as the blizzard intensified, the cold biting deep. The horse moved with relentless purpose, ascending a mountain path that was becoming increasingly difficult to discern in the whiteout. Aedelric's lungs ached, his legs ached, but he kept pace, driven by the sight of Asa, hunched in pain on the horse before him, supported by Astrid. Below them, faintly visible through the driving snow, the village glowed, engulfed in flames.

Following what seemed like an eternity, lost in the blizzard, the horse finally stopped before a small, dark shape nestled in the mountainside: a cabin, snow-mounded but solid. Aedelric, numb and windburned, watched as the horse stamped and snorted, its sides heaving with exhaustion. He looked at the animal. "Is this where we go?" he asked, though he knew he could not answer. He turned back to Asa and Astrid. "Stay put."

He approached the door and reached for the latch. It turned easily, unlocking. He checked inside, checking that no one was there. Seeing it empty, he returned to the horse and helped Asa down, then Astrid.

They stumbled inside, out of the fury of the blizzard. The cabin was small, spartan, but dry and mercifully warm. A hearth with stacked firewood, tinder ready. Someone had prepared this cabin.

Asa was immediately on her knees, groaning, her labor in full force. The sound tore out of her, low at first, then rising as another contraction seized her. Her fingers dug into the packed-earth floor, her breath coming in sharp, uneven bursts. Aedelric froze for an instant, then frantically built a fire, his hands clumsy with cold and exhaustion.

He went back out as Astrid was helping Asa, checked the horse outside, and pulled the pack from its back. The horse, its duty done, turned and trotted away into the blizzard. Aedelric watched it go for a few heartbeats, snow swallowing its shape.

Back inside, Astrid, despite her exhaustion and weakness, was still helping Asa. Her voice was quiet but firm, steady in a way that cut through the storm's roar. She had seen births before, assisted in them. Everything they needed, clean cloth, a sharp knife, pots for heating water, was in the cabin.

Asa's labor deepened. Each contraction came crashing like a wave breaking against stone, folding her forward, forcing sound from her throat. Sometimes it was a growl, sometimes a cry, sometimes only a ragged breath she fought to control. Sweat beaded along her brow despite the cold. Her hands quivered. She leaned against Astrid's shoulder, then against Aedelric's when he knelt next to her, gripping his forearm with surprising strength.

Hours went by in a blur of pain, effort, and raw, desperate strength. The blizzard outside howled and battered the walls, but inside the cabin, the world contracted to Asa's breathing fast, then slow, then fast again, and the pattern of her body working.

Aedelric stoked the fire, provided water, and held Asa's hand when she needed it. She crushed his fingers more than once, and he welcomed it, centering her, anchoring her. Astrid guided her through each stage, her voice composed even when Asa's cries rose sharp enough to echo off the rafters.

The air became dense with heat from the fire, steam from the boiling water, and the raw, human scent of labor. Asa's breath turned to gasps. Her body shook. She lay her forehead to Aedelric's chest, teeth clenched as another contraction tore through her. Astrid murmured instructions, coaxing, encouraging, commanding when she had to.

Then came the moment when Asa's cry broke into something different, a sound pulled from the deepest part of her, fierce and primal. Astrid leaned forward, hands ready. "Again," she urged. Asa pushed, trembling, breath shuddering, every muscle straining. The storm beyond raged, but inside the cabin, the world maintained its breath.

And then, finally, cutting through the blizzard's roar and Asa's cries, came another sound. A sharp, mighty cry. Small, but strong. Alive. The newborn's voice resounded in the cabin, startling in its power. Asa sagged back, tears trailing down her cheeks, her chest rising and falling in exhausted relief. Aedelric's breath caught, his eyes fixed on the tiny, wriggling life in Astrid's hands.

In this small, warm cabin high in the mountains, surrounded by the blizzard, the resounding of battle, and the cry of new life filled the night.

Part 6: Beyond the Blizzard

The sharp, mighty cry of the newborn sliced through the blizzard's sounds outside, a defiant cry of life versus the storm. In the small, warm cabin, time seemed to catch its breath. Asa lay back, utterly exhausted, tears of pain and relief tracking across the dirt on her face. Astrid, despite her weakness, worked quickly, cutting the cord and cleaning the small baby with the clean cloths found in the cabin; her movements were surprisingly competent, honed by necessity and experience.

Aedelric, hands shaking from exertion and emotion, added wood to the fire, ensuring the warmth. He looked from Asa to Astrid, then to the small, squalling bundle. Then Astrid placed the newborn into Asa's arms, telling her in a gentle voice, "It's a girl." Aedelric was shocked by the announcement. He had not been correct in his thoughts about a boy.

Asa, with tear-filled eyes, repeated, "A girl." They were four of them now. An impossible thought made real in this remote, snow-bound cabin.

Asa held the baby, her face softening with profound love, weariness momentarily forgotten. Aedelric knelt next to the bed, his look fixed on the tiny face. The baby quieted slightly, rooting against Asa's chest. Astrid watched from the side, a complex expression on her face at the new life, relief that Asa had survived the difficult birth, and the ever-present worry for their precarious safety.

Asa gently brushed a tiny, damp strand of hair from the baby's forehead. It wasn't the darker of hers, nor the dark shade of Aedelric's. It was a rich, warm brown, like varnished wood. "Her hair," Asa whispered, her voice dense with emotion, using West Saxon. "The color... of cinnamon." She looked at Aedelric, her eyes wet with a love so deep it stole his breath. "Sassa," Asa said, "divine beauty."

Aedelric repeated the name, unfamiliar but beautiful on Asa's lips, Sassa, his daughter.

He reached out a tentative finger, touching the baby's soft cheek. A wave of overwhelming love and fierce protectiveness came over him. His daughter. Born amidst battle and blizzard. He leaned down, kissing Asa's forehead gently, then pressed a kiss to the baby's head, inhaling the sweet scent of new life.

But the moment, however profound, was fragile. The cabin's warmth was a temporary shield. He was a warrior. A protector. His gaze moved to the door, to the small, oiled-clothed window. *Where were they? Who had prepared this cabin? Were they followed?* Instincts honed by months of survival refused to be silenced, even now. He rose, moving quietly to check the door's simple latch, glancing through a crack in the shutters, assessing the small, single room. Safe for now. But for how long?

Astrid, her own vision scanning the room, shared his silent vigilance. She had been through too much, seen too much, to let her guard down completely. Asa, utterly exhausted but her will unbroken, watched them, her expression grimly resolute. She had brought a life into this world; she would fight for it, no matter how weak she felt.

The blizzard raged outside, a constant roar against the cabin walls, trapping them in their mountain sanctuary. The immediate hours after the birth were a rush of attending to Asa and the baby, finding what supplies were in the pack the dark-skinned man had left: more dried meat, bread, hard cheese, a small bag of dried fruit, extra layers of rough clothing, a fire-starting kit, the bare necessities, prepared with foresight. Aedelric stepped outside briefly, the blizzard's fury a brutal strike, to check if they were *followed. No one would last long in these conditions.*

For a day and a half, the blizzard held them captive. The small cabin, though prepared, was not a larder. The initial supplies were dwindling. They needed more meat to stretch the little they had.

As the blizzard finally began to subside, leaving a world buried in deep snow, the grim reality of their situation reasserted itself. Aedelric sat by the fire, sharpening his dagger, watching Asa sleep. Sassa nestled beside her. Astrid sat opposite him, staring, seeming deep in thought.

"We need more meat," Aedelric said, breaking the silence. "Supplies will not last forever."

Astrid nodded, her gaze hard. "Hunting then?"

"Also..." Aedelric hesitated, looking towards the door. "We need to know what happened in the village."

Astrid looked at him sharply. "We should hunt first."

"The state of the village is important," Aedelric countered, his voice assertive. "We need to find out what happened if anyone followed. If it's safe." He knew the risks, the pull to get intel overriding the immediate need for food.

They debated, a quiet, grim argument fueled by necessity and different priorities. Astrid argued for the immediate, tangible need for food for Asa. She needs nourishment to produce the milk that will feed the baby. Aedelric argued for the strategic necessity of understanding the threat, whether Pall or his men had survived, whether they were being hunted, and whether returning to the village was even possible.

Finally, a decision was reached, a compromise born of their distinct skills and the pressing needs. "I will go check our bearings," Aedelric conceded. "See if I can get to the summit." He gestured towards the mountain outside. "I can try to see the village. Find out its state."

Astrid nodded, accepting his reasoning. "Fine. I will hunt."

Asa stirred, waking slowly, her body aching but her mind already sharp. She heard their conversation, saw the resolve in their faces. "I will help," she said, her voice weak but determined, trying to sit up.

Aedelric was immediately at her side, gently pushing her back down. "No," he insisted, his voice mild but firm. "You rest. You need your strength." Asa protested weakly, her warrior's spirit rebelling against her body's demands, but she ultimately yielded, trusting his judgment, her body too weary to argue effectively.

Astrid clothed herself with the spare clothing and went out first, a silent hunter disappearing into the deep snow. Aedelric prepared to follow, his gear minimal, his purpose grim. He told Asa his plan to climb high, see the lay of the land, locate the village if possible, and assess its condition. He kissed her forehead, then Sassa's, a tacit promise to return safely.

Aedelric's climb was challenging. The snow was deep, the cold bitter and harsh. The mountain was steep, requiring him to scramble over ice-coated rocks, pulling himself up with aching muscles. Hours passed. Finally, exhausted, he reached a summit offering a panoramic view.

The world stretched out below him, a vast, white landscape under a clear, cold sky. He scanned the terrain, identifying landmarks and trying to orient himself toward the direction they had traveled. And then, he saw it. In the distance... ruin.

He located the village. From this distance, it looked like a dark scar on the white landscape. He could see signs of extensive fire: charred timbers and collapsed roofs. The village, or a large part of it, had burned. He squinted, searching for signs of life, movement. It was hard to tell from this far, but it looked desolate. He estimated the distance to be a few hours of hard travel on foot, down the treacherous mountainside and across the snowy plains below.

He looked at the scene, the destruction, the silence below. And his mind was crowded with questions. Had anyone survived? Pall's forces? Had anyone from the opposing villagers caught the dark-skinned man, and his followers made it? Was Pall alive? Was the threat still there, waiting in the ruins? He needed to know. He had to know what remained, who was still alive, before they could even think of leaving the fragile safety of the cabin. He stayed at the summit for a long time, etching the landscape into his mind, assessing the impossible scale of their task. When he finally began the arduous descent, the load of his findings was heavier than any physical burden he had ever carried. He had located the village. And its state was grim.

Part 7: Morning of Truth

The descent proved arduous, Aedelric slipping on ice-coated rocks and plunging through deep snowdrifts. Hours later, exhausted and freezing, Aedelric finally made his way back down the mountain and across the snow towards the cabin. Smoke twisted faintly from the chimney.

He pushed open the door, the blast of warmth a shock against the cold outside. Astrid looked up from the hearth, where she was stirring a meager stew in a pot over the hearth. She had returned while he was gone, successful in her hunt. Two snow hares, their white fur stark against the brown of the small cabin floor, lay processed nearby. She was using what little they had, some dried herbs from Asa's pack, a bit of rendered fat from the hares to stretch the meat into something resembling a meal.

Asa lay on the bed, propped against pillows made of bundled clothes, Sassa nestled at her breast, suckling quietly. Sassa, her tiny face peaceful, stared up at her mother. Asa looked better; some color returned to her cheeks, and a measure of rest in her expression. They were doing well, considering.

Aedelric shrugged off his pack, leaning his sword against the wall, and moved to the fire, holding out his hands to the warmth. He knelt for a moment by the bed, looking at Asa and Sassa, a wave of profound love and relief flowing over him. He murmured thanks to God, offering a silent prayer of gratitude for their survival and this small, warm sanctuary. Asa looked up at him, her gaze keen with question. "What did you see?" she asked, her voice quiet.

He shifted, allowing the warmth of the fire to seep in as his thoughts settled. "I found the village. It was burned." His voice was slow, grim. "Bad fire. A lot of fire." He estimated the distance and the time required to reach it. "A few hours, maybe more." He looked at Astrid, then at Asa. "I need to know if anyone is alive." He had already decided. "I will go down the mountain in the morning. I have to see." Astrid nodded, her expression grim. "I will stay and watch over Asa and Sassa."

"Good," Aedelric confirmed, his gaze meeting hers. Despite her time in the dungeon, Astrid was still a warrior, capable of fierce defense. And she was loyal to Asa. Asa reached out, taking his hand, her expression hesitant. "Aedelric, this is too dangerous."

"It is," he acknowledged, squeezing her hand. "But it's necessary. We have to find out if the threat is still out there." He looked from her to Sassa, a strong resolve stiffening his expression.

As they ate the thin stew Astrid had prepared, the meager warmth in their bellies did little to dispel the cold reality of their situation. Astrid's eyes moved between Asa and Aedelric, sensing the unspoken questions, the gaps within their common story. It was time.

"Tell me," she said, her voice subdued, direct. "What happened… after the shipwreck? How… you two… ended up like this? With a child?" Asa looked at Aedelric, then back at Astrid. She drew a slow breath. "It's… a long tale," she spoke quietly. Aedelric nodded. "But you deserve to hear it."

In mutual glances with Aedelric, Asa began. She recounted their impossible survival from the wreck, being washed ashore, the initial enmity, and the slow, forced reliance on each other. As she spoke of the hunts, the wound she tended, her voice mellowed.

"There were days," she said quietly, "when we thought we would die. And nights when… we stopped wanting to." Aedelric added, "We learned to trust each other. Bit by bit. More than either of us expected."

Asa continued, telling of the waterfall, the bond that grew, defying the ingrained hatreds of their peoples. She hesitated only once, glancing at Aedelric before speaking of the final night on the beach, their decision to face the unknown together, their simple yet unconventional marriage, and the physical joining that sealed their fate. "It was our choice," she said, firm though soft. "Both of us." Aedelric's voice followed, low. "I love her." She spoke of the journey inland, the growing cold, the bear encounter, and finally the life growing within her, the child conceived in that moment of joint commitment. Aedelric added details, clarifying moments, his gaze often shifting to Asa, confirming the truth of her statements and the love he felt for her.

Then it was Astrid's turn. Her voice was quieter, rougher, the story darker. "I thought I died," she said. "When the sea took me under… I thought that was the end."

She described the chaos of the shipwreck, being swept overboard, the icy grip of the sea pulling her down, and the certainty of death. "But I woke," she said, "on a piece of the longship. Alone. No land. No hope. Just the water."

She spoke of drifting for days, the threat of drowning, freezing, and starving. "When the ship found me," she said, "I thanked the gods. For a breath. For an instant." Her mouth clenched. "Then I saw their faces. And I knew." "Slavers," Aedelric murmured. Astrid nodded. "Yes. They took me aboard like cargo. No name. No worth. Just a body to sell."

She told of the settlement she didn't recognize, being sold to Pall, the journey to the village, the strange customs, her arrival at Pall's Great House, and the moment she was led not to rest, but down, below ground, into the cold cells.

"The dungeon…" She swallowed. "The stone was always wet. The air is never warm. People were taken. At random. And they never came back." Asa whispered, "Astrid…" Astrid shook her head gently. "I lived because I refused to break. I held onto the fjords in my mind. To home. To you."

She spoke of the other prisoners, the silent gestures, the shared scraps of food, the huddled warmth. "We could not speak," she said. "But fear has its own tongue."

Her gaze shifted to Aedelric, lingering with a trace of confusion, suspicion. "And then… I see you here. With her. With a child. After everything." Her voice wavered. "I still don't understand it."

Aedelric held her stare. "I cannot change what happened. But I swear to you, I would die before harming her. Or the child." Astrid looked back at Asa, her look softening. "I trust you," she said quietly. "And if you say this is love… then I will stand with you. Both of you."

Part 8: Weight of Gold and Ashes

Aedelric awoke in the pre-dawn light to the soft sounds of Asa murmuring. He opened his eyes. Asa was propped up in the bed, breastfeeding Sassa, murmuring soft words to the baby girl. Sassa was awake, looking up at her mother, making tiny cooing sounds, a small, sleepy smile touching her lips; mother and daughter, bonding in the quiet dawn. Aedelric watched them for a moment, his heart rising, murmuring a silent prayer of thanks to God for their safety, for this precious new life. Asa noticed him watching. "Morning," she whispered, smiling. "Join us?" He moved to the bed, sitting beside them, reaching out to gently touch Sassa's tiny hands, a moment of joint quiet, of love, of family.

But dawn had arrived. The soft light shining through the cabin's small window acted as a reminder. He had to go. He rose, creeping to the hearth, stirring the embers, adding wood. Asa continued to breastfeed Sassa, watching him as he prepared. He packed his makeshift pack with the remaining dried meat, herbs, flint, and steel. He secured his sword, the heavy steel sensing both familiar and grimly necessary.

He moved back to the bed, kneeling, and embraced Asa and Sassa, holding them close for a moment, breathing in the fragrance of mother and child, the fragrance of hope and vulnerability. "You be safe," Asa whispered, her voice husky with emotion. "Return quickly. We need you."

Aedelric held her gaze, pouring all his reassurance into his eyes. "I will return. I will be safe. For both of you." He kissed her, then Sassa, a final, fierce promise. He gently shook Astrid awake. "Astrid. I am leaving now. Protect them."

Astrid's eyes snapped open, immediately alert despite her exhaustion. She nodded, understanding the command and the trust placed in her. "Good luck," she rasped, her voice still rough.

Aedelric left the cabin, closing the door quietly behind him. He began his descent down the mountain, the snow deep and treacherous, his mind focused on the task ahead. He traveled with caution and stealth, a lone shape against the vast, white landscape. Hours passed. The mountain gave way to the snowy plains, and in the distance, the dark stain of the village.

He approached with extreme caution, moving silently through the snow, using the terrain for cover. There were no sounds, no signs of life. The village was utterly silent. As he drew closer, the scale of the destruction became horrifyingly clear. The town was destroyed. Every building was a burnt-out shell, smoke-blackened timbers bold against the snow.

He made his way through the ruins, sword in hand, every sense alert, seeking any sign of movement, of life. But there was nothing. Only silence and ruin. He reached the site where their longhouse had stood, now just a pile of charred logs and ashes.

He moved towards the village center, where the massive rune stone had stood. It was toppled, broken in half, its intricate carvings blackened by fire. And there, grim and undeniable, was a spear hammered into the frozen ground. On top of it, a severed head. As he approached, the features resolved. Pall. His face, frozen in a rictus of death, his once jovial expression replaced by a grim, final mask. Pall was dead.

Around the toppled rune stone, and in other parts of the village center, there were piles of burnt bodies. Stacked like cordwood, then set alight. A deliberate act. He noticed that most of the bodies wore identical mail and armor to that of

Pall's guards. Pall's followers. Dead. The village was littered with discarded, broken weapons.

He made his way to the site of the Great House. It, too, was utterly destroyed by fire, leaving only the massive stone hearth and parts of the lower log walls. He walked through the burnt remains, remembering the impossible grandeur, the bewildering luxury, the disturbing sensation beneath the surface. *Why had God brought them here? Shown them this place of hidden evil?* Then he thought it was Astrid; she was the reason, had God willed them to be here?

As he picked his way across the debris near the back of where the Great House had stood, something caught his eye. A spot on the floor that didn't look right, covered by burnt planks, but lower. Curiosity prevailing caution, he removed the charred wood. A small opening, barely large enough for one man to fit through, leading down. A staircase, hidden under the floor.

He descended into the small space. It was a concealed chamber. And in it were sacks. Heavy sacks. He opened one. Gold. Silver. Precious objects. Hoarded wealth. It was apparent Pall's treasure, taken from the people he had captured, enslaved, and hidden here beneath his own house, thinking it safe even if the house above burned.

He knew he couldn't take it all. It was too much, too heavy for one man on foot, or even with a horse. But he couldn't leave it all. This was stolen wealth from victims. He struggled with the decision, taking it felt like stealing, like plunder. But this wasn't Pall's. It belonged to the lost. And they would desperately need the resources. He decided. He would take one sack. It was heavy, but manageable. He offered a silent prayer of thanks, asking God to forgive this act, promising that if he ever returned to Winchester, he would donate some of his wealth to the Church, seeking to cleanse its origins through righteous use.

He climbed back out of the secret chamber, replacing the burnt planks, leaving most of the hoard behind. As he emerged from the ruins of the Great House, sack slung over his shoulder, he heard a sound from one of the village roads, rhythmic footsteps in the snow. His heart jumped. He dropped the sack, drew his sword, and prepared for a fight.

But as the figure appeared from the whirling snow at the edge of the village, relief flowed over him so powerfully it made his knees weak. It was the black stallion. The horse that had carried them to the cabin was now returning. It trotted towards him, as if it had sought him out.

He lowered his sword, his hand going to the horse's warm neck, burying his face in its mane. "You returned," he murmured, a deep feeling of gratitude filling him. He would call him Scildfrēond. Shield-friend. The one who had led them to safety.

There was nothing more for him in the village. No signs of life, only death and ruin. Pall was dead. His followers are dead. The battle had been absolute. He wondered about the fate of the dark-skinned man and the opposing villagers; had they perished? Or had they won and left? There was no way to know from the bodies present. He considered the fate of all who had been here, the winners and the losers, the hidden evil and the desperate stand against it.

Before leaving, he had to know about the cave. With Scildfrēond following patiently, he made his way back to the hidden path. He pushed through the vines. The entrance was no longer open. It was sealed. Blocked by massive rocks and rubble, clearly a deliberate act, a monumental effort was taken to ensure no one could enter the dungeon again. Someone had wanted Pall's secrets buried for good.

He returned to the cabin while twilight began to fall, fatigued but alive. He carried a heavy sack of treasure, a loyal horse named Scildfrēond, grim news of a destroyed village, and profound questions about the fate of those who had fought for its soul. He had faced death and destruction and found wealth and a friend.

CHAPTER 5

Part 1: From Cabin to Coast

Aedelric returned to the cabin while evening darkened, a dark shape against the snow, leading the black stallion, Scildfrēond, and carrying a heavy sack slung over his shoulder. He pushed through the door, bringing with him the biting cold and the grim silence of the world outside. Astrid looked up from the hearth, where she was stirring a thin stew. Asa lay on the bed. Sassa nestled against her, both watching him with worried eyes. Asa's voice was soft, strained. "You're back… thank the gods. Are you hurt?" Aedelric shook his head, snow melting in his hair. "No. Just cold. And tired."

He shed his pack, leaned his sword against the wall, and warmed himself by the fire, his breath rising in the air. For a moment, he said nothing, gathering the words, the weight of what he had seen. Then, in low, measured tones, he recounted his journey down the mountain. "The village is gone," he said. "Burned to the ground. Nothing left but ash." Astrid's stirring slowed. "All of it?" she asked quietly. "All," he answered. "Pall… his head was on a spear. His body likely burned with the rest."

Asa closed her eyes, exhaling shakily. "So, it's truly over." Aedelric nodded. "The cave was sealed. Deliberately. Someone wanted its knowledge buried." He hesitated, then added, "I found a chamber. Hidden. A hoard of gold and silver. Payment… tribute… spoils. Whatever it was, it belonged to the dead. I took only one sack. Enough to help us survive." Astrid frowned slightly. "A secret chamber? Pall kept much hidden." "He did," Aedelric said. "Too much." He spoke of the horse returning to him from the blizzard, a loyal companion in the desolation. "He found me," Aedelric murmured, glancing toward the door.

"As if he knew I wasn't done yet." Asa reached out a hand toward him. "I'm glad you came back to us."

Astrid, her eyes open wide, had been listening intently to the description of the secret chamber. At the mention of the hoard of gold and silver, her gaze lit up, a trace of her old, avaricious spirit shining through. "Gold, you say?" she piped up, almost forgetting the grim context. "A whole horde? Oh, the gleam of it! The weight of it!" Her eyes seemed to trace phantom coins in the air. "I do love gold... and silver, too. Think of what we could do with such wealth!"

Asa, however, was quick to interject, her voice firm, cutting through Astrid's momentary avarice. "Astrid," she stated, her tone leaving no room for argument, "That hoard is blood-stained. And it is not for idle spending. We will use it *only* if necessary, for our survival and future. It will be required, not wasted. We will not squander a single piece of it, not while our path ahead is so uncertain."

Astrid's face fell slightly, but she nodded, understanding that Asa's word was final. The dream of glittering coins quickly gave way to the harsh reality of their situation.

A heavy quiet followed his words, interrupted solely by the blazing fire and Sassa's soft breathing. The grim reality of the village's fate came upon them like another layer of snow. The immediate threat from Pall was gone, but the world outside remained brutal and uncertain. Astrid finally spoke, her voice muted. "Then we rest tonight and … we decide what comes next." Aedelric nodded. "Yes, Together."

They discussed their options, the dwindling supplies, and the deep snow blanketing the mountainside. Remaining here, in the cabin, for the remainder of the winter, was the only sensible choice. It offered shelter, warmth, and a chance to recover and prepare for the next challenge. So it was decided that they would shelter here for the remainder of the winter.

The winter months settled in, a long, arduous period of confinement and mutual existence. Their days remained a rhythm of survival tasks. Aedelric and Astrid took turns venturing out into the deep snow to hunt, often returning with only small game snow hares, ptarmigan, and enough to supplement their dwindling smoked meat and the meager stores left in the cabin. Aedelric maintained the fire, a constant, vital need against the ceaseless cold, gathering wood when the weather allowed or carefully rationing their existing pile. As Asa recovered her strength, she took charge of preparing their meals, stretching their resources, and using dried herbs and what little rendered fat they had. They cleaned, Asa cut and trimmed hair, they mended their worn clothes, and they cared for Sassa.

The uneasy tension between Aedelric and Astrid remained, an unmistakable undercurrent beneath their necessary cooperation. Astrid had seen the worst of Aedelric's world, and her time in Pall's dungeon, sold by slavers, had merely deepened her suspicion of outsiders, particularly Christian ones who seemed to wield strange influence. She watched him, wary, a trace of her old belief in a spell still lingering. Yet, they worked together, hunted together, and defended their small space together. Their shared ordeal, their loyalty to Asa, and Sassa's presence created a reluctant respect, a functional, if not warm, camaraderie.

As time went past, Asa and Sassa thrived. Asa fully regained her strength, her body recovered from the rigors of pregnancy and childbirth in the wild. The gauntness of the past months faded, replaced by a healthy resilience. Sassa grew, her tiny limbs gaining substance, her cries strong, her blue eyes beginning to hint at a storm grey that would subsequently define them. Astrid, too, slowly shed the physical and mental load of her captivity. The dullness in her eyes lessened, her movements regained their warrior's edge, and her spirit, though signified by her ordeal, reasserted itself.

Their shared language, forged in the raw necessity of survival on the beach, now truly flourished in the close confines of the cabin. What began as a halting assembly of vital words had developed into a vibrant, fluid network of communication. They no longer exchanged phrases; they started to think in the interwoven rhythms of Norse and West Saxon, grasping not just vocabulary but the elaborate pathways of each other's grammar, the subtle inflections that conveyed a world of meaning beyond literal translation. Humor, once elusive, now sparked effortlessly between them, revealing a mutual laughter and understanding that transcended the spoken word. Through this deepening linguistic intimacy, they were able to share stories honestly, delving into the nuances of their pasts and creating vivid images of their separate and shared journeys for Astrid, filling in the gaps of their time apart with rich detail and emotion. The cabin became a crucible not just of their separate languages, but of their very cultures, as they mingled and melded to create a truly unique, powerfully effective tongue.

When the weather offered brief reprieves from the deepest cold, they would venture outside to train. Aedelric with his sword, Asa with her bow, Astrid with her blade. They honed their skills, their movements sharp and efficient against the backdrop of snow and ice. They took turns watching Sassa, bundled in furs near the cabin door, her clear eyes following their movements. The training sessions often became competitive, particularly between Aedelric and Astrid. Astrid, fierce and proud, constantly pushed to prove her superiority in combat, challenging Aedelric with a zeal that sometimes bordered on aggression.

"You're holding back, Saxon!" Astrid would sneer, her breath swirling in the frigid air, her salvaged blade a blur as she drove her attack. "Afraid to meet a real warrior?"

Aedelric, his sword a controlled sweep of his arm, would parry, the ring of steel sharp and distinct. "I hold back nothing, Norsewoman," he'd retort, his jaw firm, his pride pricked. "Perhaps your blows are just... light."

"Light?!" Astrid would growl, lunging forward, her eyes glaring. "I'll show you light!" Their sparring matches were sharp and tense, fueled by the lingering animosity from their initial encounters and the undeniable friction of their warrior pride. Small arguments would erupt, their voices sharp and cutting in the cold, still air, endangering to unravel the fragile truce between them.

It was always Asa, holding Sassa, bundled in her furs and watching their intensity, who would step in. Her voice, calm and firm, would cut through the competitive fervor, a steady anchor in their heated exchanges. "Enough," she'd say, her tone even, her gaze gliding between them. "You both bleed on the ground, but for different reasons. Remember why we do this. We need each other, whole and sharp. Your blades are for our enemies, not for proving who is the more foolish."

Her words were direct and always brought them back to mind. Aedelric would lower his sword, his shoulders drooping slightly in acknowledgement. Astrid would exhale sharply, her stance relaxing, though a defiant glint often remained in her eyes. The tension, though never entirely gone, would dissipate, and they would return to training with a renewed focus on their common purpose and on their reliance on each other for survival through the brutal winter.

Sassa was remarkably alert and vocal even as an infant. She watched them train, her tiny head turning, her eyes tracking their movements. Asa, observing her daughter's focus, her strength, saw the spark of a warrior spirit already present. She knew, with a conviction that filled her with both pride and a mother's worry, that Sassa would one day be as capable as any warrior, perhaps more so. Aedelric and Astrid, watching the child, saw the intelligence within her gaze, the strength in her grip.

The few remaining winter months passed in this manner. The rhythm of the cabin, the demands of survival, the presence of Sassa, the constant, quiet work of building a life together, shaped them. The sack of treasure remained, a heavy, silent presence, a token of the darkness they had escaped and the resources it provided for their uncertain future.

Finally, the grip of winter began to loosen. The snow softened, the days lengthened, and the first tentative signs of spring appeared on the lower slopes. It was time to leave.

The decision was made with a shared sense of purpose. They would journey, guided by Asa's knowledge of the coastline and the fjords, in the hope of finding familiar lands that would lead them to Njardarheimr. Preparations began. They packed their meager belongings, including dried meat and herbs, their weapons, flint and steel, and the sack of treasure, carefully secured on Scildfrēond's back. Aedelric tended to the horse, speaking quietly to him, the animal a steady, reliable presence.

While Aedelric was outside, packing Scildfrēond, Astrid spoke to Asa in a low voice, ensuring Aedelric was out of earshot. "You know what may wait if we find Njardarheimr?" Asa nodded, her look grim. "I know."

Astrid's gaze was direct and steady; her voice was urgent and compelling. "They will not accept him, Asa. Ever." She spoke of Jarl Gunnar, of the warriors of Njardarheimr, of the deep-seated hatred for Saxons, for Christians. "They will see him as an enemy. They will kill him, sacrifice him to the gods as an offering." Her voice dropped, a trace of fear in her eyes as she looked at Sassa, bundled in furs nearby. "Maybe even her." Asa's face was pale, but her voice was firm and resolute. "They will not harm my daughter."

Astrid persisted, needing Asa to face the grim possibilities. "And you, Asa? You helped him, you love him. They may exile you, cast you out. Even kill you for this." She gestured between Asa and Sassa.

Asa was quiet for a long moment, the weight of Astrid's words and the brutal reality of her people's ways falling upon her. She knew the truth in Astrid's warnings. But she also knew something else, something that contradicted logic, defied her upbringing, defied the gods she had worshipped her whole life. She looked at Astrid, her eyes shining out with a quiet, steadfast conviction, with a love that seemed to burn brighter than any fear. "I know. All these things, I know." Her hand went instinctively to Sassa, nestled against her. "But this love I feel for him... It is like nothing else. I cannot explain it. It is stronger than my thoughts, stronger than my own beliefs, stronger than my knowledge of our gods. It is like something has taken hold of me, something beyond me." She met Astrid's concerned gaze, her voice firm. "We will cross that bridge when we come to it, if we find our village."

Astrid nodded, her look softening with acceptance, with fierce loyalty. She would stand by Asa. No matter what. But the grim reality of what was coming hung tangibly in the air between them.

They were ready. Sassa was secured in a sling fashioned from the soft fur of the snow hares, nestled against Asa's chest, her tiny face peeking out, watching the world with wide, curious eyes. Aedelric, sword at his back, dagger at his belt, stood ready. Astrid, sword also at her back, a grim determination in her eyes, stood beside him. Asa, carrying the load of their supplies and the sack of treasure on Scildfrēond, mounted the black stallion.

They began their descent from the mountain, leaving behind the small cabin that had been their sanctuary. They rode and walked down the melting slopes, the air cool and fresh bearing the scent of thawing earth and pine. In the distance, the dark stain of the burnt village lay on the landscape, a grim token of the path they had traveled, the darkness they had escaped, and the unknown future that awaited them. Their time in the cabin was uneventful; they never spotted another person. They had survived, they had formed a family, but now, they were journeying towards a place that could shatter it all.

As the group traveled, the landscape slowly changed, the steep mountain slopes giving way to rolling hills and eventually to flatter plains. They followed what appeared to be a faint, overgrown track, hoping it would lead them to a more traveled road. For some time, they encountered no one; the wilderness was vast and empty around them. They hunted, they foraged, and they made camp under the open sky, their routine a known rhythm of survival. Sassa, nestled against Asa, grew stronger, her tiny cries a constant presence, a token of the precious life they protected.

Then, one fresh dawn, they saw them. Figures in the distance, moving along what looked like a more defined road. As they drew closer, they saw they were farmers, traveling with carts laden with goods. Aedelric, Asa, and Astrid immediately grew wary, their hands going to their weapons, their bodies tensing. They were in potentially hostile lands, and caution was paramount. The farmers, too, saw them, their movements halting, and their faces turning towards the armed group approaching from the wilderness.

Astrid, consistently the pragmatist, took the lead. "Stay quiet," she spoke quietly to Aedelric and Asa, her voice low and steady. "Let me speak."

They approached each other slowly, two wary groups meeting on a lonely road. Astrid stopped a short distance from the farmers, her hand visible but not on her weapon.

The farmers were a mix of ages, their faces weathered by sun and wind, their clothes practical and straightforward.

"Who are you?" Astrid called out in clear Norse, her voice resounding across the space.

One of the older farmers, a man with a long grey beard, stepped forward cautiously. "We are farmers," he replied, his dialect similar to Astrid's, but with subtle differences. "From the south. Traveling to Kaupang for the Várblót."

Kaupang. The ideal trading center in Norway. Várblót. The Spring Sacrifice. Asa and Astrid traded glances. They were familiar with Kaupang, a thriving center of trade and activity. These were not enemies. They were traveling south, towards known lands. Joy, sharp and sudden, flooded through Asa. They were in the right place. They were close.

"We are travelers," Astrid replied, keeping their identity vague. "Lost in the wilderness."

The farmers looked at Aedelric, his Saxon features, his sword. Their gazes lingered, wary, but the old farmer waved a hand dismissively. "Many people travel these roads," he said, his tone accepting. He looked at Asa, at Sassa in the sling, his expression easing slightly. "A child. May your trip be safe."

They traded brief pleasantries, wished each other well, and continued on their way. The farmers headed south, while Asa and her group headed north along the now-identified road. As the farmers' figures receded into the distance, Asa and Astrid turned to each other, their faces shining with relief and excitement.

"Kaupang!" Asa exclaimed, her voice bursting with joy. "We are close! We are in the right place!"

"Yes," Astrid agreed, a rare smile touching her lips. "It lies north of Kaupang, along the coast. We are traveling in the right direction."

They calculated the distance and the likely pace for a horse and a baby. A week. A little more. Njardarheimr was only a week or so away. The joy of knowing they were so close was immense, a burst of hope after months of uncertainty.

But the joy was short-lived, quickly tempered by a grim reality. "The land of the Hålogaland Chiefs," Astrid said, her voice sobering. "We must pass through it."

Asa's expression hardened as a powerful ruling elite in northern Norway. Not outright enemies of Jarl Gunnar, but their history was riddled with tension, uneasy alliances, and earlier conflicts. They were proud, often arrogant, and fiercely protective of their territory. Passing through their land would require extreme caution. Asa's mind went back to her conversation with Astrid in the cabin, where she had expressed fears about Aedelric's reception in Njardarheimr. Now, they had to face the potential hostility of other Norse peoples first. Would the Hålogaland Jarls accept a Saxon traveling with Norse women? Could they see him as a threat? Would they demand tribute? Or worse?

The weight of these concerns descended on Asa, dimming the joy of being close to home. She thought of Aedelric, of Sassa, of the risks they were taking. She prayed silently to Odin and Freyja, asking for safe passage and protection. Would the gods understand? Would they grant her this prayer, despite the man she loved, the child she carried? The uncertainty nibbled at her.

They traveled for a few more days, the road clearer now, their pace quicker. The landscape changed again, becoming more rugged, with steeper hills and deeper valleys, hinting at the coastline ahead. They were now in what felt like Hålogaland territory, the air becoming colder and the wind sharper. Every journeyer, every distant figure on the road, was a potential threat. They stayed alert, their weapons close at hand, their senses keen.

It was late one afternoon, the sun beginning its descent, throwing long shadows across the road, when they saw them. Six figures on horseback, approaching from the north. Young men, moving with the easy confidence of those who expect no challenge. Warriors. Astrid's hand went to her sword hilt, her body tightening like a bowstring.

"Warriors," she uttered to Asa and Aedelric, her voice subdued, edged. "Young ones. Trouble."

The riders drew closer, their silhouettes sharpening against the dying light. Their pace quickened. Their posture shifted. Intent became unmistakable. Aedelric, Asa, and Astrid moved closer together, instinctively forming a tight triangle, weapons ready. The air thickened with the kind of silence that comes before steel is drawn.

"Be ready," Aedelric whispered in Norse, his hand on his sword. His eyes never left the riders. "Pray this does not go bad."

Asa and Astrid murmured prayers to their gods, Aedelric to his. Asa tightened her hold on Sassa, nestled against her chest, her body already angled to shield the child if blades began to fly.

The young men pulled their horses to a halt a short distance away, blocking the road. Six of them, all armed, their faces young, arrogant, hungry for something to prove. Their stances were cocky, their eyes challenging, their smirks the kind worn by those who had never truly bled.

"State who you are!" the leader called out, his voice loud, demanding, puffed with inherited authority. He was barely more than a boy, but he sat his horse like he believed the world owed him obedience.

Astrid stepped forward a fraction, her chin lifting. "Who are you?" she retorted, her voice keen, cutting through the air like a blade.

The young man bristled, clearly unused to being questioned. "We are warriors of Harald Fairhair!" he declared, chest swelling. "I am Trygvi!" He spoke his name as though it should make the mountains bow.

Astrid gave a short, snide laugh. "Harald Fairhair? Who? I thought Hårek of Tjøtta ruled here." Her tone was light, but her eyes were sharp, watching every twitch of their hands.

Trygvi's face darkened with rage. He pointed at Aedelric, his voice stiff with fury. "Is this… this man-dog… allowing this bitch of a woman to speak to me in such a manner?!"

Before Aedelric could respond, Astrid's voice sliced through the tension, cold and deadly. "Call me bitch one more time, boy, and I will cut you from balls to neck."

The young warriors stared, stunned by the audacity of her threat. The moment hung, a single heartbeat where the world seemed to hold its breath.

Then Trygvi laughed. A harsh, ugly sound. He swung off his horse, his men following, boots crunching on the gravel as they spread out, forming a loose semicircle.

"I will ignore that insult, woman," he sneered, though his eyes burned. His gaze slid to Asa, lingering on her figure with leering intent. "For all the goods you have. I will allow you and your companions to live… after my men and I have had our way with them."

His gesture toward Asa and Astrid was slow, deliberate, dripping with threat.

Rage, cold and absolute, washed through Aedelric. His hand flew to his sword, drawing it in a single, fluid motion. The blade gleamed in the fading light. His voice dropped to a low, lethal growl.

"Lay a finger on them, and I'll carve your name into Hell's gate with your damned spine."

Before Trygvi could reply, before his men could react, the air sang.

Asa, still mounted on Scildfrēond, Sassa clutched against her, had drawn her bow. The arrow loosed with deadly velocity, slicing through the quiet like a streak of winter lightning. It struck Trygvi directly in the eye, silencing his sneer forever. He collapsed, dead before his body hit the ground.

Silence. Shock. Awe. The young warriors stared at their fallen leader, at Asa, at the impossible shot that had ended the confrontation before it began.

Then Astrid screamed a battle cry, raw and primal, a sound that ripped the stillness apart and charged the stunned group, sword raised. Aedelric followed instantly, his rage fueling his stride. The young warriors, their leader dead and their formation shattered, scrambled to react, drawing weapons with panicked haste.

The battle was short and savage. The young men, though armed and arrogant, were painfully inexperienced; their swings were wild, their footing unsure. Aedelric, Asa, and Astrid, hardened by months of brutal survival and years of warfare, moved with lethal precision.

Aedelric cut down two warriors in quick succession, his blade a blur of cold steel. Asa, from her vantage point on Scildfrēond, her bow singing, put an arrow through another man's chest. Astrid met a wild swing with a brutal block and drove her sword into her attacker's throat. And Scildfrēond, the black stallion, proved his worth as a warhorse, trampling one of the remaining warriors under his hooves.

In moments, it was over. All six young men lay dead on the road, their arrogance extinguished in a brutal, swift end.

Breathing heavily, adrenaline still flowing through them, Aedelric and Astrid stood over the bodies. Asa immediately checked on Sassa, who, miraculously, had slept through the entire brutal encounter, nestled against her mother. Seeing her daughter safe, Asa quickly checked on Aedelric and Astrid. Neither was harmed, their skill and the inexperience of their attackers ensuring their survival.

Astrid, her face hard but practical, immediately began to check the bodies for valuables. "Arm rings," she grunted, pulling gold and silver bands from wrists. "Sword here... good steel." She found a finely crafted sword on Trygvi's body, a valuable weapon.

Aedelric watched her, a weary grimace on his face. He looked at the dead young men, their lives ended so swiftly and brutally. "Is this... is this what it is like?" he asked, his voice subdued, speaking to both Asa and Astrid. "In this land? Always like this?"

Asa and Astrid shared a look. "For the most part," Asa replied, her voice sober. "It is the way of things here. Strength takes what it wants."

Aedelric nodded, the reality settling in. It was a harsh land, a brutal way of life. He was concerned, yes, but not entirely surprised. He had seen brutality in Wessex. This was just... different. More open.

They continued on their way, leaving the bodies on the road and taking their horses with them, the silence of the plains returning after the brief, violent storm. Njardarheimr was only a few days' ride now. As they traveled, the landscape grew more familiar to Asa and Astrid: the shape of the hills, the direction of the streams, the fragrance of the air.

Finally, after months of hardship and uncertainty, after battles and blizzards and the miracle of new life, they saw it. In the distance, nestled against the fjord, the familiar shape of the palisades, the main gate, longhouses, and the smoke rising from hearths. Njardarheimr. Home.

Asa's breath stuttered, tears blurring her vision. Months she had dreamed of this moment. Astrid rode beside her, her face furrowed with the same profound emotion. Aedelric and Astrid, now riding the captured horses, leading the others, his hand finding Asa's, shared the moment, his heart a mix of her joy and his profound fear of what lay ahead of them.

They sent a look, a wordless dialogue of hope and dread. Would this be a welcoming homecoming, a haven at last? Or would the past, the differences, the brutal realities of their worlds, shatter the fragile family they had built?

They turned Scildfrēond and the horses towards the village, beginning the final approach. Together. Bound by love, by survival, by the life of the child nestled against Asa's chest. They would encounter whatever came, together. No matter the odds.

Part 2: Njardarheimr

Salt hung heavily in the air, sharp as a blade against Asa's cheek, and stung in the threadbare wool of her cloak. Scildfrēond's flanks steamed in the cold, his breath rising in twisting clouds as they plodded forward, hooves churning the muddy road. Asa could taste the old brine on her lips and feel Sassa's warmth pressed to her chest, grounding her for one last stretch before Njardarheimr. The final reach of the road appeared both impossibly long and terrifyingly short. After months of hardship, of battling the wilderness, of forging a family against all odds, they were finally here. Relief, profound and soul-deep, warred inside Asa with a deep dread about the reception that awaited them. Aedelric rode beside her, his hand near his dagger, his look sweeping the approaching village, his features grim with vigilance. Astrid, on the other side, was equally tense, her eyes fixed on the familiar longhouses, her core a mix of longing for home and fear for the future.

As they drew closer to the main gate, figures started to emerge from the longhouses, drawn by the sight of the approaching horses and the small group. At first, they were just curious shapes, but as the distance closed, faces became clear. And then, recognition dawned. A cry went up, sharp and disbelieving, cutting through the quiet air. "Asa! Astrid!"

More people spilled out of the longhouses, their faces furrowed with shock, then overwhelmed with joy. Cries of their names resounded across the ground. "They live!" "By the gods, they have returned!" The road was filled with villagers running towards them, tears streaming down their faces, hands reaching out. The crowd engulfed them, pulled from the horses, embraced fiercely by people who had mourned them as lost to the sea.

Hands reached for Asa, for Astrid, pulling them into tearful hugs, murmuring blessings to the gods for their return. Villagers they had known since childhood, faces furrowed with grief, now transformed by joy. They were kissed, embraced, and welcomed back into their community with an outpouring of raw emotion.

In the midst of this joyous chaos, Aedelric stood slightly apart, sword still at his back, a silent, watchful presence. He saw the overwhelming love for Asa and Astrid, as well as the villagers' genuine relief. He felt hands clap his shoulder, heard voices murmur greetings in Norse he didn't fully understand, saw faces turn towards him with an array of curiosity and confusion. Who was this tall, dark-haired man with the sword, accompanying their lost daughters? One man, his face weathered in kind, paused, his eyes lingering on Aedelric's Saxon features, opening his mouth to ask a question, but the surging crowd swept him away, pulling Aedelric along with them towards the heart of the village.

Word of their impossible return spread like wildfire. It began as a murmur, then a shout, then a roar that rolled through Njardarheimr like thunder. Footsteps pounded across the packed earth outside the longhouse. A young warrior burst through the doors, breathless.

"Jarl Gunnar!" he shouted, voice cracking with urgency. "Jarl, your daughter! Asa, she has returned! She and Astrid! They live!"

The longhouse fell into stunned silence. Gunnar sat at the high seat, his face weathered by sorrow, the weight of grief carved deep into every line. His daughter, his only child, had been lost to the sea a year ago. A wound that had never closed.

Eiríkr Björnsson, towering beside him like a carved pillar of oak, went still. The warrior who had protested fiercely when the longships sailed, who had begged to go with Asa and Astrid, froze mid-breath, his massive hands curling into fists.

Gunnar rose too quickly, the bench scraping behind him. His countenance paled, his eyes wide, disbelieving. "What did you say?" His voice was barely more than a whisper.

The young warrior swallowed hard, chest heaving. "They're at the gates, Jarl. Asa… Astrid… they've come home."

Gunnar staggered a step, almost falling. His heart hammered against his ribs, a painful, desperate rhythm. "Asa… alive?" The words trembled out of him, fragile as frost.

Eiríkr stared toward the open doors, his jaw clenched, stunned into silence. For a moment, he looked carved from stone, then something cracked in his expression, a flicker of hope he had buried long ago.

Outside, the shouts grew louder, swelling with disbelief and joy.

Gunnar pressed a hand to the table to steady himself, breath shaking. "By the gods…" he whispered. "My girl… my girl has come home."

The crowd, a joyous, weeping mass, surged towards the Jarl's longhouse, carrying a group. As they reached the steps of the great hall, the crowd parted, revealing Jarl Gunnar standing there, Eiríkr beside him. Gunnar's usually stern face was imprinted with overwhelming emotion.

Asa, with Sassa clutched against her chest, saw her father. Tears streamed down Gunnar's face as he descended the final steps. Asa ran to him, and they embraced fiercely, clinging to each other as tears of happiness and relief streamed freely. Months of fear, of mourning, of loss, poured out in that single, powerful embrace. Gunnar held his daughter, kissing her hair, murmuring her name; the warmth of her presence remains a miracle against the cold ache in his heart.

Eiríkr, his visage a combination of disbelief and profound relief, moved towards Astrid. He embraced her tightly, a fierce, private clasp that conveyed a bond deeper than friendship, a secret love that had endured separation and fear. Astrid clung to him, burying her face against his chest, gaining comfort in his strength.

Aedelric stood back, watching the emotional reunions, a mute spectator in this moment of overwhelming Norse joy. He saw the love, the relief, the genuine welcome. For a moment, he allowed himself a trace of hope. *This may not be so bad.* But his warrior's vigilance remained, a chilling knot in his gut.

Gunnar finally pulled back from Asa, his gaze falling on the bundle in her arms. His eyes widened in surprise, then softened with wonder. A child. His granddaughter. "A child?" he murmured, his voice swollen with emotion. "How... how did this happen, my daughter?"

Asa looked at him, then at Aedelric standing slightly behind her, then back at her father. "There is much... to explain, Father," she said, her voice quiet, the load of their story descending on her.

Gunnar's gaze followed hers, falling on Aedelric. His expression changed, the joy tempered with surprise, then a dawning understanding. Saxon features. A sword. He was a Saxon. Here. Gunnar's mind worked quickly. The joyous welcome, so public, so emotional, would be short-lived once the truth spread. He had to act.

"Enough!" Gunnar's voice, though still heavy with feeling, held the burden of authority. He addressed the crowd, his voice loud and clear. "Praise the gods! My daughter, Asa, and Astrid have returned to us!" He raised his hands, commanding attention. "They are weary. They need rest. Return to your homes. To your lives. All will be revealed... in time." He added, his voice muted but firm, "Praise the gods for their return."

The crowd, though reluctant, began to disperse, murmuring thanks to the gods, their faces still wet with tears. Gunnar turned to Asa and Astrid, gesturing towards the longhouse. "Come. Inside. All of you." He looked at Aedelric, his look unreadable, but the command was clear.

Gunnar and Eiríkr guided them into the longhouse, leaving the dispersing crowd behind. As they entered, Aedelric caught a glimpse of a person standing apart from the dispersing villagers, watching them with a fixed, intense gaze. A man with a dark beard, rubbing his chin, his eyes narrowed. Hákon Bersason. A warrior of Njardarheimr, known for his ambition and his disdain for Asa. He had not joined the welcoming crowd. His presence and expression spoke volumes. He had not expected this. And whatever sinister plans he held were now, undeniably, changed.

They moved into the warmth and the well-known scent of the Jarl's longhouse smoke, roasting meat, and the lingering smell of ale and sweat. It was home, still, it felt subtly different. Asa's eyes scanned the room, searching for a face. Her mother. But she wasn't there, not among the household warriors, not among the women near the hearth. A cold knot appeared in Asa's stomach.

She looked at her father, his face still wet with tears of joy, but a shadow touched his eyes as he followed her gaze. "Mother?" Asa asked, her voice quiet, a sudden terror creeping in.

Gunnar's expression eased with sorrow. He reached out, taking Asa's free hand, his thumb stroking her knuckles. "My daughter," he said, his voice mild. "Your mother... she did not survive the winter."

Asa's breath faltered. Her mother. Gone. While she was lost, fighting for her own life, her mother had passed. A wave of grief, sharp and sudden, came over her, adding a new layer to the complex emotions of the day. Tears welled in her eyes again, different from the tears of joy. But even in her sorrow, there was a grim acceptance. Loss served as a constant companion in their world. Life was brutal, short. She had seen death and faced it countless times. Her mother's passing, while deeply painful, was the way of things. She squeezed her father's hand, a muted acknowledgment of their shared loss.

Gunnar, seeing her grief, nodded. He understood. Sorrow was a part of life, but life, and the living, must continue. He turned to a household slave standing nearby. "Prepare food and bring ale," he ordered. "For my daughter, Astrid, and our guests. The best we have."

One of the household slaves bowed, murmuring that it was midday and nothing had been prepared for a feast. Gunnar waved a dismissive motion. "Then prepare it now! Quickly!"

While the household prepared a meal, Gunnar turned his full attention to Aedelric. His expression, though still welcoming, held a new intensity, a directness that put Aedelric on guard. Eiríkr stood nearby, his massive frame tense, his eyes fixed on the Saxon. Astrid moved closer to Asa, a silent show of support, her gaze wary.

"Now," Gunnar said, his voice composed but firm, addressing Aedelric directly in clear Norse. "You. Please tell me who you are. And where do you come from?"

Aedelric met the Jarl's gaze, knowing this was the moment of truth. He stood tall, meeting the challenge directly. "My Lord," he began, his Norse fluent now, honed by months of necessity. "My name is Aedelric, son of Wulfric. I am a warrior... a Thegn... from the land of Wessex. From Winchester." He began to recount the events, starting with the battle at Wareham, the clash with the Norse fleet.

"The battle at Wareham?" Gunnar interrupted, his looks sharpening. He had sent his daughter and his men on that raid. He had thought he lost all, including Asa.

Aedelric nodded. "Yes, my Lord. I fought there. Against your men. Against... Astrid…against Asa." He glanced at Astrid, who remained stoic. He continued, describing the chaos of the ambush, Eadric's death, Asa's intervention, and his capture. He spoke of being taken aboard the longship, the storm, the wreck, the impossible survival.

As he described being washed ashore with Asa, the beginning of their time in the wilderness, Asa started to speak, wanting to add her perspective, to soften the stark facts of their initial enmity. "Father, it was..."

Gunnar held up a hand, stopping her. His gaze remained fixed on Aedelric. "Can this man not speak for himself, daughter?" His tone was not cruel, but it was a clear assertion of his authority, a demand for Aedelric to stand on his own two feet. He looked back at Aedelric, his look sharp. "So. You are Saxon."

Tension thickened in the hall. Eiríkr's hand closed on the hilt of his axe, his knuckles clenched. Asa and Astrid looked like they shared dread.

Aedelric met Gunnar's gaze directly, his voice steady, unwavering. "Yes, my Lord. I am Saxon."

Gunnar's expression remained unreadable for a long moment. Then, he asked the question that remained in the air, the question that could seal Aedelric's fate. "Are you... Christian?"

Aedelric did not hesitate. He stood tall, his gaze meeting the Jarl's, his voice sure and confident. "Yes, my Lord. I am Christian."

A united breath seemed to be held in the hall. Asa and Astrid braced themselves, dreading the expected explosion of rage, the condemnation, the immediate threat to Aedelric's life. Eiríkr's grip on his axe tightened further. But Gunnar's reaction was not what they anticipated. He did not roar, did not call for guards, did not order Aedelric seized. He simply... looked at him. A long, assessing gaze that seemed to penetrate Aedelric's very soul. No one moved. The quietness stretched, taut and heavy.

Before Gunnar could speak, before anyone could break the tense silence, the heavy doors of the longhouse burst open with a crash. All heads turned. Standing in the doorway, framed by the light, was Hákon Bersason, accompanied by a few of his men. He stepped inside as if he owned the place, his look of casual arrogance, a hint of a sneer hovering on his lips.

"Greetings, great Jarl of Njardarheimr," Hákon said, his voice projecting through the hall, a hint of distance, almost derision, in his tone as he addressed Gunnar.

Eiríkr's massive frame tensed further, his eyes tightening with apparent displeasure. "Hákon," he growled, his sound a quiet rumble. "By what right do you burst into the Jarl's hall and interrupt his council?"

Gunnar, his attention diverted from Aedelric, held up a hand, stopping Eiríkr. His expression remained calm, controlled. He would not show weakness or intimidation to Hákon. "It is alright, Eiríkr," Gunnar said, his voice composed. He looked at Hákon, his gaze direct. "Welcome, Hákon Bersason. You arrive at a moment of... unexpected tidings."

Hákon Bersason. Son of Bersa. A warrior of Njardarheimr, though not one who had sailed on the raid. He was not blessed with the brute size of Eiríkr or the natural warrior's grace of Asa. Hákon had learned early that brute force was not the only path to power in their world. He possessed a sharp mind, a cunning intellect, and a willingness to use influence, coercion, and gold to achieve his aims. He paid others to fight for him, relying on wealth and manipulation rather than on the strength of his arms. This was why he had remained behind, deemed more valuable for his connections and influence within the village than for his prowess in a shieldwall. Gunnar knew this about him, knew of his ambition, his resentment, his firm belief that women, particularly Asa, were unfit to lead.

Hákon's father, Bersa, had been a close friend of Gunnar's in their youth, fighting battles together and sharing feasts and sorrows. Before his death, Bersa had asked Gunnar to look after Hákon and his remaining family. Gunnar, out of loyalty to his friend, had done so. However, over time, Hákon's family had dwindled, leaving him feeling isolated and resentful within the village, where he was never truly accepted, despite Gunnar's efforts. This isolation had festered into an ingrained hatred for Gunnar's family, a burning desire to usurp their position and rule Njardarheimr himself. He had been watching, waiting, planning, and always looking for an opportunity.

Hákon's eyes, sharp and assessing, swept over the group near the hearth: Asa, holding a child, Astrid, Eiríkr, and the unfamiliar Saxon. His expression, usually one of casual arrogance, faltered with surprise, only to be quickly masked. This was not what he had expected. Asa and Astrid returned from the dead. And with a Saxon. His sinister plans, whatever they were, would indeed need to be changed. He stood there, watching a disruptive force enter the already tense hall.

Hákon stepped fully into the hall, his men following close behind him, their presence an unspoken challenge to the Jarl's authority. His gaze rested on Asa, then on Sassa, a trace of something indecipherable in his eyes before settling on Aedelric, his expression hardening.

"Unexpected tidings, indeed, Jarl Gunnar," Hákon said, his voice smooth, a predator circling. "Rumors spread quickly. Of ghosts returned from the sea. And... of a Saxon dog in your hall." His gaze was fixed on Aedelric now, openly hostile. "What is the meaning of this?"

Eiríkr's hand squeezed further on his axe. "He is a guest in the Jarl's hall, Hákon," Eiríkr rumbled, his voice as a low warning. "Show respect."

Hákon ignored Eiríkr, his eyes still on Aedelric. "Respect is earned, Eiríkr. Not given to enemies." He looked back at Gunnar, a challenging flash in his eye. "Jarl Gunnar. This man is a Saxon. Our enemy. What is he doing here? And the child..." His gaze moved to Sassa, a cold assessment in his eyes. "Whose child is it?"

The air in the hall grew heavy, thick with unvoiced tension. Gunnar remained outwardly calm, his look steady as he met Hákon's challenge. He knew this wasn't only about Aedelric; it was about Hákon asserting his influence, questioning Gunnar's judgment, testing the waters for his ambitions.

"Hákon," Gunnar said, his voice measured. "My daughter and Astrid have returned from a terrible ordeal. They bring with them a story that defies belief. This man... Aedelric... was with them. He is here under my protection."

"Your protection?" Hákon scoffed, a sneer returning to his lips. "A Saxon warrior? In your hall? After the failure at Wareham? Have you gone soft in your old age, Gunnar?"

A ripple of unease went through the household warriors and slaves gathered in the hall. Hákon's words were a direct insult to the Jarl, a dangerous escalation.

"Watch your tongue, Hákon," Eiríkr warned, taking a step forward, his massive presence a clear threat.

"Enough, Eiríkr," Gunnar said, stopping him again. He looked at Hákon, his expression hardening, the steel beneath his calm exterior showing. "My decisions are my own, Hákon Bersason. This man's presence will be explained. In time. At the Thing. When all the villagers can hear." He was asserting his authority, pushing the decision to the communal assembly, where Hákon's influence might be diluted.

Hákon's eyes narrowed further. He knew Gunnar was maneuvering. However, he had the advantage of surprise and public opinion on his side. The villagers outside, still murmuring with the news, would not welcome a Saxon. "The villagers will not wait for the Thing, Jarl Gunnar," Hákon said, his voice muted and dangerous. "Their kinsmen died at Wareham. At the hands of Saxons. What will they say when they learn you harbor one of their killers? And the child... a half-breed?" His gaze flew to Sassa again; the cold assessment now mixed with something darker.

Asa, who had been silent, listening to the exchange, her hand clenching on Sassa, spoke then, her voice lucid and strong despite her weariness. "He saved my life, Hákon," she said, meeting his gaze directly. "He saved Astrid's life. We survived because of him."

Hákon turned his full attention to Asa, his look of dismissive contempt. "You speak of saving lives, Asa?" he sneered. "While our men died on your raid? While you were lost, perhaps enjoying the company of this... Saxon?" His gaze rested on her, on Sassa, a leering, unpleasant look. "Or perhaps he took you by force? Is that the truth of this child?"

Rage, icy and sharp, flared in Asa. *How dare he.* How dare he question her honor, her choices, the legitimacy of her child? Aedelric took a step forward, his face an expression of fury. Eiríkr's hand was on his axe, ready to strike. Astrid's eyes blazed.

"Hákon!" Gunnar's voice cracked like a whip, sharp and commanding, cutting through the rising tension as he stood. "That is enough! You will not insult my daughter in my hall!" His authority, absolute and firm, filled the space. He looked at Hákon, his eyes cold steel. "You will leave my hall, Hákon Bersason. Now."

Hákon held Gunnar's gaze for a long moment, the challenge clear in his eyes. He knew he had pushed, perhaps too hard, too fast. But he had planted the seeds of doubt, of suspicion, in the minds of those who had heard him. He gave a slight, nearly imperceptible nod to his men.

"As you wish, Jarl Gunnar," Hákon said, his voice regaining its smooth, unsettling quality. "But the truth will come out." He turned, his cloak swirling, and walked towards the door, his men following. As he passed Aedelric, his gaze served as a promise of future conflict. As he passed Asa, holding Sassa, his expression was one of cold, calculating disdain.

The heavy doors closed behind him, plunging the hall into a tense silence. The air still sizzled with the aftermath of his intrusion. Gunnar stood for a moment, his expression grim. Eiríkr's hand remained on his axe, his massive frame radiating suppressed fury. Astrid's face was stern; her eyes fixed on the closed door. Asa held Sassa tighter, her face colorless, still resolute.

Gunnar looked at Aedelric, as his more stern expression was replaced by one of deep concern. Hákon had forced his hand. The truth about Aedelric, about Sassa's parentage, would have to be revealed to the entire village, and sooner than Gunnar would have liked. The joyous homecoming had quickly turned into a precarious situation, their safety hanging in the balance. The loyalty of his own, the influence of Hákon, the deep-seated prejudices against Saxons and Christians, all would come to bear at the Thing.

"Aedelric," Gunnar said, his voice tired yet firm, gesturing towards the benches near the hearth. "Eat. Rest. We will speak more later. About everything." He looked at

Aedelric, a silent apology in his eyes for the coming storm. "The Thing... it will be soon."

The household slaves, their faces wary after Hákon's outburst, began to bring food: simple bread, cheese, dried meat, and ale, the beginnings of the meal Gunnar had ordered. The threat now overshadowed the initial joy of return, the knowledge that their fight for survival had not ended in the wilderness but had followed them home.

Part 3: Gunnar's Gamble

The air still sizzled with the aftermath of his intrusion, the subtle challenge to Gunnar's authority weighing down. The household slaves walked carefully, setting out the simple meal Gunnar had ordered: bread, cheese, dried meat, and ale. Asa held Sassa close, her face wan, still resolute. Aedelric stood beside her, his look fixed on the closed door. Astrid and Eiríkr remained tense, their warrior instincts on high alert.

They ate in a strained quiet, the initial joy of the homecoming overshadowed by the forthcoming threat Hákon represented. The food, though simple, was nourishing after their months in the wilderness. Sassa, oblivious to the tension, suckled contentedly or slept in Asa's arms.

When the meal was finished, Gunnar rose from his seat at the head of the table. He looked around the hall, his gaze settling on his daughter, then Astrid, then Aedelric. His expression was weary but held the firm authority of a Jarl.

"My people," Gunnar said, his voice projecting through the hall, addressing the household. "Sharing this meal with my daughter, with Astrid, and with my new grandchild... it is a blessing that warms my heart more than any fire." He paused, his look lingering on Sassa. "For months, we mourned them as lost. Now, by the grace of the gods, they are returned." He looked at Aedelric, his expression changing to a more formal one. "Now... I must speak with this man. In private."

A ripple of unease went through the hall. Eyes shifted nervously. To speak with a Saxon, alone, after Hákon's outburst... it was unexpected. Eiríkr, his massive frame stiffening, began to rise. "Jarl," he started, a note of protest in his voice.

Gunnar held up a hand, a silent, absolute command. Eiríkr hesitated, then slowly and reluctantly sat back down.

Aedelric looked at Asa. Her eyes were wide with worry, a wordless plea in their depths. He knew, and she knew, that Gunnar's word was law here. To protest or refuse would be a grave insult, a show of disrespect that could only worsen their situation. They had no choice but to trust Gunnar's judgment, despite feeling uncertain about his intentions. Neither of them could truly read the thoughts behind the Jarl's weathered face.

Aedelric met Gunnar's gaze, offering a slight, respectful nod. He stood, his movements deliberate, and followed Gunnar towards the back of the hall, towards the private room behind the Jarl's carved throne. As he passed Asa, their hands touched, a brief, silent touch, a reassurance, a shared fear, a frantic hope.

The heavy door of the private room closed behind them, shutting out the hushed silence of the hall. Gunnar walked to a chair near a small, cold hearth and sat heavily, letting out a long, weary sigh. Aedelric remained standing, sword at his back, his posture that of a warrior, watchful though respectful.

Gunnar looked at him, his gaze direct. "You have put me in... quite the predicament, Aedelric of Wessex." His voice was low, devoid of overt hostility, but the force of his words was clear. "Now... I must decide. What to do?"

Aedelric met his gaze, choosing honesty. "My Lord," he began, his voice composed. "I understand. But... I must tell you. About Asa. About us." Jarl Gunnar's jaw stiffened. "Speak, then," he said, though his voice bore the strain of a man bracing for a blow.

Aedelric drew a slow breath. He spoke of their time in the wilderness, the brutal reality of their survival, and the way they had been stripped bare of their old lives, forced to rely on one another. He spoke of the bond that grew, defying the hatred of their peoples. He spoke of his love for Asa, a love which had grown in the face of death and despair, a love he could not explain, only feel with every fiber of his being.

Gunnar's eyes narrowed, not in anger, but in the painful effort of understanding. "You claim love," he murmured, almost to himself. "After all that has passed between our peoples." Aedelric nodded once. "Yes, and it is the truest thing I have ever known." He spoke of Sassa, the life they had formed together. "We thought… many times… we would not survive. But we did. Together."

Gunnar's breath caught at the mention of the child. "My granddaughter," he whispered, the word fragile, uncertain, as though he feared it might break if spoken too loudly. Aedelric hesitated. His voice lowered. "There is… even more. That we have not yet told you." Gunnar's look intensified, steady, and heavy. Gunnar listened in silence, his eyes fixed on Aedelric's face, assessing the truth in his words, the sincerity in his voice. When Aedelric finished, Gunnar was quiet for a long moment.

"I can see it, Aedelric," Gunnar finally said, his voice more gentle. "The love my daughter has for you. It is plain in her eyes. I know my daughter. I know her heart." He sighed again. "And I know her heart is also for her people. For the role she will one day hold." He looked at Aedelric directly. "I have no sons, Aedelric. Asa is my only child. She is the one who will lead Njardarheimr after I am gone." He explained his reasons for sending her on the raid to Wessex. "I sent her across the seas... to prove herself to the village. To show them... she had the strength. The cunning.

The warrior's heart. To lead them." He looked at Aedelric. "My people... they follow strength. Asa needs more than her birthright to command their loyalty."

He leaned forward slightly. "The fact that I can see my daughter's love for you... The fact that Astrid, fierce Astrid, has not killed you herself... that was enough for me. To not kill you on sight. To hear what you had to say." His gaze hardened slightly. "But now... Hákon has gotten involved in this. He has planted seeds of doubt. Of suspicion. Among the people. He will use you to challenge my authority. To undermine my daughter's right to lead." Gunnar's jaw stiffened. "I must find another way. To show my people... that my choices are sound. That they should not question... what has happened. What fate has brought to my hall?"

Aedelric felt a chill. He had thought he was safe, at least for the moment, under Gunnar's roof. He had thanked Gunnar for sparing him earlier. "My Lord," Aedelric said, his voice quiet. "I... I thank you for not killing me."

Gunnar gave a short, grim laugh. "Do not be so quick to thank me, Aedelric." His gaze was piercing. "That... is what I must decide... will happen soon. To give my people... the answer they seek."

Aedelric's mind reeled. He didn't understand. Was Gunnar saying he would kill him? Sacrifice him? After everything? Gunnar's expression was unreadable, a mask of grim resolve.

Gunnar looked at Aedelric, his eyes seeking. "Tell me, Aedelric. Truly. Do you love my daughter? Will you do... anything... for her?"

Aedelric did not hesitate. The answer was immediate, absolute. "Yes, my Lord," he said, his voice firm, unwavering. "I love Asa more than life itself. And I will do... anything... for her. Anything for Sassa. They mean more to me... than anything I have ever known."

Gunnar held his gaze for a long moment, assessing the truth of his words. A slow nod. "Good." He rose from his chair, his decision made. His voice was laden with the weight of it, but resolute. "Then you will agree... to what must happen."

He laid out his plan, stark and brutal in its simplicity. "I will gather my people this evening. In the square, I will tell them the story of you, my daughter, my grandchild. I will reveal your identity and your origins. And then...you will challenge Hákon. To a duel. To the death. In the square." Gunnar's gaze was fixed on Aedelric. "You... will fight him."

Aedelric's breath faltered. *A duel? Against Hákon?* To the death? In front of the entire village? He knew of duels, of trials by combat, but this... this was a political maneuver, a test of fate, a gamble with his life and their future. Gunnar was placing everything on this fight.

Gunnar explained the purpose, the brutal logic of their world. "The gods will decide. If Hákon wins... then they deem, you a true enemy. Unworthy. And Hákon... will have what he seeks." He looked at Aedelric, his look steady. "But if you win... if you defeat Hákon Bersason... then the gods have brought you here for a reason. They have decided... to allow you to live. This will prove to my people... that the gods are with you. That your presence here... is by their will."

Gunnar knew Hákon's nature. Hákon was a manipulator, not a warrior at heart. He relied on others to fight on his behalf. To refuse a challenge to a duel, particularly one sanctioned by the Jarl and presented as a judgment of the gods, would be an act of cowardice, a defiance of fate itself. It would severely damage Hákon's standing among the people. He would be forced to accept.

Aedelric stood there, reeling. A duel to the death. His life, Asa's future, Sassa's safety, all resting on his ability to defeat a man he had just met, a man who represented the deep-seated prejudices of this land. He couldn't believe this was how things were handled, so swiftly, so brutally, leaving everything to the blade and the perceived will of the gods. But he looked at Gunnar, at the grim determination in his eyes, and saw something else, a desperate hope, a gamble taken for his daughter, for his grandchild, for the future of his lineage. At that instant, Aedelric experienced a strange, inexplicable trust in this fierce, complicated man. He loved Asa. He would do anything for her.

"I agree, my Lord," Aedelric said, his voice composed despite the shock. He would fight. For Asa. For Sassa. For their chance at a life here.

Gunnar nodded, a trace of relief in his eyes. He turned and walked towards the door, opening it. The hall was silent; everyone waited and watched. Gunnar stepped back into the main entrance, Aedelric following him. All eyes turned to them. Gunnar stood tall, his voice ringing out with authority, as he addressed the assembled household.

"Gather the village!" Gunnar commanded. "Tonight! In the square! At sunset!" His gaze swept over their faces. "There will be a Thing. And a duel. By the will of the gods!" He looked directly at Aedelric. "This man... Aedelric... he has agreed to face Hákon Bersason. In combat. To the death."

A unified gasp went through the hall. Asa's eyes widened in horror. "No!" she cried, taking a step forward, her hand going to her mouth. She knew. She knew the customs, the brutal finality of a duel to the death. She knew the skill of the warriors here. And she knew Hákon, his cunning, his ambition.

But even as the protest left her lips, she knew it was futile. Gunnar had spoken. The challenge had been issued. Aedelric had agreed. It would happen. No matter what. The joyous homecoming, the brief respite, had ended. Their fight for survival was nowhere near over. It would be decided tonight, in the square, by the blade, by the gods.

The air in the longhouse remained dense with tension after Gunnar's pronouncement. A duel. To the death. In the square. At sunset. The joyous homecoming had culminated in a brutal gamble for survival and acceptance. Asa's cry of protest wafted in the air, quickly stifled by the grim reality of their situation.

Gunnar, his visage a mask of grim resolve, turned to his household warriors. "Go!" he commanded, his voice throbbing with authority. "Announce the Thing! Throughout the village! Tell them to gather in the square at sunset! For a matter of grave importance! And a judgment of the gods!"

Several warriors, their faces reflecting surprise and unease, nodded and moved quickly towards the doors, their heavy boots thudding on the wooden floor as they went to spread the news.

Gunnar then turned to Eiríkr, whose massive frame still radiated suppressed fury from Hákon's intrusion. "Eiríkr," Gunnar said, his voice calmer now, but the command clear. "Find a suitable set of mail for Aedelric. The best we have. He must face Hákon armored."

Eiríkr nodded, his expression grim, and strode towards the back of the longhouse, presumably to the armory or storage area.

Meanwhile, Astrid, her eyes still blazing with anger at Hákon's words and the danger he represented, moved towards Aedelric. She looked at the sword he carried, the one he had taken from the fallen guard in Pall's village. "Give me your sword," she said, her voice curt. "It will need a better edge for what is to come."

Aedelric, understanding the necessity, handed her the blade. Astrid took it without another word and moved towards the hearth, where a grindstone was kept, her movements efficient and purposeful.

As the household stirred around them, preparing for the unexpected Thing and the even more unexpected duel, Asa remained near the hearth, holding Sassa. The baby was wide awake now, her eyes shining wide, taking in the sights and sounds of the busy longhouse. Asa watched Aedelric, her heart burdened with fear, but her look steadfast.

Eiríkr returned shortly, carrying a heavy roll of mail armor of interlocking metal rings, gleaming dully in the firelight. It was well-made and clearly meant for an important warrior. He dropped it near Aedelric with a grunt.

Asa, still holding Sassa, moved towards Aedelric. "Let me help you," she said, her voice quiet but firm. She set Sassa down carefully on a pile of furs near the hearth, ensuring she was safe, then turned her attention to the mail.

The mail was heavy, cumbersome. Asa helped Aedelric don it. As she worked, guiding the heavy rings over his head and shoulders, helping him settle them into place, she spoke to him in a low voice, her words for his ears alone.

"Hákon is cunning, Aedelric," she warned, her hands shifting over the cold metal. "He is not a warrior of strength, but he is shrewd. He will not fight fairly. He will use tricks and feints. Be aware of his movements, not just his blade." She looked up at him, her eyes serious. "He is desperate for power. He will do anything to win."

She explained the significance of the Thing, the assembly Gunnar had called. "The Thing is where the people gather. To make decisions. To judge. By holding the duel there, Father is putting the outcome on display for everyone to see. And before the gods. The people will see it as the gods' judgment." She paused, her gaze easing slightly. "If you win... it will be seen as a sign that the gods favor you. Or at least... that they do not oppose you."

Sassa, nestled on the furs, watched them, her tiny head turning, her eyes fixed on Aedelric's face as he pulled on the heavy mail. Aedelric looked down at her. At that moment, in the midst of the tension and fear, Sassa smiled, a broad, gummy baby smile, her eyes wrinkling at the corners. Aedelric felt his heart clench. He smiled back, a grim, tender smile.

Asa saw the exchange. Her hand went to Aedelric's cheek, her thumb stroking his skin.

"She loves you, Aedelric," she said, her voice laden with a fierce tenderness. "Just as I do." Her gaze met his, unwavering. "I will pray. To the gods. That they grant you favor. That they see the truth in your heart. There is a reason for all of this, Aedelric. I feel it. A reason you were brought here. A reason we survived."

Aedelric held her gaze, his own filled with love and grim determination. In his mind, he offered a silent prayer: '*God, my Lord.' See me through this. Grant me strength. For Asa. For Sassa.* He looked back at Asa, his voice muted and firm, pouring all his firmness into his words. "I will be victorious, my love. For you. For her. I will not fall."

Just then, Astrid returned from the hearth, Aedelric's sword in her hand. The blade gleamed, its edge honed to a razor sharpness. She held it out to him, hilt first. "It is ready," she said, her voice expressionless. "Sharp enough to cut bone."

Asa looked at the blade, then at Astrid. "Thank you, Astrid."

Astrid met Asa's gaze, a trace of something indecipherable in her eyes. Then she looked at Aedelric, a grim humor in her voice. "Don't die, Saxon. I do not wish to spend the next few months consoling Asa over your loss. It would be... tiresome." Aedelric gave a short, humorless chuckle. "I will try not to."

Gunnar, seeing the preparations nearing completion, turned to his household slaves again. "Begin the feast preparations!" he commanded. "No matter the outcome tonight, no matter who stands victorious, we will feast! We will celebrate the judgment of the gods!"

Part 4: Serpent's Plan

As the evening began, the sky outside the longhouse was bathed in shades of red and violet, and the village stirred. Warriors, farmers, women, and children all were starting to gather, drawn by the news of the Thing, the promise of a duel. They moved towards the central square, their tones a low murmur of speculation and anticipation. Torches were being lit, emitting flickering light onto the ground. The Thing-stead, the heart of the village assembly, was coming alive.

Aedelric, now clad in the heavy mail, sword at his back, stood with Asa and Astrid near the longhouse entrance, looking out at the approaching crowd. The sun was beginning to set, throwing extended shadows throughout the village. The breeze was cold, sharp in anticipation. The Thing was beginning. Soon, he would walk into that square, face a cunning enemy, and fight for his life, for his family's future, under the eyes of the gods and the judgment of a skeptical people.

The square was packed, faces brightened by the faint torchlight, a subtle susurration of anticipation flowing through the crowd. Gunnar, Jarl of Njardarheimr, stood on the raised stone that served as the speaker's platform, his figure imposing in the torchlight. Eiríkr stood beside him, a silent, massive guardian. Asa, holding Sassa, stood with Astrid and Aedelric slightly apart from Gunnar, near the edge of the platform, their existence a sharp visual representation of the matter at hand.

Gunnar raised his hands, calling for silence. The murmuring ceased, all eyes fixed on their Jarl. His voice, strong and clear, carried across the square. "People of Njardarheimr! We are gathered here this evening for a

Thing of great importance!" He paused, his look drifting over the assembled villagers. "Many of you rejoiced today, beholding faces we thought lost to the sea!" A ripple of assent went through the crowd. "My daughter, Asa! And Astrid!" Cheers broke out, quickly silenced by Gunnar's raised hand.

"They have returned to us," Gunnar continued, his voice laden with emotion. "From a terrible ordeal. A storm that claimed many brave warriors." His expression turned grim. "They survived against all odds. And they bring with them a story that you must hear. A story of hardship, of survival, and fate."

Jarl Gunnar stood straight, the murmuring crowd falling into a tense hush. His voice held the burden of a man who had lost everything and somehow been given a piece of it back. "People of Njardarheimr," he began, composed but roughened by emotion. "You have heard the gossip. I will speak the truth plainly." He drew a breath, his look sweeping over the faces before him.

"My daughter Asa… and Astrid, her shield-sister… were not taken by the sea as we believed. They lived. By the gods, they lived." A quiver of shock moved through the crowd.

"They survived a shipwreck," Gunnar continued. "Thrown into the waves, washed ashore in a land none of us have seen. They faced the wilderness with nothing but their will to live. Hunger. Storms. Wounds. The cold. The kind of trials that break most men." His voice deepened, pride and sorrow intertwined. "They endured." He paused, letting the word settle.

"And in that wilderness," he said, "Asa found an unlikely ally. A Saxon warrior, Aedelric, was taken prisoner at Wareham. A man she should have hated. A man who should have hated her." A few murmurs rose; Gunnar lifted a hand for silence. "Listen," he commanded. "For this is the truth of it."

He continued, his tone resolute but not defensive. "They survived together. Fought together. Merged. And in that struggle, a bond formed between them, stronger than the old hatreds of our peoples. A bond forged in fire and fear and the will to live." He swallowed, emotion tightening his voice.

"They journeyed inland. Faced dangers I would not wish on any of you. Found shelter where they could. Fought their way free when darkness rose around them." His look softened. "And in the heart of a blizzard, in a mountain cabin far from any home… my granddaughter, Sassa, was born." A murmur of awe swept through.

Gunnar straightened, his voice increasing in strength. "I will not hide the truth. Aedelric is a Saxon. He stands among us because my daughter lives, because he kept her alive when the world tried to take her from me. The child is his. And she is blood of my blood." He let the silence stretch, heavy and expectant.

"This is the tale as it was told to me. And I speak it now so all may know: my daughter has returned. Her shield-sister has returned, and the child she carries is a gift bought with suffering and courage." His final words rang with the authority of a Jarl and the heart of a father. "Honor them."

The crowd listened in stunned silence, their faces reflecting a mix of awe at the tale of survival, sorrow for the fallen warriors, and growing unease as Gunnar spoke of the Saxon.

Gunnar looked out at his people, his voice ringing out with authority. "Fate has brought this man, Aedelric, to our shores. He has faced death and survived. He has protected my daughter and Astrid. He is the father of my granddaughter." He paused, permitting the weight of that sink in. "There are questions among you. Uneasy. About his presence here. About his faith." He looked directly at Aedelric, standing beside Asa. "This man is Christian." A murmur went through the crowd, louder this time, a wave of disapproval.

"But we are people of the gods!" Gunnar declared, his tone rising. "We believe in their will! In their judgment!" He gestured to Aedelric. "Fate has brought him here. And the gods will now decide his fate!"

Cheers burst from the crowd, a wave of approval. They understood. The Jarl was putting the matter before the gods, as was their way.

Gunnar waited for the cheers to subside, his gaze scanning the crowd. His eyes settled on a person standing near the edge of the assembly, his face somber, his arms crossed. Hákon Bersason.

"Hákon Bersason!" Gunnar's voice boomed across the square, calling him out publicly. Hákon's head jerked up, his eyes tightening. "You were the first to voice your concern! To question this man's presence! To name him an enemy!" Gunnar's voice mellowed slightly, a note of regret entering it, for the man was the son of his old friend. "Perhaps... the gods gave you that insight, Hákon. Perhaps they chose you... to be the one to test him."

Hákon's face, moments before, set in a mask of grim anticipation, paled slightly. He had not expected this. He had expected Gunnar to condemn the Saxon, or at least present him as a prisoner. He had not expected to be singled out, to be thrust into the center of this, to be named the gods' chosen instrument. He was a manipulator, a schemer, not a duelist. He was trapped. To refuse would be an act of cowardice, a defiance of the Jarl and the perceived will of the gods, a move that would shatter his standing and his ambitions.

"Jarl Gunnar," Hákon said, stepping forward, his voice rigid, trying to find a way out. "Surely... I was not the only one to notice that this man is a Christian. That he is Saxon."

"That may be true, Hákon," Gunnar replied, his voice firm, cutting off Hákon's attempt to deflect. "But you were the one who spoke it aloud! You were the one who questioned his right to be here! Therefore, the gods have chosen you to settle this matter! To face him in combat!" Gunnar's gaze was unwavering, giving Hákon no room to maneuver. "The gods will decide! By the blade! In the square! To the death!"

Hákon stood there, trapped, his mind working, searching desperately for an escape, finding none that would leave his reputation and ambitions intact. He looked at Aedelric, standing tall, clad in mail, sword at his back, his expression grim though resolute. He looked at the assembled villagers, their eyes fixed on him, waiting. He looked at Gunnar, the Jarl, his father's friend, who had just trapped him completely.

With a visible effort, Hákon straightened his shoulders. He looked out at the crowd, forcing a mask of grim determination onto his face. He knew he had to agree. Reluctantly, his voice rigid with suppressed fury and fear, he spoke. "I agree, Jarl Gunnar. I will face this Saxon. In combat. To the death. As the gods command."

A murmur went through the crowd, the tension tightening further. The duel was set.

As the Thing-stead began to be prepared for the combat, a clear space was marked out, and torches were adjusted to illuminate the dueling ground. Hákon moved away, towards a small group of his most trusted men. He spoke to them in low, urgent tones, his voice scarcely a whisper, his eyes darting towards Aedelric, then towards the edges of the square.

"Listen," he murmured, his voice rigid. "If I fall... if this Saxon dog defeats me... You will not stand by." His eyes were hard, desperate. "He is bewitched! By his Christian god! He has bewitched Gunnar! The whole village!" He looked at his men, their faces stern. "If I cannot defeat him... You must intervene. Create chaos. And if necessary... flee. Seek help. This village... it must be cleansed of this... this Christian influence. Before it spreads." He gave them specific instructions, quiet commands that would ensure disruption, escape, and a continued threat regardless of the duel's outcome.

Unseen, unheard by Gunnar, by Aedelric, by the vast majority of the assembled villagers, Hákon Bersason established the basis for treachery, making certain that even if the gods chose Aedelric, his ambition and hatred would not die with him. The duel was about to begin, but the actual battle for Njardarheimr had already started, its roots hidden in the shadows of the Thing-stead.

The Thing-stead buzzed with a tense energy, the wavering torchlight throwing long, waving shadows throughout the faces of the assembled villagers. The air appeared cold, sharp in anticipation. Gunnar stood on the speaker's stone, his presence imposing, having exposed the improbable tale of survival and the stark choice before them. Hákon Bersason stood opposite, his face wan but set in a guise of forced resolve, surrounded by a few of his closest men. And between them, the dueling ground, cleared of obstacles, awaited its grim purpose.

Aedelric stood near the edge of the platform, clad in the heavy mail Eiríkr had provided. It was well-made, offering solid protection, a strong contrast to the rough hides he had worn for months. His sword felt balanced in his hand, its edge honed to lethal sharpness by Astrid. He perceived the weight of the mail, the burden of the moment, the weight of Asa's love and fear, and the silent, watchful presence of Sassa, held close by her mother. He was a Saxon warrior, a Christian man, about to fight a Norseman, a follower of Odin and Thor, in a trial by combat sanctioned by a Jarl and judged by the gods of this foreign land. The dilemma was stark: win and potentially gain acceptance, lose and face death and the likely condemnation of his family.

Two shields were brought forward, round, wooden, bound with leather and iron. One was given to Hákon, one to Aedelric. They moved to the center of the cleared space, facing each other. The crowd fell silent, every eye fixed on the two combatants. Gunnar's voice cleaved the silence, laying out the rules, the stakes, the judgment of the gods.

Part 5: Treachery in the Square

The duel began. The air in the Thingstead square crackled with anticipation, yet a tense quiet fell as Aedelric and Hákon circled each other. Hákon, despite his Jarl-like bluster and the intimidating presence of his loyal men, was not a warrior of Aedelric's caliber. His movements were overly cautious, almost stiff; his large, round shield was held defensively high, but with a slight quiver in his grip. His swings were tentative, more for show than substance, lacking the fluid power of a seasoned fighter.

Aedelric, in stark contrast, was a veteran shaped in the crucible of countless fights and pitched battles. He moved with a controlled, deadly grace, his steps light on the packed earth, his body coiled and ready. He was patient, his eyes like a hawk's, assessing his opponent. He quickly recognized Hákon's fatal flaw: a distinct lack of actual combat experience, masked only by brute force and a false confidence. Aedelric pressed forward slowly, not rushing, testing Hákon's defense with feints and probing attacks. His sword movements were economical, purposeful, each calculated to draw a reaction, to find a weakness.

Hákon parried wildly, his shield taking the brunt of Aedelric's measured, deliberate attacks. The blows, though not yet aimed to kill, landed with concussive force, rattling Hákon's arm. Sweat beaded on his forehead, glistening despite the fresh air, and his breathing grew ragged. He attempted a few small, cunning feints, quick jabs intended to draw Aedelric's guard wide, movements that Asa had warned Aedelric to expect. But Aedelric saw them coming, anticipating each clumsy attempt. His shield, a sturdy plank of oak and iron, deflected the blows with skilled ease, barely requiring a shift in his weight. The fight was glaringly not equal. Aedelric was clearly superior, his movements flowing like water, his strikes precise and inevitable, while Hákon's were heavy, desperate, and increasingly wild. The crowd, initially boisterous, had grown quiet, sensing the imbalance.

Aedelric saw his opening, clear as a bell. Hákon, in a desperate attempt to gain more ground, overextended on a wild, telegraphed swing, leaving his entire left side exposed for a fatal moment. Aedelric moved swiftly, a streak of motion. His sword, keen and eager, flashed through the air, aimed for a killing blow, a precise thrust designed to pierce Hákon's unprotected side, straight to the heart. Hákon cried out, a harsh sound of fear and surprise, reeling backward, his shield suddenly useless, hanging slack. Victory was unequivocally within Aedelric's grasp, the duel all but decided.

But before Aedelric's sword could find its mark, before the life could drain from Hákon's eyes, a burly figure surged from the very edge of the dueling ground. It was Thórir, one of Hákon's most devoted men, his face an expression of desperation and fury. Without a moment's hesitation for custom or honor, he threw himself forward, sword in hand, stepping directly between Aedelric and his doomed leader. The clang of steel echoed sharply as Thórirs' blade, gripped with desperate strength, met and deflected Aedelric's final, lethal thrust. The sudden, stunned quiet that followed was broken solely by Hákon's hoarse gasps for air and the subdued murmur of shock among the assembled Norsemen.

The crowd shouted. A roar of outrage, of disbelief, of fury. A duel was sacred, a judgment of the gods.

Intervention was an unthinkable act of sacrilege and cowardice.

Gunnar's face, moments before grimly watching the combat, contorted with rage. "Hákon!" he roared, his voice shuddering the Thing-stead. "What is the meaning of this treachery?!" He pointed at Hákon's man. "Seize him! Seize Hákon! Do not kill them!"

Eiríkr, his massive frame already moving, moved forward, axe in hand, towards Hákon and his intervening man. Astrid, her eyes blazing, tried to push through the dense crowd near the platform, desperate to reach Aedelric, to join the fray, but the press of bodies, the low light, and confusion held her back. Not everyone in the packed square had seen the intervention clearly in the wavering torchlight, adding to the chaos.

Hákon's men, few but prepared, reacted instantly. They had been positioned near the edge of the square, near the horses they had waiting. As the crowd rushed forward, yelling, they drew their weapons, creating a small, desperate pocket of resistance around Hákon and Thórir. They fought with efficiency, not to kill the villagers, but to clear a path and buy time.

Aedelric, caught off guard by the sudden intervention, was momentarily tangled in the press of bodies, hindering his quick movement. He saw Hákon, his visage a combination of fear and desperate triumph, being pulled towards the edge of the square by his men.

Gunnar's household guards, warriors loyal to the Jarl, charged ahead, attempting to reach Hákon and his men, to follow Eiríkr's lead and apprehend them. However, the sheer density of the outraged crowd and the chaos of the moment slowed their progress. Villagers, caught between the fleeing men and the pursuing guards, stumbled and fell, adding to the confusion.

Hákon and his men fought their way through the edge of the square, towards the waiting horses. One of Hákon's men fell, cut down by a villager's axe in the frenzied scramble. But the others reached the horses, mounting swiftly.

As they galloped away into the darkness, disappearing into the night that surrounded the torch-lit square, Hákon's voice, thin but filled with venom, carried back on the wind. "I will return, Gunnar! And I will have my vengeance! This is not over!"

The Thing-stead was left in chaos. The duel was unfinished, its outcome interrupted by human treachery. Hákon Bersason, defeated in combat but saved by his men, had escaped, his ambition and hatred now fueled by public humiliation and an intense desire for revenge. Aedelric stood in the center of the square, sword in hand, the weight of the mail suddenly heavier, the cheers of the crowd replaced by the angry murmurs and shouts of the villagers. The duel had settled his fate for now, but the fight for Njardarheimr, for his family's place within it, had just become far more complicated.

CHAPTER 6

Part 1: Aftermath

Gunnar stood on the speaker's stone, his face an expression of cold fury and frustration. Hákon, the ambitious son of his old friend, had not only challenged his authority but had publicly shamed the sacred ritual of the duel. His escape and his parting threat of vengeance hung dense in the air, a dark promise for the future of Njardarheimr. Gunnar's gaze swept over the faces of his people, taking in the confusion, the anger, and the lingering unease. Hákon had succeeded, at least partially, in sowing discord.

The household guards, slowed by the chaotic crowd, were now trying to restore order, their voices sharp as they urged people to disperse.

Aedelric, standing in the center of the dueling ground, sword still in hand, perceived the weight of the mail, the burden of the moment. He had been ready to end the duel, to claim victory and the tenuous acceptance it might bring, only to be thwarted by Hákon's cowardice. The cheers that had begun to rise for him had been drowned out amid the roar of outrage against Hákon's men. Now, the villagers looked at him with a mixture of lingering curiosity and renewed suspicion. The duel was inconclusive, his fate still hanging in the balance.

Asa, her countenance pale with fear and anger, pushed her way through the thinning crowd. Sassa held firmly against her. Astrid, her attempt to intervene thwarted, followed closely behind, her eyes hard. They reached Aedelric, standing beside him, a silent, defiant front against the still-murmuring villagers.

Gunnar descended from the speaker's stone, his stride purposeful. He reached Aedelric, Asa, and Astrid, his expression grim. "This changes nothing," he said, his voice muted, for their ears alone. "Hákon's treachery... it has angered the gods. And my people." He looked at Aedelric. "Your victory was clear, Aedelric. The gods' will... it was interrupted, not denied."

He turned to the remaining household guards. "Clear the square!" he commanded, his voice pulsing with authority once more. "See the people to their homes! Eiríkr, take men. Search the immediate area. See if Hákon and his dogs can be found. But be cautious. They are desperate now."

Eiríkr nodded, gathering a few of the most capable warriors, and they moved quickly towards the edge of the square, disappearing into the darkness in pursuit.

Gunnar turned back to Aedelric, Asa, and Astrid. "Come back to the longhouse. We must speak. And decide our following steps." He looked at Asa, his expression softening slightly. "And we must care for my granddaughter. She has seen enough chaos for one night."

They walked back towards the longhouse, leaving the still-stirring Thing-stead behind. The air in the longhouse was saturated with the lingering tension from Hákon's intrusion and the chaos.

Gunnar led them to the central hearth, where a fire still burned brightly, giving warmth and a sense of fragile normalcy. Asa plopped on a bench near the fire, adjusting Sassa in her arms. Astrid sat next to her, her hand lying on her sword hilt, her gaze hard. Aedelric stood, still clad in mail, his sword at his side, watching Gunnar, waiting.

Gunnar sat opposite them; his expression marked with the load of his responsibilities and the uncertainty of the future. "Hákon's actions tonight... they were a direct challenge to my authority," Gunnar said, his voice muted and grim. "And a grave insult to the gods. He has made himself an outlaw. An enemy of Njardarheimr."

He looked at Aedelric. "You fought well, Aedelric. You proved yourself the better warrior. The people saw it.

Even those who did not see the intervention... they saw you standing victorious, and Hákon fleeing like a coward." He paused. "This... it helps. It shows strength. It shows the gods did not abandon you."

But the victory was incomplete. Hákon had escaped, and his threat of vengeance was real. Gunnar knew Hákon's cunning, his ability to gather support from those who were resentful or ambitious. He would not disappear quietly into the wilderness. He would seek allies, build strength, and return to challenge Gunnar and, more importantly, Asa's right to inherit.

"Hákon will seek help," Gunnar said, voicing his concern. "From those who oppose me. From those who resent Asa's position. Perhaps even from outside Njardarheimr. He will spread lies. Twist the truth. He will use your presence here, Aedelric, your faith, to turn people against us."

The dilemma was now more complex than ever. Aedelric's life was no longer solely on trial; their very presence in Njardarheimr had become a catalyst for internal conflict, a threat to Gunnar's leadership and Asa's future.

"What do we do now, Father?" Asa asked, her voice quiet but firm, her gaze meeting Gunnar's.

Gunnar sighed, passing a hand over his face. "We wait. We prepare. Eiríkr will search, but I doubt he will find them tonight. Hákon planned this. He had horses ready. He has allies, even here, who helped him." He looked at Aedelric. "You cannot leave, Aedelric. Not now. It would be seen as a weakness. As an admission of guilt. And it would leave Asa and Sassa vulnerable."

He looked at Asa. "Your position is stronger now, daughter. The people saw you return, saw your child, saw this Saxon fight for you. But Hákon's escape... it leaves a wound. A threat that must be dealt with."

Astrid spoke then, her voice hard. "He will return. And he will not come alone."

Gunnar nodded grimly. "I know. We must be ready. We must strengthen our defenses. We must also consolidate support within the village. Hákon's treachery tonight... it will turn many against him. But there will be others... those he has already swayed... who will side with him."

He looked at Aedelric again, a new assessment in his eyes. "You are a warrior, Aedelric a, skilled one. You have proven your loyalty to my daughter. To my granddaughter." He paused. "You are also a Saxon. A Christian. This is a challenge. For you. For us. But perhaps... it is also a strength. You know another world. There are different ways of fighting. Of different ways of thinking."

Aedelric met Gunnar's gaze, understanding the offer. He was no longer only a guest whose fate was to be decided. He was a potential ally, a warrior who could help defend Njardarheimr against the threat Hákon represented. "My Lord," Aedelric said, his voice firm. "I will stand with you. With Asa. With Njardarheimr. Against Hákon. Against anyone who threatens my family."

Gunnar nodded, a trace of approval in his eyes. "Good. We will need your strength. Your skill." He looked at Asa, then at Sassa, with a sincere tenderness through his gaze. "My granddaughter... she is a bridge. Between worlds. Between people. Perhaps... she is a sign. Those things can change. That the old ways... may not always be the only ways."

He rose from the bench, the load of his responsibilities settling back onto his shoulders. "For tonight... we rest. We recover. Tomorrow... the work begins. The work of preparing for Hákon's return. And the work of securing Njardarheimr's future."

He looked at Aedelric. "You will remain here, in my home, under my direct protection. And you will train with my warriors. With Eiríkr. With Astrid. You will show them your skill. Earn their respect."

He looked at Asa. "You and Sassa will remain here as well. Safe." He looked at Astrid. "You will remain here. By my daughter's side. And you will help prepare our defenses."

The decisions were made. The immediate crisis had passed, but the long-term threat remained. Hákon's escape had not ended the conflict; it had merely shifted the battlefield. Aedelric, the Saxon warrior, was now inextricably linked to the fate of Njardarheimr, his presence as a source of both danger and potential strength. The fight for acceptance, for survival, for the future of a family born against all odds, was nowhere near over. It had just entered a new, more perilous phase.

Part 2: Harald Fairhair's Arrival

That night, the longhouse offered a fragile sanctuary, but sleep remained a restless visitor. Aedelric and Asa, with Sassa positioned between them, retired to Asa's sleeping area, a space shared with Gunnar. It was not unlike the communal sleeping arrangements Aedelric was familiar with from his own home in Wessex, yet the tension of the evening, the lingering threat of Hákon's escape, kept his mind sharp and wary. Eiríkr and his men returned hours later that night, their search unsuccessful. Hákon and his remaining followers had disappeared into the vast, unforgiving wilderness, leaving no trace. The knowledge that Hákon was out there, plotting vengeance, was a cold weight in the darkness.

Morning arrived with a grey, piercing chill. Inside the longhouse, the household stirred slowly. Some warriors were already tending to the hearth, the smell of firewood smoke filling the air, while others still lay wrapped in furs, seeking warmth. Gunnar sat by the central fire, his face furrowed with the weariness of a sleepless night, discussing the events with Eiríkr and a few trusted men. Asa and Aedelric were also near the fire, sharing a quiet moment, Sassa awake and alert in Asa's arms. Astrid was sharpening her sword nearby, the scrape-scrape a familiar, grounding sound.

Suddenly, a disturbance broke out outside. The distant blare of a war-horn, sharp and insistent, cut through the morning air, followed by the heavy rattle of armored men at the main gate. A frantic shout resounded through the square. Moments later, the heavy door of the longhouse burst open, and a young warrior from Njardarheimr stumbled in, breathless, his eyes open with urgency.

"Jarl Gunnar!" he gasped, his voice resounding through the hall, straining against the sound of faraway shouts. "Harald! Harald Fairhair is at the main gate! With many warriors! They demand entry, Jarl! They are not stopping!"

A collective stillness fell over the longhouse. Harald Fairhair. The name alone carried immense weight. He was a powerful, ambitious Jarl from the south, consolidating his rule and demanding fealty from all who lived in what he now claimed as his kingdom, a unified Norway. Gunnar had dealt with Harald before; their relationship was a tenuous balance of uneasy respect and latent tension. They had never seen eye to eye on Harald's claims of dominance, their disagreements seething beneath the surface, but it had never escalated to open conflict.

Gunnar rose swiftly, his weariness replaced by the sharp alertness of a leader facing a sudden, formidable threat. "Eiríkr! Gather the warriors! Quickly!" He turned to Asa and Aedelric. "Come. We will meet them at the gate." It was a calculated move, showing strength by not forcing Harald to enter the heart of his hall immediately, but instead meeting him on the threshold, on neutral ground.

Asa quickly handed Sassa to Elara, the household wet-nurse, her motions fluid and calm, even as her heart quickened. Aedelric was already at Gunnar's side. Together, the three of them advanced with intent towards the longhouse doors, followed by Eiríkr and the rapidly arming Njardarheimr warriors.

They reached the main gate to find a tense scene. Outside the heavy wooden doors, Harald Fairhair sat astride a mighty warhorse, his armored retinue lined up behind him, a formidable, disciplined force numbering in the dozens. Their banners, emblazoned with Harald's raven sigil, snapped in the cold wind. Harald himself was a man of imposing presence, his gaze surveying over the fortifications of Njardarheimr with an air of absolute authority.

"Harald," Gunnar's voice was firm, carrying across the small gap. "To what do we owe this early visit?"

Harald dismounted, his boots thudding onto the earth, his look piercing. "Gunnar," he pronounced, his voice full and resonant. "I have come for answers. And for justice. My path is long, and I prefer to conduct my business within halls, not on the dirt road. Will you allow us entry, or must we speak through a locked gate?" His words were a challenge, veiled in the veneer of politeness.

Gunnar's expression remained unreadable. He assessed the numbers, the disciplined stance of Harald's men, and the so-called king's fixed gaze. Refusing would be an act of outright defiance, likely leading to immediate conflict. To allow entry was to invite a serpent into his nest, but it bought time and perhaps more information. "You are a Jarl, Harald, and you demand hospitality," Gunnar replied, his voice composed, projecting strength despite the disadvantage. "Enter. Our hall is cold, but our hearth is warm." He gave a subtle nod to the guards at the gate, who, with a grunt, began to pull open the massive timber doors.

Harald gave a slow, assessing nod, a hint of satisfaction in his eyes. He motioned for a select few of his guards to follow, leaving the bulk of his forces outside, a clear reminder of his overwhelming power. Harald stepped inside Njardarheimr's outer defenses, his look sweeping the hall with an air of absolute authority. Behind him, his chosen retinue fanned out, their movements precise, their weapons ready, their presence as a silent, undeniable challenge.

A tense standoff immediately gripped the hall. Gunnar's warriors, few compared to Harald's entourage, stood ready, weapons in hand. Eiríkr, his massive form a bulwark, took a position near Gunnar. Asa, Aedelric, and Astrid moved closer together, a small, defiant unit. Asa, her face a mask of calm resolve, quietly moved towards the youthful Elara, who held Sassa near the hearth, ensuring her daughter was safe. As she did so, she subtly drew a small, sharp dagger from her belt, concealing it behind her back.

Harald's eyes settled on Gunnar, ignoring the others for a moment. "Gunnar," he said, his voice full and resonant, carrying through the tense silence. He looked around the hall with a slow, assessing gaze. "You have done well for yourself here. Your hall is... impressive." It was a compliment, but suffused with a trace of appraisal, of measuring Gunnar's wealth and strength.

Gunnar met his gaze, his own steady. "Surely you did not come all this way, Harald, merely to comment on my hall," Gunnar said, standing taller, meeting Harald's imposing presence head-on.

Harald's expression changed, the casual assessment replaced by a grim purpose. "No, Gunnar, I did not," he agreed, his voice stiffening. "I have come seeking answers. And justice." He paused, his look sweeping over the faces in the hall, lingering for a moment on Asa, on Aedelric, then back to Gunnar. "My son... Trygvi... was found dead on the road to the south. With some of his men."

Asa, Aedelric, and Astrid exchanged quick, startled glances. Trygvi. They had almost forgotten the encounter in the face of the subsequent chaos in the village. The consequences of that swift, brutal fight had arrived, not in the form of Hákon's vengeance, but in the far more dangerous shape of Harald Fairhair's wrath. A chilling knot of fear tightened in their stomachs, but they remained silent, their faces betraying nothing. Asa's grip on the concealed dagger tightened.

"My condolences, Harald," Gunnar said, his voice grave. He knew the customs, the expectation of vengeance for a kinsman, even one Harald might not have cared for deeply. "A great sorrow."

"Sorrow is for the weak, Gunnar," Harald said, his voice harsh. "This is about justice. About authority." He advanced further into the hall, his warriors mirroring his movement. "Trygvi was my blood. His death on land I claim as mine is an insult. A challenge." His gaze was stern, unwavering. "I will find who did this. And I will bring swift justice upon them. And depending on who they are, and why they did this... I will decide if that same judgment falls upon their entire village."

The implicit threat wafted in the air, heavy and chilling. Asa, Aedelric, and Astrid perceived the weight of it, the terrifying possibility that their actions on the road could bring Harald's fury down upon Njardarheimr. They remained silent, their fear masked by ingrained discipline.

Harald's gaze, sharp and unsettling, broke from the general survey of the hall and fixed upon Asa. He hadn't seen her in some time, and his eyes traveled over her with disturbing scrutiny. A slow, predatory smile brushed his lips as he noted the woman she had become, the youthful awkwardness replaced by a striking, if still somewhat untested, maturity. "Young Asa," he said, drawling, his voice oozing with insinuation, "grown indeed." He leaned forward slightly, his eyes never leaving her face, making her skin crawl. "Tell me, girl, has some man claimed you yet? Have you been ridden?" The questions were crude, deliberately degrading, thrown as rocks into the tense silence. Gunnar had a surge of protective fury; the insult stung sharply. He saw the slight flinch in Asa, the tightening around Aedelric's eyes. But he recognized the game instantly. Harald was prodding, testing for a reaction, hoping to ignite Gunnar's temper and force a mistake. Gunnar held his ground, his expression carefully neutral, refusing to rise to the bait. He would not let Harald dictate the terms or reveal the depth of the offense. Aedelric, Asa, and Astrid remained statuesque, their silence a proof of the precariousness of the moment. They knew any outburst would be disastrous. It was Gunnar, ever the strategist, even in the face of personal insult, who broke the charged pause, smoothly drawing the dangerous so-called king's focus back where it belonged. "Again, my condolences, Harald."

Harald now had his full attention on Gunnar. "I heard the raid on Wessex did not go well," he stated, his tone carrying a note of almost casual cruelty. "That almost all of your seasoned warriors... were lost to the sea, that Rán had taken them." It was a fact, brutally delivered. Gunnar's losses were well known, a weakness Harald was aware of. "Did any return with wealth?" Harald asked, his look sharp, assessing Gunnar's reaction. Gunnar knew Harald likely had informants, spies planted in villages to report on the strengths and weaknesses of potential rivals. He could not hide everything, but he could choose what to reveal.

"Many did not return, Harald," Gunnar replied, his voice composed, acknowledging the truth of the losses. "But not all was lost. Two ships returned, and not empty-handed." It was a small fortune, enough to help Njardarheimr recover, but not enough to draw undue attention, he hoped. He wondered, briefly, who Harald's informant could be, but quickly refocused on the man before him.

Harald's expression was unreadable for a moment, a trace of something, perhaps reluctant respect for Gunnar's resilience, or simply calculation, in his eyes. "It must have been painful," he said, the words almost sympathetic, but the manner was cold, assessing. "To lose so much, so quickly." He paused, and the true purpose of his words emerged. "Summer raids are upon us, Gunnar. I would be... happy to help. To provide aid. With my ships. My men." It was an offer of 'assistance' that was a veiled threat, a statement that Harald knew Njardarheimr was vulnerable, that he saw Gunnar as weak, perhaps even ripe for conquest under the guise of protection.

Harald then shifted, a broad smile appearing on his face, though it did not reach his eyes. "But let us rejoice, Gunnar! Your daughter has returned! I heard of it. A blessing indeed." He looked at Asa again, his gaze still holding that disconcerting intensity. Gunnar knew Harald was baiting him, prodding him, looking for a reaction that would confirm his assessment of weakness. But Gunnar did not take the bait.

"I am grateful for the offer, Harald," Gunnar said, his voice composed, measured, neither accepting nor outright refusing. "We will need to think heavily on what this summer will bring. On how best to protect our people."

Harald's smile faded, replaced by his grim, purposeful expression. He seized the opportunity to shift back to the matter of his son. "This incident with my son, Trygvi," Harald said, his voice keen. "Do you know anything of it, Gunnar? Have you heard anything? Perhaps your villagers... might know something?" He watched Gunnar closely, his eyes missing nothing.

Gunnar met his gaze directly. "I know nothing of this incident, Harald," he replied truthfully. "Nor have my men heard anything." It was the truth. The encounter had been swift, brutal, and far from any witnesses Gunnar's men would have spoken to.

Harald's jaw stiffened slightly. He had expected more. "If you do hear anything, Gunnar," he said, his voice subdued and dangerous, "I expect you to come forward with any information. Promptly."

"I will do so, Harald," Gunnar replied, his voice steady, making the promise of a fellow Jarl, knowing the gravity of the situation.

Harald seemed to decide his time here was done. He had delivered his veiled threats, assessed Gunnar's strength, and planted the seeds of his purpose. "My time here is done," he said, turning towards the doors. "Other villages need to be questioned. We have a long journey."

"Ale and rest are offered, Harald," Gunnar said, extending the customary hospitality, though he knew it would be refused.

Harald waved a scornful hand. "No need, Gunnar. We must press on." It was a deliberate slight, a silent statement that Gunnar's hospitality, his food and drink, were beneath him, not worth accepting. "I will see you soon." The threat was clear: a promise of future interaction, future demands.

As Harald turned to leave, his men following suit, he stopped at the longhouse doors. He turned back, his look gliding the hall one last time before settling directly on Asa. "Asa," he said, his voice projecting through the hall, drawing all attention to her. "You returned from Wessex. How did you find your way home?"

Asa remained quiet for a moment, the weight of the question, the potential danger in her answer, bearing heavily on her. Gunnar started to speak, to answer for her, but Harald held up a hand, his look fixed on Asa. "Let the daughter of Gunnar speak for herself," he commanded.

Asa knew she had to answer. The situation was too fragile to defy Harald, to show weakness or hesitation. She met his gaze, her own steady, showcasing the leadership qualities her father had sought to instill in her. She was about to speak, but Harald cut her off. "By sea, or by land?

Asa knew the significance of the question. By sea meant a ship, perhaps salvaged, perhaps found. By land... by land meant a journey through unknown territory, a journey that might raise questions about who she was with, how she survived. She met his gaze, her voice bold and strong. "By land, Harald," she said. "We returned by land."

Harald held her gaze for a long moment, a trace of something indecipherable in his eyes. Then, a slow smile spread across his face. "By land," he repeated softly. "Truly, your return is a blessing, daughter of Gunnar." He gave a slight nod, then turned and walked out of the longhouse, his men following him, the heavy doors closing behind them with a resounding thud.

The calm that fell over the longhouse was heavy, charged with the aftermath of Harald's visit. The immediate threat had passed, but the air sizzled with the tension of what was to come. Harald Fairhair had arrived, delivered his veiled threats, and left, but his presence persisted, a dark shadow cast over Njardarheimr. The question of Trygvi's death, the unsettling interest in Asa, the precise assessment of Gunnar's vulnerability, all of it pointed to a dangerous future. The saga of Asa and Aedelric, their fight for a place in this world, had just become intertwined with the ambitions of a king-in-the-making, a man who sought to control all of Norway, and who now had reason to look closely at Njardarheimr.

Part 3: Seeds of Doubt

The heavy slam of the longhouse doors closing behind Harald Fairhair and his retinue appeared to reflect the tension left hanging in the air. The quiet that followed was not one of peace, but of a fragile calm after a storm, charged with unvoiced fears and the frightening certainty of future conflict. Gunnar stood by the hearth, his visage grim, the weight of Harald's visit settling onto his shoulders. Eiríkr, his massive frame still tense, remained at his side, his hand never far from his axe. Asa, Aedelric, and Astrid, a tight unit near the hearth, felt the lingering chill of Harald's gaze, the unsettling interest he had shown in Asa, and the veiled threats regarding Trygvi's death.

Gunnar turned to Eiríkr and Astrid, his voice subdued and urgent. "See that Harald and all his men leave our lands," he commanded. "Ensure none remain behind."

Eiríkr nodded, his expression grim. "I will take men and walk the village," he said. "Make sure none of his dogs linger."

Astrid met Gunnar's gaze, her eyes hard with resolve. "I will follow Harald from a distance," she added. "Ensure they all depart our territory. I will return and report when it is done."

Gunnar nodded, a trace of relief in his eyes at their competence and loyalty. Eiríkr gathered a few trusted warriors, and they left the longhouse, their footsteps resounding as they set out on their task. Astrid, after a brief, sharp nod to Asa and Aedelric, also departed, moving with the quiet purpose of a seasoned scout.

Asa retrieved Sassa from the Elara, grasping her daughter close, finding peace in the warmth of her small body. The terror that had tightened in her chest during

Harald's questioning slowly started to subside, supplanted by a cold anger. Harald's arrogance, his blatant disregard for Gunnar's authority, and his disturbing appraisal of her had provoked a fierce protectiveness, not just for herself and her family, but for her home, Njardarheimr.

Aedelric watched Gunnar, his expression copying the Jarl's grim resolve. He had faced powerful men in Wessex, but Harald Fairhair possessed a different kind of power, the ambition of a man forging a kingdom, a man who saw people and villages as pieces on a board to be controlled. His presence here, he knew, was now a significant complicating factor, a potential spark for the larger conflict Harald seemed intent on igniting.

Gunnar finally broke the silence, his look sweeping over Asa and Aedelric. "Come," he said, his voice quieter now, gesturing towards the back of the longhouse, towards his private quarters. "We must speak. In private."

Asa and Aedelric looked, a wordless understanding flowing between them. This was the moment. They followed Gunnar into the private room, the heavy door closing behind them, shutting out the hushed silence of the hall.

Once inside, with Sassa settled safely in Asa's arms, Asa looked at her father, her voice subdued but steady. "Father," she began, her gaze resolute. "There is something you must know. About Trygvi. About his death."

Gunnar's eyes narrowed a bit, a trace of anticipation in their depths. "I thought as much," he murmured. "Harald's look told me there was more to the tale. Speak it."

Asa, with Aedelric standing silently beside her, recounted the encounter on the road. She described Trygvi's arrogance, his leering threats, and his intent to harm her and Astrid. She spoke of their desperate defense, of Aedelric's readiness to protect them, and of her own swift, deadly shot that had ended Trygvi's life. Gunnar listened without interrupting, his jaw tightening, his breath slow and heavy.

When she finished describing the moment the arrow struck, he exhaled through his nose. "So the boy brought his own doom," he said in a low voice. "I see."

Asa continued, explaining how, in the chaos of their journey and the return, with Hákon, the encounter had been pushed from their minds, with the consequences not fully considered until Harald's arrival. "With everything that has happened, Father," she finished, her voice colored with regret, "we did not even think… to tell you." Gunnar studied her for a long moment, then shifted his gaze to Aedelric. "And you?" he asked. "You stand by her account?" Aedelric nodded once. "Every word, my Lord. I would have killed him myself had she not been faster."

Gunnar let out a slow breath, the weight of truth coming down on him. "Then it is done," he said. "And what is done cannot be undone." He looked back to Asa, his voice more gentle but still edged with the gravity of a Jarl facing the consequences of bloodshed. "You did what you had to do to live. I will not fault you for that." He looked at Asa, at Aedelric, at the innocent face of his granddaughter.

"Trygvi," Gunnar finally said, a weary sigh escaping him. "Yes. That sounds like a son of Harald. Arrogant. Cruel." He ran a hand over his face. "It is not an ideal situation, my daughter. To have the blood of Harald's son on our hands. But I understand what happened." He looked at Aedelric. "You defended them. You did what any warrior should do."

He rose from his seat, walking to the small, cold hearth, his back to them for a moment. The reality of their situation pressed hard on him. Harald's threat wasn't only about Trygvi's death; it was about dominance, about Harald's ambition to unite Norway under his rule. And

Njardarheimr, weakened by the losses at sea, was vulnerable.

Gunnar turned back to them, his expression resolute. "Harald has many warriors," he said, his voice grim. "His forces could be four times ours. Perhaps more." He turned back to them and looked at them. "We have perhaps forty capable warriors to defend Njardarheimr. Forty against a vast tide of hundreds of warriors."

The numbers were stark, the reality chilling. But Gunnar's gaze was steadfast. "We must focus now," he said, his voice firm. "On better defense. On preparation. We must strengthen our palisade. Train our warriors. And we must be ready for Harald's return. Or for Hákon to seek allies and return with force."

He looked at Asa, then at Aedelric, with an intense certainty in his eyes. "Know this," Gunnar said, his voice intense. "I am with you. I understand. And I will stand with you. With Asa. With Sassa. With Njardarheimr. No matter the cost."

Asa had a surge of relief, of fierce loyalty. Her father, her Jarl, stood with them. Aedelric met Gunnar's gaze, a quiet pledge of allegiance passing between the Saxon Thegn and the Norse Jarl. They were bound now, not just by Asa and Sassa, but by the common threat of Harald Fairhair and the need to defend their home. The conversation was over, the truth lay bare, the path ahead full of danger, but they would confront it together. The seeds of suspicion had been sown, but the roots of loyalty and determination were also taking hold.

CHAPTER 7

Part 1: Roots of Loyalty

The shadows in the longhouse had deepened considerably since Astrid and Eiríkr had burst back through the doors, their faces stern. A few hours had passed, hours spent confirming their report: Harald Fairhair's men had indeed pulled back, melting away from the village borders as quickly as they had appeared, a reprieve, perhaps, or a calculated move. Either way, it bought Njardarheimr a sliver of time.

Jarl Gunnar stood by the central hearth, though no fire burned now, only embers shining dimly in the pit. The air appeared stale and heavy, redolent of old smoke, dried fish, and unwashed wool. Around him sat Asa, Astrid, Eiríkr, Aedelric, and a handful of Gunnar's most trusted household guards, men whose loyalty had been proven in countless raids and lean winters. Their faces, scored with fatigue and worry lines, caught the low light.

"They are gone," Gunnar stated, his rough voice like grinding stones. "For now." He motioned toward a roughly drawn map scratched into the packed earth floor beside him. It depicted the village, the surrounding palisade, the slope down to the fjord, and the dense, unforgiving forest behind. "We have an unknown amount of time and hope the gods are kind, before Harald or even Hákon returns with a larger force. We cannot wait."

He knelt, tracing a finger along the palisade line. "Our defenses are... adequate for raiders, perhaps. Not for an army." He looked up, meeting the eyes of his small council. "We must strengthen the palisade. Double the height in key sections," he indicated the landward side, "and reinforce the weak points where the ground dips." "Wood will be needed," Eiríkr stated, his voice practical. "Lots of it. Felling, hauling, shaping..."

"It must be done," Gunnar cut in, his gaze hard. "Every able-bodied soul not tending essential tasks will be on the palisade. We place sharpened stakes in the ground outside," his finger jabbed at the earth before the palisade line, "angled outwards. Tripping hazards. Impaler's."

He moved his finger to the area near the fjord. "The slope is steep here, a natural defense. But they could still attempt a landing. We need archers positioned higher up, overlooking the water. And traps." He looked at Aedelric. "Your people use pits, do they not? Concealed pits with stakes?"

Aedelric, who had been listening intently, nodded. "Yes, Lord. 'Wolf pits' are simple, but effective at breaking a charge or isolating men. We can line the likely approach routes from the forest as well." His Norse accent was becoming more comfortable on his tongue; it still carried the reverberation of his Saxon origins.

"Good," Gunnar grunted. "We also need to clear lines of sight beyond the palisade. Any thick brush that could serve as cover must be cut back. And we need positions for our melee fighters. Places where a small force can hold back a larger one, funneling them into kill zones." He looked at Astrid. "You have a good eye for ground, Astrid. Where would you place the shieldwall if they breached the outer defenses? Where can we ambush stragglers?"

Astrid, quiet until now, leaning forward, her eyes examining the map. "The narrow path leading from the northern gate," she said, her voice muted but clear. "We can form a shieldwall there, bottlenecking them. And small groups, hidden in the longhouses near the palisade gaps, could strike their flanks as they enter." She pointed to areas within the village layout. "If they push too far in, the lanes between the houses can become death traps."

Asa spoke up, her look fixed on the map. "Arrows will be key, Father. We need more fletchers working constantly. And positions for the archers that give them wide fields of fire without leaving them too exposed." She pointed to the rooftops of the longhouses closest to the palisade. "Elevated positions. And small, reinforced platforms behind the palisade itself."

Gunnar listened, his head nodding slowly. "Agreed. Eiríkr, weapons and armor are yours. Every blade must be sharp, every shield sound. Any broken rings on mail must be mended. We have little new gear coming in. We use what we have, and we make it work."

He looked at Aedelric again. "You, Saxon, will take the men and women who are not seasoned warriors: the younger lads, the older men, the women who can hold an axe or spear. You will train them. Make them into fighters. They may not have the bloodlust of a seasoned warrior, but they can hold a line, they can defend their homes."

Aedelric placed a hand on his chest, a gesture more formal than the Norse were used to. "I will do my best, Jarl. I have trained men for battle before."

"I know," Gunnar said, a trace of something akin to esteem in his eyes. "Your skills are needed now, more than ever." He rose, the joints in his knees protesting slightly. "This is what we discuss among ourselves. But the village must know. They must understand the threat, and they must choose."

Jarl Gunnar emerged from the longhouse, the smaller group trailing behind him. The news, though not yet official, had washed through Njardarheimr with the speed of a tossed stone hitting still water. People were already gathering in the open space before the Thingstead stones, a nervous knot of villagers and warriors. The late afternoon light did little to warm the cold air that had spread over them. Farmers leaned on hoes; their faces creased with worry. Women held their children closer. Warriors, their usual swagger muted, gripped the hilts of their swords and axes, glances sweeping the faces around them. Unease, thick and palpable, hovered in the air like mist off the fjord.

There were whispers, furtive glances, who could be trusted? Was there a snake in their midst, perhaps still holding loyalty to the defeated Hákon, or worse, already bought by Harald?

Gunnar mounted the low, worn stone platform of the Thingstead. He stood tall, a figure of weathered oak against the grey sky, his expression stern but not devoid of grim resolve. Asa, Astrid, Eiríkr, and Aedelric stood near the base of the stones, there being a silent show of unity.

"Hear me, people of Njardarheimr!" Gunnar's voice, though not a shout, carried across the assembly, cutting through the soft talk. It was a voice honed by years of commanding, a voice that demanded attention. "The gods are testing us! How else can we explain the events of these past days? The return of Asa and Astrid, pulled from the sea's icy grip, a sign of Freyja's favor, perhaps? Followed so swiftly by the shadow of Harald Fairhair at our borders!"

He paused, letting the force of his words settle. His gaze swept over the crowd, lingering for a moment on Aedelric, who stood stoic and watchful beside Asa. "And this man, Aedelric," Gunnar continued, his voice steady, "a Saxon, a Christian, yet he stands here, having faced the sea's fury and is alongside my daughter and Astrid." A low whisper spread through the crowd. Gunnar held up a hand. "The will of the gods for him is not yet fully known," he admitted, a rare public acknowledgement of uncertainty. "But I know this, he is here for a reason. He is with me now." His gaze challenged anyone to dispute it.

He returned to the immediate threat. "Harald Fairhair seeks to grind us under his heel! He seeks to break our independence, our way of life! His scouts were here, on our land, just hours ago! And Hákon, his grip loosened, may seek to rally those still foolish enough to follow him, perhaps even turn them against us in their desperation!" Gunnar laid out the situation plainly, the stark reality of their outnumbered position hanging unspoken but understood.

"Preparations must be made!" he declared, his voice increasing slightly. "Defenses must be improved! Our palisade strengthened until it is a thorny shield against any who would assault us!" He then shifted, his tone stressing the mundane still essential. "But we cannot forget the tasks of life! The fields must be tended! The harvest is brought in! If winter finds us unprepared, we will perish, not by Harald's hand, but by our neglect!"

He outlined the immediate changes. "Hunting parties will now go out with no less than two warriors! No man or woman walks alone beyond the sight of our village! We will train! We will mend! We will prepare as if the Eye of Odin himself is upon us!"

Gunnar paused, his gaze once more sweeping across the faces before him. The anxiety was still there, a tightness in their shoulders, a lack of ease in their stances. This was the crucial moment. "Listen to me now, all of you," he said, his voice more gentle, but no less firm. "The way forward is grim. It will be hard. There will be hunger, and there will be fear. If any among you feel you cannot face this, if you wish to seek a new home, away from the shadow of Harald and the coming storm... do it now. Leave Njardarheimr now. No shame will be placed upon you. Your lives are your own to command."

He waited. The quietness lingered, interrupted solely by the cry of a distant gull. Faces looked at faces. Farmers glanced at the warriors. Children clung to their parents. No one moved. Not a single soul turned to leave. A unified breath seemed to be held, then slowly released. Loyalty. It wasn't just a word; it was the roots that tied them to this harsh land, to each other, to Gunnar.

A young warrior near the front, a man named Bjorn with a scar across his eyebrow, found his voice. "Jarl," he called out, his voice a little hesitant. "The summer raid...

How are we to earn our keep? Provide for our families? Without gold or silver..."

Gunnar knew the implicit truth behind the words. The Warriors needed the promise of wealth and success to stay. It wasn't just loyalty; it was practicality. He opened his mouth to speak, unsure how to answer truthfully without breaking their fragile resolve, when he felt a light touch on his arm.

Asa, standing close to the platform, whispered up to him, her eyes radiant with a fierce, sudden idea. "Father," she uttered, low enough only for him to hear. "I have that covered. Do not worry about the warriors' keep."

Gunnar looked at his daughter, surprise playing across his face. How could she possibly have that covered? But he trusted his daughter.

He turned back to the assembly. "Bjorn," he said, his voice firm. "There will be no summer raid this year. Our fight is here, in our home. Defending it. Listen to me: I will ensure that all my warriors are taken care of. Their families will not go without."

There was a beat of uncertainty, then a wave of acceptance passed through the warriors. Gunnar's word was their bond. He had always looked after his own, and that loyalty flowed both ways. No warriors left.

"Good," Gunnar said, his gaze roaming over his united people. "Then there is work to be done! Every hand is needed! Go now! Get to your tasks!"

He gestured to the four beside the platform. "Asa, Astrid, Eiríkr, Aedelric! You will oversee the preparations!" He pointed towards the palisade. "Asa! You know the land, you know defense! Direct the strengthening of our walls! Position our archers for maximum coverage!"

He turned to Astrid. "Astrid! You faced many men! You know the methods! Organize our ground defenses! Where the shieldwall will stand! Where the ambush points will lie! Make the ground itself fight with us!"

"Eiríkr!" Gunnar's voice was sharp. "Weapons and armor are your charge! Scour the village! Mend every shield, sharpen every axe! We fight with what we have!"

His gaze fell upon Aedelric. "Aedelric! Take the untested! The young, the old, the women who will stand with us! Train them in the ways of the shield and spear! Make every person a defender of Njardarheimr!" He knew that training them into seasoned fighters would be a monumental task, given the limited time and resources, but Aedelric's experience offered their best chance.

Gunnar clasped his hands behind his back, his gaze hardening. "I will manage the daily tasks of the village and the hunting parties. We will survive this winter, but first... we must survive battle."

The assembly began to break up, the villagers dispersing with a new sense of purpose, the anxiety replaced by a grim determination. The Root of Loyalty had been tested, and in the face of the storm, it had held firm. The work is about to begin.

Part 2: Toil and Timber

The brief, tense silence after Gunnar's address was shattered by a flurry of activity that would not cease for days. Sleep turned into a luxury, food a necessity wolfed down standing, and the rhythm of life in Njardarheimr shifted from the seasonal cycles of farming to the frantic, unyielding pulse of preparation for war. The air, already carrying the tang of the fjord, now thickened, laden with the scent of newly cut timber, plowed earth, and the biting smoke from the ever-working smithy.

Asa threw herself into strengthening the palisade with a ferocity born of desperation and an ingrained need to protect her home and the family she had just been reunited with. Under her sharp eye, teams worked tirelessly from before dawn until the light failed. The measured chop of axes resounded from the forest edge, where select trees were felled, stout oaks and sturdy pines that would become the new backbone of their defenses. The work was brutal. Men and women strained against thick ropes, hauling the heavy logs over uneven ground, their muscles burning, hands roughened and raw within hours.

Asa moved among them, her voice distinct and authoritative, directing where the new, larger posts should be set, urging on those who flagged, her gaze missing nothing. She wasn't afraid to heft a rope herself, to help roll a notably stubborn log into place, earning the respect of the villagers who saw their Jarl's daughter working as hard as any of them.

Gunnar was often nearby, overseeing the overall operation, his presence a quiet anchor. He and Asa didn't need long conversations; a mutual glance, a brief nod was often enough. He saw the competence in her, the natural leadership he had always known she possessed.

One evening, as the last light faded and the weary workers shuffled back towards the longhouses, Gunnar approached Asa as she rubbed a knot in her shoulder. "You handle them well, daughter," he said, his voice gruff while laced with genuine approval. "They listen to you."

Asa looked at him, a tired smile touching her lips. "They listen because it is their home, Father. And because they trust you."

Gunnar placed a heavy hand on her shoulder for a brief moment, a rare physical display of affection from the stoic Jarl. "And they trust you, Asa. You carry the blood of Njardarheimr." It was a simple acknowledgement, though in that moment, amid the raw timber and dug earth, it spoke volumes about their renewed bond and common burden.

Astrid, tasked with the tactical layout of the defense, moved with a different kind of intensity. Her body was still recovering from the ordeal of her captivity, but her mind was sharp, focused by the immediate threat. She worked closely with the experienced warriors, scouting the land outside the palisade, her eyes reading the slopes, the stands of trees, the natural contours of the earth like a map.

She pointed out where the main shieldwall would form if the palisade were breached, a kill zone where the enemy would be funneled into a tight, vulnerable mass. She identified hidden dips and clusters of rocks where small groups of warriors could conceal themselves for ambushes, striking at the enemy's flanks before retreating. Her explanations were concise, drawing on her brutal experiences in the shieldwall. "They will expect a frontal assault," she told the warriors gathered around her, tracing lines in the dirt with a stick. "We give them that, but we hit them where they do not expect. Like wolves from the trees."

Eiríkr was her shadow during these planning sessions, not just because he was assigned to weapons, but because he wanted to be near her. In private moments away from the others, often as the sun lowered under the horizon, coloring the sky with burning hues, they found brief pockets of solace together. One evening, as they sat on a rock overlooking the fjord, the sounds of the village preparations were a remote murmur. Eiríkr gently took Astrid's hand. "You are tired," he said, his thumb stroking the back of her hand.

Astrid leaned her head on his shoulder. "We all are. But it is good work. Necessary work." She was quiet for a moment, then spoke, her voice just a whisper. "There is something else, Eiríkr." He turned to face her; his brow knitted with worry. "What is it? Are you hurt?"

She shook her head, a small, uncertain smile flickering on her lips. Her hand went to her belly. "I do not think... I do not think I bled with the last moon."

Eiríkr stared at her for a moment, his eyes open wide. Then, a slow comprehension dawned, followed by a wave of emotion, disbelief, fear in the face of danger, but overriding it all, a profound and overwhelming joy. He pulled her into his arms, holding her tightly, burying his face in her hair. "Astrid..." His voice was heavy with feeling.

"In all this madness," she spoke quietly into his shoulder, "a new life."

They held to each other, the weight of the coming battle momentarily eclipsed by the fragile, precious secret they now shared. A new root of loyalty, growing in the shadow of the storm. They knew they had to keep it quiet for now; the village had enough to worry about. But the knowledge spurred their determination, giving them something intensely personal to fight for.

Eiríkr divided his time between supporting Astrid in planning and overseeing the urgent scramble for weapons and armor. The smithy was a place of constant, ear-splitting noise and searing heat. Broken sword blades were reforged into spear tips, dented helmets hammered back into shape, and chain mail meticulously mended, link by painful link. There were never enough raw materials, so ingenuity was key. Old tools were repurposed, scrap metal eagerly scavenged.

Aedelric, who was struggling with the immense task of turning untrained villagers into a fighting force. But with Astrid's help, while they had often been at odds, their joint love for Asa had become an unexpected bridge between the Saxon Thegn and the shieldmaiden. Since Aedelric had rescued her, they had begun to navigate a hesitant understanding, anchored by their mutual devotion to Asa and now, Sassa. They would exchange brief, meaningful glances, a muted acknowledgment of their shared protectorate over her and their newfound, fragile connection.

Aedelric's training ground was a scene of constant, often awkward, effort. He drilled the recruits in the basics: holding a shield correctly, a solid, round piece of wood, frequently reinforced with a simple iron boss presenting a spear point, moving together as a unit. It was a far cry from training seasoned Saxon warriors. These were people whose bodies were used to the rhythm of the farm, not the shock of the shieldwall.

Among the recruits was a young man named Leif. He was tall for his age, perhaps fifteen or sixteen, with sandy hair and a scattering of freckles across a nose that looked perpetually sunburnt. He was earnest and tried hard, but he was clumsy, often tripping over his own feet or fumbling with his shield. Yet, there was something in his eyes, a wide, hopeful vulnerability, a quickness to grin when he finally got a movement right, that snagged at Aedelric.

Leif, with an almost painful clarity, reminded Aedelric of his friend Eadric. Eadric, who had fallen at Wareham, was killed by Astrid's blade in a brutal ambush. The memory had troubled Aedelric for a long time, a bitter knot of grief and resentment. But being with Asa, loving her, and building a life with her had slowly, painstakingly helped him loosen that knot. Seeing Astrid now, seeing her weariness and her fierce protectiveness of this village and Asa, further blurred the sharp edges of that old pain.

Seeing Leif, however, brought an alternate kind of ache, the clear reminder of lives cut short, of potential loss. Aedelric found himself watching Leif more closely. He corrected his stance more often, offered extra pointers after training, and patiently showed him how to keep his shield up and use his body weight behind a spear thrust. He pushed Leif harder than some of the others, a silent test, a last hope that he could help him survive.

Leif, in turn, looked up to Aedelric, this foreign warrior who moved with such quiet competence. He heard attentively to Aedelric's instructions, practicing the movements repeatedly when Aedelric wasn't looking. A tentative connection began to form, built on shared effort and the tacit understanding of the danger they faced together. Aedelric, who had often felt isolated by his past and his faith in this Norse land, found a small measure of connection in mentoring this young man, a way to honor the memory of a lost friend by potentially saving another. He even noticed Astrid watching him train Leif sometimes, a somber, knowing look in her eyes that acknowledged the ghost standing between them.

Amid the relentless work and the heavy weight of leadership, Jarl Gunnar found his only genuine moments of respite with his granddaughter, Sassa. She was a small, warm bundle in the midst of the village's grim preparations. Asa would often bring her to where Gunnar was overseeing the work, checking on the progress of the palisade or speaking with the hunting parties as they returned.

Sassa, a bright-eyed child with Asa's determined chin and a curious gaze, was too young to grasp the danger that appeared fully. She saw only the bustle, the people working with focused energy. Gunnar, the stern, unyielding Jarl to his people, would soften visibly in her presence. He would scoop her up in his strong arms, the calluses on his hands a sharp contrast to her soft skin.

He would let her play with a smoothed piece of wood or a discarded feather, his eyes watching her with a fierce, protective love. These were the moments that reminded him *why* they were doing this. Not just for the land, not just for their honor, but for this new generation, for Sassa and children like her, so that they might have a future. He would bounce her gently, a rare, tired smile on his face, before handing her back to Asa, the load of his responsibilities settling back upon his shoulders, but his will strengthened.

The late spring days were long, stretching the hours of daylight needed for the frantic labor. The sun, when it appeared, was not yet the fierce warmth of high summer, but it stayed in the sky for what seemed like an age, demanding continued effort. The sounds of hammers, saws, and training shouts resounded in the air from dawn till dusk. Food was simple and devoured: stew, dried meat, dark bread, sustenance, not comfort, fuel for the weary bodies. Evenings were devoted to mending, sharpening, preparing for the next day's toil, or standing watch on the newly reinforced palisade under the lingering twilight.

The farmers worked the fields with a desperate urgency, not yet harvesting, but tending the young crops, weeding, making sure they had the best possible chance to flourish before any potential siege or conflict disrupted their growth. The health of the barley, rye, and oats was paramount; come winter, they would rely on this yield. The hunting parties, consistently at least two warriors strong, ventured into the woods under the constant twilight, keenly aware that they might encounter enemy scouts or rival hunters from other neighboring lands. Fishing in the fjord also continued, adding vital protein to their diet.

Every task, no matter how small, was now imbued with the pressure of their survival. Njardarheimr was transforming, not just in its physical defenses, but in the hardening of its people. Exhaustion was constant, but fear was slowly being transmuted into grim determination. The roots of loyalty, nurtured by shared labor and the bonds of family, nascent friendships, and even common past trauma, were indeed deepening in the hard ground of their home, preparing them to face the storm together.

Part 3: Final Edge

The frantic vigor had settled into a deep-seated weariness, but also a quiet, formidable resolve. The palisade was now visibly stronger, thicker in crucial sections, its sharpened stakes a bristling threat to anyone who approached. The wolf pits were dug and cunningly concealed. Lines of sight had been cleared, offering no straightforward approach for a hidden enemy. The physical shell of Njardarheimr's defense was nearly complete, a proof of the villagers' grueling labor.

Inside, the smithy had quieted somewhat, but the regular *clang-clang-clang* still echoed, the final sharpening of blades, the careful tensioning of bowstrings. Piles of arrows, fletched and tipped, lay ready in long, shallow baskets, enough, they hoped, to make any attacking force pay dearly for every foot of ground. Weapons were mended, armor patched; they would fight with what they had, and what they had was now the sharpest and strongest they could make it.

But a shell was useless without the strength and skill to defend it. The focus had shifted from building the defenses to training the defenders. The air in Njardarheimr now hummed not just with the sounds of work, but with the grunt of effort, the sharp commands of trainers, and the regular pound of practice weapons against shields and padded bodies.

Aedelric's training ground remained the most visceral representation of their efforts. He was molding the untrained, the farmers, the fishermen, the older men, the brave women, into a single, cohesive unit: the shieldwall. He knew, perhaps better than anyone here, the brutal reality of this formation. It was not about individual glory, but about standing shoulder to shoulder, a living, breathing wall of wood and iron, absorbing the shock of the enemy charge and presenting a bristling hedge of spears, swords, and axes.

"Closer!" Aedelric would roar, his voice harsh by midday. "Close the gaps! A gap is a weakness! A weakness is death!"

He had them stand in lines, shields overlapping, creating a solid barrier. He would take a practice spear himself, prodding at their defenses to demonstrate how even a hand's width could let an enemy blade through. He drilled them in the basic movements: stepping forward and back together, presenting their spear points as one, using their shields to absorb blows and push back, and using the seax when closer combat was needed.

It was grueling, bone-jarring work. Shields slammed together, feet were inevitably stepped on, and the air was laden with the smell of sweat, exertion, and the moist soil of the training ground. Aedelric didn't shy away from describing the grim reality. "Understand this," he would tell them, his voice subdued and serious after a particularly rough drill. "A shieldwall is a grinder. It is a bloody, snarling mess. Men will fall. But the wall must not break. You hold the line for the man beside you, and he holds it for you. Your life, his life, the lives of your families, depend on that piece of wood and your will to stand."

Leif, the young man who reminded Aedelric so strongly of Eadric, was still clumsy at times, but his earnestness had consolidated into a strong determination. Aedelric saw him practicing the footwork when he thought no one was watching, saw him modifying his grip on his spear, saw the absolute focus in his young eyes during drills. He still corrected Leif, but there was now a tacit understanding between them. Leif wasn't just a recruit; he was a charge, a promise Aedelric was making to a solid fighter. Leif, under Aedelric's focused attention, was improving rapidly; his shield was held more steadily, and his movements within the wall became more fluid. The awkward teenager was starting to resemble a warrior. Aedelric felt a trace of hope, a dangerous thing in these times, but one he couldn't entirely suppress.

While Aedelric built the solid foundation of the shieldwall, Asa was cultivating a different kind of force: the archers. Archery was often seen as a supplementary skill in Norse warfare, valuable for harassing skirmishes or ship-to-ship combat, but the core of battle was the clash of shields and steel. Asa knew better. Against their enemies' overwhelming numbers, skilled archers could be devastating, thinning the enemy ranks before they ever reached the palisade, breaking their charge, and picking off leaders.

She gathered the few experienced archers the village had, mostly hunters whose skills lay in stalking game, and a smaller group of recruits, anyone with a steady hand and the strength to draw a bow. Asa's skill was formidable. She moved with some quiet, coiled power, her movements economical and precise. She didn't just teach them to shoot; she taught them to *kill* effectively.

"The wind," she would instruct, holding up a damp finger to gauge the breeze off the fjord. "Always feel the wind. It is a friend or an enemy to your arrow." She taught them to judge distance by eye, to understand the arc of the arrow, and how to aim high to compensate for gravity over longer ranges. She showed them how to nock an arrow swiftly, to draw the bowstring back smoothly to their cheek, to release cleanly, letting the arrow fly true.

She had them practice from the newly built platforms behind the palisade, understanding the angles and limitations of shooting from a fixed position. She taught them to shoot in volleys, a hail of arrows descending on a single point, and to pick individual targets, the glint of mail that indicated a leader, the gaps in a shieldwall. Her instructions were calm, clear, and utterly focused on lethality. She transformed clumsy recruits into competent bowmen, and the competent into potential sharpshooters. One in particular, named Hrolf, who quickly became second, only to Asa. The whistle of practice arrows became another constant sound, a deadly song of preparation.

Jarl Gunnar, his visage a roadmap of the harsh years he had endured, spent his days overseeing the final touches, making sure that every task was completed and every resource accounted for. However, he took a moment to observe the training. He would often stand near the edge of the training ground, the ever-present weight of leadership eased slightly by the small, warm weight in his arms: his Sassa.

Sassa was an example of pure curiosity. She would gurgle and reach out a tiny hand towards the sights and sounds of the training, her shining eyes wide. Gunnar would bounce her gently, his stern gaze relaxing as he looked down at her before sweeping back across the scene before him.

He watched Aedelric relentlessly drilling the recruits, pushing them until they stumbled, then helping them up, his patience a surprising counterpoint to the brutal reality of the shieldwall. He saw the raw potential Aedelric was molding from reluctant material, saw the growing competence in Leif and the others. A grunt of approval would escape him.

Then his gaze would shift to Asa and her archers. He watched his daughter, a warrior woman, move with such poise and authority, turning simple villagers into a force capable of striking from afar. He saw the bundles of arrows, growing daily, a quiet pledge of death to anyone who approached. Pride swelled in his chest, pride in his daughter, pride in the strength of his people, and pride in the unexpected strength brought by the Saxon and the warriors.

One evening, as the training wound down and the exhausted recruits ambled towards their homes, Aedelric, Astrid, and Eiríkr found themselves together near the smithy, the lingering heat a welcome warmth in the chilly evening air. They watched the last of the fletchers packing away their tools.

"You work them hard, Saxon," Eiríkr said, wiping sweat from his brow with the back of his hand, a smile flickering on his lips. There was genuine regard in his tone now, the initial suspicion having long faded.

Aedelric offered a tired smile in return. "Hard ground requires a deep plow. The shieldwall is not for the faint of heart. It is... a grim mess."

Astrid nodded, her eyes faraway for a moment, recalling battles engaged in tight formations. "Aye. A dance with death. You teach them well. You understand the push and pull, the way the wall breathes."

Aedelric inclined his head, acknowledging her words. "I have seen shieldwalls break," he said, his voice muted. "And I have stood in ones that held against impossible odds. It is about trust. Trusting the man next to you will not falter." He paused, then looked at them, a new openness through his gaze. "But I have also seen how you Norse fight. You are fierce like wolves breaking from the pack. There is a wildness to it, a courage... It differs from our Saxon formations, but is no less deadly. Your skill with an axe, a sword..." He trailed off, a genuine esteem in his eyes. " Formidable."

Eiríkr grinned, a flash of his old humor returning despite the exhaustion. "We have our ways."

Astrid met Aedelric's gaze, a wordless acknowledgment of the complex history between them, the death of Eadric, the rescue, the shared concern for Asa. "You teach them discipline," she said. "We teach them... fire."

Aedelric nodded. "Perhaps," he said, a sense of fellowship settling between the three of them, "we can teach them both. The discipline to stand, and the fire to fight."

In that moment, the Saxon Thegn and the two Norse warriors stood together, their paths converging here in Njardarheimr, bound by the shared threat and a growing, hard-earned respect. The preparations were almost complete. The shieldwall was forming, the arrows were fletched, and the defenders were hardened. The final edge had been honed. All that was left now was to wait.

Part 4: Beneath a Rainy Sky

A cold, persistent rain began to fall while dusk spread across Njardarheimr, turning the churned earth around the palisade into slick mud and muting the sounds of the village. The frantic spirit of the day had finally tapered off. Exhaustion, profound and absolute, had claimed most of the villagers. The longhouses were quiet, filled with the heavy breathing of sleep.

In Gunnar's longhouse, the main hall was faintly lit by the central hearth, where the fire still glowed, throwing flickering shadows on the smoke-darkened timbers of the roof. The fragrance of damp wool, old fires, and the slight, sweet smell of roasting meat from earlier mingled in the air. The small group remained awake, gathered close to the warmth: Asa, Aedelric, Astrid, and even young Leif, who had been welcomed into their circle by Gunnar with a nod of approval, a quiet acknowledgement of his potential and his budding connection with Aedelric.

They spoke in low tones, the regular *drip-drip-drip* of rain outside a constant backdrop. Their conversation, surprisingly, had drifted to Aedelric's faith. Curiosity, not challenge, was in their questions.

"So," Astrid began, her voice mellow, "you say you have but one god? Only one? He rules everything?" It was a concept so alien to their world, with its vast pantheon of Odin, Thor, Freyja, and countless other spirits and wights.

Aedelric, cross-legged near the fire, nodded slowly. "Yes. One God. He created the heavens and the earth, the sea, and all that is within them." He paused, probing his memory for the words. "The Psalms... they speak of Him. 'The earth is the Lord's, and the fullness thereof; the world, and they that dwell therein.'"

Leif, wide-eyed, leaned forward. "But... how can one god have power over the sea, the sky, and battle? Does he not have domains, like Njörðr for the sea, or Thor for thunder?"

Aedelric grinned slightly. "We believe that His power is... absolute. He is everywhere, in all things. He commands the waves, sends the rain." He hesitated, working through the complexities of explaining his faith to those whose understanding of the divine was so different. "He is a God of love, the priests teach, but also a God of wrath. He sent His son, Jesus, to walk among us."

Asa listened attentively, her chin resting on her hand. "His son? Did this son have great power?"

"He performed miracles," Aedelric said, remembering the stories. "He healed the sick, made the blind see." He took a breath, coming to the most challenging part. "But He was... crucified. Nailed to a cross, like a criminal, and killed."

A quiet shock passed through the small group. Death was familiar, brutal, but this... "Killed?" Astrid repeated, a frown furrowing her brow. "Why would a god's son be killed? If he had such power?"

Aedelric struggled to articulate the core tenet of his faith in terms they might understand. "It is... a difficult thing to explain. It was a sacrifice. To... to cleanse us of our sins."

Leif looked bewildered. "Sins? What are sins?"

As they struggled with the alien concepts of sin and divine sacrifice, the heavy wooden door of the longhouse ajar creaked, letting in a gust of cold, rain-laden air. Eiríkr stepped inside, shaking water from his shoulders, his leather armor shining darkly within the dim light. He had been making the rounds of the guards posted along the palisade, ensuring the weary watchmen remained alert in the miserable weather. He knew how easily complacency could creep in during a cold, wet night.

He closed the door against the gale and moved towards the hearth, his boots heavy on the packed earth floor. Astrid caught his eye as he passed and gave him a look, a subtle lift of her eyebrow, and a small, private smile that implied warmth and shared closeness away from the others. She stood up, stretching. "I am tired," she announced, her voice a little louder than before. "I think I will sleep."

As she passed Eiríkr, their hands brushed, and she gave him a brief, firm squeeze, her look reinforced by a knowing wink. He met her gaze, a silent understanding flowing between them. He knew he would join her soon, but the chill of the rain clung to him.

"What are you all discussing?" Eiríkr asked, crouching by the fire, holding his hands out to the embers.

"Aedelric's god," Asa replied.

Eiríkr visibly lost interest. He grunted. "Ah. The Christian one. Never understood it myself. Too much talk, not enough feasting and fighting." He shivered theatrically. "No, thank you. Give me Thor and a good hammer any day."

Asa stood up as well, stifling a yawn. "It is late. We should rest, Aedelric."

Aedelric nodded, getting to his feet. He looked at Leif. "You too, Leif. Get some sleep." He clapped Eiríkr on the shoulder, grinning. "Though I wouldn't dare tell Eiríkr when to go to bed. A man of his size needs little sleep."

Eiríkr chuckled, a quiet rumble. "True enough. Come, Leif, share some ale with me before you turn in. Build some proper warrior's strength." He motioned to a skin of ale nearby.

Leif looked hesitantly at Aedelric, who shrugged with a kind of paternal amusement that said, *Why not?*

"Do not get drunk," Asa warned, though her voice was light. "Be mindful of how much you drink."

Aedelric smiled at her, a shared tenderness in his eyes, before heading towards the sleeping area. As he walked away, Eiríkr called out after him, a good-natured tease, "He may be young, but he knows when to let loose and have some ale!" Leif, excited to be included by Eiríkr, moved eagerly towards the ale skin.

Asa watched them for a moment, then turned and followed Aedelric towards the private room section of the longhouse. It was a small, walled-off area they shared with Gunnar and Sassa. The Jarl was already fast asleep on his sleeping platform, his snores rumbling through the small space like far-off thunder. Beside him, in a small, fur-lined wooden cradle, Sassa slept soundly, a tiny, peaceful presence.

In the hazy light filtering in from the main hall, Aedelric was already shedding his damp outer layers and sliding onto their shared sleeping platform, covered in thick furs. He watched as Asa began to undress, her movements measured and deliberate. He expected her to put on her sleep tunic, as was their norm. But she didn't. She shed everything, standing for a moment within the dim light, her form soft and strong.

He propped himself up on an elbow, surprised. "Asa? What are you doing?"

She turned to him, a look in her eyes that he knew well, a look of fierce desire that always took his breath away. "I am in the mood, Saxon," she said, her voice soft and low. She moved towards the platform, the furs soft beneath her bare feet. "I watched you train today... Watched you moving, teaching them. I daydreamed about this, about having my way with you."

She knelt on the furs beside him, reaching out to touch his face, her thumb tracing the line of his jaw. "And lately..." Her look softened, becoming more serious, more yearning. "Lately, I think more and more about having more children. About sons." She looked towards where Sassa slept. "Sassa is our little bear cub. But I want to bear you many sons. Strong sons to honor you, to stand with their sister. We need to... build our family bigger."

Aedelric's heart expanded in his chest, a painful mixture of love and the ever-present fear. He reached for her, pulling her down beside him onto the soft furs. "Asa," he murmured, burying his face in her hair. "I will have more children with you. More sons, daughters... whatever God will grant us." He pulled back slightly, meeting her gaze. "But... with Hákon's shadow, and now Harald... is this a good time to think of such things?"

Asa smiled, a sad, experienced smile that contained the wisdom of a lifetime lived on the edge of survival. "Is there ever a good time? In this life? We seize the moments we are given." Her hand cupped his cheek. "Do you miss your home, Saxon? Do you want to return?"

The question hovered in the air, heavy with implicit history. Aedelric thought of Winchester, of the green fields, the stone churches, and the life he had lost. He missed it, yes, a part of him always would. But it now appeared far away, like a dream. He looked at Asa, at Sassa sleeping peacefully beside her snoring grandfather.

"My home," he said, his voice firm, filled with an assurance that surprised even himself, "is wherever you and Sassa are. It took me a long time to understand that. I never thought it would be... here." He indicated around the longhouse, the Norse domain that had become his own. "But it is. You are my home, Asa."

And in the quiet darkness, beneath the steady pattering of the rain and the rumbling snores of Jarl Gunnar, they came together, two souls anchored to each other in the face of uncertainty. There was no time for pretense, only the raw, honest connection of their bodies and hearts. They made love quietly, fiercely, clinging to the moment, laughing tenderly against each other's skin whenever Gunnar's snoring reached a particularly impressive crescendo, hoping they wouldn't wake him or the baby.

The laughter waned into contented sighs, replaced by the sounds of the rain and the steady, strong beat of two hearts against each other. Exhaustion finally claimed them, pulling them down into the depths of sleep, entwined, safe in each other's arms for this one night.

The quiet did not last.

It was still early morning, the sky a deep, bruised grey outside the longhouse. The first faint hint of nautical twilight was beginning to push back the total darkness, rendering shapes visible but indistinct against the gloom. The rain had softened to a persistent drizzle, clinging to the newly reinforced palisade as a shroud. Jarl Gunnar, who had been awake for hours, restless with worry, had walked the perimeter himself, a silent, watchful figure in the pre-dawn gloom.

And he had seen it. Movement against the grey-on-grey of the land beyond their defenses. A lot of movement. An army.

Turning from the palisade, his heart a cold, hard knot in his chest, Gunnar moved with grim purpose back towards his longhouse. He strode through the quiet hall, ignoring the sleeping forms, and pushed aside the curtain leading to his family's sleeping area.

He reached the sleeping platform he shared with Asa and Aedelric and shook them roughly awake.

"Asa! Aedelric! Wake!" His voice was low, though urgent, cutting through the traces of sleep. There was no time for gentleness.

Asa and Aedelric were instantly awake, scrambling from the warmth of the furs, their bodies momentarily bare and vulnerable in the sudden intrusion of alarm. They could see Gunnar standing over them, his face somber and shadowed in the faint light.

"An army," Gunnar said, his voice harsh with the stark reality of his sighting. "Approaching the walls."

Asa and Aedelric were already reaching for their discarded tunics and armor pieces, their minds racing, the intimacy of night replaced by the cold shock of impending battle. The pale, grey light of dawn barely illuminated the small room, barely softened the hard line of Gunnar's jaw.

"All our preparation," Gunnar said, securing his weapon belt. "It will be put to the test now."

Aedelric fumbled with the straps of his chest armor, his heart beating against his chest. "Harald? How many of Harald's men?"

Gunnar stopped, his eyes, sharp and weary, met Aedelric's in the low, pre-dawn light, and the truth, stark and unexpected, landed amidst them like a thrown spear.

"Not Harald," Gunnar said, his voice subdued, filled with a weary understanding that gave a chill through Aedelric colder than the morning air. "It's Hákon. And he has brought many warriors with him."

The rain continued to fall, the quiet morning shattered by the news. In the faint light of twilight, the shadow that fell upon Njardarheimr was not the biggest one they were expecting, but a shadow nonetheless. Njardarheimr's fight for survival had just begun.

CHAPTER 8

Part 1: Clash at Dawn

Throughout the longhouses, figures stirred, scrambling from furs onto cold earth floors. The sounds of hurried movement spread through the air, the ringing of mail, the bump of boots, the low murmurs of urgency. There was no panic, only the grim, practiced response of a people who knew the wolf could come to the door at any time. Every man and woman with a weapon and a task was running to their assigned place.

In the heart of the Jarl's longhouse, the private room was a scene of rapid, focused action. Gunnar had already snatched his sword from the wall, its battered handle familiar in his grip. Asa and Aedelric, the soft intimacy of their night together stripped away by the brutal awakening, were pulling on their battle gear with desperate speed. The light leather of Asa's armor, the mail and padded layers of Aedelric's, replaced the feel of soft furs and each other's skin.

Asa buckled her final strap and turned, her eyes immediately seeking the small, curtained cradle where Sassa still slept, miraculously undisturbed by the commotion. Elara stood nearby, her countenance pale but resolute.

"Elara," Asa said, her voice keen with command, but her eyes easing for a brief moment as they met. "Take Sassa. Gather the other servants, the children. Take them to the storage longhouse, the one closest to us. Bar the doors. Pile anything you can against them."

Elara consented, her hands calm as she lifted the sleeping infant from the cradle and wrapped her carefully in a thick wool blanket.

Asa unbuckled a dagger from her belt, a plain but sharp blade, and placed it into Elara's hand. Their eyes met, a profound, terrible understanding flowing between them in that silent exchange. "You know what to do," Asa said, her voice muted, raw with the unspeakable instruction. "If... if they make it inside. If we fail. Do not let them take the children."

Elara's grip clenched on the dagger, her jaw setting. "I understand, Asa." There were no tears, only sober acceptance.

Asa gave a sharp nod, a final, heavy look at her daughter, then turned, hardening her heart, pushing the unbearable possibility into a locked box in her mind. She was a warrior now, with a different duty.

"Archers!" she roared, her voice ringing in the hall, already moving towards the main entrance. "To your positions! Bring extra arrows! On the walls! On the longhouse roofs overlooking the gate!" She reached outside, pointing towards the structures nearest the main entrance. "Those spots will give us the best shots if the gate is breached!"

A small group of archers and Hrolf, woken from sleep, their bows in hand, scrambled to obey, grabbing armfuls of arrow baskets. Asa joined Hrolf, pulling herself onto the wooden palisade wall, her boots getting hold of the rough-hewn logs. Twenty archers, the village's best, clambered onto the walls and the designated rooftops, nocking arrows, their eyes surveying the land beyond the palisade. Gunnar was already beside Asa on the wall, his presence as a solid, unyielding force.

Below, in the open space before the Thingstead, the shieldwall was forming. Aedelric moved with the practiced economy of a seasoned veteran, directing the placement of his recruits with ease. Astrid and Eiríkr were already taking their positions, their movements flowing and efficient. Leif, his face wan and drawn in the faint light, clutched his shield, looking desperately nervous.

"Leif," Aedelric said, his voice composed but firm as he took his place in the front rank. "Behind me. Keep your shield high. Watch my head." Leif nodded mutely, positioning himself behind Aedelric, his shield slightly lower than it should have been.

Astrid took her place beside Aedelric, their shields almost touching. Eiríkr positioned himself directly behind Astrid. Around them, the other fighters, a combination of seasoned warriors and newly trained villagers, formed the tight ranks of the shieldwall, Njardarheimr's living barrier. Other, smaller groups of warriors moved stealthily between the longhouses closest to the gate, ready to act as flanking forces.

The grey light grew stronger, pushing back the shadows of night, revealing the landscape beyond the palisade. And then they saw it.

An army. Moving steadily towards them across the open ground.

Hákon's newly made banner, a snarling wolf on a field of black, whipped in the damp morning wind at the head of the approaching force. Asa and Gunnar, their eyes alert, scanned the enemy ranks. There were many of them, far outnumbering Njardarheimr's defenders: a few hundred fighters, a frightening sight. But Asa's gaze, and Gunnar's, settled on the small number of men carrying bows. An army built for melee, for crushing force, not for a protracted archery duel. It was a crucial detail.

Hákon's force advanced, their shieldwall a dark, moving mass against the grey land. They halted just outside of the effective range of Asa's archers, a silent challenge.

From her position on the palisade wall, Asa's voice was low, directed at her father beside her. "How... how do you know it was Hákon?" she asked.

Gunnar's gaze was fixed on the figure of Hákon, who now emerged from the ranks of his shieldwall, accompanied by a couple of guards. A complex mix of emotions flickered in Gunnar's eyes: old affection, profound disappointment, and a deep, weary sadness. He glanced at Asa. "I just..." he said, his voice rigid. "I just knew."

Hákon advanced towards the palisade, stopping a short distance away, well within earshot. He stood tall, his stance arrogant, his face set in a smug, self-righteous expression. He raised a hand, demanding silence from his ranks, and addressed Gunnar.

"My Jarl Gunnar!" Hákon's voice carried across the wet ground, laced with venom and a cold mockery of respect. "I come on a mission from the gods themselves! To purge this village of rot! The Christian rot that has infected your people! The weakness that has taken root here!" His gaze, cold and hateful, seemed to bore into Gunnar, then turn towards where he knew Aedelric must be.

He spread his arms wide, addressing not just Gunnar but the entire village huddled behind the palisade. "You harbor a defiler of the old ways! A Saxon! A Christian! He and all those who stand in my way will be met with the sword! With fire! With the rightful wrath of the Æsir!" His voice rose to a roar. "But! Those who give up this... foreign stain... those who surrender now... will find a small amount of mercy! They will be allowed to live!"

Hákon's eyes narrowed, fixing on Gunnar. His voice dropped, the menace now a low growl meant for Gunnar alone, though carried on the wind. "I will see you," he promised, his gaze burning with a terrifying intensity, "blood-eagled for this defilement!"

Gunnar stood unfazed, his expression like carved stone. He didn't need to look around. He could feel it, the absolute stillness of his people, the resolute silence that met Hákon's offer of mercy. Not a single soul moved to surrender. Loyalty, forged in hardship, held stronger than fear.

Gunnar's voice was calm, steady, a clear contrast to Hákon's fury. "It does not have to be this way, Hákon," he called back, his voice bearing the weight of genuine sorrow. "I trusted your father. He was a good man. He... he only wanted what was best for you."

The words, meant as a plea, an indication of a common past, instead struck Hákon like a sudden shock. His smugness vanished, replaced by a raw, incandescent rage that distorted his features. Gunnar's mention of his father, of wanting what was 'best,' ripped open old wounds: the death of his father, the loss of his family, the years spent alone, never truly finding his place, not even here in Njardarheimr, not even within Gunnar's family, who had offered him refuge. He was the unwanted guest, the unceasing reminder of loss. Gunnar's attempt at connection deepened his festering bitterness.

"Prepare for battle!" Hákon shrieked, his voice faltering with fury. "Prepare to cleanse this place!"

A roar went up from Hákon's men, a savage, bloodthirsty cheer that promised violence and destruction. Hákon, his face an expression of enraged hatred, turned and stormed back into the ranks of his shieldwall. The dark, moving mass began to advance once more, picking up speed, a tide of armed bodies surging towards the palisade gate.

Below, in the shieldwall, the air was laden with tension. Eiríkr, ever one to cut the tension with humor, nudged Aedelric with his elbow. "Well, Saxon," he grinned, though his eyes were serious. "Thought you might not make it to the shieldwall. Sleeping in, were you? Or perhaps Asa kept you from making it quite so promptly?"

Aedelric allowed himself a brief, tight smile, a common moment of gallows humor with Eiríkr and Astrid beside him. Astrid even offered a slight, wry smirk, acknowledging the mutual joke despite the grim circumstances. Leif, however, his grip white-knuckled on his shield rim, looked bewildered. *How could they joke now?*

Aedelric experienced a pang of concern for the young man. He looked back at Leif, his look softening slightly. "Leif," he said, his voice muted, cutting through the noise of the approaching army. "Remember what I taught you. Keep that shield above you." He locked eyes with the nervous teenager. "Hold strong. If you falter... if you let a sword or axe through... it might be me it finds." It was a blunt, perhaps cruel way to put it, but Aedelric knew that fear of harming his temporary guardian might be a stronger motivator than abstract courage.

Astrid, standing beside Aedelric, overheard his words to Leif and turned her head, a glint of something inscrutable in her eyes as she looked at Aedelric. "We shall see, Saxon," she spoke quietly, just loud enough for him to hear over the growing thunder of Hákon's approaching army. "If you're single, God shows up to protect you... and us."

Aedelric met her gaze, a complex mix of their common past and present woven between them. He smiled, a small, cryptic expression that didn't confirm or deny anything. Eiríkr, hearing Astrid's teasing comment about Aedelric's faith, responded with a low growl. This familiar sound revealed his ingrained Norse cynicism and dislike of Christianity, even as he stood shield-to-shield with the Saxon.

Back on the palisade, Asa's voice rang out, sharp and commanding. "Archers! Nock! Wait for my command!"

The twenty archers on the palisade walls drew their bowstrings taut, the warm summer air still carrying the damp fragrance of the recent rain. Their arrows, fletched with goose feathers, were aimed at the approaching shieldwall of Hákon's force, a dark, undulating mass against the greening landscape. Each archer focused, their breath pluming in the clear morning, their fingers tensed on the bowstrings. As Hákon's army drew closer, their shouts growing louder, Asa gave the order.

"Loose!"

With a synchronized hiss, a hail of arrows arced through the grey, pre-dawn air, descending towards Hákon's tightly packed shieldwall. The *thwack* of shafts striking wood and leather resounded throughout the damp ground. Some arrows found gaps, glancing off helmets or finding vulnerable points in the seams of armor, but the immediate effect was less than devastating. The shieldwall absorbed much of the volley, the tightly packed shields deflecting or stopping the shafts with dull thuds. Asa noted this with a grim satisfaction that her enemies would likely interpret as a sign of disappointment. This initial volley was not meant to break their formation, but to test their cohesion and make them believe the archers posed no significant, immediate threat. Her eyes, sharp and calculating, were already scanning for the next weakness, the next opportunity.

The shieldwall moved forward, a disciplined wave of men and timber, all but missing the pits and wolf traps. As they neared the main gate, the reason for their tight, central formation became horrifyingly clear: concealed beneath the mass of shields was a battering ram, a heavy, iron-shod log, gripped by a dozen burly men. Hákon's men hefted it and slammed it against the main gate with a sickening *CRUMPH.* The heavy timbers groaned, but held. Again, they struck, a jarring impact that resounded through the very ground. The gate held firm, designed to withstand such blows, reinforced for just this purpose.

Asa's eyes, sharp and calculating, saw the opportunity. The battering ram required men to lower their shields or create small gaps in the wall as they worked, sacrificing protection for leverage. "Archers!" she yelled, her voice ringing through the rising din. "Aim for the gaps around the ram! Make them pay for every blow!"

Arrows rained down on the clustered area around the battering ram, the *thud-thud* now accompanied by grunts of pain. Some shafts found their marks, striking exposed limbs or bodies in the tightly clustered men. It caused casualties, a few men slumping, but not enough to stop the relentless battering. The gate groaned again, a noise like a wounded beast. It would not hold forever. Asa knew she needed to act decisively, to unleash the true power of her archers.

Asa made a split-second decision, a dangerous, audacious gamble that could win or lose everything. She turned to Gunnar, who stood grim-faced beside her. "Father! I have a plan! Trust me!"

Gunnar met her fierce gaze, seeing the quick intelligence burning there, remembering her words from their youth: *We use what we have, and we make it fight with us.* He trusted her implicitly. He always had. He nodded, a silent grant of command, his eyes already hardening with a fresh resolve.

"Archers on the wall!" Asa yelled, her voice resounding with haste. "Fall back to the longhouse roofs! Reinforce those positions! Quick now!"

The archers on the palisade, understanding the command, scrambled down the ladders and ran towards the longhouses, their quivers rattling. They quickly clambered onto the stout, turf-covered roofs, joining the archers already positioned there, gaining crucial height and a superior angle over the approaching enemy. Gunnar descended from the palisade as well, his sword now held ready, moving towards the main shieldwall that guarded the gate's inner approach. He would be in the thick of it. He was handed a shield from one of his warriors.

Asa took a deep breath, the summer air filling her lungs, then yelled the order that stunned everyone within earshot.

"Open the gate!"

A gasp spread through the few villagers not at fighting stations, a collective intake of breath from warriors and non-combatants alike. Protests erupted from some of the warriors near the gate hinges. *Open the gate?* As an enemy army battered it down? It seemed like sheer madness, an act of suicidal folly.

But Gunnar's voice, the Jarl's voice, cut through the protest like a summer storm, iron-hard and inflexible. He understood. He had seen the intelligence in Asa's eyes. He barked the order to the warriors controlling the gate. "Open it! Now! You heard her!" He then turned to the shieldwall, his voice ringing out across the square, a battle cry in itself. "Shieldwall! Be ready! Hold the line no matter what! By Odin's beard, we hold!"

Asa's gaze swept over the Njardarheimr shieldwall, a compact line of determined faces and gleaming steel, finding the warriors she trusted most. "Aedelric!" she shouted, her voice cutting through the din. "Break their wall! Break their line!"

They saw her, acknowledged her command with grim, resolute nods, as their shields shifted and their spears lowered.

The heavy gate groaned as the bars were lifted and swung inside, revealing the interior of Njardarheimr. Hákon's shieldwall, focused on the battering ram, paused for a moment in surprise. Then, seeing the gate open, a hoarse roar of triumph went up from their ranks. They thought their battering had succeeded, that the defenders were breaking, retreating in fear. Blinded by rage and perceived victory, Hákon yelled, urging his men forward, oblivious to the trap.

Asa watched them surge forward, a relentless wave of bodies rushing into the open gate. Her eyes, sharp and calculating, scanned the chaotic mass, ensuring none of her people were caught outside the carefully laid trap. She waited, heart beating fast, until the bulk of Hákon's shieldwall had poured through the entrance, creating a dense, packed mass just inside the palisade, caught squarely in the confined killing ground. Then, with a fierce triumph in her voice, she roared the final command to the warriors by the gate.

"Shut the gate!"

With a heavy thud, the gate swung shut, the massive timbers closing with a noise like a thunderclap, the heavy bars dropping into place with a resounding clang. Hákon's army, packed shoulder-to-shoulder inside the narrow entrance, was now utterly trapped within a small, inescapable arena.

"NOW!" Asa shrieked, her cry a high, fierce cry that cut through the sudden, confused roar of the enemy, an almost predatory sound.

Below, Aedelric's shieldwall, which had begun to fall back slightly at Asa's previous command, sensing the unfolding trap, stopped its retreat. Their shields locked tighter, their stances solidified.

"Forward!" Aedelric roared, his voice finding a new, savage power, filled with an ancient fury. "Shields locked! Spears out! FORWARD!"

The Njardarheimr shieldwall answered with a cry that shook the air, not words, but a raw, primal sound torn from the chests of men and women ready to kill or die. They surged ahead as one, a wall of wood and iron and cold, murderous resolve. The ground shook under their boots. Breath steamed from their mouths, similar to smoke from a forge.

The distance between the two forces vanished in a heartbeat.

The impact was thunder.

A bone-jarring, earth-shaking CRUNCH as shield met shield, iron met iron, and bodies slammed together with the force of colliding storms. The shock traveled through the line, rattling teeth, numbing arms, stealing breath. The two walls fused into one grinding, heaving mass, locked in a brutal embrace just inside the gate.

The melee began.

This was the shieldwall, not glory, not heroics, but a grinder. A choking crush of bodies, sweat, and terror. Spears thrust through the narrow gaps, long and hungry, punching into flesh with wet, sickening sounds. Men screamed, roared, choked on their own blood. The air reeked thick with the copper sting of fresh gore, the hot tang of iron, the rank, animal stink of men fighting at breath's distance.

Gunnar was a tree in the storm, immovable and deadly. His heavy spear thrust and struck with unrelenting force, smashing through shields, splitting skulls, and punching through ribs. He fought with the icy precision of a man who had lived his entire life in battle, no wasted motion, no hesitation, only lethal intent.

Beside him, Aedelric was controlled violence. His Saxon training showed in every movement, the disciplined shield work, the sharp, efficient thrusts of his spear. He fought like a man who had already died once and refused to do so again. Even in the chaos, he checked on Leif behind him, guarding the boy's space with the instinct of a seasoned warrior.

Astrid was a storm given flesh. Her spear flashed in brutal strikes, her movements flowing and savage. She ducked, twisted, struck, a predator moving through the crush. Eiríkr fixed her flank, a mountain of muscle and fury. His axe rose and fell with grim certainty, parrying blows meant for her, ripping open gaps in the enemy line. When he hooked his axe over a shield and tore it down, the man behind it died a heartbeat later.

Leif was terror and courage tangled together. His shield shook in his grip, held too high until Aedelric barked a correction over the din. He lowered it just in time to catch a spear that would have split his skull. The press of bodies kept him upright even when his knees threatened to buckle. The noise, the screams, the metal, the breathless grunts-battered his senses. The smell of blood and sweat and fear scratched at his throat.

He saw the enemy's faces, twisted with rage, splattered with gore, eyes staring with the madness of battle. His heart throbbed as a trapped bird. Then Aedelric's voice cut through the chaos, sharp and commanding. "Hold, Leif! Hold! Don't break!"

And he held.

He saw Aedelric drive his spear through a man's throat. Saw Astrid's weapon bury itself in a ribcage with a gruesome thud. Saw Eiríkr knock aside a blow meant for Astrid's spine and answer with a killing strike of his own.

Fueled by terror and the desperate need not to fail, Leif found a sliver of strength. He held his shield tighter against the wall, bracing against the man beside him. When a blade arced toward Aedelric's head, Leif managed a clumsy but timely parry, knocking it aside.

Njardarheimr's shieldwall, though outnumbered, had the crucial advantage of position and the desperation of defending their home. Hákon's wall was backed against the palisade, effectively using it as an immovable extra shield behind them, preventing movement and providing an advantage. Hákon's men, packed tightly in the entrance, had nowhere to maneuver, their numbers becoming a disadvantage in the confined space. The grinder worked relentlessly in Njardarheimr's favor.

Slowly, painstakingly, Njardarheimr's shieldwall began to gain ground, pushing back against the packed enemy. The pressure stayed relentless, a grinding, crushing force that made Hákon's men stumble, their shields shuddering under the weight. The enemy line began to buckle, first in small ripples, then in visible bends, the formation warping under the strain from the front and the crush of bodies on the flanks.

The sheer press of men became a curse for Hákon's warriors. They could not move. They could not breathe. They could not swing. Njardarheimr's wall drove into them like a wedge of iron.

Aedelric felt the shift, the subtle give in the enemy shields, the quiver of panic in the men pressed against him. "They're breaking!" he roared, voice harsh with battle-fury. "Push! PUSH!"

With a thunderous heave, Njardarheimr's shieldwall advanced. Hákon's line shattered.

Shields twisted out of formation. Gaps tore open. Men fell back, tripping over their own dead. The moment the enemy wall fractured, Njardarheimr's warriors moved with ruthless precision. Spears were discarded, clattering to the ground as short swords, seaxes, and hand axes flashed into their hands.

The sound changed, no longer the dull bang of spear on shield, but the brutal, intimate hacking of close-quarters slaughter.

Gunnar, Aedelric, Astrid, and Eiríkr fought like veterans carved from the old sagas. Aedelric's seax found vitals with surgical precision, each thrust deliberate and deadly. Astrid's axe split shields and helmets with savage power. Eiríkr parried and swung with grim efficiency, carving a path through the turmoil. Gunnar was a force of nature, a crushing, unstoppable presence that broke men as easily as he broke their shields.

The enemy recoiled, recoiling backward into the bottleneck of the gate. And then Aedelric saw it, the perfect moment.

"STOP THE ADVANCE!" he bellowed, slamming his shield into the dirt to halt the momentum. "HOLD THE LINE! HOLD!"

Njardarheimr's warriors obeyed instantly, locking shields once more. The sudden halt created a pocket of open ground, a killing space, between their line and the collapsing remains of Hákon's.

Above them, Asa saw the gap open like a gift from the gods.

From his position at the back of the trapped shieldwall, Hákon saw it too. He saw his men falling, saw his line breaking, saw the closed gate behind him and the towering palisade walls trapping them. And on the longhouse roofs, positioned with ruthless intent, he saw the silhouettes of archers drawing their bows.

Asa and her archers, now with a clear, devastating view into the packed mass of Hákon's shieldwall, drew their bowstrings back with grim satisfaction. There was no wood to hide behind, no open ground to maneuver, no escape. Hákon's men were a dense, helpless target.

"LOOSE!" Asa shrieked, her cry primal and fierce, vengeance and defense woven into one.

The volley fell like a storm.

Arrows rained down into the struggling melee, finding necks, shoulders, undefended backs, piercing helmets, piercing mail. Men screamed, stumbling and collapsing within the merciless press, creating more gaps, more chaos, more terror.

Another volley followed.

Then another.

A relentless, whistling rain of death.

Hákon watched in horror as his army was decimated around him. The ground inside the gate became slick with blood and littered with fallen bodies. His warriors, trapped and exposed, were being cut down by the score, not primarily by the shieldwall they faced, but by the arrows they had fatally underestimated.

From her vantage point on the longhouse roof, Asa drew her bowstring back until it trembled like a breathing creature. The winds tugged her hair, the screams below ascending like a tide. She could see everything: the crush of bodies, the splintering of Hákon's shieldwall, the blood pooling in the churned earth.

And she saw him. Hákon. The man who had tried to take her home, her people, her life. The man who would never stop unless they stopped him.

Her jaw stiffened. Rage burned hot in her chest; still beneath it, a quieter ache pulsed. She did not kill lightly. But this man had chosen his path, and if she spared him, he would only rise again to destroy everything she loved. Her fingers steadied on the bowstring.

This ends now.

Below, Hákon staggered among his dying men, his shieldwall collapsing around him. He looked up, seeing her, and for a second their eyes met across the chaos. Asa exhaled. Her first arrow flew. It struck him in the chest with a brutal, thudding force. Hákon jerked back, shock twisting his features. He clutched at the shaft, blood spreading over his mail.

As the volleys from her archers rained down, Asa did not look away. She nocked another arrow, her breath sharp, her heart throbbing with fury and sorrow intertwined.

"This is the only way," she whispered, though no one could hear her.

Hákon reeled, arrows striking around him, but he still clung to life, staggering, refusing to fall. His rage kept him upright, the same rage that had driven him to this moment. Asa drew her final arrow. Her hands did not shake.

"For Njardarheimr," she breathed.

"For my father."

"For Sassa."

She loosed.

The arrow flew straight and true, cutting through the storm of shafts. It struck Hákon in the throat, burying itself deep. His eyes widened, the last trace of defiance dying in them. He collapsed to his knees, then fell forward into the blood-soaked earth, the life leaving him in a slow, shuddering exhale.

Asa lowered her bow.

Her rage ebbed, leaving only an empty ache, even one so steeped in violence. She closed her eyes for a second, honoring the gravity of what had just taken place.

Below, the battle in the entrance grounds sputtered out. The shieldwall fought on for only a few more brutal moments, dispatching the last stunned enemies. The bulk of Hákon's force lay dead or dying, caught in Njardarheimr's deadly embrace.

The brutal dawn had ended, and Asa's arrows had begun and finished Hákon's fall.

Part 2: After the Thunder

The roar of battle died down, replaced by a sudden, echoing silence, interrupted solely by the persistent, pained moans of the dying. Inside the main gate of Njardarheimr, the scene was one of brutal carnage. The narrow space was a knotted, bloody mess of bodies, broken shields, shattered wood, and discarded weapons. The victory was decisive, achieved with swift and horrifying efficiency, but the cost, though smaller than it could have been, was still paid in blood.

From her position high on the roof of the longhouse overlooking the gate, Asa, her arms aching, her hands shaking gently, not from exertion, but from the sheer, brutal finality of the scene below. The timbers under her feet. Around her, the other archers on the rooftops, their expressions pale and stunned, lowered their bows, the quiet enhancing the ringing in their ears. Their arrows, loosed with such devastating effect, had ended it swiftly.

Below, in the killing ground inside the gate, the shieldwall of Njardarheimr slowly, wearily, lowered its shields. Gunnar, Aedelric, Astrid, Eiríkr, and Leif, along with the others in the formation, stood in the middle of the carnage, their armor slick with blood, their faces stern. A wave of raw emotion flooded the survivors, a shaky, overwhelming relief that they were still standing, quickly followed by the nauseating jolt of grief as eyes scanned the fallen forms of their own. There were few, mercifully few, of Njardarheimr's people among the dead in the killing ground, but even one was too many. A low, keening wail rose from a woman who had run forward, recognizing her husband among the still figures. Other villagers, their faces wet with tears, knelt near their fallen, uttering choked cries of sorrow. The grim joy of survival was instantly combined with the bitter taste of loss. Then the rain began to fall again, like tears, to match the carnage they all just witnessed.

Gunnar, his chest heaving with the effort of the fight, surveyed the scene from within the remnants of the shieldwall. His gaze found Asa high on the longhouse roof, a dark shape against the grey sky, her bow lowered. He had a surge of profound pride, so strong it momentarily eclipsed the grim reality around him. He gave her a short, sharp nod, a silent acknowledgement of her key role.

Asa descended from the longhouse roof, her boots finding the familiar path down the wet timbers. She met her father as he emerged from the shieldwall, wiping rain and blood from his brow with the back of his hand. Aedelric, Astrid, Eiríkr, and Leif, appearing utterly spent but alive, were just behind him.

"You did well, daughter," Gunnar said, his voice coarse but heavy with emotion as Asa reached him. He wasn't one for effusive praise, but his following words held immense weight. "Your thinking... your quickness... It saved us. You will lead them well one day. You already do."

Asa met his gaze, seeing the weariness and pride there, as well as the deep trust. "We did it together, Father," she said, her voice quiet. "All of us. Those who stood in the shieldwall," she glanced at Aedelric, Astrid, Eiríkr, and the still-shaking Leif, "and those who loosed the arrows."

As the immediate shock began to recede, the victorious warriors dispersed from the killing ground. Villagers, cautiously emerging from the longhouses, joined them, some rushing to aid the wounded, others to claim their dead. The air teemed with a mix of hushed voices, quiet sobs, plus the rhythmic *drip, drip, drip* of rain hitting the blood-soaked earth. There was no triumphant cheering, only the somber, shared weight of survival.

Gunnar, with Asa and Aedelric now beside him, began to saunter through the carnage inside the gate, Astrid and Eiríkr joining them, their faces stern yet unharmed. They stepped carefully over bodies, the sounds of their boots squelching in the mud and blood.

The sheer number of Hákon's dead was staggering in the confined space. As Gunnar moved among them, his experienced eye noticed something. "Look," he said, gesturing with his sword handle towards the bodies. "Their markings... the patterns on their shields, their clothes... They are not all from one village. Not even two." He crouched next to a fallen warrior, examining a distinctive arm ring. "This one... he is from the east. And him..." He pointed to another. "...from the north. From beyond the grey peaks."

The three followed his gaze, seeing the truth of his words. The dead wore the colors and symbols of disparate communities.

"How did he gather so many?" Astrid murmured, her voice laden with a cold wonder. "And why did they follow him?"

"Gold and promises," Gunnar said, his voice dull. "Hákon promised them loot, land... and perhaps the chance to spill Christian blood." He looked at the dead faces around them, the vacant stares fixed on the grey sky. "They were mercenaries, rallied by hate and greed."

Gunnar straightened, a weariness settling deep in his bones. The immediate threat was gone, but the questions persisted, dark and unsettling. He surveyed the scene, grimly aware of the task ahead.

"Eiríkr, Astrid," he commanded, his voice regaining some of its Jarl's authority. "Begin the clean-up. Go through them." He gestured to the bodies of Hákon's men. "Take what is valuable, arm rings, necklaces, coins. Armor, if it can be salvaged." He paused, his look sweeping over the many bodies still gripping their weapons even in death. "But leave their weapons in their hands. A warrior should go to the next life with his blade or axe ready." It was a small mercy, a nod to a belief in Valhalla, even for their enemies. "Pile them here, near the gate. We will burn them."

Eiríkr and Astrid nodded, their expressions resolute, already moving to organize groups of villagers for the grim task of stripping the dead.

Gunnar then turned to Asa and Aedelric, his voice easing slightly, though the sadness remained carved on his face. "Asa. Aedelric. Find Hákon's body. Prepare him." His gaze went beyond, towards the fjord. "He will have a ship burial. Before nightfall. It is the least I can do... for his father."

A trace of surprise crossed Asa's face, and Aedelric's. A ship burial for Hákon? The man who had just tried to slaughter them all, who had threatened to blood-eagle her father? There were murmurs among some of the listening villagers. Surely, Hákon didn't deserve such an honor, such a show of respect. But no one dared voice their dissent to Gunnar. His reasons, rooted in a history he fully understood at the time, held sway over him.

A wave of sorrow came over Gunnar as he thought of Hákon, of the boy he had known, the lost, angry man he had become. "He was lost," Gunnar said, his voice laden with regret. "Completely lost. There was no other choice."

He then looked for Leif, spotting the young man standing shocked near the edge of the killing ground, his face ghostly, his shield still in his trembling hand. "Leif!" Gunnar called out, his voice kind. "Go. Go to the storage longhouse. Check on the children. Tell Elara to bring Sassa to me."

Leif nodded, relief sweeping over him, grateful for a task that took him away from the sight and smell of death. He turned and ran, his feet splashing in the puddles.

As Asa and Aedelric began the grim task of searching for Hákon's body among the fallen, and Astrid and Eiríkr organized the stripping and piling of the enemy dead, the full weight of the day settled upon Njardarheimr. The thunder of battle had passed, leaving behind a heavy, somber silence. The cost of their defense was visible in the few still forms of their own, in the exhaustion and grief carved on every face, and in the harrowing realization of the enemy they had faced, not a single, unified force, but a desperate, greedy collection of men rallied by one man's venomous hatred. The victory was won, but the scars, both seen and unseen, would remain. The long task of survival had just entered a new, somber phase.

The grim, necessary work continued through the afternoon. The bodies of the enemy dead were stacked high, from the morning's brutality. Weapons placed in hands, broken shields salvaged for wood, and armor assessed for repair. The air, even washed by the rain, still carried the iron tang of blood.

As the sky deepened from grey to shades of purple and orange in the west, throwing a strange, mystical light over the fjord, the village gathered near the water. The surviving warriors stood together, their faces still imprinted with the exhaustion of battle. Villagers, their relief at survival tempered by the loss of their own, stood silently. A small, older fishing boat, sturdy but past its prime, had been hauled to the water's edge, prepared for its final journey.

Asa and Aedelric approached, guiding the rough wooden stretcher bearing Hákon's cleaned and roughly dressed body. It felt strange, unsettling, to show such care for the man who had hours ago sought their destruction, who had threatened her father and their lives. But Gunnar's command had been clear, and his reasons, however layered with history, held firm. Together, with quiet, heavy hearts, they carefully lifted Hákon and placed him in the center of the small vessel, arranging the crude grave goods, the sword, the arm ring, and the horn around him.

There existed a palpable sense of questioning among some of the onlookers: a ship burial? For Hákon? The betrayer? The attacker? Whispers exchanged among a few, but no one dared voice their doubts aloud when Gunnar was present. His will was law, especially today.

Gunnar stood near the boat, his shoulders heavy, his look fixed on the darkening water. He looked down at the still face of the man who had been both kin and enemy. The anger and fear Hákon had inspired seemed to dissipate in the face of death, leaving only a great sadness for what might have been. He thought of Hákon's father, a man he had respected, a friend lost to the harsh realities of their world. This burial was for him, a concluding act of respect for a bond broken not by death, but by the corrosive power of bitterness and ambition.

"Hákon…" Gunnar's voice was low, rough with emotion, audible only to those closest to the boat. "You chose your path. A dark one. You were lost to us long before this day." He didn't offer forgiveness — not for the attack, not for the threats — but there was a deep lament in his tone. "May your trip… wherever it takes you…find a better end than your life here."

He stepped back.

Strong hands, belonging to Gunnar's trusted warriors, pushed the boat away from the shore. It slid smoothly into the dark water of the fjord, drifting out a few paces, the still form of Hákon lying among the furs and kindling prepared for him.

Only once the boat had begun to drift did two warriors step forward, chosen for their skill with a bow, flaming arrows nocked. At a silent nod from Gunnar, they drew their bowstrings taut and loosed.

The flaming shafts arced through the twilight air, two fiery streaks against the deepening sky, and landed in the boat among the furs and kindling. Fire blossomed instantly. The dry wood caught quickly, flames licking up the sides of the ship, curling around Hákon's still form as the vessel drifted farther into the fjord, the water glowing orange and red beneath it.

They watched in silence as the burning ship drifted slowly out into the fjord, carried by the gentle currents. The fire grew, consuming the vessel, transforming it into a blazing pyre against the backdrop of the dark mountains and the dusk sky. Smoke twisted upwards, a dark column against the bright hues of the sunset.

The villagers lingered together, a somber crowd, their faces brightened by the trembling, distant flames. Asa stood close to Aedelric, his arm a soothing pressure around her shoulders, both of them watching the fiery spectacle as the brutal morning receded slightly before this ancient ritual. Astrid and Eiríkr stood a little apart, their expressions unreadable, reflecting on the many warriors they had seen die and the many fires they had watched consume the dead.

Gunnar remained standing there for a long time, even after the boat had burned down to a low-lying glow on the water, watching the fire on the fjord, the quiet guardian of his people, carrying the weight of the living and the dead into the coming night.

Part 3: Hunter's Secret

The raw wounds of battle began to scab over during the days that followed. The pyres of Hákon's men burned for a day and a night near the gate, a constant, heavy smoke rising into the sky, carrying the smell of death. The few fallen of Njardarheimr were mourned with traditional rites, their bodies prepared and placed in their family burial mounds, their spirits commended to the care of their ancestors and the gods. Slowly, painstakingly, the village began to return to a semblance of normalcy. Defenses were repaired where the gate had been battered, broken palisade logs replaced, and wolf pits checked. The level of alert remained higher than before, sentries posted vigilantly, but the frantic urgency of the past weeks had subsided. Life, as it always did, reasserted its quiet, daily demands.

A couple of mornings after the battle, with the sky a clear, crisp blue for a change, Gunnar decided a hunt was needed, for fresh meat, yes, but also for a short escape from the heavy air of the village and a specific purpose only he knew. He asked Aedelric to accompany him. Aedelric readily agreed, also sensing the need for space away from the village.

They moved through the familiar forest that surrounded Njardarheimr, the sounds of their boots on fallen leaves and the snapping of twigs the only disruption to the quiet of the woods. Gunnar moved with a practiced, silent tread despite his years, his eyes examining the undergrowth for signs of game. Aedelric, equally skilled in the hunt, moved with a different economy of motion, the quiet precision of a Saxon. They hunted in quiet silence for a time, eventually sighting and taking down a young deer.

They found a small clearing near a bubbling stream to clean the kill and rest before the haul back. The sounds of the village were distant now, muffled by the trees. The only immediate threat was the lingering, unseen shadow of

Harald Fairhair, a knowledge that kept their senses sharp even in this moment of relative peace.

As they worked, Gunnar paused, leaning against a moss-covered rock, watching Aedelric expertly skin the deer. "You fought well, Aedelric," Gunnar said, his voice quiet, breaking the natural silence of the woods. "In the shieldwall. You held strong. You kept the fear from young Leif's eyes."

Aedelric looked up, surprised by the direct praise from the usually reserved Jarl. "Thank you, Jarl," he replied, wiping a hand on a patch of grass. "The training was held. For all of us."

Gunnar nodded, his look lingering on Aedelric for a moment. "I see the care you have for Asa," he continued, his voice thoughtful. "For Sassa. It is clear. You are... hers, now. And she is yours." He paused, choosing his following words carefully. "Your home... it is in Wessex, is it not? Your people? Your faith?"

Aedelric met Gunnar's gaze, understanding the implicit question beneath the words. He knew the path he had chosen, the life he had built here, meant leaving another behind. It wasn't a decision taken lightly, but it was one he had come to accept, even embrace, amid the quiet hours since the shipwreck. He answered with confidence and was both peaceful and absolute.

"My home was in Winchester, Jarl," Aedelric said, his voice composed. "My people are there. But... since the sea took me and brought me here... since I found Asa... this," he motioned vaguely around them, towards the forest, the distant fjord, "this is my home now. Wherever Asa and Sassa are... that is my home." He met Gunnar's eyes directly. "I may never return to Wessex. And I have come to terms with that."

Gunnar held his gaze for a long moment, searching for any hint of doubt or regret. He found none. A slow nod of understanding spread across his face. He had suspected as much, seen the deepening roots Aedelric had put down in this harsh soil, but hearing it spoken aloud, with such certainty, was... necessary.

"I thought as much," Gunnar said, his voice lower now. He shifted on the rock, his expression growing serious, the casual air of the hunt dissipating. "I have been testing you, Aedelric. I've been watching you closely since you arrived with Asa. Your skills, yes, but more... your heart. Your loyalty. Not without reason."

Aedelric set down his knife, his full attention on Gunnar, noticing the shift in the conversation, the weight gathering behind the Jarl's words.

"I did not just bring you out here to hunt," Gunnar stated, his gaze scanning the surrounding trees, his voice sinking to a low, confidential tone. "I needed to speak with you where no ears could overhear. Where no one could know what I am about to reveal." He looked directly at Aedelric, his expression stern and utterly serious. "What I tell you now... You cannot tell anyone. Not Asa. Not Astrid, or Eiríkr. No one. Can I have your word on that?"

Aedelric didn't hesitate. He understood the gravity in Gunnar's voice. "You have my word, Jarl. You can be sure I will keep it to myself."

Gunnar studied him for another long moment, then nodded, a decision made. He reached into the leather satchel he carried, the one that held his flint and steel, some dried meat, and other necessities for the hunt. He pulled out a small, leather-bound object, carefully wrapped in oiled cloth. He unwrapped it slowly, revealing a book. Not a saga written on vellum, but a bound volume, its cover worn, its pages clearly old.

Gunnar presented it to Aedelric.

Aedelric took the book, his brow knitting in confusion. It was small, unlike the larger scrolls or texts he was used to seeing. As his fingers touched the cover, as his eyes registered the familiar script on the aged pages... his breath caught in his throat. His eyes widened, fixed on the words, on the layout, on the very *feel* of the book. It was impossible. His gaze shot from the book to Gunnar, his head whirling.

The Gospel of Matthew.

Here? In Njardarheimr? In Jarl Gunnar's possession? Confusion warred with a powerful feeling of shock. Where did he get this? Why would he have it? Questions streamed his mind, unspoken, tumbling over each other.

Gunnar watched Aedelric's reaction, the stunned disbelief on his face. He took a deep breath and spoke, his voice quiet, but the words resounding with unbelievable weight in the peaceful forest clearing.

"I am a Christian, Aedelric," Gunnar said. "And I have been... for many years now."

Aedelric stared at him, the world revolving on its axis. *A Christian? Jarl Gunnar? The formidable, pagan Jarl who ruled this remote Norse village?* It couldn't be real. It must have been a dream, an illusion of the light, a consequence of exhaustion.

"Lord..." Aedelric began, the old, respectful address slipping out in his shock. He corrected himself. "Jarl... how... how is this possible?"

Gunnar settled back against the rock, his look distant, looking back into the years. "Years ago," he began, his voice muted, spinning a tale Aedelric could never have imagined, "while on a raid... across the great sea... in the land of the Scots. We sacked a small chapel near the coast. Took what little gold they had, some silver, and... prisoners. Among them were monks. One of them... he was different. Not like the others. He held onto a book," Gunnar gestured towards the Gospel in Aedelric's trembling hand, "like it was his life."

"We brought them back here," Gunnar continued, his eyes seeing the ghosts of the past. "And I came to find... this monk was no ordinary monk. He was a warrior turned monk. He had wielded a sword, shed blood, before deciding to serve his God differently." Gunnar allowed himself a small, wry smile. "He also spoke our tongue, strangely enough. So, I allowed him to keep his book."

"He became my slave," Gunnar stated, the harsh reality of their world entering the story. "His life was not easy. No slave's life is. But the more time I was around him, the more we spoke. Asa was only a small child then." Gunnar's look softened slightly at the memory of his young daughter. "But the monk... his name was Colm."

Aedelric absorbed the name, the story developing like a saga, unbelievable yet utterly authentic. Colm. A warrior monk in the service of Jarl Gunnar.

"Colm served in the longhouse," Gunnar went on. "Did the tasks of a slave. But late at night... after the others slept... I would have him brought to the hearth. And I would ask him questions about his God. And he would answer. He would tell me of his one God, of his son Jesus." Gunnar paused. "In time... Asa's mother, Yrsi... she would join us. She was... curious. She saw something in Colm, in his reserved strength, even as a slave."

"And over the years," Gunnar's voice dropped further, becoming more intimate, revealing the depth of their secret. "Colm would read to us from that book. This book." He nodded towards the Gospel. "From the Gospel of Matthew."

"Colm... he was quiet about his faith, mostly," Gunnar said. "He did his work. But one night... he told Yrsi and me... that he knew what his mission was. He said God had sent him here. To Njardarheimr. And that his mission was to convert us. To Christianity."

Gunnar's jaw stiffened at the memory. "It angered me." He ran a hand over his grizzled beard. "Deeply. This slave... this foreign monk... telling me, a Jarl, what my fate was, what my gods should be." His voice grew rougher as he relived the moment of rage. "One night, late... in a fit of anger... I beat him. Almost to death. I meant to kill him."

Aedelric flinched, picturing the scene, the formidable Jarl in a rage, the defenseless monk.

"But even as I struck him," Gunnar's voice was low, filled with a lingering awe, "even through the blood and the pain... he told me... he would pray for me. That, even in death, he would ask his God to let me see the light. It was... unnerving."

"As I stood over him," Gunnar said, his look distant, "about to finish it... Yrsi... she stayed my hand. She pleaded with me. Said something was not right about killing him. That she could feel it... intensely. And I..." Gunnar trailed off, shaking his head slightly. "I wanted to kill him. I wanted to silence him. But I could not. Something I had never felt before... came over me. A wave of..." He struggled for the word. "Of... sorrow? Of regret? Of something more extensive than myself. It brought me to sobbing tears. I had not wept like that ever."

"Yrsi nursed Colm back to health," Gunnar said, a note of tenderness entering his voice at the mention of his late wife. "And I... I fought the urge to try to kill him again for months. But then... something changed. His quiet faith... his forgiveness... it softened something in me."

"Yrsi and I... we asked him to teach us more," Gunnar revealed, the secret laid bare between them. "In secret, of course. For a few years, before an illness finally claimed him... Colm taught us. He taught me... to speak and read Latin. So I could read this book." Gunnar nodded towards the Gospel. "And I... I memorized it. The Gospel of Matthew. Every word."

"Before he died," Gunnar said, his voice quiet with the memory of Colm's last days, "he baptized us. Yrsi and I. One night, down by the fjord. We accepted Christ into our lives." He looked at Aedelric, a trace of the Jarl's authority returning. "And he told me... that my mission now... was to spread the Gospel to my people. To use this book."

Gunnar's expression turned to one of deep regret. "I have not fulfilled his mission, Aedelric. Not truly. The fear... The fear of what would happen if my people knew. The fear for Yrsi, for Asa... for myself. It held me back. The old ways are strong here. Any sign of weakness... of foreign faith... would be exploited. By rivals. By men like Hákon." He gestured towards the village gate, the recent battle a clear reminder. "He spoke of purging Christian rot... He did not know... how close he came to the truth."

"I have tried," Gunnar added, his look distant. "Over the years, I have tried to acquire other books. Other Gospels. To learn more. But I have never come across another one I could get my hands on." He looked at Aedelric, his secret finally shared after so many years of silence.

Aedelric sat in stunned silence, the weight of the Gospel of Matthew heavy in his hands. His mind tried to process the impossible truth: this Norse Jarl, this man who embodied the strength and tradition of their pagan world, was a secret follower of Christ. The rain that had fallen during the battle, the unexpected victory, the quiet moment of peace in the woods... It all seemed to converge on this single, unbelievable revelation. He had come here seeking refuge among pagans and found... this.

Aedelric sat utterly still, the leather-bound Gospel of Matthew heavy in his hands, the weight of Gunnar's confession bearing down on him. Jarl Gunnar. A Christian. It was a truth that appeared to warp the reality of everything Aedelric had seen and experienced in this land. He stared at the Jarl, studying his face, his timeworn features, the lines formed by sun, wind, and sorrow, seeing now not just a pagan Jarl, but a man who had carried an impossible secret for years.

Gunnar watched Aedelric, giving him a moment to process the sheer impossibility of the revelation. Then, he spoke again, his voice more subdued now, quieter, as if the confession had lifted a small part of his immense burden. "There is... one more thing, Aedelric," Gunnar said. "Something else Colm gave me."

Aedelric could only nod, his mind still struggling to grasp the first revelation. More? How could there be more?

Gunnar reached back into his satchel. This time, he pulled out not a book, but a piece of faded, carefully folded cloth. He handed it to Aedelric.

Aedelric opened it. It wasn't just cloth; it was old, treated hide, supple despite its age, and upon it, a drawing. A map. His eyes, not fully trained in navigation at sea and reading terrain on land, immediately recognized the rough shapes. It was a coastline, islands... The northeastern part of the North Sea, as best he could tell. His gaze fell upon a cluster of islands clearly marked and labeled. Written in Norse, familiar to his ears now: *Orkneyjar*. The Orkney Islands.

Tucked within the folds of the cloth map was a small, tightly folded piece of parchment. Aedelric opened it carefully. It was written in neat, precise script, but in a language neither he nor Gunnar recognized. It was Gaelic, the tongue of the Scots, *the monks' homeland?*

Gunnar saw Aedelric's confusion as he looked at the map and the letter. "I asked Colm about them," Gunnar said, his look distant, remembering that night. "The night he died. He was weak... the illness had taken hold. I showed him the cloth, the letter. I asked him what they meant. What place is this? What do these words say?"

Gunnar paused, the memory sharp and painful. "He looked at the map... at the letter... He looked at me. And before he drew his last breath... all he said was, 'If you need refuge... find it.'" Gunnar's voice was heavy with years of unanswered questions. "And then... he was gone. He gave me this map, this letter, and those few words. Nothing more."

Gunnar explained his attempts to understand. "I knew 'Orkneyjar' was a cluster of islands. North of the land of the Scots, where Colm came from. I thought... perhaps it meant something. A safe place he knew of? A place where others of his faith might be?" He ran a hand over his face. "I tried to find it after Colm died. Took one ship, a trusted crew. Told them we were scouting for new raiding grounds far to the north. Never told them my true intention. But the seas... they were against me. Storms. Rough weather I had never seen. We were driven back, time and again. I had to abandon the search. Never found the place."

He looked at the map in Acdelric's hand, then at the illegible letter. "For years... they have been a mystery. A final, unanswered question from a man who changed my life."

Gunnar's gaze grew even more somber, revealing the lonely burden he had carried. "I had plans, Aedelric. After Yrsi and I... after we accepted Christ... I thought... one day... I would tell Asa. Tell her about us. About her mother's faith, and mine. About Colm." He sighed, a sound of deep regret. "But I never found the right moment. I didn't know how she would take it. This world..." He motioned around them. "It is harsh on differences. On weakness. On foreign ways."

"So I kept raising her as I would have anyway," Gunnar continued. "Teaching her the old ways. The strength, the fighting, the ways of our people. I sent her on that raid to your land..." His gaze met Aedelric's, a trace of wonder in his eyes. "Perhaps... perhaps there was a reason for that, after all. Perhaps God had a hand in it. Sending her to cross your path."

He lowered his head slightly, his voice laden with remembered pain. "Then... the news came. The two ships that returned... telling me she was lost to the sea. It brought such doubt. Such despair." He paused, his voice growing quiet, raw with the memory of that time. "And then... her mother passed. Yrsi." He closed his eyes for a brief moment. "Suddenly, I was utterly alone with the secret. With the grief. No one... not a single soul to confide in."

Gunnar's voice dropped almost to a mutter, revealing the depth of his gloom. "It brought on thoughts... of ending it. Of ending my life. Seeing no path forward. Alone. Burdened by the secret. Surrounded by those who would turn on me if they knew." He looked out into the quiet woods, seeing not trees, but the edge of an abyss.

"But then," Gunnar said, his voice regaining some strength, a note of awe entering it. "The morning Asa returned... I was... pleading. Not to Odin, not to Thor. But to God. Pleading for a sign. For a way forward. And seeing none... I had decided. I was going to end it that night." He met Aedelric's gaze, his eyes clear and steady. "Then Asa walked through that gate. Alive. With you. And Sassa." He shook his head slowly, a wonder that still touched him. "It gave me... a fresh purpose. A reason to live. A reason to fight."

He looked at Aedelric, a new, delicate hope in his eyes. "And now... You are here. Aleman of my faith. With the book." He gestured to the Gospel. "I feel... perhaps... There is a path forward, a way to fulfill Colm's mission. But I am unsure what it is. Or how?"

Aedelric sat, silent, stunned, the map and letter forgotten for a moment in his hands. The sheer weight of Gunnar's story, the depth of his hidden life, the despair he had faced, the unexpected twist of fate that had brought them together... It was almost too much to comprehend. He looked at the fierce, weathered face of the Jarl, seeing him in an entirely new light, not merely a leader of men, but a man of secret, profound faith, carrying a burden no one else knew.

Aedelric's mind raced with the implications. A Christian Jarl in pagan Norway. The hatred Hákon had shown towards his faith, towards any hint of "Christian rot." If this were ever revealed... He thought of Asa, of her strength, her loyalty to her father. He thought of Sassa, their precious daughter. They would all be in unimaginable danger. Dead, or worse. It would be devastating. They needed to tread with impossible care.

He needed a moment. Aedelric closed his eyes for a brief second, the map and letter clutched in his hand, and silently, instinctively, prayed. He prayed for guidance, for wisdom, for protection. He prayed for this man, this secret brother in faith, who had endured so much alone.

He opened his eyes, feeling a gentle resolve settle within him. He looked at Gunnar, seeing not just the Jarl, but the fellow believer who had entrusted him with his deepest secret. He collected himself, the shock still there, but now overlaid with a sense of common destiny.

"It is late, Jarl," Aedelric said, his voice composed despite the unrest inside him. He carefully folded the map and letter and placed them back into Gunnar's satchel, then returned the Gospel to its oiled cloth wrapping, holding it reverently. "We should return to the village." He met Gunnar's gaze, and a new depth of understanding and solidarity was exchanged between them. "But know this. You are not alone now. You told me... You needed to know I would not abandon Asa. My home is here. And my faith... is here too. With you. With God. We will manage this... together."

Gunnar looked at Aedelric, a slow nod forming on his face, a relief he hadn't realized he was carrying easing in his chest. The burden was not entirely lifted, but it was now, finally, shared.

They finished processing the deer in a quiet, efficient rhythm, the mundane task grounding them after the extraordinary conversation. As they shouldered the weight of the kill and turned back towards the village, the forest appeared different. The way forward was still full of unseen dangers; the shadow of Harald Fairhair loomed; and the secret they carried was a heavy one. But they walked now together, two men bound by blood, love, and a shared, hidden faith, their relationship forged anew in the quiet of the woods.

CHAPTER 9

Part 1: Family Deepens

In the months that followed, Njardarheimr settled into a new rhythm. It was a deceptive calm, a fragile peace built on the muddy, blood-soaked ground of their recent victory. Life, with its insistent demands, returned. The remaining crops were tended with fresh diligence under the strengthening sun of summer, the promise of a harvest, a powerful motivator. Fishing boats returned to the fjord, their catches a welcome addition to the village stores. Hunters ventured back into the woods, albeit in larger, more cautious groups.

Yet, the quiet was highlighted by a constant, low whirr of vigilance. The defenses, guards on the palisade, remained watchful, their gazes constantly sweeping the horizon and the forest edge. Every far-off sound was noted, every stranger eyed with suspicion. The memory of Hákon's unexpected attack, and the ever-present specter of Harald Fairhair's ambition, were constant reminders that the storm could return at any moment.

During this wary return to normalcy, life within the longhouses continued. Relationships, tested by fear and forged in joint struggle, deepened. Sassa, now a sturdy, bright-eyed infant, grew day by day, her innocent presence a source of quiet joy and a powerful symbol of what they were fighting to protect. Gunnar, the stern Jarl, often found moments of peace simply by holding her, his rough hands gentle on her soft skin, the weight of his secret faith a silent prayer for her future.

His bond with Aedelric had undergone a profound transformation. The shared secret of their faith was a powerful, unseen current flowing between them. In the still moments they shared, reviewing the palisade repairs, discussing hunting strategies, or simply sitting by the hearth late at night after the others had fallen asleep, their conversation took on a new depth. They conversed about mundane things, of the village's needs, still beneath the surface ran the implicit recognition of their shared truth. Aedelric, in turn, found a confidante in Gunnar, a fellow believer in a world that otherwise demanded secrecy. He could ask questions about Colm, about Gunnar's journey, strengthening his understanding of this hidden corner of faith in the Northlands. Their mutual respect had deepened into a quiet trust, a brotherhood created not just in arms but in the common vulnerability of their secret.

Asa watched the growing ease between her father and Aedelric with calm satisfaction. She saw the respect Aedelric had earned, not just from Gunnar, but from the villagers. His skills in training, his courage in battle, and his calm strength had all chipped away at the initial suspicion of the foreigner. She saw the love between Sassa and Aedelric deepen with each passing day, a love now rooted not in the shared responsibilities of their lives and the calm rhythm of their family.

One evening, as the longhouse slowly emptied for the night, Asa found herself alone with her father by the dying embers of the hearth. Sassa was sleeping soundly inside their shared sleeping area. The quiet stretched between them, comfortable and familiar, before Asa broke it, her voice mild, almost a whisper.

"Father," She began, tracing patterns in the ash with a bare finger. "I... I did not think it possible. To feel this way. For a man from across the sea, a Saxon, a Christian." She paused, searching for the words to explain the inexplicable. "When he was my prisoner, I felt it. A pull. A... connection which had no reason to be there. I fought it, Father, with all my strength. It was wrong, against all we believed, all I had been taught. But I could not stop it. The feelings grew. Unbidden. Unexplained."

Her voice fluttered, just slightly. She looked up at him then, her eyes vulnerable within the dim light, looking for understanding. "It was like the ocean drawing the tide, silent and powerful. There was an understanding between us from the start, a kinship of spirit that overcame our differences. I cannot explain it. No god, no custom, no logic should have allowed it, yet... here we are. Aedelric. My husband. The father of my daughter." A small, bewildered smile curved her lips. "How can such a thing be?"

Gunnar listened, his look fixed on the embers, his face unreadable. The firelight carved deep shadows throughout his features, making him look older, heavier with memory. He heard the sheer honesty in her voice, the resonances of his own past, the quiet truth he had carried alone for so long. He felt the known burden of his secret, the Christian faith he had hidden, the forbidden love he had formerly known, the choices which had shaped him.

He understood her completely. More deeply than she could ever know.

He understood the magnetic pull of a soul recognizing its own, even across the widest chasm of belief and blood. He understood how love could defy every law of the clan, custom, and god. But he kept his truth close, unwilling to burden her with it now, unwilling to reveal a vulnerability that could endanger them both.

Slowly, he reached out, his calloused hand gently covering hers, still tracing patterns in the ash. His touch was warm and grounding, the same one that had steadied her since childhood.

"My fierce daughter," he said, his voice low and steady, carrying the weight of a Jarl and the tenderness of a father. "The heart does not always follow the path laid by custom or by the old gods. Sometimes, it forges its own. Sometimes, a bond is... meant to be. Stronger than any sea, older than any custom."

He paused, his thumb stroking the back of her hand, a rare gesture of affection from a man who had spent a lifetime hiding softness behind iron.

"It is a mystery, Asa. And sometimes, the greatest strength resides in embracing what the world sends you, even when it defies all you thought you knew." His voice became softer further. "You are strong. And you have found a good man. That is all that matters. Trust what your heart tells you, daughter. It rarely lies about what really sustains us."

Asa leaned her head against his shoulder, a silent acceptance of his wisdom, a profound relief pouring over her. Gunnar closed his eyes for a moment, letting himself feel the weight of her against him, his only child, returned from the dead, a mother now, a woman grown. He rested his cheek lightly against her hair, a gesture he had not made since she was small.

During that quiet moment, the longhouse around them appeared to fade. There was only the warmth of the hearth, the soft breath of the sleeping child nearby, and the silent bond between father and daughter, a bond shaped in blood, loss, and love.

Asa knew her father understood, even if she could not apprehend the depth of that understanding. And Gunnar knew that no matter what storms came, she had discovered her anchor, not only in Aedelric, but in the unbreakable strength of her family.

Life, even under the constant threat of Harald Fairhair, found its rhythms, knitting new threads into the pattern of daily existence. Moments of quiet introspection blended with the steady hum of village life, where shared tasks often led to unexpected revelations.

One afternoon, as Asa and Astrid worked together near the storage longhouse, sorting through cured hides, a quiet moment fell between them. The sounds of the village were a quiet drone around them, the distant ring of a hammer, the call of a child, the bleating of sheep. Asa looked at Astrid, her look lingering for a moment. Astrid was talking about the quality of the hides, but something about her seemed... different. A subtle softness around her middle, a fatigue in her eyes that wasn't just the exhaustion of hard work. Asa's own experience as a mother, and the intuitive link they shared, made her notice the nearly imperceptible changes.

"Astrid," Asa said softly, interrupting their task. Astrid looked at her, a question in her eyes. "Yes?" Asa hesitated for a moment, then spoke, her voice mild. "Are you... with...child?"

Astrid froze, her hands still on the hides. Her eyes widened slightly, a trace of surprise, then a wash of vulnerability crossed her face. She hadn't thought it was noticeable yet. She looked at Asa, seeing only understanding and quiet support in her friend's expression.

Astrid lowered her voice, moving closer so only Asa could hear. "How did you know?" Asa grinned slightly. "I see you, Astrid. I have eyes. And... I know the look."

Astrid hesitated for another moment, then made her decision. She trusted Asa with her life, and with this. She nodded slowly, a combination of fear and fragile joy in her eyes. "Yes," she whispered. "I am."

A flood of warmth went through Asa, combining with a knot of concern given the dangerous times they lived in. She reached out, taking Astrid's hand. "Astrid... That is... That is wonderful news."

Astrid squeezed her hand, her gaze searching Asa's. "It is... a complication. With Harald's shadow always present." She took a deep breath. "And... the father is Eiríkr."

Asa's eyes widened again, this time with genuine surprise, then understanding. She had seen the closeness between Astrid and Eiríkr, the way they gravitated towards each other, the quiet communication that passed between them. It made sense. A wave of protective affection for both of them came over her. "Eiríkr?" Asa said, her voice mild. "Does he know?"

Astrid nodded, a small, soft smile touching her lips. "Yes. We... we discovered it just before the battle with Hákon. That night." She looked around instinctively, even though they were alone in their task, lowering her voice further. "We have not told anyone else. Not yet. It feels... too vulnerable. Too soon." She looked at Asa, her plea clear. "You cannot tell anyone, Asa. Promise me."

Asa squeezed Astrid's hand firmly, her loyalty absolute. "I promise, Astrid. Your secret is safe with me. Always." She held Astrid's gaze. "A child... in these times... It is a heavy worry. But also... a great hope."

They held the promise between them, another shared secret woven within the fabric of their lives. The vulnerability of Astrid's pregnancy and the quiet love story unfolding between her and Eiríkr added another layer to the personal stakes in Njardarheimr's survival.

Part 2: Roots and Routes

Peace, however fragile, was a gift they knew would not last indefinitely. Harald Fairhair was consolidating his power, his shadow extending across Norway. They could not simply wait for him to arrive. Gunnar knew they needed information. They needed to know Harald's movements, his strength, and maybe, find allies among other Jarls who might also resent Harald's ambition.

He called a council, not a formal Thingstead gathering, but a meeting of his closest advisors. The air in the longhouse was heavy, permeated by the scent of drying herbs and the ever-present smoke from the wood.

"Harald will come," Gunnar stated, his voice dull, accepting the inevitable. "It is not a matter of if, but when." He looked at the faces around the table. "We cannot stand alone against his full might."

"We need eyes and ears," Asa said, her gaze keen. "In the villages to the north, the south, and along the coast. We need to know what Harald is doing."

Gunnar nodded. "We send out parties. Small groups. Trusted warriors. To gather what information they can. To see if Harald's reach has already touched those places. To see if others might feel the same threat we do." He paused, his gaze holding Aedelric's for a fraction longer than the others, a silent communication shared between them about the *other* potential reason for seeking information, the refuge in Orkney that remained a distant, uncertain possibility.

"We do not reveal our hand," Gunnar instructed. "We are simply... trading parties. Visiting kinsmen. Whatever cover is needed. But they watch. They listen. They bring back every scrap of information about Harald. And they gauge the temper of the other Jarls. Are they for Harald, or against him? Are they strong, or weakened?"

Eiríkr, ever practical, leaned forward. "Longships will be needed, Jarl. To travel quickly, along the coast. Our fleet... it was weakened by the storm that brought Asa and Aedelric to us."

Gunnar's expression grew grim. The state of their longships was a constant worry. A jarl's strength was measured, in part, by his fleet. Raiding, trade, travel, and defense all relied on swift, sturdy ships. Their losses had crippled them.

"Aye, Eiríkr," Gunnar said. "We must rebuild the fleet. It is vital. Every able hand not essential for farming or defense must contribute."

The need to rebuild the longships became another focal point of village life. The sounds of axes biting into timber shifted from felling trees for everyday use to selecting and shaping the long, curved keels and ribs of the ships.

Shipbuilders, whose skills had been developed over generations, oversaw the painstaking process; trees were their wood carefully shaped and seasoned. Planks were split and smoothed, ready to be clinker-built, overlapping and fastened with iron rivets. Tar was brewed to seal the seams. It was slow, arduous work, needing precision and immense effort, an ongoing reminder of their vulnerability and their determination to regain their strength at sea.

"These ships..." Gunnar said one afternoon, watching men work on the curved ribs of the new vessel. "They are our lifeblood. Our defense... our freedom." He paused, then added, his voice subdued, meant only for Aedelric, "And perhaps... one day... our route to refuge. If needed."

Aedelric met his gaze, the tacit reference to the map, the letter, and the Orkney Islands moving between them. "We will build them strong, Jarl," Aedelric replied, his voice equally low. "Strong enough for any sea."

He knew the meaning of those words. They were building not just longships for raiding or defense, but potentially, a vessel to carry them towards an uncertain future, guided by a mysterious map and the earnest hope for a haven.

As time passed, the longships slowly began to take shape on the shore, their roots deepening in the hard ground, while the routes they sent out charted the growing threat beyond their borders. The storm was indeed gathering, and Njardarheimr was preparing, in ways both seen and unseen.

As groups of warriors were chosen and prepared for their intelligence-gathering missions, Gunnar assigned Eiríkr and Astrid together for one such journey. It was a logical pairing; both were skilled warriors, discreet, and their bond was well-known and trusted by Gunnar. They were tasked with traveling south along the coast, visiting several smaller villages and homesteads, ostensibly for trade and news.

Their journey proved a test of their skills and their relationship, away from the known confines of

Njardarheimr. They sailed in a small, sturdy knarr, a trading vessel, less conspicuous than a longship, its single square sail pushing them south along the rugged coastline. The sea air remained sharp, the waves sometimes rough, and they relied on each other for navigation, for watchfulness, and companionship during the long days and cold nights. The secret they carried, the knowledge of the life growing within Astrid, added a profound facet to their mutual moments, a quiet intimacy among the practicalities of their mission.

Eiríkr's protective instincts towards Astrid were heightened, a constant, subtle presence in his demeanor, though he had to mask it carefully. Astrid, in turn, saw Eiríkr's calm strength, his constant loyalty, and his growing maturity through the lens of their shared future.

In the villages they visited, they played their roles, trading furs and dried fish for grain or tools, and asking seemingly innocent questions about coastal raids, travel conditions, and prominent Jarls in the area. But their eyes and ears were sharp, listening for any mention of Harald Fairhair, his ships, his men, any signs of unrest or submission in these smaller communities. They gathered piecemeal information, reports of Harald's growing fleet near the fjords to the south, rumors of smaller Jarls submitting to his rule rather than facing his wrath, and stories of communities facing harsh demands for tribute. It was not a clear picture, but it confirmed the direction of the gathering storm.

In the quiet evenings, camped on a lonely stretch of beach hosted in a smoky, unfamiliar longhouse, their bond intensified further. The shared danger, the need to rely entirely on each other, stripped away any lingering pretense. They talked of their pasts, their hopes, their fears. The secret they carried, the knowledge of the life growing within Astrid, added a profound facet to their mutual moments, a quiet intimacy among the practicalities of their mission.

One night, huddled close by a small, crackling fire on a secluded cove, the soft lapping waves the only sound, Astrid leaned her head on Eiríkr's shoulder. "I never thought... this would be my life," she uttered quietly, her voice unexpectedly soft. "A shieldmaiden, yes. But... a mother? And with you." She turned her face to look at him, her eyes reflecting the firelight. "You've changed, Eiríkr. You carry yourself differently. More... sure."

Eiríkr wrapped an arm tighter around her. "And you, Astrid," he replied, his voice harsh with emotion. "You are still fierce, but... There is a gentleness now, too. A warmth I didn't always see, beneath the warrior's pride." He paused, gazing into the flames. "This child... it changes everything. Makes the risks we take, the future we fight for, feel... real." He took her hand, his thumb tracing the lines on her palm. "Are you afraid?"

Astrid sighed, a long, shaky breath. "Always," she admitted, her voice faintly whispering. "For the child. For us. For what Harald will do. But... with you, the fear feels different. Not crippling. Just... sharp. It reminds me of what I have to protect." She looked up at him, a rare, unguarded smile adorning her lips. "And you, are you ready for screaming babes and sleepless nights, for a life that isn't just axe and shield?"

Eiríkr laughed quietly, pulling her closer. "I'm ready for anything, Astrid," he said, pressing a kiss to her hair, "as long as I'm facing it with you. And if it means a future for us, for our child... then yes. I am more than ready."

Their mutual laughter, quiet and hopeful, drifted out over the waves, presenting a new perspective on the life taking root inside the shadows of war.

Part 3: Harvest and Haralds

The summer deepened, and fall became evident, painting the hillsides in bright greens and golds, before slowly, inevitably, beginning its graceful retreat. The long days, once dedicated to frantic shipbuilding, returned to the ancient rhythms of farming, hunting, and fishing. The exceptional harvest this year felt like a blessing from the gods, a reward for their fortitude and hard work. The barley house and storage pits filled with grain, dried meat, and preserved fish, a tangible promise of survival through the lean months ahead.

The harvest celebration of Vetrnætr (Winter Nights), held under the crisp, clear skies of early autumn, honored Freyr, the land spirits, and the ancestors in hopes of a mild winter and continued prosperity. It was a rare pause in the year, a night of feasting, laughter, and shared warmth after months of strain. Horns of ale and mead passed freely from hand to hand, fires crackled beneath roasting meat, and music rose into the cool air, loosening voices that had been tight with worry for too long. It was an earthy, exuberant gathering, a moment to give thanks for the land's bounty and the strength of their community, and to acknowledge the gods who governed the turning of seasons and the fragile balance between plenty and scarcity.

Yet, also amidst the feasting, the vigilance remained. The palisade was still manned; the warriors' eyes still scanned the horizon. The threat of Harald Fairhair was a shadow that no amount of ale could entirely dispel.

One of the most significant changes in the village landscape was down by the Fjord. Over the summer months, the sounds of boat building had become a constant presence. The skilled hands of the shipwrights, aided by many willing villagers, had labored tirelessly. Now, resting near the water's edge, there were six new longships, sleek and strong, their wooden ribs gleaming, their sails waiting to be hoisted. Minor details, the carving of figureheads, the final finishing of the oars, remained, but the ships themselves were, for the most part, complete and seaworthy. With the two older vessels Gunnar still possessed, Njardarheimr's fleet now numbered eight longships. It was a far cry from the massive fleets commanded by Harald, but it was a significant increase in their strength and potential mobility.

The village itself had grown. Word had spread along the coast and through the valleys, accounts of a Jarl who had stood against Hákon, of a community which valued strength and independence, a place where not everyone bowed to Harald's growing power. Seeking refuge, or perhaps drawn by Gunnar's reputation, families and warriors had arrived over the summer, adding to Njardarheimr's numbers. Their warrior strength had swelled to around three hundred and fifty, a strong force for a single village, but still a small wave against the rumored tide of one to two thousand men that followed Harald.

In the calm of the Jarl's longhouse, late into the night, only the hearth's embers and the soft moan of oak beams broke the silence. Gunnar, Aedelric, and Eiríkr bent over a patch of earth marked with campaign lines and faded hides inked with crude cartography, their fingers following Harald's path beneath the flicker of torchlight. The missions had not delivered the allies they'd hoped for. Yet, every fragment of gathered intelligence now lay bare before them revealing Harald's relentless advance and the vastness of the force they could soon confront.

"He is building his strength," Gunnar uttered one evening, his finger gliding along a line along the coastline to the east. "Subduing the smaller Jarls, demanding tribute. His fleet is growing. When he turns his full attention here..." He didn't need to finish the sentence.

Their conversations were often grim, centered on contingencies, on survival. The newly built fleet was central to their most desperate plan.

"If he comes by land, overwhelming our defenses," Gunnar explained, his gaze meeting Aedelric's, a wordless acknowledgment shared between them about the Orkney map, "we use the village as a shield. Buy as much time as possible." He looked at Eiríkr. "Get as many people, the women, the children, the elders, onto the ships as we can. Stocked and ready." He turned back to Aedelric. "You, Eiríkr, Leif... you will oversee that. Ensure each ship is ready to sail at a moment's notice. Food, water, furs, weapons for defense at sea."

"And if he comes by sea?" Eiríkr asked. "If his ships fill the fjord?"

"Then we cannot use our ships for escape here," Gunnar said grimly. "We fight on the beaches, at the water's edge, to buy time for the village to flee into the forest. Find refuge in the mountains." He pointed towards the rugged peaks behind the village, a harsh but familiar sanctuary. The plan for using the forest as an escape route, while discussed, was less detailed, an urgent dash rather than an organized departure.

The worst possibility hung unspoken in the air, a simultaneous attack by land and sea. In that scenario, there was only one plan: they would all fight to the death, defending their home to the last breath. That was a given.

As the men went over these grim possibilities, tracing routes and discussing timings, the women of the longhouse, sensing the heavy turn of the conversation, decided a walk in the fresh autumn air was in order. Asa, Astrid, and a few others rose and moved towards the door. As they passed through the main hall, their eyes fell upon Leif and Elara.

Young Leif, no longer the terrified recruit of the battle but a hardening warrior, was whispering alongside Elara, the servant girl who had cared for Sassa during the attack.

They were leaning close together by the now-cold hearth, sharing a quiet laugh, a perceptible warmth and fondness evident in their easy smiles and lingering glances. Their relationship, a shy, budding romance born in the shared fear and relief of the past months, had become a small, sweet note in the otherwise tense atmosphere.

Asa smiled, seeing the innocent connection between them. Astrid, too, watched them with a gentle expression. One of the older women in the group, a perceptive flash in her eye, nudged Astrid. "Look at those two," she spoke quietly. "Young love blooms even in hard times."

Asa, feeling a rare moment of happiness, turned to Astrid. "Why don't you two," she said, addressing Leif as well, along with Elara, with a kindly smile, "Take a walk with us? Or... perhaps you would prefer a walk on your own? The air is fresh outside." Her meaning was clear: an invitation for them to have some private time.

She and she exchanged shy, eager glances, blushing. "Oh... well..." Leif stammered.

Eiríkr, overhearing from the planning table, let out a bark of laughter. "Careful there, young Leif!" he called out, his voice projecting slightly in the hall. "Don't be humping her too much! You'll have her pregnant before winter!" It was a crude joke, but made with a familiar affection for the young man.

Aedelric rolled his eyes good-naturedly, while Gunnar's gaze, sharp despite his years, fixed on Eiríkr for a moment, then glanced to Astrid. A slow, cunning smile spread across the Jarl's face.

"Or perhaps," Gunnar said, his voice composed, deliberately loud enough for Eiríkr and Astrid, and indeed everyone in the hall, to hear, "he should take your advice. Eiríkr, it seems *you* had no such caution yourself."

A stunned quiet descended over the hall. Eiríkr's laughter died in his throat, replaced by a look of absolute shock. Astrid froze by the door, her hand halfway to the latch, her face draining of color. Asa stared at her father, bewildered. Leif and Elara looked between the adults, their eyes wide and their expressions confused.

Eiríkr found his voice first, a hoarse whisper. "Jarl... How...?"

Gunnar's smile held a trace of amusement. "I might be old, Eiríkr, but I am not blind. And I see everything." He looked pointedly at Astrid, then back at Eiríkr.

Astrid turned to Asa, her eyes swelled with dismay. "Asa? You told him?"

Asa shook her head vehemently, as shocked as Astrid. "No! Astrid, I swear! I did not tell him!"

The sudden, deeply personal revelation lingered, completely derailing the preceding discussion and the planning session. Eiríkr looked from Gunnar to Astrid, a flush creeping up his neck. Aedelric watched the unfolding scene with wide eyes, a combination of surprise and understanding.

Gunnar, perhaps sensing the awkwardness he had caused, cleared his throat loudly. "Right then," he said, his tone abruptly shifting back to the practicalities of survival. "The forest route. We need to map out the best paths. Consider how quickly we can move the less able." He gestured for Eiríkr and Aedelric to return to the map.

The men, visibly relieved by the change of subject, quickly bent their heads back over the rough map, muttering about terrain and timings, leaving the women and the young couple standing in the charged silence.

Asa, Astrid, and the other women traded glances, the implicit question hanging between them: How indeed did Gunnar know? Astrid appeared completely shaken, her carefully guarded secret revealed in such a public, albeit accidental, manner.

Taking their cue, Asa put a comforting arm around Astrid's shoulders. "Come," she uttered softly. "Let us take that walk." They stepped out into the fresh autumn air, leaving the men to their grim planning along with the lingering shock of Gunnar's unexpected announcement. Leif and Elsa, perceiving the change, decided their private walk was no longer a good idea and stayed close to Asa and Astrid, casting questioning glances back inside.

They walked through the village, past the longhouses, the drying racks, the repaired palisade. The air smelled of smoke and fall.

"I did not tell him, Astrid," Asa said again, her voice earnest. "I promise you."

Astrid hugged herself, her expression troubled. "I believe you. But... how? How did he know?" The question stayed unanswered between them, adding to the uncertainty of their situation.

As they walked through the northern side of the village, the familiar path toward the fjord curved away from the longhouse and led them toward the main gate. The ground rose slightly there, forming a natural rise beside the palisade, not part of the parapet, but high enough to give a clear view over the land beyond.

They followed the wall eastward, the timber logs towering to their right, the faint scent of the fjord drifting on the breeze from farther down the slope. Their steps were unhurried, enjoying the brief respite from the longhouse and the cool bite of early air.

But as they reached the rise beside the gate, the view opened northward across the rolling ground beyond the village.

And that was when they saw them.

Riders.

A small company, approaching from the north with a deliberate, unhurried pace.

Asa's hand went instinctively to the dagger she carried on her belt, her posture stiffening. Astrid stiffened beside her, her gaze sharpening. Almost simultaneously, a sharp cry cut through the air from above; one of the guards on the palisade, high on the rampart, had spotted them. His voice carried clearly on the breeze.

"Riders! Approaching the gate!"

Asa's eyes narrowed, scanning the figures on horseback. They rode at a deliberate, almost arrogant pace, their formation loose and unconcerned. As they drew closer, her look fixed on the banner fluttering in the breeze, a raven, stark and black against a field of white.

"Harald," she spoke quietly, the name a bitter taste on her tongue, recognizing the hated emblem of Harald Fairhair's 'Landwaster' banner.

A guard was already scrambling down the interior ramp of the palisade, running towards them. "Asa! How many?"

"Only a handful," Asa replied, her voice keen and controlled. "Not a raiding party." She could see their casual formation, their unhurried approach. It was not a force meant for battle, but for display. "Arrogance," she commented to Astrid beside her, a grim set to her jaw. "You can see it from here."

She turned to Elara, who had followed them out, Asa still holding Sassa close. "Elara, take Sassa back to the longhouse. Go quickly." She handed the child to her gently. "Leif!" she called out, now standing near the palisade gate. "Hurry! Get my father!"

Leif, galvanized by the urgency and authority in Asa's voice, turned and ran back towards the longhouse, Elara scurrying behind him with Sassa held firmly.

Leif burst into the longhouse, interrupting the planning session along with the lingering awkwardness that had been present. "Jarl!" he called out, breathless, his chest heaving. "Harald's banner! Approaching the gate!" She was standing just inside the door, clutching Sassa, her eyes open wide with apprehension.

The conversation about escape routes was instantly forgotten. Weapons were grabbed, faces hardened.

Gunnar's gaze was sharp, decisive. "Warriors!" he roared to the household guard and any other fighters in the hall. "With me! To the palisade!"

They ran through the longhouse and out into the cool fall air, moving swiftly towards the main gate. Asa and Astrid were there, joining the guards who were watching the approaching figures.

Gunnar climbed onto the palisade wall, where Asa and Astrid were watching the riders approach the gate. They looked out, their eyes fixed on the handful of riders drawing closer.

"It's them," Asa confirmed to her father, her voice subdued. "Only a few. Not an army. Not yet." She watched their confident, almost leisurely approach. "They ride like they own the land." Her earlier comment to Astrid stayed with her.

Gunnar watched the riders approach the gate of Njardarheimr, his countenance unreadable. They did not slow, yet neither did they come with blades drawn. Their pace was steady, purposeful, the kind carried by men who bore messages heavier than their weapons. Even from a distance, there was something in the way they held themselves, an undercurrent tension beneath their controlled movements, an authority that bore upon the air akin to the first shift of wind before a gale.

They were Harald's warriors, that much was clear, heralds by duty, but their presence carried more than simple news. Something rode with them, unseen but palpable, a weight that hung over the village like a shadow extending long across the earth.

Gunnar felt it in his bones, the way old warriors do when the world begins to tilt. Whatever tidings these men brought, they were not small ones. Their arrival was the first trace of something huge moving beyond the horizon.

Part 4: Harald's Demand

The handful of riders approached the gate at a confident, unhurried pace, their horses' feet being heard in the autumn air. High on the palisade wall, Gunnar, Asa, and Astrid watched them, flanked by a few watchful guards. Below, the gate remained shut, its heavy timbers a solid barrier. Gunnar's gaze was steady, assessing the approaching figures. He did not recognize any of them, not their faces, not their gear, beyond the unmistakable banner fluttering overhead.

One of the archers on the palisade wall, a young man who was not thinking, drew his bowstring back instinctively, an arrow nocked and ready. With a swift, decisive motion, Asa raised her arm, her hand flat, signaling him to stand down. The archer paused for a moment, then slowly relaxed his bow, though his eyes remained fixed on the riders.

The Harald's warrior-messengers pulled their horses to a halt a short distance from the gate, their mail gleaming dully in the afternoon light. They were indeed seasoned fighters, their postures relaxed but alert, their vision scanning the palisade, noting the repairs and the watchful faces atop the wall. The one who appeared to be in charge, a large man with a weather-beaten face and a cruel flash in his eye, wearing mail and a good helmet, looked up at Gunnar. Called Sven, one of Harald's most trusted men.

Sven sat tall on his horse, emitting an arrogance that seemed to precede him like a wave. He spoke, his voice reaching clearly to the palisade, adopting the same mocking tone Harald had used months ago in the longhouse. "Jarl Gunnar," Sven called out, a smirk tugging on his lips. "Do you meet all your guests with a closed gate these days?"

Gunnar's expression remained unreadable, his voice composed and level. "Times are dangerous," he replied.

"Caution is wise for everyone, and," his gaze narrowed slightly, "I do not recognize the man I am speaking to."

Sven chuckled, a low, unpleasant sound. "Indeed. But you should know Harald Fairhair's banner, surely?"

"I do," Gunnar said. "And I recognize it. But that does not tell me who stands before my gate. State your name and purpose."

Sven's smirk widened. "I am Sven," he announced, his voice conveying the force of his master's authority. "One of Harald Fairhair's most trusted warriors. And these are my men." He gestured to the warriors flanking him.

"Sven," Gunnar acknowledged with a curt nod. "Why this late visit?"

"We are sent," Sven explained, his voice shifting from mock pleasantly to blunt command, "to visit the villages and homesteads in these lands. To ensure that when Harald Fairhair arrives to visit his new subjects, they have their tribute ready." He motioned vaguely. "All the other villages have seen the wisdom of cooperation. Yours is the last on our list."

The words landed like bricks, heavy with implied threat. Gunnar felt the cold hand of fear grip him for a momentary second, a fear he instantly suppressed. This was not a visit; it was a declaration, a warning. Harald was coming, not to parley, but to conquer. And Sven's presence, his arrogant demeanor, the mention of other villages bending the knee, it was all meant to intimidate, to make Gunnar understand that resistance was futile, that Harald expected him to submit or be crushed. Harald was using this moment to assess the defenses and the spirit of the village.

But Gunnar did not show the slightest bit of fear. He remained a figure of firm strength on the wall, his voice composed, almost dismissive. "Tribute?" Gunnar said, lifting an eyebrow slightly. "I was not aware I was a subject of Harald Fairhair. This... this is new to me."

Sven's eyes narrowed, the humor draining from his face, replaced by a hard glint of annoyance. "You should have known, Jarl. It is disappointing that this information has not reached you. But you will have the tribute ready regardless."

"And what does Harald Fairhair expect as tribute?" Gunnar asked, his voice still calm, but with an edge of steel that disguised his easy tone.

Sven's cruel smile returned. "You will know," he said, his voice muted and menacing, "when Harald arrives."

That was all Gunnar needed to hear. This wasn't a negotiation for tribute; it was a clear declaration of war. Harald did not seek Gunnar's fealty; he sought his destruction. Harald saw Gunnar as a potential rival, a strong Jarl in a strategic location. Harald intended to eliminate him and take his land and resources. And his family... There would be no reason to spare them. Asa and Sassa would be threats, symbols around which others could rally in the future.

A dangerous glint entered Gunnar's eyes, a flash of the old warrior's fire. He turned to the guards by the gate hinges. "Open the gate," he commanded, his voice resounding with quiet authority.

A quiver of surprise went through all on the palisade. Open the gate? To Harald's men?

Gunnar turned back to Sven, his expression hardening into a challenging stare. "The gate is open, Sven," Gunnar called out, his voice projecting clearly. "You are welcome to enter my village." It was an invitation, plain and simple, an invitation to fight. And Gunnar had every intention of accepting, of having Sven and his men cut down the moment they set foot inside.

Sven, for all his arrogance, was not foolish. He saw the look in Gunnar's eyes, the sudden tension in the warriors on the wall, the small shift in the air around the gate. He understood the challenge; the trap being offered. The smirk vanished completely, replaced by a look of cold fury.

"We decline your invitation, Jarl," Sven said, his voice rigid with suppressed rage. He knew he had been seen, that his attempts at intimidation had failed against the old Jarl. "But I promise you... We will see you again soon. When Harald arrives."

His gaze swept over Gunnar, then lingered on Asa, standing beside her father, her face resolute. A repellent smirk returned, fouler than before. "And your daughter," Sven added, his voice sinking to a vile purr that gave a chill through everyone who heard it. "Harald will deal with you, Jarl. But I... I will make sure she is taken care of properly."

The air sizzled with instant, violent rage. Archers on the wall tensed, drawing their bows. Warriors held their weapons, their faces contorted with fury at the blatant, sickening threat against Asa. They were ready to lose, to charge, to tear these men apart.

But Gunnar, his face an expression of iron control despite the surge of protectiveness and care and fury that roared within him at the threat to Asa, raised a hand, palm out, a single, decisive gesture. The archers held. The warriors stilled, their rage simmering, held in check by their Jarl's command.

Sven saw their reaction, saw the leashed fury he had provoked, and a trace of unease crossed his face. They had pushed too far, misjudging the old Jarl and his people. He kicked his horse, turning it sharply. "Your defenses are... impressive, Jarl!" he yelled back, the bravado returning, though a visible tension remained in his shoulders as he rode away. "That gate... and the wall! We will see them again soon!"

He and his men turned and rode back the way they had come, their retreat swift and purposeful now, leaving behind them an air dense with unspoken threats and smoldering rage.

As the sound of their horses faded, the tension in Njardarheimr did not ease. Harald was coming. Soon. And his intentions were deadly clear.

Gunnar turned from the palisade wall, his eyes hard, his mind already racing. He looked at Eiríkr, who had joined them on the wall, his visage grim.

"Eiríkr," Gunnar said, his voice keen urgently. "Find the quickest rider in the village. And the fastest horse. They need to scout ahead. Ride south. Find Harald's army. Get eyes on them. And then ride back here like the wind. We need to know how much time we have."

The period of waiting was over. The storm was no longer only gathering on the horizon. It was on its way.

Part 5: Jarl's Plan

Sven's words and his vile threat against Asa had given a jolt of icy fear through Njardarheimr, a fear that Gunnar knew, left unchecked, could easily become panic. His mind, however, was not gripped by fear, but by a thousand racing thoughts, possibilities, strategies, the terrible burden of responsibility for every soul in his village. Eiríkr was already gone, running towards the stables to find the fastest rider and the swiftest horse, Scildfrēond, Aedelric's horse, whom they brought back with them from Pall's village. His steps echoed the desperate urgency that now permeated the air.

Aedelric, Asa, and Astrid turned to Gunnar, their faces knitted with grim resolve, but with a trace of the fear that Sven's visit had just reignited. "Jarl," Aedelric said, his voice stiff. "What do we need to do?"

Asa and Astrid matched his question with their eyes, ready for orders, but the implicit question hovered between them: *Are we ready? Is there anything more?*

Gunnar saw the fear, saw the potential for it to spread rapidly through the village. He needed to stem it now. He took a deep breath, and when he spoke, his voice was calm, steady, a deliberate counterpoint to the rising tension. Still beneath the calm lay the firm authority of the Jarl, a stern command that demanded immediate action.

"Aedelric," Gunnar said, his look locking firmly with the Saxon's. "Your task is the ships now. Go to the Fjord and take charge. Work with Leif and the others. Make certain every vessel is ready to sail at a moment's notice, stocked, provisioned, sails checked, and lines secured. Everything in order. When the time comes, we cannot afford delay."

Aedelric nodded, grasping the weight of the order; the escape plan was now not a distant contingency, but an immediate possibility. "Yes, Jarl. They will be ready." He turned and moved swiftly towards the path leading to the fjord, his mind already cataloging supplies and tasks.

Gunnar turned to Asa. "Asa. Your archers, all of them. Get them organized. Check their quivers. Make sure every arrow is accounted for. Then get them into position: the longhouse roofs, the palisade walls… anywhere they can strike hardest when Harald's men show themselves."

Asa's face hardened, her fury cold and controlled. "They will be ready, Father."

She pivoted sharply, her voice escalating with the unmistakable edge of command. "Archers! With me!" The warriors snapped to attention as she strode through them, checking quivers with quick, practiced motions. "Full count on arrows, no one goes short! Move! Roof lines and wall positions, now!"

Gunnar looked at Astrid, his look easing slightly. "Astrid. Gather the warriors: every warrior and the rest of the village. Get everyone to the square. Now."

Astrid nodded, her gaze grim. She knew what this meant: a village-wide assembly, a moment to face the inevitable together. "It will be done, Jarl." She moved through the village, her voice sounding out over the rising susurration of worry, calling people towards the central square.

Throughout Njardarheimr, the shift was immediate and profound. The semblance of everyday life vanished. Villagers hurried, not in panic, but with a grim, focused purpose. Warriors grabbed their weapons, their faces hardening. Children, perceiving the shift in the adults, clung to their parents. The sounds of hurried movement, low voices, and the ringing of armor resounded in the air as everyone converged on the square.

Gunnar watched them go, saw the fear in their eyes, the resolve in their strides. He began to stroll towards the square, his pace deliberate, outwardly calm despite the tempest raging within him. In his mind, a silent, fervent prayer rose. *God.* His thought was raw, simple, born of desperate need. *Now. Now is the time I need you to show up. Give me strength. Give us a way.*

As he reached the square, the villagers and warriors were already gathering, a tense, watchful crowd. They looked at Gunnar, their Jarl, their leader, their faces showing a mixture of apprehension and trust. Eiríkr arrived back at the edge of the square, his chest heaving slightly, confirming to Gunnar with a quiet nod, "He is on his way, Jarl. Our fastest rider. On the fastest horse."

Gunnar's thoughts raced. The scout's report was crucial. Knowing the size of Harald's army, their speed, and their route could mean the difference between survival and annihilation. It could inform their final desperate choice: fight here, flee to the ships, or vanish into the forest. But even without the scout's report, Gunnar knew they had done almost everything they could to prepare. Their defenses were as strong as they could make them, their ships as ready as possible, their warriors as trained as time had allowed. The rest would be in their courage, their unity, and perhaps... the hands of God.

He mounted the low stone platform of the Thingstead, the center of their community, the place where decisions were made and their shared identity affirmed. Silence dropped over the square; everyone's gaze set on him. The air snapped with tense anticipation. Gunnar knew, with an eerie certainty, that this was one of the most critical moments of his life. He had to be strong. Show no fear. Be the anchor his people needed in the face of the coming storm.

He looked out at them, his voice resounding with strength and strong determination. "Hear me, people of Njardarheimr!" Gunnar's voice, though not a shout, carried across the square, filled with fire and a fierce, unyielding confidence. "Harald Fairhair sends his demands! He seeks to make us bend the knee! To take our land! To take our freedom!"

He didn't sugarcoat the threat, but he immediately offered them a path forward, a sense of agency in the face of overwhelming odds. "We are not helpless!" he declared, his look gliding over the assembled faces, instilling courage with his very presence. "We have prepared! We have built! We have trained!"

He laid out their grim strategy, weaving it within a narrative of resistance and cunning. "Our ships are ready!" he announced, his voice strong. "Ready to carry the women, the children, the elders to safety if Harald's fleet is not here to trap us in the fjord! We will know soon if that path is open to us!" The uncertainty was acknowledged but framed within a potential action framework.

"If Harald's army comes by land," Gunnar continued, his tone hardening, "we will use this village as a shield! We will use the defenses you have built! The gates will hold against their initial rage! Let them waste their strength against our walls! Let them stumble into the wolf stakes, the traps you have dug!"

He spoke of the fighting force, of the warriors, and the newly trained. "Asa and her archers," he announced, gesturing towards the longhouses where the archers were taking position, "will rain fire upon them! From above! On land or at sea, their arrows will bite deep!"

He then spoke of the plan for the fighters if the gate was breached, outlining a desperate, vital role. "Astrid, Aedelric, Eiríkr," he named them, the core of his fighting leadership, "and the warriors in the killing ground!" He looked at Aedelric, a shared understanding flowing between them. The shieldwall had served its purpose against Hákon, but against Harald's likely numbers, a static defense inside the gate might be a death sentence for the entire village trapped behind them. Their role now was different. "You will not stand as a single wall to be broken! You will spread out! You will be a distraction! A storm of resistance in their path!"

He emphasized the goal: time. "Every moment you fight them inside the gate, every enemy you draw away from the crucial task," he said, his voice climbing with intense resolve, "buys time! Time for our people to get to the ships! Or time for them to make for the forest, for the safety of the mountains!"

He looked out at his people, his firm gaze, fire in his eyes. "This is not our end!" he roared, his voice ringing with conviction, instilling hope, pushing back the fear. "This is not the day Njardarheimr falls! We will see another day! Yes, some will fall!" The harsh reality was acknowledged but faced head-on. "That is the price of resistance! But we are not weak! We are not alone! We are stronger than Harald Fairhair thinks! We are the roots that have held firm in this land for generations! And we will not be easily broken!"

A wave of raw emotion surged through the crowd, fear, yes, but also a rekindled determination, a fierce pride in their Jarl's steady strength. His words and confidence pushed back the advancing panic. They looked at each other, seeing not just their fear, but the common resolve in their neighbors' eyes.

He stressed the need for readiness and the importance of the human element. "We will all sleep in shifts!" he ordered. "You will need rest! But when you are called... You will be ready! We will all be ready!"

The crowd dispersed, not with the panicked flight of the defeated, but with the focused energy of a community facing overwhelming odds with their eyes open. The air, minutes ago charged with fear, now pattered with a grim, determined purpose. The fate of Njardarheimr hung in the balance, awaiting the return of a single scout and the arrival of a storm they could no longer outrun.

Part 6: Long Watch

Only a few hours after Harald's man, Sven, had delivered his chilling demand at the gate, and the fastest rider in Njardarheimr had galloped south, the scout returned. The scout's face coated with sweat and grime, Scildfrēond lathered and blowing hard, rode straight to Gunnar's longhouse. He dismounted heavily, his legs stiff from the ride, and was quickly ushered inside, where Gunnar, Asa, Aedelric, Astrid, and Eiríkr waited, their faces tight in anticipation.

He didn't waste words. His voice was strained, grim. "I found them, Jarl. South, a night's walk. Camped... there are many." He paused, taking a deep breath. "Two thousand, Jarl. Maybe more. It is... a great army."

A stunned quiet descended over the longhouse. Two thousand. The number remained in the air, a crushing weight. Gunnar felt a chilling knot tighten in his gut, even though he had expected a large force. *Two thousand.* He thought of his own three hundred and fifty warriors, brave and ready, but so few against such a tide. *Almost every warrior in the region,* the thought rang in his mind, a terrifying confirmation to Harald's power and the reach of his ambition.

Asa's hand reflexively went to Aedelric's, their fingers intertwining, a silent show of shared fear and solidarity. Astrid's face turned pale, and Eiríkr's jaw clenched, his gaze hardening. Leif, who had been standing nearby, helping to secure the longhouse, looked visibly shaken, his earlier youthful confidence momentarily evaporating in the face of the overwhelming numbers.

The scout's report came over the village as a shroud. There was no more frantic preparation to be done. The ships were ready by the fjord, stocked and waiting. The archers were positioned, their quivers filled. The warriors knew their roles, grim as they might be. All that was left was the waiting. The long, agonizing watch through the night for the dawn that would bring Harald Fairhair's army to their doorstep.

As the night deepened, a heavy quiet came upon Njardarheimr. Fires burned low in the longhouses, emitting flickering light on weary faces. The air was laden with unspoken fear, but also with a fierce, strong resolve. Families clustered together, gaining comfort in proximity. Guards stood vigilant on the palisade, their eyes strained against the darkness, listening to the sounds of the night, the hoot of an owl, the distant cry of a fox, sounds that now seemed full of menace.

In Gunnar's longhouse, the central hearth offered a pool of warmth and dim light. The scout's report had been delivered, the immediate shock absorbed, and the final hours extended out before them.

Asa and Aedelric retreated to their small, curtained-off space with Sassa. The air inside the curtain felt warmer, safer, a tiny sanctuary against the vast darkness outside. Sassa was asleep in her cradle, her soft, even breaths a heartbreaking counterpoint to the tension that gripped her parents. Asa sat on their sleeping platform, leaning against Aedelric, his arm around her, both watching their daughter.

"Two thousand," Asa murmured, the number still feeling unreal. "How can we...?"

Aedelric held her tighter. "We fight," he said, his voice quiet but firm. "We fight for her." His gaze moved from Sassa to Asa, his love for them a fierce, protective fire within him. He thought of Gunnar's secret faith, of Colm's dying words, of the map to Orkney. Was this the night they would need that refuge? He offered a silent prayer, a prayer for strength, for guidance, for a miracle in the face of impossible odds. "Whatever comes, Asa, we face it together. As a family."

Asa leaned into him, drawing strength from his presence and the solid reality of his body next to hers. She reached out and gently touched Sassa's cheek, her heart breaking with love and fear for the future. Gunnar entered the space quietly, watching them for a moment. He saw their fear, but also their deep, unshakable bond, centered on the innocent life of his grandchild. This, he thought, was what they fought for. This was the future they desperately needed to protect. He offered them a rare, slight smile, a silent show of support and common purpose, before retiring to his sleeping platform, the load of his Jarl's responsibilities heavy upon him, his secret faith, a quiet comfort, and a silent hope.

In another corner of the longhouse, Astrid and Eiríkr discovered a quiet space away from the others. Astrid's pregnancy, no longer a carefully guarded secret, appeared impossibly vulnerable now. The knowledge of the life growing within her made the prospect of battle terrifyingly real, but also imbued her with a fierce, protective resolve.

Eiríkr watched her, his gaze filled with love and unspoken fear for her and their unborn child.

"It is many," Eiríkr said, breaking the silence, his voice subdued. "Two thousand."

Astrid nodded, wrapping her arms around herself. "Too many for a shieldwall."

Eiríkr reached for her, pulling her close. "Then we fight differently. We fight smart." His hand went to her belly, resting there gently. "We fight for this."

They looked at each other, the tacit weight of the night and the coming dawn heavy between them. This might be their last night together. The thought remained in the air, raw and painful. They were seeking the comfort of each other's bodies in the face of such overwhelming uncertainty. There were no elaborate words, only the quiet sounds of their shared breathing, the gentle touch of their hands, the silent promises whispered against skin. They held each other close, finding peace and strength in their physical closeness, a desperate affirmation of life in the face of impending death, praying silently in their ways for a future they might share as a family of three.

Leif, together with Elara, young and their love still new and shy, found a corner near the wall, away from the leading group but not entirely alone. The fear they felt was raw and visible.

"Two thousand," Leif whispered, his voice fluttering slightly. "That's... so many."

Elara consented, tears filling her eyes. "Are we going to die, Leif?"

Leif didn't have an answer. He pulled her close, holding her tightly. "I don't know, Elara." He thought of Aedelric's training, of the shieldwall, of the grim plans Gunnar had laid out. He thought of Elara, her kindness, her calm strength. He had never felt anything like this for another person. The thought of losing her was unbearable.

"I..." Leif began, his voice uncertain, shy. "I want to... to be with you, Elara. Truly." The crude joke Eiríkr had made earlier felt miles away. This was about something else. Something honest and vulnerable.

Elara looked up at him, her gaze wide and solemn, understanding the implicit depth of his words, the gravity of the night. "I know, Leif," she whispered. "I want that too."

In the quiet, fear-filled longhouse, among the sleeping forms and the watchful guards, these two young souls, facing the terrifying uncertainty of the dawn, found a moment of desperate connection, a quiet act of resistance against the death that approached outside. They lay together on their furs, two bodies seeking warmth and peace in the cold night, their burgeoning love a fragile flame in the darkness.

Throughout the longhouse, people found their ways to endure the waiting. Some sharpened their weapons, while others tended to the wounded from past skirmishes; most lay awake, listening to the sounds of the night, their thoughts weighed down by a blend of dread and hope. The ships were ready, the archers were in place, and the warriors knew their tasks. Every possible preparation had been made. Now, all they could do was wait.

The hours passed slowly by, marked only by the changing of the guards on the palisade, archers, and the gradual dimming of the fires. The sounds of the night remained, but now, every rustle among leaves, every distant snap of a twig, was amplified, potentially the harbinger of the approaching army.

Slowly, agonizingly, the deep black of night commenced to soften. The stars faded. A faint, grey light appeared on the eastern horizon. The long watch was nearing its end. The dawn was coming. And with it, Harald Fairhair's army.

CHAPTER 10

Part 1: Dawn of the Storm

The long watch had ended. The night merged into the cold, grey light of pre-dawn. On the palisade wall of Njardarheimr, Jarl Gunnar stood, a single figure against the broad expanse of the morning sky. He had been there for hours, watching the southern horizon, his mind a whirl of strategy, faith, and terrible possibilities. The village behind him was a hive of quiet, tense readiness, warriors at their posts, archers positioned, families clustered in the longhouses near the escape routes, the ships waiting by the fjord.

As the initial rays of sunlight started to paint the eastern sky in pale, cold hues, Gunnar's eyes, sharp and steady, caught a movement on the southern road: a single rider.

He watched him approach, a single figure on horseback, moving with a deliberate, almost leisurely pace. It wasn't a scout; Gunnar didn't raise the alarm yet. He waited, watching, a knot of anticipation tightening in his gut.

The rider drew closer, and as the distance narrowed, the morning light illuminated the figure more clearly. The set of the shoulders, the confidence in the posture, the way the rider held himself… Gunnar knew him. A chill, cold, and sharp, traced its way down his spine. It wasn't a messenger. It was Harald Fairhair himself.

Harald pulled his horse to a halt a short distance from the closed gate, looking up at Gunnar on the palisade wall. There was no army visible yet, only him, the Jarl, and the man who sought to be king, facing each other across the silent ground.

Harald smiled, a thin, chilling expression that didn't reach his eyes. "Expecting me, Jarl Gunnar?" he called out, his voice distinct and surprisingly pleasant in the quiet morning air.

Gunnar met his gaze, his expression impassive. "I have been," he replied, his voice composed, betraying nothing of the unrest inside him. "For some time now."

Harald's eyes, sharp and assessing, swept over the palisade, noting the reinforced sections, the sharpened stakes, the vigilant guards discreetly positioned. "You have been busy, Jarl," he commented, a note of reluctant respect in his voice. "Word travels, even in these remote fjords. They say you are doing well for yourself here. Building your strength."

"The gods have been good to the village," Gunnar said, acknowledging the hard work of his people, ascribing it to the higher powers his people still worshipped.

Harald laughed, a short, sharp sound devoid of humor. "The gods?" He shook his head. "I hear other whispers, Jarl. Talks of a Saxon Christian you harbor. They say he has... *humped* your only daughter." Harald's voice oozed with casual cruelty, designed to provoke. "And that you have allowed this... defilement. That she has even borne him a Christian whelp, and you let them live, here, in your hall."

Gunnar did not deny it. There was no point. Harald clearly knew more than he had let on. He met Harald's gaze directly. "My affairs are my own, Harald. Why such interest?"

Harald leaned forward slightly in his saddle, his smile returning, colder than before. "Your affairs are *my* affairs, Jarl. I am always interested in what goes on in my kingdom. In the lands I have united."

Gunnar's jaw tensed. "Kingdom?" he repeated, a hint of challenge in his voice. "Subjugating free people is no kingdom. Only fools declare themselves kings."

Harald's laugh rang in the quiet morning, a sound of pure arrogance. "Only the strongest of men make themselves kings, Gunnar. And I have done so. All bends to my will now. Save you."

"My people will not be subjugated," Gunnar stated, his voice flat, resolute.

Harald's smile vanished. His eyes turned cold, hard as flint. "Then this is why they will die, Gunnar. All of them." His voice dropped, becoming dangerously low. "I knew it, months ago. When I visited your hall, I should have killed you then. Put an end to it." A hint of frustrated rage entered his voice. "Perhaps Hákon would still be alive if I had simply... removed you."

Gunnar felt a cold clarity settle over him. Harald was aware of Hákon's attack and appeared to be involved in some way. *So there is a spy,* the thought registered, calm and confident, even as Harald stood before him, threatening his life. He did not betray this knowledge, did not give Harald the satisfaction of confirming a leak in his village. It mattered little now. The inevitable was at hand.

Harald continued, explaining his knowledge, his motives. "Hákon came to me," he said, his voice projecting, spinning a narrative of treachery. "After you cast him out. Bitter. Angry. He knew you were weak, Gunnar, under the spell of a Christian. He wanted to root it out. To cleanse this place." Harald's lip curled in disdain. "I gave him a mission. Gold. To find others who would join him. To rid your village of the Christian rot." He shook his head. "But he was too weak. He failed."

He looked at Gunnar, his gaze keen. "I came here, months ago, to size you up, Gunnar. To see what kind of man defied me. And when I saw the defenses, you have built," he gestured to the palisade, "and heard how your numbers have grown... I knew." Harald's voice hardened, becoming utterly merciless. "I knew a simple demand would not suffice. I needed a great army. To rid you from this land for good, Gunnar. You, and all your kin."

"The fates will decide this day," Gunnar replied, his voice composed, fatalistic, placing the outcome in the hands of powers beyond mortal men.

Harald threw back his head and laughed again, a long, mocking sound. "Fate!" he sneered, his eyes smoldering with contempt. "You know nothing of the gods, Gunnar! You are a dirty Christian!" He pointed up at Gunnar on the palisade, his voice climbing to a freezing roar, his words a torrent of pure, unadulterated malice. "And you will suffer for it! I will take your daughter! Your precious Asa!" His smile remained a horrifying rictus of pure evil. "I will take her here! In front of you! Then I will have every man in my army do the same!"

The guards on the wall held their weapons, their faces contorted with fury. Below, unseen by Harald, warriors along the palisade, drawn by the raised voices, listened in horror, their hands going to their axes.

Harald's voice grew even more vicious. "Then, when they are done with your whore of a daughter, I will take the whelp! Your granddaughter! I will kill her here! In front of you! Crush the life from her tiny body!" He paused, letting the monstrous words hang in the air. "Then... I will butcher your followers! Every last one of them who denies the true gods!" His gaze returned to Gunnar. "And you, old man? You will not have a warrior's death. You will be strung up on my longhouse in my village and left to starve! To rot! A feast for the ravens!"

Gunnar stood utterly unfazed, his visage a mask of iron control. He did not flinch, did not cry out, did not show the slightest hint of the devastation the words wrought within him. The horror of the threat against Asa and Sassa was a cold, burning fire in his gut, but he would not give Harald the satisfaction of seeing his pain. His composure was a shield, a last act of defiance.

Harald watched Gunnar, his rage mounting as his horrific threats failed to elicit a reaction. Angered by Gunnar's stoic silence, he spun his horse around sharply.

"See you soon, Gunnar!" Harald roared over his shoulder, his voice as a promise of impending destruction, and spurred his horse into a gallop.

Harald rode back the way he had come, disappearing swiftly over a low hill that marked the edge of the visible horizon. The moment he vanished, the silence was broken. Not by a single sound, but by the growing, rumbling roar of thousands. The sound of an army on the move.

Gunnar stood on the palisade; his eyes fixed on the hill Harald had just crested. The sound grew louder, deeper, the unmistakable thunder of countless feet. And then, over the crest of the hill, they appeared.

A vast, dark mass of bodies, spreading out across the landscape as a tidal wave. Shields, helmets, the glint of steel, it stretched further than Gunnar could comprehend. Two thousand had appeared insurmountable. This was more. Many more. Three thousand strong, perhaps even four. The accurate scale of Harald Fairhair's army, the force he had brought to crush Njardarheimr, was revealed in the cold light of dawn.

Part 2: Dawn of the Great Wave

The sound of Harald Fairhair's army cresting the southern hill was not a murmur, but a growing, terrifying roar, a sound of thousands of voices, the drum of countless feet, and the rattle of weapons. Gunnar stood on the palisade wall, the sound flowing over him, as he watched the dark mass spread across the landscape. It felt like the entire world was marching on Njardarheimr. The sight should have broken him, should have sent a flood of despair through his heart. But Gunnar experienced a strange, cold calm settle over him. The waiting was over.

The time for agonizing over possibilities was past. Now was the time for action. For the plan, Gunnar looked out to sea and saw nothing; this was their chance. They had to be on the ships soon and now.

He turned from the palisade, his face set, his gaze resolute. He descended quickly, his boots thudding on the wooden steps, and strode towards his longhouse, where the core of his command, his family, waited. He entered the great hall, where Asa, Aedelric, Eiríkr, Astrid, and Leif were gathered, their expressions grim, reflecting the terror gripping the village outside.

Gunnar wasted no time. His voice cut through the tense air, calm but carrying the absolute authority of the Jarl. "Now," he declared, his gaze roaming over them. "Now is the time for the ships. Get everyone to the ships. Make way for the sea."

There was no hesitation. This was the plan they had rehearsed, the desperate contingency they had prepared for. Everyone knew their job. A controlled rush began. Villagers, clutching bundles of essential belongings, dried food, furs, weapons, cherished tools, hurried towards the fjord, guided by those assigned to the task. The warriors moved with grim purpose, preparing for their roles in the desperate delaying action.

Gunnar's eyes found Aedelric. He grabbed the Saxon's arm, pulling him aside for a brief, crucial moment, away from the immediate chaos of people gathering their things. "With me," Gunnar said, his voice subdued and urgent.

He led Aedelric quickly to the private area at the back of the longhouse, the small, walled space that had been their sanctuary. Ignoring the scattered furs, Gunnar went straight to his satchel. He retrieved the oiled cloth wrapping, revealing the Gospel of Matthew, the aged hide map, and the folded Gaelic letter. He pressed the bundle into Aedelric's hands.

"Hold on to this, Aedelric," Gunnar said, his voice firm, stressing the weight of the charge. "Keep it with you. At all times. Keep watch over it." His gaze held Aedelric's, a deep intensity of shared faith and purpose exchanging between them.

Then, Gunnar did something rare. He pulled Aedelric into a fierce, heartfelt embrace, a warrior's, a father-in-law's, a brother-in-faith's. Aedelric, surprised by the gesture, felt a sudden, terrible understanding dawn in his heart, a cold premonition. He embraced Gunnar back tightly.

"You know your job," Gunnar murmured into Aedelric's shoulder, his voice heavy with feeling. "The ships. The people. See them to safety." He pulled back, meeting Aedelric's eyes, his own filled with unshed tears, still resolute. "I will see you... on the ships."

Aedelric opened his mouth to protest, to question, but Gunnar was already turning, moving back towards the chaos of the main hall, his purpose clear. Aedelric stood for a moment, the weight of the bundle in his hands feeling impossibly heavy. He understood. He knew.

Out in the village, the rush towards the fjord continued, a desperate, controlled flow of humanity. The path to the docks was a river of hurrying figures, their faces creased with fear, their movements driven by the primal instinct for survival. Warriors, their numbers bolstered by the summer's arrivals but still agonizingly few against the coming tide, gathered at the Thingstead, Astrid and Eiríkr organizing them, their expressions grim but determined. Leif stood beside them, no longer shaking, his jaw set with resolve.

Asa, her own heart beating, directed her archers, now fifty strong, towards the palisade. "On the walls!" she commanded, her voice cleaving through the din. "Reinforce the positions! Bring every arrow!" Her leadership, honed in the heat of battle, shone through the fear. She saw Elara, clutching Sassa tightly, guiding a group of mothers and children towards the docks, her face colorless, still resolute. Asa gave her a quick, encouraging nod before turning back to the grim task of preparing the archers.

Aedelric, clutching the satchel and its precious contents, made his way through the stream of villagers towards the docks. His eyes scanned the grey waters of the fjord, a desperate search for any sign of Harald's longships that would trap them here. There was nothing. The fjord was empty, save for their fleet, bobbing impatiently at the water's edge, sharp and sudden, pierced through his dread. The path to the sea was open. He began barking orders, his voice loud and authoritative, directing people onto the ships, urging them to hurry.

Meanwhile, Gunnar made his way back to the palisade. Harald Fairhair's army was closer now, the ground vibrating along the rhythm of their march. The massive shieldwall, a dark, seemingly endless tide, advanced steadily towards the main gate. They were still just outside effective archer range, but the distance was closing rapidly.

Asa and her archers were finally on the wall, their fifty bows nocked and ready. She had spent months drilling them until their movements were as natural as breath. Not only accuracy, but speed. Nock, draw, loose. One motion flowing into the next, a rhythm she had carved into them with tireless training.

"Ready," Asa called, her voice rigid and sharp. The gust carried it along the wall, steadying the hands of her archers. She watched the approaching force with a hunter's focus, gauging distance, the rhythm of their march, the moment when their shields would be most exposed.

She waited.

Waited.

Her breath clenched tight in her chest.

"Loose."

The command shattered through the air.

Fifty bowstrings snapped in unison. Fifty arrows rose in a sweeping arc, a dark cloud of fletching that gleamed in the light before plunging toward the massive shieldwall. The first volley struck with a noise like heavy rain on wood and iron. Men staggered. A few dropped. The line shuddered.

"Again," Asa shouted.

Another volley soared. Then another. She had them firing in rapid succession, each archer moving with the precision she had hammered into them. Quivers emptied at a brutal pace. The air filled with the hiss of arrows and the cries of men who could not hide behind their shields fast enough.

It was a relentless rain, a storm of wood and iron. Even with the tight shieldwall, the sheer number of arrows meant many found their mark. Men stumbled, fell, were dragged aside, or trampled as the formation struggled to hold. Every move forward costs them blood.

Asa did not relent. Her voice rang out over the chaos, commanding, unyielding. She drew and loosed with a fury that burned through her arms and shoulders. Each arrow she sent carried the load of her rage, her fear for her people, her determination to break the enemy before they reached the gate.

Her bowstring thrummed again and again, her fingers raw, her breath sharp. She watched every arrow strike, watched the shieldwall waver beneath the punishment she delivered. She felt no triumph, only the cold necessity of the moment.

Gunnar watched with a grim satisfaction that mixed uneasily with the dread tightening in his chest. His daughter's skill, the precision of her archers, was carving bloody lines through Harald's advancing force. Every volley struck with punishing effect. He saw the traps they had laid outside the gate spring to life, wolf stakes catching men by the legs, hidden pits swallowing them whole.

Confusion rippled through Harald's ranks as warriors stumbled, fell, or vanished into the earth. Each fallen man, each moment of hesitation, bought precious seconds for the villagers fleeing toward the ships.

Then the sky darkened with returning fire.

Arrows began to rain down on the palisade. Harald's army had archers of its own, far more than Hakon had ever brought. Their shafts hissed through the air and hammered into the timber walls with vicious force. Some found flesh. A few of Asa's archers cried out, struck where they stood, stumbling or tumbling from the wall. Gunnar felt a shaft tear past his ear, close enough that the wind of its passage chilled his skin. Asa ducked instinctively as another arrow buried itself in the timber beside her head, quivering inches from her cheek.

"Archers," Asa shouted, her voice keen and commanding. "Target their archers. Behind the shieldwall. Silence them."

Njardarheimr's archers shifted instantly. Their arrows now arced high over the massive shieldwall, seeking the less protected ranks of Harald's bowmen. Asa's training had been relentless, teaching them to judge distance, to find the smallest opening, to strike with speed and certainty. The effect was immediate and brutal. Harald's archers, exposed and unprepared for such accuracy, fell quickly. Some dropped their bows and fled behind the shieldwall. Others collapsed where they stood, arrows jutting from their chests or throats. It was a modest yet crucial victory, removing a threat that could have torn the defenders apart.

With Harald's archers silenced, Asa's archers turned their attention back to the main force. The battering ram was now visible, a massive shape driven toward the gate by a determined knot of Harald's men. Asa's archers rained arrows down on the ram operators and the warriors shielding them. Men staggered under the assault, some falling, others forced to raise their shields and slow their advance. Every move forward cost them blood.

The gate moaned under the impact of the ram, the timber splintering under each heavy blow. It held, but only barely. Gunnar watched from behind his shield, his jaw clenched, praying silently for the wood to endure a little longer.

Every heartbeat mattered. Every arrow mattered. And the storm pressing against their walls was only growing heavier.

He yelled down to Eiríkr, who, with Astrid and Leif, stood ready at the Thingstead with the leading group of warriors. "Eiríkr! Spread them out! When the gate breaches, draw their fury! Buy time!" The plan was not to hold a shieldwall in the confined space, but to create chaos and distraction, giving the villagers more time to reach the docks.

Harald's army was being decimated in the bottleneck at the gate, men falling in droves to arrows, traps, and the crush of bodies. Yet their sheer numbers pressed on, a tide that refused to break. Throwing spears and axes began to arc over the palisade, hurled with frustration and fury. The projectiles banged against the timber, tore through the air, and found flesh. More of Asa's archers cried out, struck down where they stood. Gunnar and Asa had narrow escapes, the air around them alive with the hiss of death.

Then the enemy changed tactics.

Figures started to scramble up the palisade walls, clawing their way upward with frantic determination. They used the rough timber and the sharpened spikes as handholds, ignoring the danger. Some slipped, screaming as they fell onto the stakes below. Others pushed past the fear, driven by numbers, desperation, and the promise of plunder. Their fingers hooked over the top of the wall. Their faces appeared, snarling and wild.

The first few who made it over were met instantly by the warriors stationed along the wall and by Eiríkr's group, who moved forward like a hammer striking iron.

Eiríkr hit the first invader with the force of a charging bull, his axe cleaving through helm and skull in a single brutal motion. He kicked the body back over the edge before the next man could climb through. Astrid was beside him, her movements sharp and deadly, her axe hissing in vicious arcs. She caught a man by the wrist as he tried to pull himself over, severed his grip, and sent him tumbling backward with a scream.

Leif fought at their side, fear racing in his chest, but he held the line. He blocked a blow meant for Astrid, his shield shuddering under the impact. Eiríkr grunted approval and stepped past him, driving his axe into another man who had managed to swing a leg over the wall. Blood sprayed across the timber. The invader collapsed, dragged back by the mass of his own dying body.

But more were coming.

Hands clawed over the edge. Boots scraped against the timber. The wall shook with the weight of men trying to climb it. Eiríkr's group acted like a single organism, shifting, striking, pushing bodies back over the edge before they could gain a foothold. Every kill was immediate and necessary. Every throb mattered.

Still, the pressure grew.

Gunnar saw it all. The gate was splintered and grinding under the ram. The scaling increased with every passing moment. The defenders were thinning. Their delaying action at the gate was reaching its limit.

The storm was breaking over them, and the wall could not hold forever.

"Asa!" Gunnar roared over the din of battle, his voice ragged. "Get your archers off the wall! To the docks! Now!"

Asa, her expression grim, nodded, realizing only then, as she looked around, how few of her fifty archers remained less than half. The cost of their devastating fire had been high. She gave orders to Hrolf, guiding the surviving archers down from the palisade and towards the path leading to the fjord. Hrolf repeated her calls as they started their rapid descent.

"Eiríkr! Leif! Astrid!" Gunnar yelled over to the group, which was fighting off the scaled invaders. "Fall back! To the docks! Go!"

Eiríkr, seeing the increasing number of Harald's men making it over the walls, gave the order. His group, still fighting fiercely, began a fighting retreat towards the docks. Gunnar watched them go, then turned, making his way down from the palisade. As he passed the main gate, he saw its condition, splintered, hanging precariously, held together by sheer stubbornness and perhaps his silent prayer. *Just a little longer, Lord,* he thought, the prayer instinctive, a plea from the depths of his soul. *Hold just a little longer.*

He reached the docks, his chest heaving. The scene was a mix of controlled urgency and near-panic. Villagers were still boarding, helped by Aedelric and the remaining warriors. Aedelric spotted Gunnar and rushed towards him.

"Jarl!" Aedelric yelled over the noise of the approaching army, the screams from the village, and the creaking of the ships. "Boarding is almost complete! But... some are still coming... slow... fear..." He gestured back towards the village, where scattered figures could be seen, some running, some frozen in terror, unable to make it to the docks in time.

Asa, Eiríkr, Leif, and Astrid had made it to the docks, their expressions somber, as they looked between the ships and the sounds of the approaching slaughter from the village. The air was laden with the odor of smoke and the terrifying shouts of Harald's advancing army.

Gunnar's gaze swept over the desperate scene, the ships bobbing at their moorings, the few remaining villagers still struggling towards the docks, their faces furrowed with terror, and the horrifying din of Harald's forces pouring into the heart of Njardarheimr. His decision, already made in his heart on the palisade, solidified into grim, absolute resolve. There wasn't enough time for everyone. Not without a final, desperate sacrifice.

He moved with urgent purpose, his voice ringing through the chaos. "To the ships!" Gunnar bellowed, his voice projecting above the din. "All remaining warriors, board the ships! Move! Now!" He shoved a few hesitant men towards the gangplanks, his immense presence as a force of nature. He ensured the last stragglers, the wounded, and the youngest villagers were pushed aboard the various vessels. He saw to the lines, guiding the disorder into a semblance of order, his movements economical and swift.

"Aedelric," Gunnar said, his voice firm, unwavering, as he came to the side of the ship where Asa, Aedelric, and Sassa were now aboard. "Asa. Eiríkr. Leif. Astrid." His gaze met each of theirs, holding their eyes for a brief, final moment, conveying a depth of love, a lifetime of memories, and a farewell that words could not fully express. "Board your ships. Cast off the lines. Start to depart. Now."

A wave of protest rose from them, unspoken but clear in their expressions. *Leave him?* After all they had been through, all the battles they had fought side-by-side? The thought was unthinkable. Eiríkr took a step back towards the dock, but Gunnar's eyes, blazing with a tacit command, stopped him.

Gunnar turned, putting his shoulder to the stern of Asa's ship, straining against the heavy timber. "Push off!" he commanded the men still on the dock. He heaved with all his might, the muscles in his back coiling, helping to send the vessel further into the water, gaining precious feet from the shore. The ship moaned, slowly pulling away. Gunnar's direction was made clear, resolute, and undeniable. He stayed on the dock, watching them go, his choice made.

Asa, her heart lurching with sudden, terrible understanding, saw what he was doing. He wasn't getting on the ship. He was staying. "Father!" she screamed, her voice ragged with anguish. "No! Please get on the ship!" She lunged forward, trying to jump from the deck back towards the shore, back towards him.

"Aedelric!" Gunnar roared, his voice faltering with emotion, though his will remained iron. "Hold her back! Hold her!"

Aedelric and Leif, their faces creased with grief and understanding, grabbed Asa, restraining her as she struggled and screamed, reaching out for her father, unable to reach him. "What are you doing?" she shrieked, tears streaming down her face. "Father! Why?"

As the ship drifted further from the shore, powered by the first few oarsmen finding their rhythm, Gunnar stood at the water's edge, watching them go. Tears streamed down his aged face, combining with sweat. His voice, though strained, carried across the widening gap. "I love you, Asa!" he yelled, the words a tearing from his soul. "I love Sassa! Aedelric!" He met Aedelric's gaze, a profound farewell.

On the ship next to theirs, Eiríkr and Astrid watched, horror-struck. "Jarl!" Eiríkr roared, his voice laden with anguish. "What are you doing?"

Gunnar looked at them with his look of heartbreaking love and pride. "Eiríkr! Astrid! I love you both! More than you will ever know!" His voice rose, addressing them all, the ships pulling away, carrying the future of Njardarheimr. "Stick together! Stay strong! I will see you... In the next life!"

His gaze returned to Asa, struggling against Aedelric and Leif, her screams a raw sound of despair. Gunnar offered her a final, tearful smile, a smile of absolute love and sacrifice. "My daughter," he called out, his voice saturated with a depth of emotion that encompassed a lifetime. "You are the light of my life! You are the reason I live! I love you... more than life itself!"

With that, as Asa's screams continued, as tears streamed down the faces of everyone on the departing ships, warriors, villagers, friends, family, witnessing their Jarl's final, heroic act, Gunnar lifted a hand in a final wave, a silent farewell to the people he had saved. His eyes, filled with love and sorrow, held theirs until the distance grew too great.

Behind him, the sounds of slaughter in the village intensified. A mighty snap resounded through the air, the horrific sound of the main gate finally giving way under the unyielding battering. Harald's army was pouring through, a dark, unstoppable flood. Over the walls they swarmed, killing any who remained. Those who had not made it to the docks, those who had stayed in their homes, were being dragged out, their screams joining the sounds of the invasion. Torches were being tossed on and into the longhouses. Fires are lit on every standing building.

Seeing they were now in open water, the ships gaining speed, Aedelric, his heart a leaden weight in his chest, roared the command. "Oars!"

On the other ships, Eiríkr and the other ship masters echoed the call. The remaining villagers who had made it to the docks scrambled aboard the last few ships, some having to be pulled on board as the vessels pushed off, leaving the horror behind.

Gunnar turned from the water's edge. His face, though still wet with tears, was now set with a fierce, resolute resolve. He drew his sword, the metal glinting dully in the morning light, leaving the sheath on the ground; he would not need to sheath it again. The sounds of Harald's army filled the village. The few remaining villagers who had not escaped or been caught were likely dead or hiding in terror. Only Harald's army remained within Njardarheimr, save for one man.

Gunnar.

His plan had worked. By staying, by becoming the ultimate distraction, he had drawn the invaders' immediate focus away from the docks, giving the last ships those precious moments to board and push off. Harald's men, flooding the village, saw the lone figure standing defiant among the carnage, yelling a challenge.

"Harald!" Gunnar roared, his voice echoing through the burning village. "Harald Fairhair! Face me!" His voice roared like the roar of a beast.

Harald, entering the village with his vanguard, saw Gunnar standing alone, sword drawn, seemingly inviting his death. A look of savage satisfaction spread across Harald's face. He pushed through his men, who parted for him, anxious to see the demise of the defiant Jarl.

"Gunnar," Harald said, a cruel smile on his lips, stopping a short distance from Gunnar. "So glad to see you. Alone. Defiant to the last." His voice dropped, menacing. "And now... You will die. But do not worry. I will hunt your ships down. There will be no escape for them. They will be burned at sea."

Gunnar stood tall, astonishingly composed, giving off a quiet power that seemed to halt the tide of invaders for a moment. He had faced death before, but never with such certainty, never with such purpose. He said a silent prayer, not for himself, but for his family, for their journey, for the secret faith they carried. *Lord, I give my life to you. I give my soul into your hands. Let my family live. Let them find you. Guide them.*

Harald noticed the unshakeable calm in Gunnar's eyes, the lack of fear that angered him profoundly. "Your God will not save you now, Christian!" Harald sneered, raising his sword, a magnificent, ornate weapon befitting a king.

"I am not asking Him to save me," Gunnar replied, his voice composed. He raised his sword, a well-used, practical blade, not as grand as Harald's, but sharp and accurate.

With a roar, Harald charged. His men cheered, eager to see their king dispatch the defiant old Jarl.

The two men met in the center of the ravaged village, a whirlpool of violence swirling around them, surrounded by the dead and the surging tide of incoming warriors. The clash of their steel rang out, sharp and clear, a singular, resounding note above the guttural shouts of Harald's men, the screams of the dying, and the crackle of burning longhouses. Gunnar, though older, moved with the unyielding grace of a seasoned warrior, his presence a calm, collected anchor in the storm. His sword was an extension of his will, each movement economical, precise, born of a lifetime of hard-won battles.

Harald, in contrast, was a roaring tempest, a physical embodiment of the conquering wave. He was immense, powerful, his heavy, ornate sword a streak of destructive force, each swing meant to cleave through bone and shield. He bellowed challenges, his voice ragged with rage and the certainty of victory, relying on brute strength and the sheer momentum of his invading army. His blows were loud, intimidating, and designed to shatter, but they lacked the subtle finesse and deeper understanding of balance and timing that Gunnar possessed.

They circled, their blades a dizzying display of steel and death. Harald attacked with a furious, relentless assault, pressing Gunnar back with sheer weight and aggression. His sword banged on Gunnar's sword, the *THUMP-CRACK* resounding with bone-jarring force. But Gunnar was a master of defense, his parries, his movements flowing, deflecting blows, absorbing the shock, and using Harald's ferocious momentum against him. He was a stone in a torrent, unmoving, unbreakable. He parried, he dodged, his eyes never leaving Harald's, searching, always searching for the chink in the mail of Harald's raw power. The air around them sizzled with the sheer force of their blows, the ground underfoot slick with mud and blood.

Slowly, imperceptibly at first, Gunnar began to turn the tide. He wasn't merely defending; he was wearing Harald down, forcing him to overextend, to breathe harder, to commit to attacks that yielded no reward. Each parry from Gunnar subtly shifted Harald's balance; each block drained his prodigious strength. Harald's shouts became more ragged, his powerful swings a fraction slower, his footwork less agile. He pressed, swinging his heavy sword in wide, devastating arcs, but Gunnar was always there, a solid presence, deflecting blows, redirecting the force, his blade flashing in quick, probing feints that kept Harald on the defensive.

Then, Harald, in a fit of frustrated rage and genuine fatigue, made a mistake. He overcommitted to a sweeping overhead strike, leaving his left side exposed for an instant longer than prudence allowed. Gunnar saw it. His eyes, icy and keen, widened almost imperceptibly. His sword moved, not like lightning, but with the inevitable, crushing power of a falling avalanche. With a brutal, backhanded slicing cut, Gunnar's blade bit deep into Harald's left thigh, severing muscle, not a clean cut but a tearing, devastating wound that instantly buckled Harald's leg beneath him.

A cry of agony, raw and primal, ripped from Harald's throat. He staggered, his magnificent weapon clattering uselessly against Gunnar's sword as he clutched his bleeding thigh, his roaring fury replaced by a sudden, shocking pain. The fight shifted irrevocably in that moment. Harald, the unstoppable wave, was now wounded, brought to his knees by the silent, unyielding rock that was Gunnar.

Before Gunnar could deliver the final killing blow, before Harald's scream had even faded, Harald's men reacted. Seeing their leader wounded, seeing their king in mortal danger, they advanced as one.

Gunnar was swallowed instantly, a lone shape against a wave of steel. He fought like a cornered bear, every swing of his sword fueled by a lifetime of battle and the fierce love he held for his people. He cut down the first man with a brutal stroke, then another, then a third. Blood sprayed across his face. He pivoted, parried, struck again. Four. Five. Each kill bought another heartbeat for those fleeing toward the ships.

But the blades found him in return.

A spear tore into his side. A sword slashed across his ribs. Another blade punched through his back. Pain flared through him, bright and searing, but he did not fall. He roared through it, driving his sword into the throat of the man before him. His legs trembled. His breath came ragged. Still, he fought.

More weapons pierced him. Steel sank into muscle and bone. His strength began to ebb, but his will did not. He forced himself upright, forced his arm to lift his sword one last time. He saw Harald collapse.

And he knew he had done what he needed to do.

A final spear thrust drove him to his knees. The world tilted. The roar of battle faded into a remote murmur. Gunnar lifted his eyes to the grey sky above, the clouds sailing like slow-moving spirits. His lips parted, forming a silent prayer, the one he had whispered in secret for years. A plea for mercy. A plea for his daughter. A plea for the child she carried in her arms.

He felt the cold seep into him. Perceived the weight of his body begin to slip away. Yet there was no fear, only a strange, quiet peace.

Jarl Gunnar exhaled one last time and let himself fall among the bodies of his enemies. His life ended not in defeat, but in a last act of sacrifice that held the line long enough for his people to escape. His courage, his plan, and his last stand saved his family, his friends, and the future of his people.

He died as he had lived, with strength, with honor, and with a prayer on his lips.

Out on the fjord, the ships were gaining speed, the oars biting into the water. Those on board, looking back at the village, saw the smoke rising, heard the distant sounds of slaughter, and saw, with horrifying clarity, the final moments of their Jarl. They saw Gunnar standing alone, confronting Harald. They saw the duel, the battle of steel, illuminated by the flames of the burning village. They saw Gunnar, the old bear, fighting like a man possessed. They saw Harald falter, saw Gunnar's sword flash, saw Harald recoil, clutching his bleeding leg.

A unified gasp passed through those watching. Gunnar had wounded Harald. He had almost won.

Then they saw the rush of Harald's men, the single figure of Gunnar disappearing beneath the tide of steel. They saw him fall, overwhelmed, his life ended in a final, desperate struggle.

On the ship with Asa and Aedelric, Asa's screams were raw, heartbreaking sounds of utter despair. She continued to struggle against Aedelric and Leif, who held her tightly, tears streaming down their faces, watching the impossible horror unfold.

Aedelric held her close, burying his face in her hair, murmuring words of comfort and grief, his own heart torn by the loss of the man who had become a father and a brother in faith to him. He watched Gunnar fall, an intense sorrow and an intense determination settling within him. Gunnar's sacrifice would not be in vain.

Astrid and Eiríkr, on the ship beside them, watched with equally devastated expressions. Tears streamed down Astrid's face as she grasped her belly, the life within a clear contrast to the death they had just witnessed. Eiríkr stood beside her, his jaw clenched so tight it ached. His eyes, usually so clear, were misted by a storm of grief and rage.

He watched, helpless, as the Jarl who had welcomed him, who had stood by his side, who had accepted him into his family, now gave his life. The image of Gunnar, defiant and alone against the approaching tide of Harald's men, would be seared into his memory forever.

Everyone on the ships watched, saw their Jarl's final stand, saw the price paid for their escape. The heavy emotions, grief, shock, horror, but also a dawning understanding of the magnitude of Gunnar's sacrifice and the loss of those who were lost, engulfed them. They had lost their Jarl, their protector, the roots of their community. But he had bought them life. He had bought them a chance.

With the sounds of battle and death resounding behind them, and the image of their fallen Jarl seared into their minds, the ships of Njardarheimr rowed east, towards the open sea, towards an uncertain future, carrying the heavy legacy of Gunnar's final, defiant stand.

Part 3: Sea Wolf's Trap

The eight longships of Njardarheimr, a desperate, overcrowded fleet, drove their oars into the water, gaining speed and heading into the grey waters of the fjord. The sounds of slaughter from the village, the roars of the invaders, the screams of those caught in the onslaught, grew fainter with distance, but the horror of what they had left behind was seared into the minds of everyone on board. The image of Jarl Gunnar, standing alone against the tide, his final, tearful farewells resounding in their ears, was a raw wound in every heart. Grief was a tangible burden on the decks, none heavier than on the ship carrying Asa and Aedelric. Asa was curled on the deck, sobbing uncontrollably, her hands clapped over her face, trying to shut out the brutal image of her father's last stand, the sound of his voice proclaiming his love. Aedelric held her, his own eyes wet, the shock of Gunnar's sacrifice leaving him numb. Yet, the feel of the sea wind on his face, the spray of the water as the ship gained speed, and the familiar feel of the ocean was a bitter contrast to the unnatural scene they had just fled.

Then, Leif's voice, sharp with alarm, cut through the sounds of grief and rowing. "Aedelric! Ships! On the horizon!"

Aedelric's head jerked up. He released Asa, scrambling to his feet, his grief momentarily overridden by the young warrior's cry. He moved quickly to the side of the ship, shielding his eyes against the light, scanning the distant line where the sky met the water.

Leif was right. Barely visible, just emerging from the haze of distance, were other ships. Dark shapes against the lighter grey of the horizon. Not one or two. More. Many more. Aedelric strained his eyes, counting. Twenty? Perhaps more than that. A fleet.

A sickening wave of dread rolled over him. They weren't safe. Not yet.

He ran to the prow of the ship, joining the few warriors positioned there, trying to get a better look, his gaze fixed on the approaching vessels.

From the ship closest to them, riding the waves just off their starboard bow, Eiríkr's voice, strained but clear, carried across the water, almost lost in the wind and the sounds of rowing. "Aedelric!" Eiríkr yelled, pointing towards the approaching shapes. "Harald's ships! It's Harald's fleet!"

The Sea Wolf. Harald's power wasn't confined to the land. He had anticipated this. He had set a trap.

Aedelric turned back to the people on his ship, his visage grim. "Harald's ships!" he roared, his voice loud, urgent. "Twenty or more! They are waiting for us! We are not out of danger! Prepare yourselves! We need to defend the ship!"

The news sent a quiver of renewed fear through the overcrowded vessel. People looked out at the horizon, their faces blanching as they saw the distant shapes. The relief of escaping the village was instantly crushed by the terrifying reality of a fight they couldn't run from on the water.

Aedelric went to Asa, who remained on the deck, her hands clamped over her face, lost in her sorrow. "Asa! You need to hear me! Harald's ships are here on the water. We must prepare to defend ourselves. Your archers... we need them." He spoke to her, urging her, but she didn't move, didn't speak, her body still wracked with sobs. He tried again, pleading with her, but it was to no avail. She was unreachable, submerged within the depths of her sorrow.

Not knowing how else to penetrate her sorrow, understanding that action was needed now, Aedelric turned to the others. His ship was packed, a fragile vessel carrying a mix of villagers, women, and children, and only a handful of warriors and Asa's archers. "Those not on the oars!" he commanded. "To the prow! Shields up! Archers behind them! Women and children to the stern! Get low! Stay down!"

The few warriors on board grabbed shields and moved to the front of the ship, forming a thin line. The archers positioned themselves behind them, bows ready. The women and children, their fear evident, huddled together at the back of the ship, seeking any sense of safety.

As Aedelric directed the defensive positions, he saw Asa move. She rose from the deck slowly, her body stiff, her head lifting. When she turned, her face was no longer consumed by grief alone. The sorrow was still there, deep and raw, still beneath it, burning and reshaping her features, was a fierce, cold anger. Ignoring Aedelric completely, as if he weren't there, as though the earth was only her pain and the threat before them, Asa moved with a swift, decisive purpose. She walked past Aedelric towards the stern, her look fixed. She went directly to the steering oar, where one of the remaining boatmen was struggling to maintain their course in the choppy water. Without a word, she reached out, gently but firmly moved the man aside, taking the heavy steering oar in her own hands. The boatman yielded instantly, recognizing the absolute authority in her movements, the steely resolve in her eyes.

Asa held the steering oar, her body rigid with purpose, her eyes fixed on the approaching fleet. Her voice, when she spoke, was clear and sharp, cutting through the sounds of the ship and the far-off battle on land. "Archers!" she commanded. "All of you! To the starboard side! Now!"

The archers, survivors of the fight on the palisade, responded instantly, moving as one to the starboard side of the ship, their bows ready.

Aedelric watched her, momentarily stunned by her sudden emergence from grief, by the cold fury that now empowered her. He knew nothing of maneuvering a longship in battle. But Asa did. He had seen her skill on the water. Trusting her completely, recognizing that her experience was needed now more than ever, Aedelric grabbed a spare shield and joined the small rank of warriors at the prow, bracing for impact.

"Warriors!" Asa yelled again, her voice resounding with command. "Low stance! Shields locked! Form a shieldwall on the deck!"

The few warriors, including Aedelric and Leif, moved in, squeezing together, raised their shields, and created a small, makeshift shieldwall on the open deck, offering what little protection they could against arrows or boarding attempts from that side.

Asa then looked out at the other ships of their fleet, calling out across the water until she found the one carrying Astrid and Eiríkr. She yelled Astrid's name, her voice urgent, her look locking with her friend's. Astrid, positioned on the deck of her ship, her face furrowed with grief and fear, saw Asa, saw the fierce resolve in her eyes. Asa lifted her hands, bringing them together, then motioning them up and apart, a pre-arranged signal, a naval tactic understood between them. Astrid nodded, her expression grim, acknowledging the command.

Aedelric watched as the other seven ships in their small, desperate fleet, mirroring Asa's commands or reacting to Astrid's relayed instructions, began to adjust their courses and shift their defenses. Warriors and archers moved on their decks, preparing for the inevitable clash. They were all doing the same thing: turning to face Harald's oncoming fleet, the eight small ships, overloaded with refugees, sailing straight towards twenty or more enemy longships.

The distance closed rapidly as Aas commanded the oarsmen, "ROW!" The terrifying shapes on the horizon resolved into sleek, deadly longships, packed with Harald's warriors, their shields gleaming along the gunwales. The lead ship was larger than the rest, more ornate. Aedelric and Asa both saw the figure standing at its prow, Sven, the one who had delivered Harald's demand at the gate. He was leading the attack.

The tactic Asa had signaled became clear as the ships drew closer. Two Njardarheimr ships would charge one of Harald's longships, aiming to pass on either side, raking the enemy deck with arrows. It was a bold gamble, relying on speed and surprise to inflict damage without being boarded or rammed.

Asa steered their ship towards Sven's lead vessel, with Astrid's ship running parallel and matching their speed. They drove their oarsmen mercilessly: "ROW!" The wooden blades bit into the water, pushing the ship forward at breakneck speed.

As they neared Sven's ship, Asa barked commands to her oarsmen, adjusting their course by a hair, a precise movement that sent them angling towards the enemy vessel. At the very last moment, the two Njardarheimr ships split, one veering to starboard, the other to port, leaving Sven's ship caught between them.

"Archers! Loose!" Asa yelled.

Arrows flew from the decks of both passing ships, explicitly aimed at the oarsmen pulling the enemy ship, at the steersman at the stern. It was a frenzied, point-blank volley. Men cried out, hit, slumped over their oars, or fell into the water. The goal was to cripple the enemy ship's mobility, leaving it vulnerable for the others to bypass.

The maneuver worked, but the density of Harald's fleet meant there was no clear path through. As Asa's ship shot past Sven's crippled vessel, they immediately ran into *another* of Harald's longships, unable to avoid it in the tight confines.

The impact was jarring, a harsh CRUNCH of wood against wood. Asa's ship, moving at speed, struck the enemy longship midships. The effect wasn't a clean ramming blow, but enough to splinter the enemy's timbers, sending a shock through both vessels. The other longship groaned, listing sharply, men thrown off their feet, some tumbling into the cold fjord water.

A roar went up from the enemy ship as those not knocked overboard recovered. Seeing Asa's ship momentarily tangled, they hurried to board. Warriors, axes and swords in hand, leaped across the gap, attempting to gain the deck of Asa's vessel.

Aedelric, already at the prow with the warriors, met the boarding party with brutal efficiency. He fought with a cold, focused rage, his sword a blur, cutting down the enemy as they hurried onto the deck. The small shieldwall held, pushing back against the borders, the narrow confines of the deck limiting the enemy's numbers. Leif fought beside Aedelric, his earlier fear replaced by a grim determination, as he swung his sword to defend their ship.

On Astrid's ship, the maneuver was similar, though they managed to pass alongside one of Harald's ships without a direct collision. But Harald's warriors, eager for the fight, immediately attempted to board. Astrid, her face set, expertly handled the steering oar, trying to keep their vessel from being overwhelmed, while Eiríkr and the warriors on deck engaged in a gruesome melee. Eiríkr was a force of nature with his axe, its heavy blade smashing through shields, its momentum carrying men over the side into the water. It was a desperate, close-quarters fight, the deck slick with seawater and blood.

Throughout the fjord, the other ships of Njardarheimr were engaged in similar brutal skirmishes. Two ships, caught between multiple enemy vessels, were quickly overwhelmed. Harald's warriors swarmed over their gunwales, the sounds of fighting giving way to screams and the eventual, frightening silence as the ships were taken or sunk. Everyone on board, warriors and villagers alike, was killed.

Asa, having disentangled their ship from the wreckage of the one they'd hit, maneuvered their vessel with desperate skill. She used their speed to her advantage, weaving between Harald's larger, less agile longships, avoiding being pinned down. Her archers, though few, continued to fire, picking off exposed oarsmen and disturbing enemy movements. Aedelric and the warriors on deck fought off any further boarding attempts, their shieldwall holding firm.

Then, as Asa saw it, Astrid and Eiríkr's ship, locked in a brutal boarding action, was surrounded by Harald's warriors. They were fighting fiercely, but the numbers were against them. A new purpose seized Asa, her anger turning into a dangerous resolve.

"Take the rudder!" she yelled at the steersman she had replaced earlier, stepping back from the steering oar. "Aim it there!" She pointed towards the ship that was overwhelming Astrid's vessel. "Aim for the middle! Ram it!"

Asa grabbed her bow, joining her archers at the starboard rail. As they approached the enemy ship, speeding towards its broadside, Asa and her archers unleashed a point-blank volley, raking the enemy deck, aiming to disrupt their boarding action and prepare for the impact.

Their ship struck the enemy vessel with a jarring impact, though less forceful than the earlier collision. It was a deliberate ramming, designed to cripple. Timbers groaned and splintered. Men on the enemy ship cried out, thrown off balance, the boarding action on Astrid's ship momentarily faltering.

Harald's warriors on the damaged ship recovered quickly, their fury turning towards the vessel that had just rammed them. They attempted to board Asa's ship, leaping across the narrow gap. Aedelric and the warriors met them directly, their swords and axes rising and falling, cutting down the attackers with brutal efficiency.

From Astrid's ship, now gaining a moment of respite, Eiríkr saw Asa's ship, saw Aedelric fighting on its deck. "Asa! Aedelric! Thank you!" he yelled across the water.

Aedelric, cutting down another border, yelled back, his voice grim. "Don't thank us yet, Eiríkr! There are still more! We need to help the remaining ships!"

With Astrid's ship now partially freed, the two vessels maneuvered in concert. "Oars!" Asa roared to her crew. "Row hard! We help the remaining ships!" Eiríkr echoed the command to his oarsmen. They turned their ships towards the clusters of fighting where the last few Njardarheimr vessels were desperately fending off multiple attackers.

They rowed towards the chaos, joining the fray, engaging the Harald ships that were attempting to overwhelm their people. They fought alongside the remaining Njardarheimr ships, harrying Harald's vessels, buying precious moments, inflicting damage where they could.

However, despite their intervention, the odds were still overwhelmingly in favor of the other side. Even as they fought, they saw it happen. Two more Njardarheimr ships, caught between multiple attackers, were finally overcome. Their defenses collapsed as Harald's warriors swarmed over their decks; the sounds of battle on those vessels gave way to the deadly silence of defeat. Now, only four ships of Njardarheimr remained: Asa's, Astrid's, and the two they had just attempted to help. Half their fleet is lost.

Within the desperate, turbulent chaos of the battle, Acdclric's eyes scanned the enemy fleet, searching for any possibility, any weakness. And then he saw an opening. A slight gap had formed in Harald's formation as several ships converged on the lost Njardarheimr vessels, a narrow passage to the open sea.

"Eiríkr!" Aedelric roared across the water, his voice laden with desperate hope. "The opening! There! Make for the opening!" He pointed towards the gap in Harald's line.

Eiríkr saw it too. His face, grim with battle, broke into a look of intense resolve. "Astrid!" he yelled to her at the steering wheel. "Steer us to the opening! Now!"

The command was relayed to the last two remaining Njardarheimr ships. The four surviving vessels, battered and overcrowded, changed course, turning their prows towards the narrow gap, rowing with a desperate, unified purpose. Harald's other ships, seeing the sudden shift, attempted to turn and engage, but they were momentarily scattered, still dealing with the aftermath of earlier clashes.

Aedelric, standing at the prow of his ship, urged his oarsmen on, his eyes fixed on the opening, the promise of escape. He spoke to Asa, who was back at the steering oar, her wear a mask of grim concentration. "Keep us true, Asa! Aim for the opening!"

Just as they were gaining speed, just as the opening seemed within reach, their ship was struck. Not a ramming blow, but a sharp impact against their hull, sending a jarring shockwave through the vessel, making them all stumble, almost capsizing the ship. Aedelric cried out, thrown off balance. He looked to see who had struck them, who was trying to stop their escape at the last moment.

And his blood became cold. The ship that had hit them, now pulling alongside, was smaller than Harald's main longships, but fast and agile. Its warriors were already scrambling to board. And standing at its prow, sword in hand, leading the attack, was Sven: Sven, the Thegn from the gate.

Sven, ever the opportunist, had anticipated their escape, attempting to cut off their only route to freedom.

Aedelric experienced a wave of cold fury, a primal instinct to protect those he loved. He charged towards the rail, sword drawn, meeting Sven's boarding party with a savage roar. The clang of steel against steel erupted instantly as the first of Sven's men, a burly raider with a grim grin, leaped onto the deck, only to be met by Aedelric's relentless blade.

The deck of the ship, already pitching on the waves, became a scene of desperate, hand-to-hand combat. It was a confined, bloody stage where life and death were measured in inches. Aedelric and the few remaining Njardarheimr warriors, bolstered by the desperate fight for survival, fought with brutal ferocity against Sven's borders. Every swing was imbued with the weight of all they had lost and all they had to protect. They were outnumbered, but their defiance burned like a raging fire.

Asa, bearing a mask of determination, drew her sharp, sleek blade, a langseax, its polished steel shining even in the subdued light of dawn. With a silent, deadly precision, she plunged into the fray. Her movements were fluid, graceful, yet utterly devastating. She was a warrior of controlled violence, her langseax a whistling arc of death. She moved amongst the enemy, a low growl escaping her lips with each graceful strike. One man, attempting to flank Aedelric, met her blade as it swept across his chest, a deep, tearing wound that sent him gurgling to the blood-slicked deck. Another, caught mid-swing, found her langseax piercing his gut with a sickening *THWIP*, her twist of the wrist affording a swift, agonizing end. The shouts of Sven's men, initially confident, began to mix with cries of pain and alarm as Asa cut a bloody path through their ranks, a true warrior in her element.

Amidst the churning melee, a sudden lurch of the ship, combined with a carelessly placed fallen body, sent Asa stumbling. She went down hard, the deck slamming upon her ribs, her langseax clattering just out of reach. Before she could recover, a large, brutish warrior, his face contorted in a snarl of bloodlust, was on her. He straddled her, his hands like iron clamps seizing her throat, attempting to choke the very life from her. Asa struggled beneath him, raking at his arms, her breath slowly being cut off, her eyes wide with desperation, fighting against the crushing darkness.

Aedelric saw it. A red mist descended before his eyes, obscuring the edges of the raging battle. The world constricted to that single, terrifying image of Asa beneath the brute. A primal roar ripped from his throat. He charged towards the man, his sword thrusting forward with impossible speed and power, driven by a raw, unadulterated fury. The blade plunged into the warrior's back, just below the neck, piercing through muscle and bone. The man gurgled, a wet, choking sound, his hands releasing Asa's throat as the bloodied blade exited the front of his throat in a grotesque display. Aedelric, his face contorted with rage, yanked his sword free with a vicious twist, ignoring the continuing fight, pulled the dead man's heavy body off Asa, tossing it aside like a rag doll. He knelt, grasping her arm, pulling her quickly to her feet.

"Are you hurt?" he demanded, his voice laden with desperate concern, his eyes searching over her for any wound.

Asa shook her head, gasping for air, her lungs aflame, her eyes open in shock, as well as the lingering terror of near-death. Without a word, she snatched up her langseax. They rejoined the fight, side-by-side, their blades moving in brutal, synchronized concert, fighting as one against the approaching enemy.

Then, Aedelric saw Sven again, fighting his way towards them. Their eyes met across the struggling bodies. Sven yelled insults, challenging Aedelric, his face contorted with effort and aggression. Aedelric returned the challenge, his rage simmering, ready to face this surprising betrayer.

Before Aedelric could reach him, Leif, seeing Sven's advance, stepped in front of him, shield raised, sword awkwardly but bravely swung at the veteran warrior. Sven, seeing the young, inexperienced fighter, taunted him, his voice oozing with scorn. "Out of the way, whelp!"

Leif pressed his attack, trying to protect Aedelric and prove himself. But Sven was a seasoned killer, faster and more skilled. He parried Leif's clumsy swing, sidestepped the shield, and with a swift, brutal thrust, drove his sword through Leif's chest. Leif's eyes widened in shock, a silent gasp escaping his lips as the life drained from him. He crumpled to the deck, his shield clattering beside him, his sword falling from his hand.

"LEIF!" Aedelric roared, a sound of absolute fury and heartbreak.

Elara, who had been huddled at the stern with the women and children, saw Leif fall, saw the sword in Sven's hand. "NOOO!" she screamed, a raw sound of pure anguish.

Asa, fighting near Aedelric, saw Leif fall and saw the look on Leif's face, a look of terror and surprise. "NO!" she yelled.

Leif's death, following so swiftly after Gunnar's sacrifice, broke something within Aedelric. The controlled rage shattered, replaced by a terrifying, primal fury. He screamed, a sound that was not human, a sound of pure, unadulterated pain and vengeance. The sheer ferocity of his scream, the terrifying look in his eyes, struck fear even into Sven, who had just killed the young man.

Aedelric came at Sven like a berserker, moving with impossible speed, fueled by grief and a terrifying madness. Sven barely had time to raise his sword. Aedelric's blade, used with blinding speed and power, beat Sven back to the prow, giving him no quarter. A brutal cut severed Sven's sword hand, sending his weapon and his hand spinning through the air. Before Sven could even cry out again, before he could react, Aedelric's sword swung; with a single, powerful swing, he decapitated Sven. The Thegn's head flew from his shoulders, landing with a horrifying thud on the deck, his body collapsing lifelessly over the rail, tumbling into the fjord.

The brutality of Sven's death, the sheer, terrifying fury Aedelric had released, sent a wave of terror through Sven's remaining men. They faltered, their will to fight evaporating. Asa and the other warriors, seeing their fear, pressed the advantage, cutting them down mercilessly. Some of Sven's men, seeing the hopelessness of their situation and the terrifying rage of Aedelric, jumped into the cold water to escape the slaughter on the deck.

The fight was over. Sven's boarding party was defeated. Aedelric, his chest heaving, his face covered with blood and grime, his eyes still burning with a terrifying intensity, turned from the rail. His gaze found Leif's still form on the deck.

The rage drained from him, replaced by a crushing wave of grief. He stumbled to his knees beside Leif, the young warrior who had reminded him so much of Eadric, who had fought bravely, who had died trying to protect him. Aedelric could no longer hold back the storm of emotion. Tears streamed down his face as he reached out, pulling Leif's body into his arms, his sobs expressing the raw anguish he had witnessed moments before.

Elara, her screams fading into choked sobs, stumbled forward and reached Leif. She crouched next to Aedelric, her hands reaching for the young man she had shared calm moments and shy smiles with, holding him as she cried aloud, her body shaking with grief. Aedelric wept with her, holding Leif's lifeless form, two souls united in their sorrow for the brave youth lost.

Asa, her face stained with tears and the grimness of battle, watched Aedelric and Elara for a moment, her heart breaking with shared grief. But the ships... the escape... was not yet complete. She swallowed her pain, her father's sacrifice, Leif's death, hardening her will. She went back to the steering oar, taking control of the ship once more.

"Oarsmen!" she yelled, her voice harsh but firm. "Row! Row hard! Make for the opening! Now!"

She steered their ship, damaged yet still afloat, towards the gap in Harald's fleet, her eyes fixed on the promise of the open sea. The other three surviving Njardarheimr ships had already made it to the opening, their oars digging desperately into the water, propelled by the same desperate hope for survival.

Harald's remaining ships, seeing their intended prey slipping away, attempted to turn and pursue, their oars churning the water in a frantic effort to cut them off. But the gap was extending, and Njardarheimr's ships, driven out of desperation and Asa's skillful navigation, were fast.

They rowed with all their might, the sounds of battle on the fjord slowly dimming behind them, replaced by the rhythmic splash of the oars and the cry of gulls. They cleared the opening, leaving Harald's frustrated fleet struggling to keep pace. The vast, grey expanse of the open sea stretched before them, an unknown future.

They had survived. Battered, grieving, and forever changed by the horrors they had witnessed, but they had survived. Four ships, carrying the remnants of Njardarheimr, leave behind their burning village, their fallen Jarl, many lost, and the brutal, bloody waters of the fjord. They rowed towards the unknown, towards the promise of refuge hinted at in an old map and a dying monk's last words, leaving the Sea Wolf's trap behind them. They had outrun Harald's ships, but the journey remained far from over.

CHAPTER 11

Unknown Shore

The four ships sailed together, a small, battered fleet against the immense stretch of the open sea. The rage of the fjord battle was behind them; now, the sounds of pursuit faded into the rhythm of the waves and the wind. Harald's ships were no longer anywhere in sight. They were truly alone now, afloat on the cold northern waters, with no clear destination, only a direction, eastward.

On each ship, the immediate aftermath remained a mixture of exhaustion, grief, and the grim necessity of survival. The wounded were tended to, cuts bound, broken limbs splinted as best as possible with what materials were at hand. The dead were prepared for burial at sea. Valuables were taken from both their fallen warriors and the bodies of the enemy who had met their end on the decks, arm rings, coin purses, functional weapons, and anything that might be of use in the uncertain future. The brutal practicality of survival dictated that, also in death, the fallen would contribute to the living.

On the lead ship, the one that had carried Asa and Aedelric, the deck was being cleaned, the blood washed away by buckets of seawater. Asa and Aedelric sat together near the prow. Sassa held securely in Asa's arms, a small, warm weight of innocent life among the cold reality of death. Elara rested with them, her face buried in her hands, sobbing softly for Leif. Aedelric, his grief for Gunnar and Leif a heavy pain in his chest, reached out and gently placed an arm near Elara's shoulders, offering quiet comfort. He and Asa sat in mutual quiet, their hands linked, finding peace in each other's presence and drawing strength from their physical connection and the small life they shared.

The four ships sailed in a loose formation, keeping each other in sight. They were navigating by instinct and the general direction indicated by Aedelric, who kept checking the sky and the feel of the sea beneath them. The immediate danger had passed, but the acute pain of loss and the trauma of the day's events hung dense in the air. They were trying to recover, to breathe, to simply endure the transition from the maelstrom of battle to the vast, indifferent peace of the sea.

After some time, Astrid's and Eiríkr's ship, the one that had fought so fiercely alongside them in the fjord, drew closer, its battered timbers groaning softly. Ropes were thrown between the two vessels, tying them together so they could sail side by side, close enough to speak and offer mutual support.

Astrid was the first to cross the gap between the ships. Her face looked pale, marked with grime and tears, her eyes showing the deep sorrow she carried. She went straight to Asa, her gaze finding her friend and Sassa. Without a word, she knelt, her arms reaching out. Asa shifted Sassa into one arm and embraced Astrid tightly, the two women holding onto each other, sharing the deep, wordless grief for Gunnar, for their lost home, for all that had been taken. They held each other for a long time, their tears merging into one, a powerful expression of their shared history and strong bond.

Eiríkr followed, his massive frame moving carefully across the connecting ropes. He went to Aedelric and Elara, seeing their mutual grief for Leif. He didn't say anything, just extended his arms. Aedelric, still holding Elara, met Eiríkr's embrace, a warrior's hug filled with grief and fellowship. Elara, seeing Eiríkr, her grief fresh and raw, stumbled into his massive chest, burying her face in his armor, sobbing uncontrollably. Eiríkr held her gently, allowing her to weep, his large hand resting comfortingly on her back.

Soon, other villagers and warriors from the two ships crossed over, sharing embraces, checking on one another, and offering quiet words of comfort and support. It was an instant of collective mourning and desperate reassurance; they had survived, they were together.

After some time, when the initial wave of shared emotion had passed, Asa stirred, pulling away from Astrid, her face bleak though resolute. "We need to take care of the dead," she said, her voice quiet but firm, looking at the fallen forms on the deck, especially Leif. "It must be done."

Aedelric nodded, releasing Elara, his face wet with tears. "Yes. You are right."

The other two ships drew closer, and the grim task began. Below the vast, blue sky, the survivors prepared their fallen for burial at sea, according to customs they knew, adapting them to the circumstances of a ship and the scarcity of materials. Their fallen were treated with care, bodies washed as best as possible, wrapped in spare cloth or furs, weighted down. Leif's body was handled with particular tenderness by Eiríkr and Aedelric, their grief evident in their movements. Elara crouched next to him, saying her final, tearful goodbyes, a raw sound of young love and devastating loss. With quiet prayers to their gods, or in Aedelric's case, his God, the weighted bodies were committed to the deep, sliding over the side into the cold waters of the sea.

The bodies of the fallen enemy, however, were treated with less ceremony. They were stripped of any valuables that might be useful, armor, weapons, anything of worth, and then tossed overboard, their final journey stark and unadorned. The difference in treatment was clear, a subtle testament to the bond of fellowship and the harsh realities of their world.

With the dead committed to the sea, and the wounded tended, the grim necessity of planning for the future asserted itself. There were four ships, adrift, with no home to return to and no clear destination.

Asa, Astrid, Eiríkr, and Aedelric, the surviving core of Njardarheimr's leadership, gathered near the steering oar of Asa's ship. The vastness of the sea around them appeared to amplify the seriousness of their decision.

"We are here now," Asa said, her voice tired. "Away from Harald. Away from the fjord. But where do we go?"

Aedelric reached into the satchel Gunnar had given him, his hand closing around the bundle. He took out the hide map, opened it carefully, and presented it to the others. He chose not to reveal the Gospel or the letter yet. Now was not the time for secrets of faith, only for a path forward.

"Before... before Gunnar stayed behind," Aedelric said, his voice laden in emotion, "he gave me this. And he told me... to find it. For refuge." He pointed to the marked cluster of islands on the map. "He called them Orkneyjar."

Asa, Astrid, and Eiríkr leaned in to examine the map. Their eyes traced the coastline, the islands. They recognized the general shape of the Scottish land to the south, but the islands themselves were unknown to them personally. None of them had raided or sailed extensively in that specific area. But the name, Orkneyjar, was spoken of, a place of islands far to the north of the Scottish mainland.

"Orkneyjar?" Eiríkr said, his forehead creased. "I have heard tales... Islands far to the north. A place of wind and sea birds."

Astrid studied the map intently. "The land of the Scots," she spoke quietly. "We know the coast... but the islands..."

"My father gave you this?" Asa asked Aedelric, her tone brimming with surprise. "When? I never heard him speak of any map, any place called Orkneyjar for refuge."

"Just before... before he went back," Aedelric replied, his gaze meeting Asa's, acknowledging her unspoken pain. "He gave it to me in the longhouse. He said... Colm gave it to him." He chose not to elaborate on who Colm was for the time being.

"Colm?" Asa looked puzzled. "Who is Colm?"

Aedelric hesitated. "A man your father knew. Years ago." He kept the answer deliberately vague. "Gunnar believed... this was a place of refuge. Colm knew. He tried to find it years ago but couldn't."

They looked at the map, then at each other. "What are our options? Sail randomly into the vast sea? Try to find another Jarl who might shelter us, risking sailing into Harald's expanded territory? Try to make it all the way back to Wessex?"

"Wessex?" Eiríkr questioned, sensing Aedelric's unspoken alternative. "That is a long voyage, Aedelric. Across the great sea. And who is to say Harald's reach does not extend even there by now?"

Aedelric shook his head. "It is not a good plan," he agreed, his doubts about returning to a home he had already accepted losing firm in his mind. "Too far. Too uncertain."

"This map..." Astrid said, her finger gliding over the marked islands. "Gunnar trusted it? Trusted this... Colm? He believed this was a place for us?"

Aedelric looked at them, his face weary though steadfast. "He did. He gave it to me, his last act... to guide us. To find refuge." He met their gazes, one by one. "I believe... this is what he wanted. What he intended for us."

They weighed the map's uncertainty against the known terror of Harald and the impossible task of finding another haven in Norway. The choice, even though fraught with unknowns, became clear.

"Then we go to Orkney," Asa said, her voice decisive, the leader emerging from the depths of her grief. "If Father believed it was our path... then it is our path."

Astrid nodded, her expression grimly determined. "I can navigate us there," she said, looking at the map, estimating the course. "It should be... three, perhaps four days' sail with good wind. To reach the area, at least. I can get us that far."

"But we know nothing of these islands," Eiríkr stated, voicing the shared apprehension. "Who is there? Are they friends or enemies? Are they under Harald's rule? We are sailing into the unknown."

"Yes," Aedelric agreed, his look fixed on the horizon, on the direction they would now definitively take. "We know nothing. But we go together. As Gunnar wished."

Asa turned to the others on her ship, then looked towards the other three vessels, linked by ropes, with their people watching. "We have a plan," she announced, her voice conveying the new direction. "We go to Orkney. To the islands north of the land of the Scots. This map will guide us."

The decision was relayed to the other ships. There were questions, hints of apprehension about sailing into the unknown, but Gunnar's name, the belief that this was his final plan for them, his last act to save them, settled their doubts. They trusted Gunnar, even in death.

The four ships tightened their formation, their sails unfurled to catch the wind, as oars pulled steadily. Asa and Astrid, the two warrior-leaders, took command of the navigation, guiding the small fleet southeastward, then west. They sailed for three days, then four, the voyage blessedly free of major storms, the seas relatively calm. They maintained vigilance, watches posted constantly, scanning the horizon for any sign of pursuit or unexpected danger.

On the morning of the fifth day, through the lifting sea mist, they saw them. Islands. The low-lying shapes of land break the broad horizon. Orkney.

As they drew closer, the details began to emerge. Green hills, rocky coastlines. And then, as they rounded a headland, they saw something that brought a new surge of uncertainty and apprehension. Built into the natural slopes and stone outcroppings was a large, formidable fortification. Not just a simple longhouse or a small collection of buildings, but a well-built, defensible structure overlooking a natural harbor.

Aedelric stood at the prow with Asa, his look fixed on the fortification. His heart throbbed. This wasn't just a wild, uninhabited island. There were people here. Power here. "Asa," he said, his voice quiet. "I think... I think this is it. The place on the map."

Asa's eyes, sharp and assessing, took in the sight of the fortification. It looked strong. Occupied. She turned to Aedelric, her expression grave. "Are you sure, Aedelric? Is this... is this the right move? We know nothing of who built this. Who lives there?"

Aedelric looked back at the sea they had crossed, at the ships following them, carrying the last hope of Njardarheimr. He thought of Gunnar, his sacrifice, his final charge. He thought of the map, the dying monk's words. He didn't *know*. He couldn't be *sure*. But he had to trust.

"I don't know, Asa," Aedelric admitted, his voice subdued. "I don't know if it is the right move. But Gunnar believed... he believed this was refuge. He trusted this path for us." He met her gaze, his own filled with the weight of their common journey, their shared loss, and the uncertain future before them. "We will go together. We will face it... together."

With the distant sounds of the sea, the cry of gulls, and the promise of the unknown shore before them, the four ships of Njardarheimr, the last remnants of a destroyed village, turned towards the fortification on the Orkney Islands. Their voyage had ended, but the most significant test of their survival was perhaps beginning.

End of Book One.